LOVE YOU TO DEATH

Love You to Death

Max McCamish

BLKDOG

www.blkdogpublishing.com

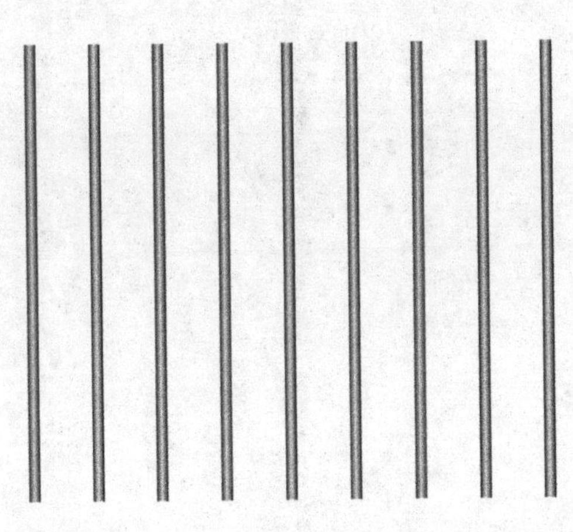

CHAPTER ONE - STEPHEN MINETT

Stephen Minett was love, life, art, all that there is to live for, and I hated him for it.

I couldn't remember when I met him for the first time, because when I met him, he didn't matter. He was as much background noise as anyone else; I knew him in the same way I knew anyone. It was important, I had discovered quickly in my life, to make as many friends as possible. Friends were people you talked to regularly. Friends allowed you to call in favours, friends talked about you positively to others, and friends built you a good reputation that protected you if and when you did bad things. I was everyone's friend. I acted happy and jovial, even though it tired me. I talked to everyone, and I listened to what they said, so I could bring it back later and make jokes that everyone appreciated. None of them knew me that well, but I knew them all. I heard much talk of the power of friendship, and it was certainly a useful tool, but I found no joy in it.

I knew about Stephen Minett. I knew he was well-known and well-loved. Nonconfrontational, friends with many and attractive to many others, although he took no notice of suitors whatsoever. He was surprised whenever someone took interest in him. He had a keen eye, he had a wit, he was gentle, he was kind. He was weak-willed and had something of a watery personality, unfixed, shifting with everyone he spoke to. So did I, but I was distinctly unlike any other human being around me. We were friends; not enough to hang out every week, but enough.

What changed everything about him came out of nowhere. There's no way I could've ever seen it coming.

It was cold and dark, as it always was. Some of my friends invited me out; Madison, Kai, and Ava. Madison was an extroverted girl who quickly grew attached to me. Kai was her boyfriend. Madison was trying to set me up with Ava. I pretended to be open to dating, when in truth, I knew I could never hold feelings for another human being. People were no different to me than intelligent animals; like dogs, giving them treats could teach them tricks. Humouring Madison and pretending to be at least somewhat interested in Ava meant that later on in English she would help me cheat. I needed to get good marks in all subjects to get into medical school, after all, and I didn't care how legitimate those marks were.

It was a movie we were going to see, at the movie theatre Stephen worked at. I knew that, but I didn't make a note of it at the time. I had no reason to care. Ava was trying to lean on my arm, and I let her, because I didn't care. Dating was fine. If she seemed overly involved or interested I'd reject her. Low maintenance partners tended to be useful to me, but too much interest could lead to my honest self being exposed. That wouldn't do.

Kai and Madison walked ahead, Ava and I behind. Ava was talking about the band she was in, and I was listening, even if I couldn't be interested. As the couple walked through the door ahead of us, Ava stopped, patting her pockets down. "I left my wallet in your car," she said, her hand slipping from my arm. "It has my ticket in it."

"Do you want me to go get it?" I suggested, gesturing

back towards the car park. Being kind and thoughtful usually turned out benefits in the long run.

Ava thought for a moment. "I can go," she offered weakly, unsure. Rather than accommodate her uncertainty, I instead made the decision for her.

"Hey, it's fine. I'll go get it." I gently patted her arm, before heading back towards the car park. I was brisk as I shuffled along the icy footpath. I intended to be fast, so that my friends would not be kept waiting, and I knew I was unlikely to fall, even on the ice. Normally I paid attention to everything, calculating everything. It was all I did, since I had no desire to do anything at all. So I just paid attention.

I noticed the couple loitering by their car, discussing something under their breath. I noticed the theatre worker on her break, sitting with a phone on a bench, shivering without adequate warmth. I noticed the raccoon flitting along the ground, holding something that was recently trash in its little fingers. Nothing that mattered.

Locating the car, unlocking it, and grabbing the wallet was easy. I found myself staring at my feet as I walked back; the ice was beginning to thicken in the new year's frost, and it would only get worse from here. I wondered if we'd get a snow day soon, and get time off of school. That would affect my plans.

I said that I paid attention to everything, but that was not always as true as I'd have liked it to be. In that moment, I did not look up.

And the next second seemed like it lasted absolutely forever.

I felt my sense of gravity overturn first. I didn't trip, I didn't fall, but suddenly my proprioception was warning me that something was off. My arms flew up in self-defence, and there was something hot leaking through my clothes and dripping down my skin, cooling as it settled. The falling feeling that caught me suddenly stopped in split second, and with a racing heart I noticed that someone was gripping my wrist. Strong fingers against my pale skin, warmth in every groove of a unique fingerprint, holding me upright. Something struck my chest, knocking the breath out of me so hard it was almost as though I had actually hit the sidewalk. My body stiffened, some sort of defence mechanism, and my eyes caught his. Stephen Minett.

I felt my heartbeat in every extremity, but I hardly even noticed. His eyes were blue, and I knew that already, but for the first time I noticed the veins of grey running around his pupils, the hints of green edging around the outside of his iris. I noticed for the first time that his eyelashes were long and elegantly beautiful, and along with his eyebrows they were slightly darker than the golden blonde of his curly hair. Hair that I hadn't paid much attention to prior to that moment, but it suddenly struck me as the softest thing I'd ever seen. He was strong enough to hold my entire weight, and as he pulled me upright, I caught on that something was very, very wrong. I didn't care if his hair was soft or if his eyes had streaks of grey and green or how pretty his lashes were. I shouldn't care. None of that was information that would do me any good. It was not important, so why was I thinking of it? Why did I want to touch his hair?

Other people got random, unasked for thoughts like those. I did not. I had never cared about anything in my life.

"I'm so sorry," he said, and the gentle, low lilt in his voice had not changed, but how charming it was to me suddenly had. There was a strange unsettling feeling in my stomach to accompany this new knowledge. There was a moment where we stared at one another and I struggled to form words. "Are you alright, Alex?"

"Uh." I finally broke contact with his eyes, and my own appearance struck me as not good enough for the first time in my entire eighteen years of existence. I gazed at the huge coffee stain across my shirt, and although I didn't feel embarrassment- not that I would know what any emotions felt like- I didn't want him to see me looking anything less than perfect. Why? I had never cared before. "It's fine," I managed to gasp, although the way my voice came out was just so wrong. I always chose to have a strong and confident voice, but I was breathy and quiet in those words, and I knew from the outside how this looked. How he must think I felt about him, in that moment.

But I didn't like people, not like that. I couldn't feel anything.

There was a pause, where Stephen eyed me up and down, and there was the tiniest quirk of his lips, and something in my gut swooped as though I'd just fallen a great distance. I didn't believe this could be happening. His hand was still around my wrist, and the way it made my heart beat was stirring up new, entirely unpleasant... things. I wanted to run. I felt like I had to run, or perhaps fight him. I needed to make these butterflies go away by any means necessary.

Finally, he spoke, gaze flickering over my shoulder at something behind me. "Uh- come with me, I'll help you, uh. Get cleaned up." There was a blush of embarrassment spreading across his face, and he dropped my wrist, finally aware he was still holding it. I noticed another presence at my back, and for a moment, I was filled with a desire to attack. Someone was intruding on this moment, and I inexplicably wanted to kill them for it. I closed my eyes and tried to breathe properly.

A realisation passed, barely recognised in this flurry: I was experiencing emotions. I didn't know their names, because I'd never felt them before.

"Are you alright?" asked a gentle voice I could find nothing but grating. I wanted to slam its owner through the concrete. It was the girl who was on her break, presumably who Stephen was bringing coffee to. She circled around to face me, and I didn't see any of her features the same way I saw Stephen's. She had eyes, but I couldn't find them any more interesting than I did five minutes before. She had lips, but I didn't feel strange things looking at them. The emotion I retroactively named fear grew stronger at the realisation that Stephen was unique.

"I'm okay," I nodded, regaining my learned charisma in a sudden swoop. If I pretended Stephen wasn't there, I almost felt fine. But I couldn't pretend he wasn't there for long. I couldn't.

"It's fine, I've got it under control," Stephen told his co-worker, and she backed off. When he looked at her, there was this characteristic wide smile that he always had, but when Stephen looked at me, it felt fake. I didn't want his smile towards me to be fake.

I spoke to him the day before, and I didn't think I felt anything then. I was doubting myself all of a sudden. Surely, that much emotion didn't come out of nowhere?

When I followed him into the movie theatre, I didn't see Ava, or Kai, or Madison. They were right there, but my eyes were on Stephen, and it was only when Ava came up to me that I remembered I didn't arrive alone.

"What happened?" she asked. Stephen was right next to me, and it would've been so easy to reach out and grab his hand. I didn't like thinking of it. Those emotions were quickly going to get in the way if they continued. I had spent a long time building up the life I had, and frankly, I enjoyed not having feelings for anyone or anything. It made life so, so much easier. Stephen Minett would not ruin that for me.

"Just an accident, it's fine." My words felt hollow in the air; the emotion in them had always been faked, but usually I was at least a little convincing. Not then. Ava blinked, confused, but when I handed her her wallet, she took it and went to the relatively quiet counter, unbothered by whether or not I was with her. It mattered little if she wasn't interested in the date either; after feeling actual… emotion, I didn't think I could even pretend to care about anyone other than Stephen.

"I'm, uh." I struggled to sound normal. It was a little easier when he was turned away, but when he looked at me, it was so hard to speak. I couldn't live like this. "I'm not sure how much you can help me," I managed, forcing each word out. I fixated on a spot right over his shoulder, but it didn't last long; soon, my gaze was drawn to his face again, noticing freckles along his cheekbone and following their path down to his jawline. He had a nice jawline.

Why did I care, though?

Stephen led me behind the counter, and while I was staring in a daze at the spot where he was merely a moment before, he procured a towel from somewhere. "I... I just feel I should help," he said distractedly, taking my wrist in his hand again and gently dabbing at the coffee where it was beginning to cool on my skin. I was hardly paying attention to what he said. I could only stare at him. There was some queasy feeling not unlike the earlier fear when I looked at him. There was no good reason I should be afraid of Stephen Minett, unnoteworthy classmate of mine who happened to work at the movie theatre I was visiting.

Except he was no longer unnoteworthy. This feeling somewhere deep in my chest belonged to him, was caused by him, was his fault. This new *emotion* I couldn't put a name to stirred me in uncomfortable ways. I liked being cold, I liked being emotionless; it meant things were easy. Looking at him was hard enough in that moment, and I couldn't imagine lasting long around him if it stayed. He was in half of my classes, and if I couldn't get over this soon, I wouldn't be able to live with it. It had to go away.

As I watched him, finding myself almost absentmindedly admiring the curve of his hair around his face, I knew this couldn't go on. If this was some stirring of romantic feelings- in me, of all people!- I would give it a week to go away. If it didn't go away within a week, I'd do anything I had to do to *make* it go away. There was one certain way of achieving that, in my belief; and if it made that horrible squeezing on my heart disappear, it would be well worth it.

I'd just have to kill him.

Chapter Two - Alex Keen

I committed my first murder when I was seven years old. I was the oldest sibling of five, two years older than my brother and six years older than my triplet sisters. My sisters were young enough that they did not bother me, and in fact, looked up to me. It was my brother, Bailey, that was the problem.

See, he caused issues in my life. My parents disproportionately believed him in arguments, even though he always started them, hitting me when I didn't comply with what he wanted. When the triplets were born he and I had to share a room, and he always rummaged through my stuff and damaged it, or kicked my bed in the middle of the night from the bunk below. He was loud, and when he broke things he blamed them on me. I would be better off without him. That is the only reason I ever killed anyone.

Even at seven, I had a sophisticated idea of who I was and what I wanted. I was stubborn and got my way, and when people got *in* my way, I pushed them out of it. My parents were concerned when I was younger, but I quickly discovered that making friends made that concern go away. The concern almost returned when I admitted to my teachers that I didn't know what happiness nor sadness felt like, that I had never felt anger nor fear, that the concept of love didn't make sense to me. At first, teachers thought I was simply too young to understand abstract concepts. With my growing social presence I was able to lie and put them on. Nobody questioned me again after that, and by middle school, I had accepted that other people felt things I did not, and that those things didn't matter to me.

When one of my friends' cats died, he cried for a week. I asked him if he was in pain, as that was the only time I had ever cried, and he said it was a pain in his chest, emotional pain. I told him 'that must be horrible', knowing I'd never feel it myself. When my grandfather died, I mimicked him, pinching myself under my sleeves so hard that I cried. I was able to convince my parents I was upset by my grandfather's death. I couldn't say I was happy about it- I didn't know that feeling either- but it was a net gain for me. He smelled weird and I was always bored whenever we went to his house. My mother was distraught at the loss of her father, and I simply didn't understand how that felt. She said it was horrible because she'd never see him again.

It was that admission that gave me the idea to kill Bailey.

I knew I could get away with killing him, because I could easily make it look like an accident, and nobody would believe a seven-year-old had the capacity to kill. All I needed was an opportunity- a method that wouldn't be overly obvious. After all, if I just stabbed him, or grabbed my dad's gun and shot him, it would obviously be murder. That wasn't the end of the world, if it wasn't clear who murdered him, but it would be. Unless I could frame someone whose jailing wouldn't affect my life, or make it appear random, I didn't want it to be seen as murder.

The family trip to Lake Michigan in the spring was perfect. There was minimal intervention on my part. From paying attention, I'd learned that my baby sisters were allergic to cow's milk, when my parents had tried to use it as a basis for their baby formula and they'd all broken out into hives. All it took was feeding them some milk the morning we arrived at the lake. It was easy enough. While my dad was showering and my mum was distracted with Bailey, I slipped some to them. Then, all I had to do was wait.

The triplets soon burst out into both tears and hives, and with three of them to contend with, both of my parents were occupied. They could only give my brother and I a passing comment, telling us to look after one another. With my parents' attention taken away from me, I had my chance.

I walked over to the door, gesturing to Bailey. I can easily recall the feeling of the iron handle on my little fingers, Bailey's pale face watching me with a smirk of mischief. "Hey Bailey, you wanna go to the lake?" I asked, knowing full well he couldn't swim.

"Yeah." He never cared about whether or not we were breaking any rules, and technically, my parents hadn't said we couldn't leave. I swung open the door of the cabin and walked out into the morning; there was still a bite of cold, but that could only work in my favour. A shame I couldn't have had the chance to kill him in the winter, to freeze him under the ice- that would have been a more certain death. But this would still be quick.

"Race you to the lake," I challenged him. I figured speed was important in a murder. If I was caught pushing him into the water, I could always cry and claim I didn't mean to hurt him, but the less hassle this was for me, the better.

"Yeah!" he accepted my challenge and took off running. I followed, and we took the stone path all the way up to the boardwalk.

"First to the end of the pier wins!" I called, and his determination was set. He sprinted along the wood, half a metre ahead of me, a grin on his face, knowing he would win.

He skidded to the end of it, bare feet kicking up the moss on the wood. It wasn't unreasonable that he would go swimming in the clothes he was wearing at that moment. "I win!"

he announced, in the shrill voice of a child. I quietly registered Bailey's last words; I'd be the only person to ever know them. *I win.*

I scanned the area and saw no one. And so, I pushed him into the lake, where it was far too deep for him to stand, knowing he couldn't swim. I would've expected him to scream or shout, but the shock locked his vocal cords shut.

It took a while for him to thrash, as the sudden cold stunned him. When I watched him struggle, unable to reach his head above the water to scream, I didn't feel like I'd done anything bad. Unlike the vast majority of the human race, I did not feel guilt. On the flipside, however, I didn't get any kind of adrenalin rush or sense of enjoyment from the act. It wasn't even satisfying, really. I viewed it as a relatively tedious task completed, like homework.

I didn't stick around to watch him die. I made it back to my parents in the cabin as quickly as I could, and hung around in the kitchen as they dealt with my sisters. They hadn't even noticed that Bailey and I had gone, as far as I could tell, so I opened up a book and pretended I had never left.

After a good fifteen minutes, they finally came to speak to me. "Where's your brother?" my dad asked, looking around the room with a rising sense of panic. Dealing with my parent's grief was going to be a long process, but it would last at most a few months, and I'd never have to deal with my brother again. The issues he would present to me as we both got older would only increase. I knew that much.

"I don't know," I lied. "He went outside and said something about the lake, but he never came back."

I sat in the cabin as my parents went to search for him, and at some point, discovered his body in the lake. I pinched myself so hard I cried again, and faked sadness for a few weeks. Our trip was cut short, but the police were never even called. Bailey was reckless and independent, enough so that they believed he could've run off to swim on his own, even though he didn't know how. Once my parents began to act normal again, so did I. Never again was I hit by my brother, or fought with, or blamed for things I didn't do. I no longer had to share a room. I knew that in the future when my life got more complicated, he would not be an extra complication in it.

And my life did get more complicated. Bailey was not the only person I murdered.

My dad has been an accountant my entire life, but until my mom found work as an attorney when I was thirteen, we weren't very rich. We rented a unit, and when I was ten, our landlord at the time proved the exact same type of trouble that warranted murder.

My father was supporting four kids and a wife, and he was paying off old loans from university. Of course, it was at this time that our landlord decided to increase our rent to extortionate prices. After hearing my parents argue about whether or not we needed to move to the countryside, and realising that killing my landlord would actually be quite straightforward and easier than restarting my social life in a new town, I knew what I wanted to do.

The plan I came up with for him was quite simple. He lived just down the road, and I had previously observed his schedule. I knew that he went for a run every evening, flaunted his wealth in just about everything he did, and ran past parts of town with a relatively high crime rate for our city. I found an old grey hoodie in a dumpster, put on plastic gloves, took a knife from my parent's kitchen and went out into the street. My dad was on a work trip and my grandmother was over at our house, giving my mother an alibi; there was no way either of my parents could be blamed, and they would never consider the ten-year-old. I told my mother I was sick and locked my bedroom door so that nobody could possibly check on me.

I was four foot ten at the time, and the landlord was over a foot taller. That didn't stop him from being terrified when he felt the knife against his back. Mr Hough, his name was. It was dark, I was behind him, and when I spoke in the lowest voice I could, forcing it to sound gravelly and smoky, he could never have possibly recognised me. "Hand over all your valuables," I threatened him. Robbery was not the motive; the point was to make it *seem* like robbery was the motive.

He threw his phone and wallet on the ground a few metres away, and tried to plead with me. "I don't want trouble, I- I have a wife and kids. I'll give you anything you want, just- please. I don't want to die, I- I love my family."

I stabbed him as hard as I could through the back. The knife plunged into the muscles around his spine with some resistance, increasingly solid the deeper the knife went. I pulled it back out with more strength than I thought I would've needed, and plunged it back in again. On each subsequent stab, I made sure to puncture both of his lungs. I would've liked to have gotten his heart, but I could tell the lungs would be enough. I collected the valuables and hung around just long enough to make sure he was dead.

Mr Hough's last words were, *I love my family*.

Blood covered my hands and the hoodie I had stolen. I went several streets over and dumped the knife, the hoodie and the valuables in the bottom of a stranger's trash. The plastic gloves I washed when I got back home, knowing my DNA would be on the inside of them; I disposed of them the next day on the way to school, again leaving them in a stranger's trash.

Mr Hough left all of his assets to his children. His wife was too distraught over her husband's death to worry us about rent, and we were able to keep the house. We would move when I was fifteen, but it would be to a nicer area, close by, and for those five years, I got to keep my hard-earned social life at school. I got to ride it into high school, and it was only good for me.

The second murder was the closest I came to being found. The police realised that it was not actually a robbery, due to the nature of the stabbing, and while my parents were briefly considered suspects, both were ruled out as their alibis were rock-solid. Mr Hough's children, Ezra and Ophelia, go to the same high school as me now. Despite the fact that they were nine and ten respectively at the time, they tend to look at me strange; just strange enough that I have to keep a watchful eye on them. They both avoid me, but I catch Ezra giving me disgusted glances and Ophelia telling people something's not right in my head. Thankfully, nobody listens to her.

The third and most recent murder happened in freshman year. This one was the hardest to conceal, the hardest to get away with, but I executed it perfectly. I would like to say I'm proud of how I achieved it, but in reality, I feel nothing about it. It's simply a fact that I achieved it better than I did my previous two.

This one was a girl, a classmate of mine. Even with my pristine reputation carried over from middle school, someone saw a weak point, and found a target in me.

Her name was Amanda. I remember how her eyes were wide-set and large, pale and always staring a little too hard. I caught her odd stare on me a little too often. She was never smart in school, skipping out on classes all the time, but she was smarter than all of her classmates in the sense that she recognised something was different about me.

Her friends were the 'bullies' of the school, subtly and covertly picking on those who didn't have the same amount of social skill. I was not a conventional target. I was not weak, nerdy, shy. I was not the lanky boy with acne who doesn't get jokes, or the quiet girl with rumours about her sex life spreading quickly through the class. I had no traits to whisper about to your friends, nothing really believable to make up about me, and enough people found me charismatic that I was hard to exclude entirely. This was all by design. The truly mean children, the ringleaders, never chose me as their target.

But Amanda chose me. She saw the emptiness behind my eyes, and when her friends were all snickering about people behind their hands, it was me she spoke about.

It didn't take long, during freshman year, for things to get less than ideal. It was bearable at first, just some strange glares and whispered words; and then she was trying to trip me and pretending I had done the same to her, telling people I'd said things I hadn't said, and trying to stop me from talking to people I tried to befriend. The first time she stole my books and I found them in a bin, I recognised that this was a pattern that would only get worse. I knew killing her would be harder than either of my previous murders, mainly because a murder at my age was plausible to police officers. I couldn't make it look like an accident or a robbery, and I still wanted to avoid the implications of it being an obvious murder.

Her bullying gave me the idea.

It was a complicated plan. The first step was finding out through the Internet how to create chloroform, writing it down, and deleting my search history, with the few weeks it would take for the rest of the plan to commence as enough time to fully bury that search. I had to learn how to copy her handwriting after stealing an assignment of hers off of the teacher's desk; that was the easier part. I socially engineered a few things, as required. I got between her and her boyfriend, for one. Letting one of her friends see me kissing him was enough to drive that wedge, until she was screaming at him, disgusted and outraged with the both of us, and they were broken up. Then, I turned some of her tricks on her, coming to a particularly dumb teacher and faking concern about Amanda's 'drug habit' and saying I thought she might be self-harming. It was possible, I realised at that point in the plan, that simply ruining her social life might make her let up; and since I'd thus far gotten away with it, it might've been safer to leave it there. I had no desire to kill her specifically. All I wanted was to remove the complication she brought into my life.

But it only got worse. Once her reputation as a fragile drug-user had begun to spread, she knew exactly who to blame, and her friends took her side. The bullying became physical; twice I was beaten up, and once it was far worse than that. After I was left in the school bathroom bleeding from my throat after two of Amanda's friends, and her brother, made me swallow razorblades at the threat of drowning me, I knew my original plan had to go forward. Not only that, but I had been given the perfect tools to forward it.

I threw up as many of the razorblades as I could into the sink, and took a photo. I got rid of the evidence then, and after going home and telling my parents the true sequence of events, I went to hospital. I asked that my parents not tell anyone, even the teachers, what had happened, giving the excuse that Amanda was very fragile and even if she'd hurt me, I didn't want to get her in trouble, as I was afraid for her own mental state. My parents fought me on the issue, but conceded, calling me noble and selfless for the decision I'd made. I told them I was neither, and it came across as humility, but it was the truth.

The second day back at school, I showed the same teacher the photo I'd taken, pinching myself as I told the story to make myself cry. I told her I'd found Amanda in the bathroom with all these razorblades, and that she'd run off and I just didn't know what to do. The teacher comforted me and asked if I thought she should speak to Amanda; with her being dumb, it was easy to convince her not to, playing it off like I had thought it would be best, but I'd changed my mind. This concern not only set up a precedent for Amanda's suicide, but it also painted me as being close to her. With teachers' complete lack of concern for actual bullying in the school, this story, that we were friends, would be more believed than the observable truth of her attacks on me.

When I got home, I made the chloroform and wrote her suicide note.

The next day was when it happened. I spoke to Amanda briefly before the last period began, telling her I wanted to speak to her in private, near the dumpsters. Telling her before the last period gave the least chance of her telling anyone, and the private location was believable for what she probably suspected the conversation was going to be about. It wasn't actually the private location that was so important, although of course, it was necessary. It was the fact that it was so close to the school bathrooms.

I stood behind the dumpster, and that's where she found me. "So, freak," I remember her saying as she rounded the corner, already seething with anger, "you gonna come clean on why you're fucking up my life? Or whatever the fuck is so wrong with you? You gonna kill me, huh?"

Amanda's last words were, *you gonna kill me, huh?*

She was so perceptive, and yet she never knew how smart she was. While she was definitely shocked when I slammed the chloroform-soaked rag over her mouth, there was a kind of recognition in her eyes. An acknowledgement that her assessment of me was entirely correct this whole time. She tried to struggle, but could only scream so much, and her grasping at me desperately and kicking with all her might turned to spasms, and then nothing. It was difficult to overpower her for the several minutes it took for chloroform to work, but I did it.

When she finally passed out, I planted the suicide note on her. I had written about how 'I' had been growing more and more depressed, unable to feel anything, how the good things in my life were disappearing, and how tiring it was to stay alive, and death was preferable, how I couldn't take it anymore. I had talked about drugs, losing 'my' boyfriend, how life was hurting 'me'. I'd written about how much 'I' loved 'my' family, and how 'I' wanted them to be happy without 'me'. It was perhaps a little without heart, but it was the best I could do. I could only imitate the feelings of others in my writing.

With a note plausibly written by her, in her handwriting, I got her fingerprints all over the pages and the pen, and then folded the note and put it in her shirt pocket. With that, I could only wait. I'd observed already that our school had two janitors, and that their routines began by going through each classroom beginning at opposite ends. We sat by one end, and as soon as the first janitor was occupied, I made my move. I had planned a route such that I avoided open areas and security cameras, knowing if I was seen with her, I would be done for. This was the riskiest murder I had committed.

I first carried her with her arm around my shoulder, as though I'd just found her and was trying to take her to a safe place. I snuck in through a back door and hurried to the girls' bathroom, sitting her down on the floor with her back cradled against me. I took out the razorblades- I used the ones her friends had forced me to swallow, simply because it was convenient- and slashed her wrists. It would've been more effi-cient to do deep cuts longways, but I made it look messy, rough and desperate, doing several sideways first until her arms were a messy criss-cross of blood and cuts. She shifted and groaned in her unconscious state, but didn't wake up. Then, finally, I made a deep enough cut straight down her arm, until the blood gushing from it was beyond sufficient to kill her. I knew the janitors would come here in about thirty minutes, but to be sure, I put her body up against the door and prepared to leave out the window any moment now. I changed my bloody clothes in the stall and watched her as she died; as soon as her breathing had stopped, I pushed my bag out of the window and followed it out. I went home knowing my most difficult murder had been completed.

There was no police investigation, as her death was de-clared a clear suicide. The teacher's statements backed up mine, and to my surprise, many people admitted she'd been acting weird, depressed, suicidal. Her ex-boyfriend and brother said this wasn't a surprise. Some of her friends, though, looked at me with suspicion; there was no confronta-tion, but I did overhear one of them blaming me. They didn't suspect me of murder, no- they thought I'd driven her to kill herself. The idea quickly died down, and it was forgotten in less than two months. My life was back to normal.

I didn't want to kill again. As I got older, I found it more difficult to hide my crimes, especially as they piled up and made each one more suspicious. The more people who died around me, the more likely it was that someone would come to suspect me, and I couldn't have that. Each death was riski-er than the last, and as such, the benefits became less and less compared to the negative consequences.

Stephen Minett did something to me that nothing had ever done to me before. I had suddenly developed the capaci-ty to feel things, but only in relation to him- sadness when he was gone, happiness when I saw him, anger when anyone else got close to what felt like mine, fear that someone would take him from me. But there was also anger, and fear, that stirred from these emotions themselves. It took me a while to truly come to grips with the fact that, after eighteen years of life, I was experiencing emotions for the first time. Even when I came to realise it, and understand it, I couldn't accept it- not as my new reality.

I never hated Bailey, or Amanda, or Mr Hough, or anyone else who had ever done me harm. Their actions were, to me, as neutral as any of mine. I ascribed no moral value to anything, evaluating actions simply based on how they affected me. Bailey, Mr Hough, and Amanda were inconveniences, easier removed than dealt with. I felt the same about them as I did my parents, my sisters, my friends; which is to say, nothing.

But I knew what it is to hate now. It was a feeling that followed every jittery, shining emotion that struck me like a bullet as soon as Stephen came into view. It was an indiscriminate kind of hate. I hated him, and myself, and the world, and everyone around me, as soon as he was out of view. I hated my feelings most of all, and whilst the hate itself was a feeling, I could tell that things were worsening due to my emotions. My life was changing. I found it hard to focus in class, as every little thing brought my mind back to Stephen Minett. Things that others did, that always seemed like pointless wastes of time, now had inherent value that didn't make sense. I never wasted so much time as I did thinking about the various ways kissing Stephen Minett might go. I tried to catch myself, to force myself to stop, but it was more difficult than anything I'd ever done.

Some inherent part of me wanted to get closer to him, wanted to love him, but far more of me simply wanted this distraction gone. It was a hateful nuisance, and any benefit I could gain from loving him would never outweigh how weak this feeling made me. I was vulnerable as long as I loved him. It was unbearable.

The only question was, how to kill him?

CHAPTER THREE
- ATARAH
ADEBAYO

The plan for killing Stephen was to be complicated, and most of that was not my fault.

For the first few days of this new... thing, I did the only thing I could think of to do, which was to learn as much about Stephen as I possibly could. I went back to the theatre that night after the movie, after gracefully rejecting Ava, and I waited until his shift was over. Without a plan, I chose not to risk going in the building. As I sat in my front seat, I watched him leave out the main door and get into a car which I quickly memorised as his. I followed that car at a reasonable distance until I found out where his home was. Knowing his address was easy, but it was nowhere near enough to decide what to do next.

I hardly slept that night. All I could think about was Stephen, and I knew by four in the morning that he was going to have to die for certain. There was simply no avoiding it. I thought perhaps it was best to just murder him openly and deal with the police investigation, because I couldn't figure out a way to make it seem like an accident. That, and violence felt necessary. I didn't know if that's how emotions worked, but it was something I found myself wanting, to just enact some kind of violence towards him. To make him bleed, bleed out these feelings. Or at the very least, to make his death up close and personal, with my hands around his throat.

The next day, most of my friends couldn't tell anything was off about me. In fact, nobody questioned a thing. My acting was good. I watched Stephen all day. I just had to last the few weeks it would take for my plan to come together; loving Stephen was a thousand times harder than enduring Amanda's bullying had ever been, and I wanted nothing more than for it to end. To stop feeling.

There is usually no spanner thrown into the works of my plans. When there is, it's almost always something I can adapt to. I was not prepared for this spanner.

Three days after my feelings for Stephen emerged, my sisters were all invited to a birthday party. Some girl I learned the name of for conversation's purposes, but otherwise knew nothing about. Dayo. My parents sent me to pick them up when the party was over, and I was invited inside. It was in that house that my relationship with her began.

I knew of Atarah in the same way I knew of everyone. She had switched schools a few times, although she was currently attending mine, in my year level. I had not spoken to her before, but I had seen her around- she was difficult to miss. If her bright blue dreadlocks and multitude of piercings didn't make her stand out, her loud voice and willingness to speak to anyone about anything would do it. She was well known for something of a lack of shame, and stories circled about her hobbies and personality that many found distasteful- stalking of internet celebrities and unwillingness to take rejection, for example. She seemed to live in a world where criticism of her actions could never find her. I could definitely say I knew who she was.

It seemed like she didn't really know me, however. Atarah was Dayo's older sister, this I knew, so I wasn't surprised when she opened the door, peering around it awkwardly at first. "Oh, hi! You're here for...?" she asked, the flicker of recognition not yet reaching her dark eyes.

"The triplets. They're my little sisters." I gave her a smile and a nod, unsure of whether or not she was the hand-shaking type, but guessing rather safely that she was not. "How are you doing, Atarah?"

For a moment, I saw her panic as she struggled to remember who I was; but then, a grin crossed her face. She wore thick-rimmed black glasses and scarlet lipstick, bright against her dark mahogany complexion. "Alex, right?"

As I nodded, she opened the door and gestured for me to come in. "The kids are playing a game right now, so it might be a few minutes. Come inside while you wait."

With no reason to decline her, I followed her inside the house. We went through a long hallway with undecorated beige walls and ruddy tiles, into a kitchen with food and dishes sitting all over the counter. Atarah's mother- a woman who appeared like a taller, thinner, older version of her, without the hair dye and piercings- was slowly making headway into cleaning this up. A particularly fat ginger cat lounged in the light of the window. Three kids who had already lost sat at the dining table, snacking on chips. One of my sisters was among the three. She looked up as I came in, processed that we were leaving soon, and visibly bit back a complaint about it. "Alex? Are we leaving now?"

"Soon. Let Darcy and Ellis finish playing first." As Atarah sat at the table beside the children, so did I. My keys jangled on the wood, and a giggle was heard from one of the rooms, a giggle I recognised as belonging to one of the triplets.

"Can we wait until the game's over, so I can say good-bye to Dayo?" she asked, and I capitulated.

"Okay." I smiled at her, convincing the room that something about her charms me. I didn't care.

Atarah looked between me and my sister, taking a moment. The game was apparently hide and seek. When those around the table were distracted, as the searcher relegated another child found, Atarah turned to me and said, "do you have another sibling, or is it just you and the triplets?"

It wasn't a question I had ever had before, and the answer was confusing. I didn't think Bailey counted. I never talked about him, simply because it never came up. To the best of my knowledge, nobody knew. "Why do you ask?"

Atarah didn't seem bothered by my confused response. She pointed at me. "A." She then gestured to Charlie, the first triplet. "C. And the other two are D and E. I hope there's a pattern there, or else that's mildly infuriating."

I didn't understand the general obsession with patterns that people had. At that time, I had felt anger exactly once since the day I fell in love, when I saw someone flirting with Stephen from across the yard. It was an overwhelming static in my ears that needed some kind of violence to settle. It was intense, hot and painful, blistering, triggered by something that felt devastating. I found it hard to believe that my parents not naming their children in perfect alphabetical order was, in any sense, infuriating to anyone.

But I humoured her, and when she pointed it out so directly, I may as well mention it. It was the trade-off I always did; offering information as a form of social currency, to make her trust me. I would regret this in the short term. "We did have a brother, Bailey." I inflect my voice with the necessary sadness and pause before his name, in a practiced dance of emotions I did not feel. Grief was not a thing I had come to experience yet; the closest I had come was something I believed to be longing and sadness, keeping me up at night as I imagined what Stephen might've been doing.

I expected, even for someone known to be somewhat rude, a level of backing off, or at least some kind of sympathy. When she didn't immediately offer some form of condolences, I thought perhaps she didn't understand. She leaned closer, and in a conspiratory tone of voice, she asked, "how did he die?"

It took me a moment to process what she said, to figure out how to respond. My blank expression slipped through, my empty response was noticed, and I tried my best to rectify it in the next moment. I wasn't sure if I should be offended, or to just answer her question, and my uncertainty made it a little hard to properly act. "It was an accident. He was five, I was seven. He- fell into Lake Michigan. Couldn't swim, and nobody was around to help him." In the last two sentences, I was able to inject some mimicry of sadness, a faint echo that she would hopefully pick up on. Watching her, she nodded slowly as I told her what happened, and honestly seemed more disappointed than anything.

Nobody knew what happened to Bailey, except now Atarah.

"Sorry if that was kind of a rude question. I'm just interested in death." She didn't seem sorry at all as she said that. It was the common misuse of the word as a pointless statement.

"It's a fair thing to be interested in," I told her, my trained reaction, but as I thought about it, it seemed like a risk to let her too close. Death was something I was unusually surrounded by, and she had a chance of noticing.

"Most people would disagree on that," she answered, gazing at me over the rim of her glasses. She was silent for a moment, pausing as Ellis came into the room, caught. I could feel Atarah's gaze boring into the side of my head. I thought it was best to not draw her attention to me, but extracting myself with any degree of subtlety would be nearly impossible until the kids' game was over. So I sat and waited, and struggled with something to say.

"Well, you didn't say you actually kill people, so." I shrugged at her, offering something of a smile. I didn't want to alienate anyone; that was how I had trained myself, and it was often best. I tried to remain amicable to her, but at that point, I knew I couldn't risk befriending her. A shameless girl with an interest in death was not safe for me. My words to her might've been humorously ironic, if I cared about humour.

Atarah smirked at me a little. One of the guests gazed over at us in curiosity, having heard the words 'kill people';

when she disregarded us Atarah's gaze fell back to me, considering. I could feel her judging me, deciding what to think of me. "If I had-"

"Alex?" Ellis pulled on my sleeve, accidentally saving me from an even longer, tougher conversation. "Are we going now? I feel sick."

"As soon as the game's over," I told her, gently running my fingers through the ends of her hair in a way I knew she liked. She rested her head in the crook of my arm, groaning gently at her apparent sickness.

Atarah was watching the movement of my fingers through Ellis' hair. She studied me for one long moment, and said, "why don't I see you around school more often?"

"Maybe I just blend in," I shrugged. She nodded slowly.

"I'm not sure about that," she responded somewhat cryptically, straightening up as the last two children entered the room: Dayo and Darcy.

Darcy looked upon me with interest. "Oh, we're going?"

"Yep. Sorry Dayo," I said with a little smile. Darcy went about hugging the birthday girl, Charlie got up and approached some of her friends, and Ellis began to wave and say her goodbyes whilst still leaning on my side. Atarah offered my sisters her own goodbyes, offering a high-five, which Charlie and Darcy both took.

I was able to extract myself and the triplets in a reasonable amount of time, but as Atarah showed us out, I knew she had twigged that something was off about me. It was the little glint in her eyes, that way she was looking at each movement of mine, inspecting my actions for something discordant with the normal humanity she'd find in anyone else. It was the same look that Amanda used to have, although Atarah's was not quite as tinged with disgust. When she waved a final goodbye, she watched as I got into the car with my sisters. It was a warning. She was paying attention.

My second encounter with Atarah was two days after the first. I had spent my days at school watching Stephen from a distance, trying to get an idea of his routine. It was regular and uninterrupted, and actually seemed to naturally intersect with mine a lot. He drove to school, passing by my house on his way, and tended to park in the same section of the carpark as I did. I'd see him everywhere around school. He looked considerably happier at school than at work, and the times I'd catch a glimpse of him taking out the trash at work were just about the only times I saw a scowl from him. His work closed at ten, and he'd finish at eleven, and drive home. I had his address memorised.

He spent most lunches sitting only a table or so away from mine, and we shared three of our classes, all electives. I would often find myself facing him and gazing at him like some lovestruck idiot.

It was lunchtime, and he was sitting two tables away with a group of kids I knew to be drama nerds. Every time I tried to get a good look at him, he'd suddenly meet my eyes. So I focused on what my friends were saying, in their entirely meaningless conversation, and tried not to feel upset because I wasn't with Stephen.

There was five of us sitting there. Madison, Kai, Chloe and Ben. Madison and Kai were there when I fell in love, and in a sense, I could almost blame them for taking me to the theatre in the first place. Ben and Chloe were other friends I'd gotten to know through Madison; she was the most gregarious person in the class, the easiest to befriend. Kai I had known previously, but had drifted away from due to circumstance- he was Amanda's boyfriend, who I'd stolen from her before I'd murdered her.

"And like- I guess it upset her that Ben didn't want to go? I get that, but it's up to-" Madison was saying, the tail end of some story about Ava, when the empty spot at our table was suddenly filled by an unexpected visitor. I didn't expect her to return, or at least not to be so bold about it, and none of my friends knew why she was here.

"Sorry if I'm interrupting," Atarah said, absolutely not sorry. She looked at me before anyone else, a smile lurking just beyond her expression. "I just have a few questions."

"For... all of us?" Madison looked around, a little confused. Chloe gave me a glance, silently asking if I knew why she was here. There was no way for me to answer her except with a shrug.

"Well, mainly you two." She had a pen in her hand, and she used it to point to me and Kai. As I tried to draw the connection, she did it for me. "You both knew Amanda McIntosh, didn't you?"

My first interaction with her was about one of my murders, although she didn't know it, and the second was about another. Something occurring once is happenstance, and I wouldn't ascribe any meaning to it; a second time might be a coincidence. But when it comes to suspicious deaths I've been close to, it wasn't a risk I was very willing to take.

"What about her?" I asked, tinging my words with what felt appropriate. Pain, and confusion, but only a little bit. A long distant memory. Kai's eyebrows knitted together as he stared at Atarah in disbelief, unable to form the words to ask a question. His ex-girlfriend, who, as far as he knew, killed herself not long after he cheated on her with me (or at least, what counted as cheating in freshman year). He didn't want to remember her.

"I do this video series on unexplored mysteries, and I've heard talk that her death wasn't actually a suicide." Alarm bells were ringing loud enough to deafen me inside my head. "I was told you knew her at the time. I just wanted to get your stories. They'll be anonymous-"

Kai asked the question, saving me from finding a way to worm it into the conversation somehow. "Who the fuck is making up those kind of conspiracy theories? She's been dead for like, five years. Can't people leave it alone?"

"If it bothers you, I can go. I didn't mean to upset you." There, again, she said an apology she absolutely did not mean. She didn't seem bothered at all by the odd gazes she was receiving, the fact that she was probably being rude.

"It doesn't bother me, I just don't get why you're digging it up," Kai answered, doing a poor job of lying about his emotions on the matter. He and I broke up not long after Amanda died, and he never told me how he felt about things. Of course, I made no effort to find out, but it was put behind us pretty quickly. I didn't need to know.

Atarah turned to me, her gaze intensely focused. I suspected, even if I could not be sure, that this was more about me than anything. "Alex?"

"Maybe later," is what I said. I didn't mean it, but with the tone I said it in, that should've been obvious. It was a dismissal, and Atarah must've known that.

"Who told you it wasn't a suicide...?" Madison asked, or perhaps demanded.

"Oh, I just heard." She shrugged off the question. "I was just investigating. I do a video series on unsolved mysteries," she repeated, like maybe everyone was reacting strangely because they simply didn't know what was going on. "I thought this might've been an unsolved mystery."

She was in a position I'd been before. Around other human beings, not understanding why they reacted to strongly to things I found entirely meaningless. I had gone through that when I was a child and learned from it, however.

"There's no mystery," I told her, completely lying to bar her from digging too deep. She was already flagged in my mind as dangerous, and this was only making me warier. I knew to avoid her from then on.

"Okay, well." She fixed her glasses and put her pen away. "Sorry for bothering you guys, then." She was staring at me, and I tried to look away, but my eyes caught on Stephen's, and whatever Atarah said next, I didn't catch it. Stephen's eyes were gorgeous, and it took all of my strength to pull my gaze away from his. I stared at my fingers for a moment, hoping there was no blush in my cheeks, until I could compose myself enough to meet the eyes of those around me again. My friends didn't notice; they allowed me to fade into the background like furniture, at least when I wanted to.

When I looked up, Atarah had left, and Madison went to me for an answer. "Why did she... What?"

"She's just weird like that," Ben said, scowling a little as she left. "I don't get it."

"She's been at this school for like, a year and I've never talked to her," Chloe said, watching her leave. "I see her around a lot and I think she's just... like that. Like Ben said. Maybe she gets off on weird shit, I don't know."

I decided not to join in the complaining, because it might mean telling them about the one proper interaction I'd had with her where she'd asked me about my brother. I could've mentioned her strange obsession with death that was evident through only two interactions with her. But why would I tell my friends the truth?

For a little over a week, Atarah didn't ask me any strange questions. In the classes we shared, she'd take a moment to talk to me before the teacher arrived, but when I sat with my friends, she didn't attempt to join us. Talking to her was the kind of situation where I might've been annoyed, had I cared; she seemed to mostly talk about herself, but she was always watching me, paying too much attention. It was strange, and I couldn't quite figure it out. She would make comments about my friends, lean on me, or nonchalantly bring up some serial killer from decades ago, and she was clearly testing for my reaction. I did everything in my power to keep up the persona I'd built, easy-going, fluid and a little dumb, but it was difficult with how far she pushed it. Every time I couldn't quite get it right, she'd get this self-satisfied smile.

And then, one day as I was at my locker, I felt a hand on my arm. It was Atarah, because of course it was.

"Are you ready to talk about Amanda?" Atarah asked. She was significantly shorter than me, and had to tilt her head up to look me in the eye, but I felt like I was the one being looked down upon. I was often somewhat intimidating by accident, but not to Atarah. "Something was odd with her death, wasn't it?"

I sighed, leaning on my locker. "I don't know anything about Amanda's death that wasn't-" I began, but I didn't get very far before she interrupted.

"I asked Ophelia Hough about you." Her honesty was surprising. "Not Amanda, you. She told me to ask you about Amanda's death. She said, kind of cryptically, that Amanda's death might not have been a suicide. That's not all she said, either."

Immediately, I needed a moment to think through those words. As far as I knew, ever since I killed their father, Ophelia and Ezra Hough had only vaguely suspected me, or at least, hadn't been able to do anything about their suspicions. Ophelia was a little too quiet and odd, and Ezra a little too loud and obnoxious, for people to really trust them over me. I'd been perfecting an estimation of perfect trustworthiness for my entire life. My occasional slip-ups tended to go under the radar. Nobody would believe I had really killed someone, not when it was a tale that someone like Ophelia was telling.

Atarah, however, was just crazy enough to believe it. And while Ophelia wouldn't tell just anyone, it didn't surprise me that, when pushed, she'd point someone like Atarah in the direction of my misdeeds.

What was surprising was that she suspected me of Amanda's murder, too. Not just her father's. I didn't think she was that smart.

"I was kind of in close proximity when she died." I built my lie quickly out of pieces of the truth. "But it was a suicide. She was on drugs, and depressed, and she and her boyfriend had just had a falling out. I'm guessing Ophelia told you Kai was her boyfriend." Atarah nodded to that, and I tried to make my story just long enough that she'd buy it and leave me alone. "She was bullying me, but I find it hard to blame her when her life was as bad as it was. Why, what do you think happened?"

"She was bullying you?" Atarah confirmed, and I nodded. "Just out curiosity… did anyone think you killed her?"

"She slit her own wrists in a school bathroom and wrote a suicide note. I was thirteen. There's no way I could've done it." I told lies as easily and effortlessly as I did the truth. I had no tells, as it all felt the same to me. Atarah shouldn't have been able to figure out I was lying to her, at least not from my behaviour.

Over her shoulder, I saw the only face I cared about, and my heart began to beat again. Atarah opened her mouth to speak, but she didn't get a word out, as Stephen stepped up to us and said, "Atarah- sorry, do you know what the home-work is for this week?"

The rest of the world was silent and colourless as soon as Stephen was around. It wasn't even me he was speaking to- although he offered me a cursory glance and a smile- but I was frozen in place. I had avoided all one-on-one interaction since falling for him, and my reaction to seeing him up close was so, so much worse than I'd imagined. I froze up in fear and couldn't move, my face burning as he waited for Atarah's answer, somewhat impatiently. Which was weird, because he was a patient person- or at least I thought. I had to remind myself I didn't really know him at all.

"For geography?" Atarah was clearly distracted as she answered him. She looked between us for the long moment it took her to think of her answer. "Oh- just the last pages of the exercise." She seemed to snap into the present then, turning to face him. "Although our projects are due in two weeks. I haven't even started mine."

Her response was amicable, but a little forced, injecting a degree of friendly banter that wasn't earned. Stephen's smile and nod might've been forced or they might've been genuine; I wasn't paying attention. I was too distracted by his smile itself, a gentle curl of his lip that flipped over my stomach and made me want to run away. If this was what love was sup-posed to feel like, how did anyone tolerate it for even a moment? How did anyone find it pleasant? How did anyone want more of it?

"Thank you," he said in that velvety voice of his, step-ping away a little. "Yeah, I haven't started mine either. I don't know where to begin."

I was still gazing at Stephen, unable to break my eyes away. The curl of his hair around his brow was mesmerizing in some strange way. With Atarah thoroughly distracted from me, I had the chance to slip away, but Stephen was here, and it was nearly impossible to force my body to move. Was this why people spent their lives with the ones they loved? Be-cause their hearts held them prisoner, and it was a kind of Stockholm syndrome that drove them to talk about love's greatness?

He was so beautiful, and it was the worst. These new ideas of beauty felt like thorns to be picked from my side. Beauty wasn't a real thing; it was illusory, and I wouldn't let Stephen deceive me.

"Neither." As Atarah turned to break off the conversation with him, and return to questioning me, the bell rang throughout the hallway, signalling that we were supposed to be in class. Stephen caught my gaze, and I dropped whatever book I was holding, scrambling to pick it up as it banged loudly on the metal bottom of my locker.

I refocused my eyes on my books, cheeks blazing, and ignored the two beside me. I felt for the first time embarrassment. I knew a clumsy act such as that was normal, but somehow the idea of Stephen thinking I was clumsy was mortifying, and I wanted to escape the very event, to erase it from history. Thoughts of worry filled my head: what if he realised my little crush on him through that small act? What if he's weirded out by me because of it, what if he hates me for it? What if he's laughing at me right now on the inside?

None of it mattered. I was going to kill him, wasn't I?

I couldn't convince myself that none of it mattered.

"We should probably all get to class. Bye, Alex," Stephen said, and I let his voice run warmly through me, before I brought my walls back up. The sound of him saying my name shook me to my very core, despite the fact it was just common politeness. I mumbled a goodbye, but stumbled over every syllable.

"Yeah," Atarah agreed, and I heard Stephen go. I felt empty and weak when he walked away.

I avoided looking at Atarah. "I need to go," I said, before she could ask me any other questions. My heart was quivering, and my emotions were welled up in my throat; I couldn't manage to talk to her. I stared blankly at my books, unable to remember what class I had next. All I could remember was Stephen's little smile.

"Oh...kay." Atarah's confusion was noticeable. "What's up with-"

"Don't ask me any more questions." I didn't intend to say those words. I didn't intend the panic, the frustration I was hiding, to creep into them. I didn't intend for my hands to shake, and I desperately wanted to run and hide in the bathroom. I needed the world to go away. I had no experience controlling my emotions; I had to learn very, very quickly in that moment. I leant into my locker and closed my eyes, trying to block out the rest of the world. Emotions were tiring.

Atarah was quiet, and after a long second, I checked and she was gone.

I was already wary of Atarah, but it grew even stronger after that point. She never finished her thought on Ophelia, and I knew she was suspicious. My reaction to Stephen couldn't have gotten past her, and I needed to know what she thought, at the very least. I needed to know how much of a threat she was to me.

I could guess, though, that she was going to return. I didn't think Atarah was one to give up.

It did take longer than I thought, but then again, I didn't give her many chances. I managed to avoid her for a week before she got through to me again.

I was following Stephen after school; his routine was a little different depending on the day of the week. He usually drove home, and then went to either dance practice or work a few hours later, unless it was a Monday, in which case he stayed home. It was a Thursday, and he should've been going home before work, but he was heading to the school gym.

The reason for this was, at first, unclear, until I remembered that signups for queer club this year were open. I used to join every year, but I'd simply forgotten this year, as Stephen took up every waking moment.

Atarah was signing up, which wasn't surprising; she'd briefly mentioned being bi, after all. But I was wary of her, and I stuck myself right to the side of the first friend I found, Chloe, hoping Atarah wouldn't get a chance to talk to me. I didn't want Stephen to notice me either- even though I had all the right in the world to be here, I was afraid he'd catch on that I was following him. If he did, it would become difficult to get enough information to have a strong murder plan. I was already having to be extra careful, as he'd caught me staring more than a few times. I could take no risks.

I thought I blended into groups of students well enough; Atarah walked past me, laughing with a friend of hers, and didn't so much as glance my direction. I watched as Stephen signed up, and soon after him, Atarah. Stephen walked past me to leave, although I kept my attention towards Chloe and invited no conversation from him; I didn't even know if he saw me. There was a pang in my chest as he left, somehow hurt that he hadn't spoken to me, even though that's what I wanted. Being hurt by that wouldn't even be logical for a normal human being.

Atarah walked by, and again, I didn't look up at her as she walked out the door. I had intended on following Stephen home again, and I quickly signed up and left, leaving Chloe with an excuse. I thought I'd make it out of the gym and to my car in time to catch him, but before I could make it out, Atarah walked back in, this time alone. For a moment, she glanced around, but as soon as she saw me, she headed straight for me.

I prepared myself for a confrontation, but the words I heard her say were not the ones I expected. I wasn't sure exactly what I expected, but it was not, "hey Alex, I think someone's trying to break into your car."

"Excuse me?" I asked, thinking perhaps I'd misunderstood. She gestured for me to follow her, and I did.

Standing just outside the door, she pointed in the direction of my car, and sure enough, a nondescript person dressed suspiciously unremarkably, with a hat and glasses to unsubtly disguise their features, was peering into the back window of my car.

"How'd you know that was my car?" I asked her quietly, even though the person was a fair way away and wouldn't have heard us speaking at normal volume.

"You picked your sisters up in it," Atarah explained, looking on at the scene with a detached curiosity. "Any idea why someone might be... I can't tell if they're trying to steal it or just snooping on you."

"It's a pretty cheap car." As we watched, they took a step back and noted my license plate. The only thing I could really tell from this distance was that it wasn't a police officer.

"Yeah, they're taking your license plate. Did you do something illegal, or what?" Atarah asked. More questions from her were not what I needed, but she had gathered the same thing I had; someone was investigating my car, and therefore, probably, me.

"No," I lied easily. It was partially true, as every murder I'd committed had been five years ago or more. There was no way the police were still investigating Mr Hough's murder, and the other two cases were already closed. "I have no idea what's going on. Thank you for telling me, though."

The investigator gazed around the parking lot and spotted us by the door, watching. They quickly pretended to have dropped their keys on the ground, picked them up, and made a swift exit.

"I don't have a lot of time, so..." Atarah paused, checked her pockets, and thought for a moment. "Give me your phone."

"Why?" I asked, even as I was unlocking it and handing it to her. I didn't take my eyes off of the investigator as they retreated into an inconspicuous black car. That was a higher priority than whatever Atarah was going to do. Atarah didn't want to hurt me, she just wanted the truth, and there was no way in hell I was going to give her that.

She was silent for a moment, and when she handed it back to me, a new contact page was open. She'd inserted her name with a little heart emoji beside it and her number. "You're going to call me later. I want to help you, but I need to know the truth first."

"What the hell are you on about?" I did my best to feign some kind of offended or confused reaction. I was as close to confused as someone could be without feeling; I was numbly unsure of what was going on. "What truth?"

"Just call me, I've got to go," Atarah said, heading off

quickly away from me. Calling over her shoulder, she added, "call me after seven, but before nine!"

When I checked my car, it was fine. Nothing was taken, it wasn't unlocked, and there were no new marks on the outside. I was just being snooped on.

I had two things to think about as I drove home. I didn't follow Stephen that night, knowing I might be being watched myself.

By the time I had helped Darcy set up a new game of hers on the computer, eaten dinner, and done all the homework I had planned, it was seven thirty, and I spent a while staring at my phone, mulling over whether or not I should call her. In the end, the decision was easy; I needed to know what it was that she knew, and in the worst-case scenario, I could always kill her if necessary. In fact, an accident wherein she and Stephen both died could be easily engineered, by working queer club into the plan. She would still know what she knew even if she didn't tell me; it was worth it to find out. The fact that she had given me her phone number, as opposed to messaging me on public social media, was telling. This was something kind of personal.

So I called her.

"What did you want to talk about?" I asked her in the nicest voice I could procure as soon as she picked up the phone.

"Alex! Just one moment," she said. It was unclear if she was saying that to me or whoever she was in the room with. There was a background noise when she first picked up the phone, but it quieted down significantly after she spoke a few sentences away from the receiver, and apparently walked into another room. "Okay. What's up?"

"You gave me your number to talk about something," I reminded her, and she laughed like I'd just told a joke.

"Oh, yeah. So." She paused. "Forgive my forwardness here, alright? So after you came to pick up your sisters, and I asked you about your brother, I realised I'd never actually seen you around much before. Like, I'd seen you, but never talked to you, and you seemed cool in a way most people aren't. So I asked my friends about you, and the consensus was that you seemed nice, just quiet. But then someone mentioned that there were rumours you were actually secretly bad. I wasn't sure I believed them."

I almost hoped this was something lame, like her asking me on a date. That would be easy enough to get out of. In the background, I could hear the sounds of what might've been driving.

She continued. "So I asked Ophelia what was wrong with you. You know her. She said you weren't what you seemed, and I should ask you if Amanda's death was a suicide. I don't think talking about Amanda bothered you, no, but I still didn't get the truth on that. That was part of what I wanted to ask you. My first question is: what really happened with Amanda?"

There was a pause, and I realised it was my turn to speak. "She killed herself. I told you-"

"How did you know her?" Atarah asked, and the pause after her words was painful to sit through. I didn't know what to tell her. There was the practiced lie from five years ago, but it took a moment to remember. I hoped she mistook my hesitance in remembering the lie as a show of emotion.

"She bullied me." I told my peers one thing, and the teachers another. "I think it was, you know, because she was depressed, she was taking her emotions out on me. It's fine. I don't blame her. She was a good person at heart, I'm sure."

"You know, Alex, I can tell that's rehearsed, and you don't mean it." I knew she would think as much. It was hard to figure out her feelings when she wasn't physically there with me, but her voice conveyed enough. "You weren't angry at her, even a little, for what she did? Didn't she put you in hospital once? Don't you feel even a little bit like she deserved to die? Bullies, well, they're not good people. They use their strength in cowardly ways. If I was you, I'd be glad she's dead. I might've even killed her myself, were I in your position."

"Nobody deserves to die." I kept up the persona, but she was saying something I'd never heard anyone say before. She was justifying, in her moral brain, my actions. I knew normal human beings committed murder, but it was usually a release of anger, much like my killing of Stephen, or for money. Murderers were beyond ousted by society. Saying something like Atarah just said was, morally speaking, wrong, as objectively as morals could be objective.

"Ophelia thinks you killed Amanda. And she thinks you killed Amanda because she thinks you killed her father." Atarah's voice had taken on a different quality, something almost reverent. "Ophelia wouldn't admit this, but he was a bad person too, apparently. Very cruel to anyone but his own family, his children, his pride and joy. I don't think he necessarily did anything wrong, actually. I imagine he must've been a strong man, using his resources to beat the competition and take what he wanted. He was your landlord, Ophelia said, and there was trouble. Your dad couldn't pay, and you were going to be kicked out, right?"

I couldn't answer her, but she wasn't looking for an answer. She kept talking. "He might've been strong, but there was someone stronger. Someone who stabbed him to death."

"Atarah, what are you saying?" I demanded. The worst-case scenario was fast approaching.

"Before I go any further, go out into your front yard."

"Why?"

"We can never know for sure if our phone calls are being monitored. Or will be monitored. Also, you left your location on, on like, every social media account you have."

She hung up then, and I did as she said, because she was heading into dangerous territory and I couldn't afford to let this go. I ran out into my front yard, half-dressed without my coat for the winter weather and my hair in the messiest of plaits. She was standing by the side of the road, leaning against her car, twirling her keys in one hand. I knew she'd been driving, but I hadn't guessed she'd been coming here.

"What the hell?" I asked her, feigning the emotion that felt appropriate, but she raised a finger as a silent 'shut up'.

She continued the conversation as though nothing had changed. "And Bailey. His name was Bailey, right?" she clarified, and I nodded slowly. Why was she smiling? "That's three deaths you were kind of close to. Isn't that a little interesting?"

"Atarah, I was seven when Bailey died, ten when Mr Hough died, and like, thirteen when Amanda died. Bailey's death was an accident and Amanda's was a suicide. Maybe Amanda's and Mr Hough's benefitted me by coincidence, but I was far too young to have done those things, and I wouldn't kill my own brother." With just the right inflections, just the right tone, maybe I could convince her. Maybe it would seem real. It sure sounded believable to me.

"Maybe you didn't kill him. Maybe you only killed the other two. Or maybe only one of them." Atarah's accusation was finally put into words, but her actions didn't seem to correlate with what she was saying. She was almost laughing, barely hiding her glee.

"You're accusing me of murder? You barely know me." The disbelief with which I riddled my words was pretty plausible, and in truth, it was hard to believe. She didn't have enough information to say that, did she?

"On that information alone, no. It could be a coincidence, sure. And any person other than me might've missed it." She was smug, almost. "Even the stranger investigating your car I probably could've put aside, although that really does make you seem kind of suspicious. But I've been watching you, and you never act quite right. It's close, but not quite right. And- I can't believe this- when Stephen came to talk to me, you fell apart. It was *so* obvious that you liked him, and not normally. I think I saw that actual, real you for a moment. I have another question for you."

"You just accused me of murder, but okay, go ahead." I forgot who I was supposed to be, sometimes, what I was supposed to be like. I wasn't sure if I was supposed to be the kind of person who got angry at this, or upset, or just reacted with confusion. My reaction ended up being a mix of all three.

"Did you know," she said, "that Stephen has a girlfriend?"

"What? Who?" The words flew out of my mouth before I could catch them. It occurred to me, even as I spoke, that she might've been lying, but fear and anger were overwhelming, even more so when they were together. I had fifteen different things I wanted to say all at one time. "How the fuck did I not- know- what the hell- I-"

"Jessie Monthouse," Atarah grinned, expectant gaze fixated on me, I didn't feel like my actions were under my control. I knew what I did next, but I did not plan to do so beforehand; it was what they called a knee-jerk reaction, something I had never experienced up until that moment.

As Atarah raised her hand- to do what, I don't know- I grabbed her by the wrist and slammed her against her car with a bang, gritting my teeth and demanding through them, *"you better be lying to me."*

Her shock afterwards was not surprising, but the glee that followed it was. Anger was seething behind my eyes, and I couldn't seem to let her go; ideas of Stephen so much as looking at anyone but me burned. I had never actually felt desire to hurt or kill anyone before- I killed for convenience. I knew what desire to kill felt like in that moment, that sadistic anger. It took hold of me when I thought about Jessie Monthouse.

"I am. Alex, I'm lying, he's single, and not even close to dating anyone." She spoke softly, and her words soothed the burning anger into a sizzling ember. I let her go, backing away and staring at my own hands. I had made a mistake, due to my emotions.

"Atarah, I'm so sorry. I didn't-" I began, trying to recover my reputation with her before anything worse could happen. She laughed, cutting me off.

"I was just confirming. I know what you are, Alex, you don't have to lie anymore." Her words were spoken with a strange degree of softness. "I'm not going to harm you. Like I said, I want to help, actually. But you've got to be honest. So, tell me the truth."

I had to make a split-second decision, without much time to consider the evidence or what to do. In that moment, the truth was what she wanted, and I had made all my choices in friendships by giving people what they want. I wasn't going to tell her she was right about everything, not yet, but I could give her a smaller truth. She didn't have to know I was a murderer yet- knowing what was wrong with me would be enough.

And so, for the first time in eighteen years, I looked another human being in the eye and I dropped the act. I let my face go blank. I relaxed my muscles and stopped trying to appear angry and confused. I stared her straight in the eyes, unbothered by what that made her feel. Unbothered by anything. Honest.

"Atarah. I truly didn't mean for my anger to get the better of me." When I spoke, I made no effort to force emotion into the words. They were spoken plainly, like reading a noticeboard. "Tell me plainly what you know."

Chapter Four - Alex and Atarah

Atarah's grin stretched throughout her whole face, lighting up her eyes. She fixed her glasses as she took me in; as quiet, empty, and still as I was. There was a second of silence, for which I waited, allowing her to consider me. To consider the truth.

And then, she spoke. Her voice, generally quite loud, high and distinct, was low and reverent. "Can I just... I won't offend you if I say something incorrect, will I? I mean, I've come this far, I may as well say it anyway."

"No, I won't be offended." The simplicity with which those words were spoken seemed to surprise her, even as she might've expected it.

"I will admit I had you a little wrong. I thought you were a yandere, but clearly that's at least a little off." Atarah's gaze still raked over me, taking in every little abnormality in my behaviour and tallying them all up.

"I don't know what that means," I told her.

"It's like... someone who's normally sweet and gentle, but becomes totally deranged when it comes to the person they love. The second part may still apply, I don't know." Her eyes finally returned to my face then, the same searching look in them. I didn't move or speak as she studied me.

"What do you know about me?" I asked again, when she was silent for a moment. There was no sound except the rustling of trees in the light breeze; all the houses were silent, and the road was dead.

"I know that you're in love with Stephen Minett." Atarah seemed nervous as she said that, wondering if perhaps she'd anger me again. The sound of his name only drew up a faint echo of longing in my heart, which despite its weakness, was felt like a seismic tremor. "And I know... I know you killed at least one of those three people. And I think you're going to kill again."

"And why should I trust you?" I asked of her before I decided what to do. Atarah had been, I thought, a threat to me, and she might've still posed one; this knowledge, if used against me, could potentially be life-ruining. But as it stood right now, she had accused me of murder with a grin on her face. She was a girl known to be a little obsessed with death, who was widely thought to be fucked up. She might've been on my side. I could kill her if she wasn't, but in that moment, she might've been something entirely unprecedented: an ally. A true one.

"I won't tell anyone whatever it is you tell me. And if you *are* going to kill... again," she spoke with such caution, shifting from foot to foot. It hadn't yet sunk in that I wasn't going to hurt her or be angry, if it wasn't about Stephen. Her voice was quiet and hesitant, and with the next words she spoke, it made complete sense. "I... can... help."

I nodded slowly. An ally; a risk worth taking. What a strange and complicated person, for a normal human. "I imagine it took a lot of courage to say that. It would be a pretty absurd thing to say, had you said it to anyone else." I was shivering slightly in the bite of the cold, and loose strands of hair were blowing in my face, but I didn't mind. "I'll trust you, Atarah, and tell you the truth. I'll hold you to that promise to keep quiet about it."

"Yeah," she breathed, awe still present in her dark irises. The worst-case scenario was that she had lied, and she was going to be horrified when she discovered the truth. But I could deal with that.

I looked around one last time, making sure we were alone. "I have, up until about three weeks ago, never felt emotions."

I expected her to interrupt, but she was enraptured, and said nothing. So I continued. "I'm sure that's hard to imagine for you, but it was normal. Without emotions, nothing mattered to me, and I made all my decisions based on what would make my life easiest, without being bored. Even boredom isn't really an emotion I can feel, but I have energy, and so I want to put it to things, where possible. But truly, there's no difference to me in almost any action. I can feel physical things as good or bad, and I'll relieve pain and seek pleasure when those things arrive, but I have no drive in regard to either of those things, behind the immediate situation. That is my background, which you would need to understand before you can understand why I've done the things I have."

I paused to let her ask questions, but she simply nodded for me to continue. She was usually talkative. This was a rare moment.

"My brother was a nuisance. My parents favoured him, and he loved to lie and blame things on me. He physically injured me a lot, and I had to share too much with him. It was such an inconvenience. I made the logical decision that my life would be easier if he were dead, and so I pushed him into Lake Michigan and he drowned."

At the confession of my first murder, Atarah's face changed, but not in a way I could comprehend. "Go on," was all she said; no questions, no condemnations. Awe was all she had to give me.

"Okay. I expected you to react differently, I'll admit," I

told her. "I'm not sure what I expected from you, but it wasn't this. You're strange."

"So you're surprised?" Atarah asked distractedly, still staring at me.

"As much as I can be without being able to care." I shrugged lightly. "So Bailey died. Everyone was upset, of course. I learned throughout my childhood how to fake emotions, and when each was appropriate, so I could pretend to be grieving. When I was that young, murder was easy to get away with. At least, Bailey's was. It got harder as I got older."

"You're good at faking emotions, I'll give you that." Atarah nodded at me. "I got the feeling you were a compulsive liar, but I had no idea all of your emotions were fake. Most people don't even realise there's a single thing strange about you. I was the odd one out for thinking so."

"Okay." I felt no need to add anything to that. "I'll continue the explanation-"

"Shit, yeah, sorry. I was trying not to interrupt." Atarah bit her lip, shifting a little where she stood. "I'll ask all my questions later. Oh, fuck, I just interrupted again, didn't I? I'm sorry."

"Atarah." Every time I used her name, it seemed to make her increasingly antsy, or perhaps excited at the honest me. An emotionless human being must've seemed like such an exotic concept to her, and she loved it. "It makes absolutely no difference to me how rude you are. I *cannot* care."

"I know, I'm just not quite used to the idea yet," Atarah said. "Anyway, go on."

"Okay. With Mr Hough, he was my landlord, yes. The case was such that he was pricing us out, and we would have to move. I didn't want to start again at a new school, and have to rebuild all of my social relationships. Building friendships is difficult, and although it's what I choose to spend a lot of my energy doing, I still wanted my life to be easy. I wanted to stay where we were living, and I could see an easy way to kill him, and so I did. We ended up moving anyway later on, although it was for favourable economic reasons, as opposed to unfavourable ones, and not as far as we would have moved. The case on his murder is technically still open. His children might think I killed him, although they can't prove it. It wasn't a life-ruining mistake, but it's a loose end that's still hanging. My reasons were not really worth the consequences of the murder."

"So you regret that one?"

"Again, Atarah, not truly. I can't feel regret about it. I can just logically think that it may not have been the best decision I could have made. I probably would still have done it, just better."

"Right. Sorry, I said I wouldn't ask questions, go on."

I ignored her meaningless apologies, acting as though she'd never said anything. "Ophelia, clearly, is still fixated on the idea enough to tell you about it. I'm not sure about Ezra. I avoid them both."

"Ezra's in the year below us, right? They look like twins. Her face is all red all the time and he's just as bad." As Atarah's frenzy grew, so did the difficulty she had in keeping her mouth shut. "He's fucking annoying, too."

Her lack of sensitivity was something I would have had to pretend to be bothered by in any other context. "If you were to react that way in a discussion of their father's death with anyone else, they would very likely be offended. I can see where your reputation comes from."

"Tell me about Amanda's death," Atarah demanded instead of answering, although she seemed amused by my words.

"Amanda was like you, in some ways. She knew I was not normal, but unlike you, she didn't like it."

"I thought she was like, a dumb bimbo or something. That's the mythology I've heard, anyway."

"Maybe. She was smart enough to figure me out, at least. She translated her fear of me into bullying, and after a time, it became more trouble than it was worth to let her live, although her death was the hardest to orchestrate."

"How does a thirteen-year-old believably fake someone's suicide?" Atarah was still in awe, and it seemed like she was only getting more thrilled as I spoke. "That's so impressive."

"It was risky, as it involved tricking my teachers into believing one thing, my peers another, and my parents another again. I homewrecked her and her boyfriend, first of all. She was incredibly offended that he would pick someone like me over her or anyone else he could've had, but he broke up with her, and from there, it was easy to paint her as depressed and unstable. She got her friends to make me swallow razorblades, and I used the outcome to frame her as self-harming in the eyes of the teachers, while telling my parents how unstable she was. Nobody at school ever knew either of those things. I copied her handwriting and wrote a believable note, and then I chloroformed her, took her into a school bathroom, and slit her wrists. I left through the window and nobody ever knew."

"Wow." Atarah breathed. "You really did that, huh? That's amazing."

"You're calling a murder amazing," I reminded her, but she didn't even seem to mind. She shook her head slowly, taking a step towards me and reaching for my hands. I let her take them.

"I'm calling you amazing. Yeah, I know what you did was bad, but that's not really how I see things." Atarah's eyes glittered. "The world is for the taking. You're unafraid of anything that should stop you, and you're fighting a battle against a society that doesn't seem to have a place in it for your authentic self. I can understand that. You didn't kill because you're evil or because you wanted to. You killed to conquer the things that stood in your way. When soldiers and great generals, politicians and police do that, we call it heroism."

Not a word of what she said meant a thing to me, but I had to wonder how a normal person can be so ousted from the norms of society that they believe such things as she did. I had no idea if she was right or wrong. In questions of morals I held no stake. But for my purposes, her beliefs were in my benefit.

"I guess I should thank you," I said, and she dropped my hands. "I'm guessing you would like to know about Stephen, too?"

"Absolutely. Go on."

"You have me wrong, about Stephen." I rubbed my cold arms, wondering if we should have this conversation inside; but then again, I didn't want my parents to know about her, not yet. Her involvement in my life was something I had yet to decide on. She was wearing a black faux-fur coat and thick woollen stockings, properly protected against the cold. Looking at her then, it seemed like she had plans for tonight. I met her eyes again. "I have fallen in love with him, yes. Three weeks ago, completely unexpectedly. He makes me feel things; he's the only thing that can. That's exactly why I have to kill him."

She furrowed her brows. "Come again?"

"I hate feeling things." There was a bitter tinge on my words; a weak emotion all in all, but stronger felt in my eighteen-year-long emotional emptiness. I was bitter because Stephen was my weakness. "I'm making stupid and irrational decisions now. My emotions are overwhelmingly negative. His presence is the only thing that brings me happiness, and yet, every time he's not around, I can be sad, I can miss him. And this... *longing*." I clutched at my chest as the snake I knew to be desire clutched at my heart, squeezing down. It was all in my mind, yet I felt a very real ache in my ribs. "It's completely unliveable. I need to get rid of it. I need to get rid of him, Atarah. I can't bear it."

"You don't want to be with him?" Atarah asked, as though it was completely unimaginable that I really wanted him dead. "I mean, that would get rid of the longing, and you'd only feel good things, right?"

"Those good feelings are blinding, misleading. They're lies. Maybe to you it's normal, but to me? It's equivalent to hallucination and delusion. And if Stephen and I were to..." even thinking the words 'get together' conjured up images of his hand in mine, his arms around me, things that generated a deceptive warm glow where that snake just was. The hope overcame the despair, but they were both alien influences, and did not belong. "Those good feelings won't last. He won't love me when he finds out the truth. If I begin to trust him, and let him in, when he leaves it'll hurt so much worse. I don't want..." the despair returned, crushing the hope like stepping on a snail. I didn't have to finish my sentence; Atarah understood.

"I get it. I mean, I don't really, but I do." She went to touch me, but decided against it, realising it made no difference to me. "But hey, I have a suggestion."

When I was silent, she took it as her cue to continue. "Don't kill him straight away. Killing him might not even be the best idea. What if you kill him, and then you're grieving for ages? That's surely worse, right?"

"That depends how bad grief is," I said, but even as I said it, I was thinking back on how my parents had responded to Bailey's death. Several years after the fact, I could still find my mother occasionally staring wistfully at the photos we had of him, and my father refused to get rid of any of his possessions for a year. I'd heard both of them accidentally say they had five children, as recently as three years ago. Even my sisters, who never knew him, had mentioned before that they'd wished he was alive. They didn't know what they were talking about, of course, but it affected them.

And Ophelia and Ezra were still so clearly bothered by their father's death. Ophelia was still telling people it was my fault, and if the events of earlier that day were anything to go by, she may've begun her own investigation, somehow. She still felt the effects of his death eight years later.

"Grief is horrifying." Her choice of words was so clearly a deliberate one. "When... look, you don't want that."

"You're right." After that long moment of consideration, I realised the wisdom of her suggestion. I wondered, briefly, about the mechanisms of her mind, how she was unbothered by the three lives I'd taken, when she had felt grief herself. Maybe I was wrong to presuppose that every other human being was far less self-interested than I was. "But what do you propose instead?"

"Well, you probably will kill him. But first, kidnap him." Her eyes glittered with the promise of the idea. "You can take out all your anger with him, and then you can kill him when you're certain you won't miss him. It'll be harder, but you won't have to do it alone. I'll help you." She grinned as she said that, like I would somehow be doing her a favour by allowing her to help.

"Why would you help me, Atarah?" I had to ask; I was learning, to some degree, that Atarah was not anything close to a normal human being, as I understood it. Like me, completely at odds with a peaceful society. That still didn't explain her decision in any satisfactory way. "Wouldn't you only be putting yourself in danger?"

"Danger makes me feel alive. I guess you wouldn't get that, but it doesn't matter. You're someone unlike anyone I've ever met before, Alex. I've always been interested in serial killers, and why they do the things they do. I half-lied, when I first asked about Amanda- I *do* do a series where Amanda's death might be relevant, but it's a series on murder. We've all got a morbid fascination with it, we just don't admit it. We watch those true crime shows, and although we never say it-" she leant in close, like this was the real secret, like we hadn't just been talking about actual murders I'd committed- "we all think of how we'd do it. We've all considered it. What if we just snapped, you know? At heart, we're animals. And animals are brutal. They kill, maim, and hurt whenever they need to. Most animals like doing it, too."

"What do you say to the majority of people who disagree with you?" I asked her, trying my best to understand this person in front of me. Most times, I never bothered, but she was such an odd case; and if she was going to be by my side, I needed to know what I was dealing with.

"The majority of people are hypocrites. Like I said- soldiers and police officers kill, but they're heroes, aren't they? What people don't realise is that they're a slave to their own morality. Morality they didn't make, that doesn't reflect reality." She seemed really into what she was saying. She truly meant it. "No life is worth more than any other. No death is any different. The strong, the brave, will do whatever they please to the weak and cowardly. The cowardly control us far too often. Mr Hough was a coward, trying to use his power to control you without giving you a chance to fight back- and you defeated him as a ten-year-old child. Amanda the same. I can't say much for your brother, but what I can say is that through none of your actions did you act with malice. You're just acting in this worldly stage, and the actions you chose were not underhanded, they were fair, and you made them based on logic. I can't hate that, only respect it. You're not bad, Alex, only neutral."

She seemed proud of herself, completely fixed in her belief. I could only shrug. "And what about Stephen?"

"Kidnapping Stephen will be doing what you need to do. Like a lion eating meat. You're fighting how you need to. And I don't need to help, but I want to. Besides, there are so many ways this can go. I'm not necessarily in favour of killing Stephen, because I think you're wrong when you say it'll be more pain than it's worth- but hey, I'd like to see a murder. Although maybe he'll even come to love you, after all."

I shook my head. "I highly doubt that, if I kidnap him."

Atarah shrugged. "I mean, it wouldn't put me off of someone. It'd be kind of cool, really."

"You're not most people," I reminded her.

She pushed her glasses up on her face and shook her head. "No, I'm not. I'm better than most people," she said with a little laugh. "Now, are you coming or not?"

"Coming where? If we're going anywhere, at least give me a moment to get properly dressed," I told her. She took a moment to look me over and blinked in surprise, like she hadn't expected me to come outside in so little. Like she expected me to know I was about to be invited out somewhere.

"Oh, of course, go get dressed." She paused expectantly, and when I didn't move, it took a long moment for her to realise she hadn't answered the question I'd asked. "I'm going out with some of my friends, and I thought you might want to come. Or- well, I want you to come. May as well be honest. I feel like we have a lot to talk about. Do you... need a reason to come, since it won't be fun for you, or....?"

"I may as well be out with you. It's as good as doing anything else. And we do need to discuss things, you're right."

I turned around at that point to go back inside and get myself dressed, and she let me go. As I walked back inside, all the calculations I'd been making on what to do about Stephen were thrown out the window, and indeed, so was a large amount of my future.

I planned on being fundamentally alone forever; I would have casual friends, be liked in my community, but I never wanted real friends. I never wanted to marry anyone or have children. Nobody would every truly know me; I wanted aid and maybe admiration, not companionship.

And I was making no guesses on how long Atarah would stick around, not yet. I knew people's relationships rarely lasted for a long time, and I'd been talking to Atarah for a matter of days or weeks, honest with her for minutes. I could guarantee nothing.

This was a very special case, however. She knew a secret of mine, perhaps the biggest secret anyone could have, and she had just volunteered to help me kidnap and kill somebody. That was not normal, and she'd be sticking around for at least a little while.

Maybe she could help me come up with a new plan tonight.

I found myself a coat and pulled on my boots. I told my mother I was going out, and she told me to have a good time, unbothered. I was an obedient and trustworthy child, and so my parents never questioned me much.

When I got back outside, Atarah was already in her car. I got in beside her, watching her face to try and gauge her emotions. She had an air of giddiness about her, as before, and I could tell she was bursting with questions. It didn't take long for them to come out.

"So you just... if you feel nothing, nothing bothers you, does it?" was the first thing she asked as we headed down the road. She drove a little faster than might've been recommended in the icy conditions, but I didn't call her up on it.

"No. Anything related to Stephen is the exception to those rules, of course. I can be in pain, or inconvenienced, and I dislike my freedom being restricted, or my work undone. I don't feel annoyed, though. Innocuous things that trigger annoyance or anger in others mean nothing to me."

"Right. Like, most people think I'm annoying, but nothing I could ever do would bother you? Like talking to much or whatever?"

"No." I counted her piercings; one in her nose, one in her eyebrow, three in each ear. They were all gold studs and rings, glittering against her skin like flecks of colour in an opal. Something must've caused her to go through the pain of getting those things done, something I couldn't understand.

"And you're totally honest with me, then?" she confirmed. She wasn't driving downtown, contrary to what she told me, but I could assume we were meeting her friends.

"If you would prefer me to be, then yes. I often tell people what they want to hear, but since you know my secret and want me to be honest, I will."

"I do want you to be honest. All the time. So, like..." she paused, considering her next question carefully. "So if you feel absolutely nothing, does that mean you can't like, like people? I mean, other than Stephen, you know."

"I have never loved anyone, other than him. I never loved my parents or my siblings either. I can like people on something of an objective basis, based on how easy it is to spend time with them. Since I can be entirely honest with you, and drop my facade, I suppose that as of ten minutes ago, I like you more than anyone else I know."

"I'll take that as a compliment," Atarah grinned. "Can you like people, as in, like, dating them?"

"I can, and do, find people sexually attractive, but dating is usually not a good idea. I will if there's no commitment." As soon as she mentioned dating, my mind went to Stephen, and I hated it. "I dated Amanda's boyfriend for a while, Kai, but that was strategic. Since then, I've dated two girls and another boy, and in every case, I had a relatively short, low-effort relationship with whoever asked me out. I always planned on breaking it off if anyone got too close, but they always broke up with me. Not that I actually felt anything about it."

Atarah raised her eyebrows. "Wow, okay. I'm not surprised that many people are interested in you, actually. I'm just surprised you said yes to anyone. Everyone seems to like the persona you put forth. They're always talking about how you're nice, and funny, and easy-going. And you're, well." She gestured to me, like I should be able to figure out her opinion of my appearance on her own. "You've got like, this elvish kind of beauty going on. I can see how they liked you."

I blinked at her. "Okay."

She quickly waved aside the fact that she had just said that, like she was embarrassed to compliment me. "Okay, but while I'm at it, do you think I'm attractive? 'Cause I've never gotten someone to honestly, objectively tell me, that's all-"

"Are you one of those people that finds serial killers attractive? Is that what's going on here?" I asked her, interrupting her rambling sentence.

I meant it without offense, but she sputtered with embarrassment, pointing a finger at me. "First of all, no, no, no, that's not what I'm saying!" Her attention was slightly too focused on me and not the icy road for my liking. "Second of all, that is not the only reason people are interested in true crime! Thirdly, I don't want to fuck you, so don't insinuate it again! I've known you for like, two weeks!"

"We met when you first moved here two years ago," I reminded her offhandedly, "but I didn't mean to upset you when I said that. I misunderstood. *Please* focus on the road."

Atarah took a breath and followed my advice, for long enough to calm down a little. "Sorry. I overreacted. My stepdad says that a lot and it pisses me off." Atarah turned into a side road, a court, that I recognised as containing her house. She pulled up in front of her driveway, turned the engine off, and climbed out of the car.

As I got out myself and followed her up the path, I said, "oh, and I guess I would say you're attractive. Not outstandingly so, but enough."

Atarah shrugged, a little smile on her lips. "I'll take it."

CHAPTER FIVE - EZRA HOUGH

By that time of night in winter, it was already pretty dark outside; dark enough that I almost missed a step I didn't see and stumbled onto her porch. I could hear voices inside, laughing about something. Atarah opened the door and waved me through, directing me towards a door in the entrance hallway that seemed to hold the voices behind it. The outside of the door was as characterless as the rest of the house, with only a black A on it, but when I went through it, it was obvious that this room was Atarah's.

There was too much furniture to properly fit in this room. Against one wall was a black double bed, with black gauze and fairy lights hanging around the walls; a tripod was set up to point towards the bed, although no camera sat on it. A cluttered desk, at which sat a computer surrounded by papers, various knick-knacks, and nerdy things I couldn't hope to understand, was opposite a built-in wardrobe overflowing with clothes that hadn't been properly hung up. The room also contained a bookshelf that was filled up to the brim with books, and still left some of her novels sitting longways on top of the others. There was a full-length mirror in one corner, and beside it a dresser, which was itself covered in more papers and small items, although there was a somewhat-organised makeup collection taking up one section of the space. One wall was covered in posters for various bands and movies, and there was a large section of another that was made up of newspaper clippings that, I could guess, reflected her interest in criminals. I had to put off my inspection of those, however, as there were two people sitting next to each other on Atarah's carpet who were all looking up at me in curiosity.

Atarah quickly came to introduce me, saving me from figuring out what I had to say. "Ladies, hello. I did tell you I'd be able to get Alex to come, didn't I?"

"Hey Alex," said one of them, like we'd already met a while ago and we'd just been reunited. She was a redhead, her hair in an undercut. She had freckles and dramatic, skilfully done eye makeup. She didn't go to our school. "I'm Kenia."

"Hi, Kenia, it's nice to meet you." As soon as I was no longer alone with Atarah, the facade went back up. It wasn't bad; it was my life, after all. It was just that little bit more tiring.

"Alex? What's that short for?" asked the other girl, fixing her glasses. She had short, curly dark hair and a bad case of acne that was the only visual hint she was any older than thirteen.

"Nothing," I said, watching carefully for her response, but she seemed willing to accept it when I said it.

Atarah waved her hand at her friend. "Don't mind Maisie," she told me, heading over to her dresser and sifting through it for something.

Kenia stood up, coming over to me. She was significantly shorter than me, but so was just about everyone. "Ooo, your hair is so long," she said, admiring it. She took the plait over my shoulder and ran her fingertips along it. "Can I do your hair? Please?"

The apparently instinctual reaction in a lot of people, usually girls, to want to play with my hair was the only real reason I kept it so long in the first place. "Sure," I told her with something of a smile, and she grabbed my wrist, pulling me to sit down on the floor beside Maisie. Like Atarah, she seemed very inclined towards physical touch, and completely unbothered by how others felt about that. She sat me down on the carpet, turned by back to her, and began undoing my hair, and that was that. I was already accepted into the group.

The conversation between the three girls picked up easily. What I quickly gathered was that while Atarah seemed, to my mind, to talk a lot, Kenia was just as bad, and when the two of them spoke, it seemed like constant tangents, with little returning to the point. It was Maisie's injections into the conversation that seemed to save matters from going completely off track. Atarah gave Kenia a box of pins from her dresser, and as this rapid discussion was going on, she was pulling on my hair and pinning it as she desired. All I was able to gather was that we were going out, although to where I still didn't know.

There was a long conversation revolving around friends of theirs that I didn't know, didn't ask about, and didn't really understand. All I knew what that these were Atarah's friends from her old school, and that they were a well-established group. Atarah had mentioned nothing special about me to them. I didn't know how close they were, but I could tell Atarah would never breathe a word of my secret to them. Her laugh at most of Kenia's jokes was fake.

There was mention of Ophelia, and that surprised me. "You know that girl I was telling you about? Ophelia?" Atarah said to her friends, and they both nodded. I received no indication of exactly what it was that Atarah had said to them. "She works at the department store in the mall."

"Isn't she, like, super rich?" Kenia asked. I failed to figure out exactly when Atarah had had this conversation with her friends, but they were up to speed already.

"Oh, she is. I think her mom made her work before she turned eighteen - I don't know, she told me and I wasn't listening. She's just got all her dead dad's money under her control now, so she's probably quitting soon. But what I'm saying is, we should go and talk to her." There was an implication in Atarah's words, one of mischief.

"So are you pretending to like her or not?" Kenia questioned, accidentally revealing more of the story that I didn't yet know.

"I mean, I was, but I just don't give a shit. It's too much effort. I wanna fuck with her." Atarah looked at me as she said that. It was something I had yet to understand, her spite towards Ophelia. "She hates Alex, you know. For no good reason. Also, I'm pretty sure her brother hangs out with the junkies."

"The ones at the skate park?"

"Yeah, I've seen him go there."

"We've got to stop by the skate park." Maisie spoke up then. "Maybe we'll see him."

"Two-for-one twins tonight," Atarah said, with a wink towards me that her two friends didn't see. This was an intentional decision she'd made, to rub our apparent newfound friendship in the faces of the Houghs. It made little sense to me, but clearly there was a kind of fun in it that I simply would never make sense of.

"They're not twins, though, are they?" Maisie corrected, unconcerned with seeming pedantic.

"They look the same," Atarah scoffed, hand-waving her away. "Anyway, we should go."

I wasn't sure if Kenia was done with my hair and was just running her fingers through it, or if she was still attempting to do something with it. She seemed reluctant to move just yet, at least.

"We have to stop at the skate park first," Maisie said, standing up and shrugging on a grey jacket. "I don't want to be caught with anything on me." She slung on a shoulder bag, and I had at least a hint of what was going on.

"Hang on one moment," Kenia protested, hurriedly placing one more pin in my hair, before pulling away. "There. Done. Do you like it, Alex?"

I stood and moved over to Atarah's mirror, gazing at myself. I knew I wouldn't really feel anything about it, but I took the time to consider it, for appearance's sake. It was pretty much just several braids going into one. I smiled. "Yeah, it's good," I said, the words empty on the inside.

"Good," Kenia grinned, standing up herself and grabbing a coat. "You're not bothered by petty crimes, are you, Alex?"

"Victimless crimes," Maisie added.

Atarah rolled her eyes at both of her friends as she grabbed her keys. "Would I have brought them along if they did care? No. Let's get a move on."

"Just asking," Kenia said, exasperated, as she headed towards the door. I followed her, and Maisie behind me. Maisie held a protective hand over her bag, like she was worried someone was going to snatch it. It may've been instinct, or it may've been me.

"Have a good time! Don't get into trouble!" called a masculine voice. Maisie called back a response, but Atarah didn't even turn, pretending she hadn't heard. I vaguely recalled Atarah mentioning a stepdad, but I decided not to ask.

Atarah stepped into the driver's seat and slammed the door behind her, a show of annoyance. I let her friends get in first, clambering into the empty seat in the back; Atarah somehow made putting the car into gear a bitter action. My decision was a good one.

The drive was uneventful. Kenia was able to quickly start up the meaningless conversation again, drawing Atarah back from annoyance with practiced ease, and maybe later I'd be able to ask her what was wrong. It didn't take long to reach downtown. Atarah parked in a central spot half a block from the skate park, and by the time we got out, she was entirely focused again.

"There they are." Kenia not-so-subtly pointed towards a group of teenagers sitting on one of the skate ramps, huddled under a streetlamp with abandoned skateboards beside them. There were roughly five of them, chatting idle.

Maisie lead the group towards them, and I followed

without question. Atarah naturally fell into step with me behind the other two. "Are you deliberately parading me in front of the Houghs?" I asked her quietly, as soon as Kenia began talking to Maisie and they'd both likely be distracted.

"Yes, absolutely. I hate those rich brats," Atarah grinned, slipping her arm around my elbow like a lady at a debutante ball. "They're *so annoying*."

I had no time to answer that, as the first of the group noticed us coming and perked up. "Hey, Maze! What's up?"

Despite Maisie's quiet, somewhat shy demeanour, she seemed fully comfortable approaching this group. "Hey, dude."

"Whatch'you got for us?" the kid asked casually. We finally arrived properly beside them; three of them were people I knew from school, one of which was, indeed, Ezra Hough. I stood at the foot of the ramp, and he sat atop it; at first, he wasn't paying attention to me, having an in-depth discussion with a girl I didn't recognise. As the new arrivals drew his attention, so did my blank gaze. His eyes narrowed, and I could see him notice Atarah's physical closeness to me, see the connection made behind his eyes.

As Maisie opened her bag to show the first guy, and the others gathered around to look, Ezra didn't move, not yet. I didn't pay attention to him, instead focused on what I could now tell for sure was clearly a drug sale. Kenia was on the watch for anybody around, as was Atarah, although she still clutched my arm absentmindedly. Ezra entered my field of vision, standing just far enough away that his friends could tell something was up.

"E-Z!" called the first kid. "Are you coming or nah?"

"Yeah, I'm comin', I'm comin'." He gave a shifty glance between Atarah and I as he stepped closer, like he was afraid we were infectious.

Atarah caught his eye and gave him the smuggest of grins. "How are you, Ezra?"

He was confused more than anything. His ruddy brown hair was half-covered by a hood, and as he ran a hand through it, he knocked the hood off. "Hi Atarah." Uncomfortable. "Alex." Bitter, suspicious, but unsure.

Atarah was right; Ezra and Ophelia looked almost exactly the same. Their voices were different, and Ophelia had long hair, but they could almost pass as each other if they tried. They had the same round green eyes, long nose, thick eyebrows, all traits they'd also shared with their father. Ezra's eyes were familiar. I stabbed Mr Hough in the back, but it took a while for him to bleed out; I got a good look at his eyes when I was waiting for him to die.

"Hello, Ezra." I put on my normal, every-day polite voice. Even if he suspected that the persona I put on was a lie, that didn't mean I could be my true self around him. Suspicion is not knowledge, and he clearly didn't know for sure. The longer he could doubt I'd killed his father, the safer I was.

Atarah seemed to take some spiteful glee in my false politeness, chuckling to herself in full visibility of Ezra. It was no wonder she had a reputation for oddness, as she seemed to take no notice of his somewhat disgusted reaction. He subsequently backed away and quickly busied himself with talking to Maisie.

When I felt nobody was paying attention, and Atarah had taken a moment to stop her own laughter, I asked her, "would you like me to teach you how to act normal and likeable?"

"Is that a dig?" Atarah asked, offended and completely serious, before she remembered who she was talking to. She found that funny, too. "No, Alex, I know that pissed him off. I don't care. I know you care what people think of you, but I sure as hell don't."

"Doesn't that make your life harder?"

"I think pretending to be someone I'm not would be a lot harder," she argued, and without another word, she dragged me towards her friends and into their conversation.

Money and paper bags were switching hands between Maisie and the teenagers. Kenia was in an avid discussion with a girl I vaguely knew, about a show I'd never seen. Atarah quickly threw her opinion into the mix before walking me around them, towards where Ezra had fled. As I watched him, Ezra took something from Maisie and handed her a wad of green bills in return. She counted his money briefly and nodded to him, and he slipped the package into his pocket.

"Uh uh uh," Atarah teased, sidling up to him. "Does your sister know you're smoking the devil's lettuce?"

"I don't think it's any of your business," Ezra snipped, "and it ain't hers either. Does she know what *you're* up to? I thought you were friends with her."

"Who said I wasn't?" Atarah quipped, and I got the feeling that some message was passing under my awareness. That happened a lot. When I couldn't be invested in things, it was hard to pick up on tiny emotional cues.

Ezra ignored her in favour of turning to me; his fiery gaze might've been uncomfortable to anyone who had the emotional capacity to care.

"What are you doing here?" Ezra asked. His voice was exasperated and tired.

My persona was one of innocent friendliness towards just about everyone; apparently, acting innocent at certain times lead others to read my actions as oblivious or even stupid. That was fine by me, and I upheld that, deliberately misreading his question. "I'm just hanging out with Atarah. I'm not here to buy drugs or anything."

He narrowed his eyes, seeing through me, although he doubted if what he saw was real. "It's been a long time since I actually talked to you, Alex, but last time I checked, you didn't *hang out* with anyone."

"I have friends." Ezra was both right and wrong at once; he could tell I didn't really care for anyone, but I did have people who liked me around. None so much or so quickly as Atarah, it seemed, but people like Madison who gave me their time in passing. "You don't need to be so rude about it."

"I think I've got bigger fish to care about than that." I let his failed metaphor and clumsily disguised distaste of me slide with my persona of ignorant kindness. "Are you two gonna stick around for long?"

"Jeez, Ezra, you don't have to be a dick," Atarah said,

loudly, so that his friends all gave pause and turned to stare at him. "You don't even know Alex."

"I- I'm not being a dick." Ezra looked furtively between the eyes now turned on him; Atarah seemed pleased with her own power move, a smirk still on her face. "I don't know if you know this, Atarah, but we used to be neighbours. I *know* Alex better than you. We used to be neighbours."

Atarah stepped forward. "Oh, I know. Your family was going to kick Alex's out to live on the street because of greed, and then you thought it must've been Alex's fault when your dad kicked the bucket, even though Alex was fucking ten at the time."

Atarah's defence of me would've been astonishing. It was not something I expected, even from her. Atarah made a lot of assumptions about the situation, but that wasn't the strangest thing. Atarah was defending my murder of Ezra's father with implied lies, but the emotion behind it was very real.

Atarah didn't just believe through some odd ideology that my murders were okay; there was some emotional stake in it. Something complicated, I could guess, judging by the way Atarah shook a little at the words, yet came away from it with the tiniest of smiles. She reached for me, finding my elbow again, and I let her hang off my arm. I could hardly believe someone like Atarah actually existed, that I actually had an ally like her.

And because Atarah spoke first, and her lies were more believable than the truth, Ezra had to let it drop as gracefully as he could. "You're high," was all he managed to say, before making a point of walking away. Atarah decided to take his hint, mostly as Maisie was done, and was now talking to Kenia about some gossip I could not care about.

"Let's go," Atarah told her friends, pulling their attention back towards her. "We've got shit to do."

"Well we don't have a time limit on doing that shit, and it's not super important, so we could've stayed, but I saw what happened, so it's fair, it's cool," Kenia said rapid-fire as we were walking back to the car. "Sorry Alex, I didn't know you had beef with E-Z or I would've gone and distracted him or something. What's the beef?"

"Oh, I don't have any *beef* with him. It's all a misunderstanding, really." I pushed the good-hearted, somewhat idiotic persona on her as well. "We used to know each other. Some bad things happened, and I think he thinks I could've stopped it? I don't know." Playing innocent meant pretending I didn't know so much. Kenia seemed to buy it. She clearly wanted to know more, but she didn't ask any more questions.

Instead, she turned to Atarah. "So we're going to the mall now?"

"Yeah," she said. "I don't want anything. Just going to bother Ophelia, really."

And Kenia went off on another tangent that I couldn't have cared about. It seemed like neither Maisie nor Atarah really cared either, but they both tolerated her random divergence that somehow ended up at her cousin's girlfriend's ski trip. It filled the silence, anyway.

Long before she was done, we arrived at the oversized building and climbed from the warmth of the car into the cold bite of winter air. As before, Maisie and Kenia naturally fell together ahead of us, perhaps by Atarah's intention. She was almost desperate to talk to me alone.

"I've got so many questions," she whispered when they were far enough ahead not to hear. "I hope you don't mind. I *know* you don't mind."

"I've actually got questions for you too," I told her as we approached the sliding glass doors. "You're a unique person."

"Oh, really? Go on."

I was almost afraid to ask the question. After all, it was still possible to alienate her. "My immediate question is, why are you okay with what I've done? I've never met anyone who thinks murder of any kind is genuinely okay before. That's why it's illegal."

"The law sucks. It's not fair." Atarah scoffed at the very idea that it could be. We finally arrived at the doors of the department store itself, far behind Kenia and Maisie.

"In my experience, it at least attempts fairness," I countered, but she waved me away without a second's thought.

"In your experience, maybe. But the law is built to keep power in the hands of a few, and anything people can do to get some of that power back for themselves is only fair, and often, right. That's all you ever did, at least with Mr Hough and Amanda- with Bailey, you were so young you can't even be said to be truly at fault." My disagreement with that statement went unspoken. "Like I said. The police kill, the military kills, even doctors kill- it's all about justification. If the law is a justification to kill, I don't see why self-defence shouldn't be."

"Okay." Understanding was all I asked for, so I didn't press further. They were moral questions, and I never had any grasp of morality. So I went to my next question. "How do you know Ophelia?"

"We're actually kind of friends. I wouldn't blame you for not knowing that." Looking over at the store attendant- who wasn't Ophelia- it seemed like Atarah might've been over-heard talking about murder, as we were being watched with far more intensity than I expected. "I mean, I don't... like her. I talk to her in class, and get along with her friends, I guess, but it's not real. She had a little get-together not too long ago that I went to, and that's where I heard about you. I've heard whispers of Ophelia's investigation into her father's death, but the fact that she thought it was you didn't reach me until re-cently. She's weird, and not in a way I like. She's never speaking, acting like she's shy, but she's always thinking, you know? I pretend to be her friend, but, like... she sucks."

The store attendant moved away from us when some-thing crashed in a nearby aisle. We'd lost track of Maisie and Kenia, but I could guess that was them.

"So," I said, as the distraction reminded me, "are Kenia and Maisie your real friends?"

Atarah took a long moment to consider, and her voice was much quieter in the next sentence. "They're my real friends, yeah. I don't fully trust them, though, we're just... fundamentally different. I'm not going to tell them about you, because they just won't get it. There's a lot of stuff they don't get. I want... I want someone to truly know me, that I can be honest with, and that's not them."

The thread left hanging open was one I had to pursue. "Is it me?"

"I mean, I don't know." Just asking that question seemed to throw Atarah off balance. "I haven't known you that long. But I like that you're honest and you aren't bothered by the weird things about me."

It was strange, Atarah's worldview. Stranger still was the fact that the way I was- this emotionless existence- was preferable to her than many others, because those others had, in some way, rejected her. "What about you bothers people?"

Atarah sneered at some thought those words brought up in her mind. "Just about everyone is bothered by my interest in crime. My voice grates people. I talk too much. I don't sit down and shut up when they want me to. I make things political too often. I'm not funny, I ask too many questions, and I don't leave people alone when they want to be left alone. I'm lonely enough that it's hard for me to change some of those things. Everyone treats me like they secretly know I'm gonna become a serial killer of babies. People think I have ethical issues, but they can't seem to truly explain to me why I'm wrong. I've never hurt anyone who didn't hurt me first, but they..." she trailed off, sighing a little. We were standing in the middle of the baby clothing section, looking entirely out of place, but she didn't seem to mind.

"So everyone thinks you're annoying or strange." I summarised. Atarah met my eyes, and it seemed I hit a note of understanding somewhere within her head. She nodded sombrely. Her phone began to buzz with texts, but she ignored it.

"Yeah. Everyone but you, really. I mean, my sister likes me, and Maisie and Kenia like me well enough. But, you- you're the only one, who... you know."

"Okay. I understand you."

CHAPTER SIX - OPHELIA HOUGH

Atarah finally checked her phone and read the incoming texts. She grabbed my arm, buzzing, walking down the aisle and pulling me with her.

"They think they might've found her," she said as we headed towards the middle of the store. It was laid out so that that was where the cashiers were, and Maisie and Kenia were idling at a display nearby, not yet willing to approach the cash registers. From the angle we approached, the cashier's back was turned.

"You should've seen what happened," Kenia whispered almost as loud as normal speech, pulling Atarah over to talk to her. "We knocked over a whole bunch of pots and pans and it was a huge mess. And then we ran away over here, and she totally saw us knock all that stuff over, and she didn't even really care. I'm not sure if it's Ophelia, but you did say she had brown curly hair, right?"

I had noticed, in all my time in school, that many social groups had a leader. It appeared, watching those three, that

Kenia and Maisie both naturally defected to Atarah's will, although Atarah made no effort to enforce this. She was not so much a natural leader as a naturally strong personality; she was always going to be the loudest in the room, in every sense of the word. She didn't accept the role of leader- she simply didn't notice that it was what she had, by default, become.

"I'm pretty sure it is her. I knew she was working. I know when most of my friends are working. For example, my friend Stephen is working tonight too, I think. Do you know, Alex?"

It was a weird detour to take, but the question she said wasn't the one she was truly asking. If we were going to go to Stephen's work tonight, we'd have to most likely ditch Kenia and Maisie, or risk them seeing an emotional outburst of mine, which I did not want. So I answered her question factually, considering what I had gathered about Stephen's schedule in the past three weeks, and ignored her real meaning. "Most likely he is, yeah," I confirmed, telling Maisie and Kenia nothing of importance at all.

"You've never talked about this dude before. How do you know him?" Kenia asked, a glimmer of curiosity in her eyes that was inconvenient. I didn't want any talk of Stephen. Somehow the very thought of others knowing about him stirred up feelings. It was hard to even decide if it was positive or negative, the way I felt.

"He's a friend of Alex's." When she said that, I briefly wished it was true. It took only a second to squash that feeling as best as I could. I was slowly learning how to limit my emotions, even though it wasn't all that effective, not in the way I wanted it to be. "He's in my class, but other than that I don't know him that well."

At least she kept the questioning off of me. I was struggling to keep my mind in the present, as I was any time Stephen was mentioned. I wouldn't have been able to come up with a convincing act.

"Anyway," Atarah said, "let's go talk to her."

Maisie was watching me with glossy eyes for a moment, and I could see that there might've once been an intelligent girl under there, but she'd lost something important; nothing physical, something mental, entirely tied to her potential. Kenia was the same, but the empty look in her eyes seemed to me to have always been there. It was a different emptiness from mine, a more usual kind, but one so common that I knew it well. Maisie and Kenia would never see the truth about me.

Atarah didn't have that emptiness, and she had seen the truth. Ezra didn't have it either.

Neither did Stephen, and that was sweet and biting all at the same time. Perhaps it signified that he was something special, unlike everyone else, and in that way, better to fall for than someone like Maisie or Kenia. But at the same time, it meant he could see through me, see the truth, and react the way almost every normal human being reacted: with fear, or worse, anger. Like Amanda, not like Atarah.

I briefly wished I had fallen for Atarah instead. If I had, though, I'd just have to kill her, and that's what I needed to remind myself of. Deceitful emotions tricked me into thinking I wanted this. My heart lied.

Behind the register, there was a forced edge to the overly polite voice that asked, "how may I help y'all today?"

Ophelia was not empty behind the eyes either. She had on lipstick, and her hair was pulled into a bun, but as Atarah had said, she otherwise looked almost exactly like her brother. Her pleasant smile was entirely forced, but it was done well, and I couldn't see what was behind it.

"Ophelia!" Atarah put on the biggest of grins when greeting her, almost smug. Knowing how much the average person appreciated subtle taunting, Atarah was deliberately making the situation worse. "How's it going? I didn't realise you were working tonight!"

Everyone present knew that wasn't true, but it didn't seem to bother Kenia or Maisie, and I couldn't care. Ophelia might've been hiding anger, if the twitch of her lips was anything to go by. "Atarah, hello." Her gaze turned to me. "Hi, Alex." Better at hiding her emotions than Ezra. Very good, in fact. "And you two, it's nice to meet you. Are y'all friends of

Atarah's?"

That last question was spoken while Ophelia stared at me, but it wasn't me who answered. "Yeah, hi," Kenia said somewhat distractedly. She had a bag over her shoulder that she hadn't had before.

"Is there anything-" Ophelia began, trying to return to her job to avoid the questioning, but Atarah began to speak before even realising Ophelia had opened her mouth.

"We saw your brother at the skate park." Atarah put some emphasis on 'skate park', pretending not to be saying what she was saying. Everyone knew that the kids who hung around the skate park were the ones that did drugs.

Ophelia knew this was what Atarah meant, but pretended she didn't. "Oh, really?" It was dismissive, but perhaps not on purpose. She was known to be shy and awkward. She paused for a moment, and ultimately decided more needed to be said. "He's an idiot, but I love him."

"That's true," Atarah said, as though she wasn't insulting Ezra. "How've you been? How's work?"

Atarah had put her in the worst position possible, and was deliberately keeping it that way. Ophelia seemed to be in good control of her emotions, though, saying, "it's been fine, although I probably got to get back to it, if you don't mind. It's just that my manager will be mad if I'm caught slackin' off." While the words themselves were not spoken with confidence, that added to her air of innocence.

"Alright." Atarah wasn't happy with letting it go that easily, I could tell, but she didn't have any plausible reason to keep Ophelia waiting. She handed her a small candy bar she'd clearly grabbed at the last minute as an excuse. "Alex, did you get anything?"

Atarah kept drawing Ophelia's attention to me, hoping for some stronger reaction than well-covered annoyance, if that was even what Ophelia was feeling. Ophelia had a certain hardness about her gaze, despite her outward shyness, and it was impossible to tell what she thought of me. I shook my head and stepped back.

Kenia pretended she'd had the bag when she walked into the store, and Ophelia either didn't notice or didn't care that Kenia was absolutely stealing it. Perhaps she was simply too afraid to mention it. Atarah didn't try to strike up a conversation with her again, instead just leading the group out of the store.

She was looking at Maisie and Kenia somewhat pointedly. "Can you two give us a moment? I want to go back and talk to her properly. She doesn't know you guys, so she'll be a bit weird about if it you're there."

It was absolutely a lie, and while Atarah may have been bad at hiding her emotions, when it came to garden-variety lies like that one, she sold them well. Kenia said something about how that'd be fine and they'd be out the back together, adding something that might've been slang for smoking, but I could only guess from context.

As soon as they were gone, Atarah turned to me. "That sucked. I thought it would be more fun than that to mess with her, and I kind of want to spy on her now."

"How do you propose spying on her exactly?" I asked, keeping my voice down as we re-entered the store. The store attendant by the door noted our return alone, but didn't seem to care much.

"I *know* she sent that dude to snoop on you this afternoon. She's up to something. As for how? I don't know, how do you spy on Stephen? I thought you'd know."

We stood in the cosmetics aisle, with Ophelia in our sights, although she couldn't see us. Watching and waiting.

"I make it up as I go along," I told Atarah.

And I did. Ophelia was tagged out by another employee, and we watched as she headed towards a back door. I headed after her, and Atarah followed quietly, letting me lead the way. I kept us behind at a safe distance, so safe we almost lost her a few times.

When Ophelia opened the door, I could see that it led to a small storeroom. She closed the door behind her, and when I sidled up to the side of the door, Atarah following, I couldn't see her, but I could hear her through the thin walls.

There was the sound of a few buttons on her phone, and

then her voice. "I only got a few minutes, so if you need a long time, call me in a few hours. If not, tell me what you got."

Atarah raised her eyebrows at me, a wide grin on her face, before Ophelia spoke again. "No, I suppose it makes sense you wouldn't find nothing there. Have you checked the house yet?"

If she was speaking to the person who was inspecting my car, then Atarah was completely correct, and she was truly investigating me. That was full of complications. Was she really so suspicious of me that as soon as she had the means, she hired someone to find proof that I was a murderer?

"Okay. That's fine." Ophelia's voice was oddly flat in how she spoke on the phone. "I'm not bothered if it takes you time. I-uh-ack..." she stuttered over her words. "Well, actually, do be quick." Those words *were* filled with emotions.

There was another long pause. I heard the voice of the person on the phone, but not a word they said. "I get it, and I'm sure sorry. But you get my situation, too."

Her voice was quiet, and I had to strain to hear her, until she said, "oh, snap, I've got to go." Her voice quieted again after that, but she spoke quickly. "Look, let me know as soon as you find anything, okay? Bye."

I expected for her to hang up the phone then, to go back into work, but she spoke again, only this time her whole demeanour had changed. It wasn't her customer service voice, and it wasn't the vague boredom of the previous phone call. "Hi! How are you?"

She paused for much longer than she did on the previous phone call, and the voice on the other end went on for a lot longer. Until finally, she said, soft and almost too quiet for me to hear, "I know. They came here just now."

The caller answered loud enough that I could hear him, and my suspicions were confirmed. I heard Ezra say something that was probably 'what the fuck is-', and a few moments later Ophelia laughed. "I know, I know. She's always been weird, and untrustworthy, so she probably did it just to make me mad. It's pretty much proof there's somethin' wrong with Alex, 'cause if Alex was a murderer we should've expected Atarah to suddenly be friends with them."

With our names dropped, there was no question of what she was talking about. Atarah was visibly enjoying this.

Ezra spoke for a long moment before Ophelia answered. "I know. I agree. I ain't got long, but we'll talk about it tonight, okay? I love you."

She was closer to her brother than I pretended to be to my sisters. She was definitely closer to her brother than I had ever been to mine.

As soon as she hung up, Atarah backed away from the door, something I quickly realised I should be doing too. I hid behind a nearby display of children's toys, and almost immediately after, the door opened. I waited until the sound of Ophelia's footsteps had faded away before I left my hiding place and re-joined Atarah.

I could only wonder what Ophelia was trying to achieve. How could she find evidence of a murder case eight years old?

"Oh, that was pretty much what I expected," Atarah admitted, her words at odds with the excitement in her steps. "I mean, at least what she said. Kinda gross how close she is to her brother."

"Losing your father could easily do that to someone," I reminded her. We quickly escaped to the front of the store, on watch for Ophelia, avoiding her by sheer luck.

"Yeah, I guess." Something about what I said wasn't what I intended. Atarah's voice was dulled compared to how thrilled she had just been.

"What?" I asked as we headed out the back of the mall to meet her friends, espionage mission successful. She hesitated, fixing her glasses instead of speaking for a long moment.

"What-" I began, halfway through insisting, before Atarah cut me off.

"Look." At first I thought it was a literal instruction, before I realised she was buying herself a moment to think. "Ophelia's not got some hopelessly tragic backstory, alright? So what if her father's dead? She's all woe is me, trying to get revenge like eight years later, but apparently I-"

When I looked over at her, I realised she was on the verge of crying. Not crying yet, but close. She stopped herself, choking back her words to save from it all pouring out.

"If it's too hard to discuss whatever it is you're trying to say, you don't have to tell me." I had never cried for any reason other than pain, not yet, but I knew what that emotional build-up was like, and I detested it. I was going to kill Stephen just to end it.

"But I want to." Atarah rubbed at her eyes, and if the mall wasn't so empty right now, I'd be worried we'd catching a lot of negative attention. She spoke softly. "I- my dad. He was murdered, too."

"Oh. I see." Atarah's blatant disrespect towards the Hough's loss both made more sense, and less, at the same time.

"But, he wasn't murdered by a ten-year-old kid. He was murdered-" every instance of the word 'murder' got more bitter, more painful. "-by a police officer, who claims he felt *threatened*. Lies." She spat the words with vitriol. "My dad was murdered for no reason, and everyone knows who did it, but he got away with it. He got away with it because everyone decided he should. Ophelia's fucking lucky, because she's got a pretty good chance of convincing everyone you shouldn't get away with it. There's no justice in it. There's justice for whoever society as a whole *feels* like giving it to."

Atarah saw her friends, but paused before approaching them, taking a moment to breathe. She didn't tell me that just so I'd know her dad was dead.

"It's like the universe wants to piss me off," she said after a moment. "My dad couldn't just die for no reason and never have justice. My mother also decided that making a cop my stepdad would be a great idea. And then on top of all that, Ophelia thinks *she* deserves some kind of revenge? *Please.*"

And without waiting for me, she headed off towards her friends. I followed, thinking that she wouldn't be able to hide the remnants of anger from them, but by the time we got there, it was skilfully covered up and ignored. She leapt into

Kenia's meaningless conversation easily and pulled them away to take them home. It was evident that Atarah was tired of them, but she had the good sense to pretend otherwise.

Atarah kept up the act until they were both dropped off and it was just the two of us. "Ugh. Sorry. They're my friends, and I love them, but I can only do it for so long, you know? Moving schools did wonders for my friendship with them."

"Why do you hang out with them at all if you don't like them?" It was all the same to me, but now that I knew what unpleasant emotions were, I would not choose to put myself through them.

"Oh, Alex. You have a lot to learn yet about how real social relationships work. We have a history and I care about them, and to everyone else, that's something." Atarah shook her head, like I was being illogical, not her. "Though I don't trust them at all with this shit. I couldn't talk to them when my dad died and I can't fucking talk to them now."

Although she didn't say anything about her dad again, I definitely noticed when she started to cry. I asked her if she was alright, and she insisted she was, in a tone that suggested I don't ask again.

I had noticed, as we spoke, where we were driving, and it made the rare emotion of nervousness churn in my stomach. After a few weeks, it was not quite as overwhelming as it was when it was new, but it was still unpleasant.

I hadn't gone back to the movie theatre since I felt for the first time. The simple knowledge that I was about to see Stephen was torture of the worst kind.

Chapter Seven
- Alex and
Stephen

Atarah was still somewhat upset as she parked the car. She pulled the handbrake bitterly and got out without stopping to wait for me. I ran after her, crossing the fateful ground where I first fell, literally, for Stephen. That felt like a whole other era, that day.

"Atarah. Don't go in upset." My voice stopped her, allowing me to catch up and turn her towards me. "Is there anything I can do to help?"

A strange look crossed her face. "No, not really. You're oddly thoughtful for someone who doesn't feel anything."

As I gently wiped the tears from her face, all I was thinking was that it would draw attention if she were seen crying; and attention, especially Stephen's, was the last thing we needed. As her words sunk in, I realised how my actions appeared.

Caring. It was strange, that; if I was thoughtful, what went on inside the head of someone who was thoughtless?

"Well, let's just wait a moment, until you feel fine," I advised. There weren't so many people in the movie theatre; there was only one worker behind the counter, who wasn't Stephen. The showtimes for all the movies were on a board above the counter, and it appeared we had fifteen minutes until the latest showing of anything. It was an animated kid's movie, one I had no more interest in seeing than any other.

There was one couple that walked past us, the only other patrons I could see, who went up to the counter and began to order tickets. After a few moments, Atarah fixed her glasses and sighed. "Let's do this. Where do you reckon he is?"

"No idea," I told her as we walked through the glass doors. "Do you think... uh..."

"He's definitely working, if that's what you were going to ask," Atarah said, quieting her voice as we approached the counter. It wasn't what I was going to ask. In fact, what I was going to ask was an incredibly pointless question, that didn't ultimately matter: did she think he'd be happy to see us?

Then the door behind the counter opened, and out of it came the key that had unlocked something inside me that nothing else ever could. He was carrying cups to restock with, but he caught my eye quickly. I probably imagined his smile, but nevertheless, it filled me up with some euphoric drug, and I had to fight off a reckless, stupid grin. Atarah gently touched my arm, and I was annoyed that she'd dare draw my attention away from Stephen for even half a second. The annoyance caused my uncontrollable smile to drop for long enough that when Stephen had put the cups down and came over to speak to us, my face contorted into something that looked normal. It might've been an accident, or Atarah might've been very, very smart.

"Hey guys!" Stephen seemed cheery, more so than I would've expected. "How's it going?"

He was too optimistic for his own good. Too kind, too beautiful, too amazing; it was a shame he was going to die. I shouldn't kill him, I thought. I dug my nails into the skin of my palm to try and keep myself afloat, in reality: those very thoughts were why I was going to kill him. Why I had no choice.

"It's going great, how about you?" Atarah said, and I realised too late that I needed to speak.

I tripped over my words, and they were forced in at the wrong time. "Great, good, how are you...?"

In that moment I hated Atarah for bringing me here to make a fool of myself. In front of Stephen, no less, the only person I'd ever cared about. The only person I was capable of loving. She was going to make him hate me. It was going to be her fault.

But Stephen didn't seem to notice, or at least care, about my awkwardness. "I'm good, actually. Long shift, but it's fine, I'm used to it." There was an airy quality to his voice, something that made him sound all the more angelic. He already looked like an angel. "So, uh, what are you guys up to?"

"Definitely not watching a movie," Atarah said, laughing at her own joke. Stephen gave her a very fake little laugh, and it almost pissed me off. I couldn't pin down exactly why Atarah's joke falling flat pissed me off, but it did, and the only thing that kept me from acting on it was the knowledge that this rollercoaster of emotions was incredibly irrational and that Stephen could not, under any circumstances, see me acting irrationally. It would make everything, including my emotions on the subject, far, far worse.

"Well, I guess I can't help you then." Stephen made a show of leaving, catching my eye to see my reaction to his little joke. Now I knew, on some level, that it wasn't funny, it was predictable and stupid and it wasn't witty. Normally I wouldn't have laughed, if anyone but Stephen had said it. I had perfected the art of learning what most people found funny a long time ago, and that joke deserved a smile at most.

But in that moment, it was funny. Genuinely, truly, funny.

I had never laughed for real before.

It felt like a hiccup at first, and it shook in my chest. The noise that came out of my mouth was unexpectedly ugly and choked, and it came out as a hiss through my teeth, bitten back simply because I hadn't expected it. There was something so inherently pleasant about it as it happened, but as soon as I was aware of it, I was mortified: was that normal, the sound I'd just made? Did Stephen think I was weird? Or worse, did he find it unattractive?

But then the dust settled, and I was able to reign myself in. Stephen wouldn't care how my laugh sounded, right? In fact, he seemed impressed that his little joke had actually found any kind of appreciative audience. Impressed with himself. And that made me happy for so many reasons I couldn't pin down. I was floating, in that moment.

There was a second that seemed to last a whole day, for which Stephen held my gaze, and we were smiling at each other, big and real, and I felt a happiness that I can only imagine was the driving force that everyone but me lived for. It was amazing, and I wanted more. I wanted every day to be like this.

And then it ended, in a way that I hoped was mutually hesitant, as Stephen said, "I should probably do my actual job, shouldn't I?"

I wanted to say no, wanted to say he should've just come away with me then and there. Where, I don't know, and to do what, I knew even less. I just didn't want to even begin doing anything that might lead to us parting.

"Only if you want to," Atarah said. While I knew she'd brought me here for this reason, and she wasn't trying to say "yes", that was what Stephen heard. He looked at her with something completely unnameable in his eyes, and I felt uneasy. I could've been wrong- the words he said, the way he acted, went against this theory, after all- but it seemed like Stephen disliked Atarah. It may've been complicated, in the same way Atarah's relationship with her friends was complicated, but the uneasiness remained. I didn't want Stephen and Atarah disliking each other, because what if Stephen came to dislike me by association? Would I not be able to associate with Atarah publicly, lest Stephen come to hate me?

It didn't matter, I reminded myself. I was going to kidnap and eventually kill him. It didn't matter.

But to my heart, it mattered.

As Atarah bought the movie tickets, I could only watch Stephen. Taking in every detail I had memorised before once again, cementing his face in my memory. He smelled a little like coconut, I think, and the buttery scent of freshly-cooked popcorn that hung around in the air probably didn't come from him, but it was forever connected to my mental image of him now.

"Enjoy the movie, guys. I'll talk to you later." His smile was everything. My heart fluttered, and it was so good and so bad at the same time. Is this what everyone who was in love felt like?

"Okay! Thanks!" Atarah said, and I stumbled to say something before he thought I was ignoring him.

"Thank you." My voice was so quiet, but I could tell he heard me. It didn't sound like my voice. It was neither the true, flat, emotionless speech nor the peer-approved niceness I defaulted to with almost anyone.

I had no control over the sound of my voice, the way my laugh sounded, the way he made me smile. I was out of my depth. I needed that control back, desperately. When we walked away, it felt good to gain control again; my face, my voice, my laugh, it was all mine again when Stephen wasn't around.

Being in control was good, but along with it came a sense of loss. Despite the objective fact that I was better off away from him, I wanted nothing more than to turn around and run back.

"Come on," Atarah whispered to me as she walked ahead, and it took me a moment to realise how slow I was walking. I matched her pace, throwing one helpless glance back over my shoulder to see Stephen watching me. My gut twisted and I had to look away.

"I hate this so much," I muttered to Atarah as we headed towards the theatre. "I hate being out of control."

"I saw how much you were struggling," Atarah answered, reaching for my arm. "Can you imagine what it's like for everyone else?"

"Surely you can't feel like this all the time." My heart was racing, and I clutched at my chest as though that would make it stop. "This is unbearable."

"Not all the time, but this happens to everyone, eventually. Maybe not falling in love, but..." she gestured vaguely at me, and I understood her to be talking about these feelings. "Most of us dealt with emotional pain when we were kids, though. We're experienced by now."

I didn't respond. I didn't know how to respond.

When we'd gone into the theatre and chosen our seats- at Atarah's insistence of sitting in the very back, and my indifference- I had returned to what I would say was my normal state of emotionless nothing. There was a lot about what just happened that I very much wanted to think about, but I stopped my thoughts from even heading in Stephen's direction as much as humanly possible.

"Hey," Atarah whispered in my ear, as though we weren't in an empty theatre alone. "Where do you think that door goes?"

I followed where she was pointing, and indeed, there was a door beneath the canvas of the screen. "It's an emergency exit, so, outside, I suppose."

"We should see where it goes," Atarah said, without further explanation.

"Why?"

"Well, it might be useful. We'll have to see at the end of the movie," she answered, somewhat cryptically. I could tell it would be left at that, so I dropped it.

We were the only ones in the theatre, bar one. A silhouette entered after the lights had dimmed and the movie was about to begin, and sat several rows ahead of us. Throughout the movie- which I had, evidently, no interest in- Atarah whispered comments to me, about how strange the animation was, how the jokes weren't funny, and asking my opinion.

"Do you agree, that their eyes are weird? Do you even have opinions about that kind of thing?" she asked, overly incessant. I imagine if anyone was watching a movie with her and they actually cared about the film itself, they would be annoyed very quickly.

"I mean, their eyes are weird, I just don't... have any feelings about it. My opinions exist, they're just weak, and I can't base on them on whether or not I personally enjoy something."

"So what do you base them on? Like... I'd expect an emotionless person to put no effort into their appearance, or to like anyone, or have any hobbies or anything. Do you even have hobbies? I'm so confused."

"I put effort into my appearance because people like me more for it. Most people, regardless of their preferences, find me visually appealing, in part because of how I dress. I don't know why I'm attracted to the people I am, but there seems to be absolutely no pattern, whatsoever, and up until Stephen it was purely physical." As I watched her, her attention was splitting between me and the screen, but my words were clearly more interesting to her than the movie. "I spend my time working on useful skills. I speak three and a half languages, I'm a skilled chef, I understand computers very well, and I used to be a gymnast. I gave up regularly doing it last year, but I'm still very flexible."

"Woah." Atarah was looking at the screen as she spoke, the blue light flickering across her face. "Shit, I have no idea what's going on. Who's this dude?"

"No idea," I answered, and with that we returned to the movie.

It was towards the end of the film that Atarah commented, squinting at the rows of seats in front of her, "who watches a movie alone at this time of night?"

I examined the silhouette of the lone stranger and tried to figure it out for myself. From the way Atarah talked, I could tell she'd been thinking it since they entered. "I agree it's uncommon, but why would it matter to us?"

"Because someone was investigating your car earlier today," Atarah muttered. "I'm suspicious."

"Do you want to take a closer look?"

"At the end of the movie," Atarah decided. "I don't

want to chase them off."

When the movie did end, and the lights came up, Atarah didn't move, so neither did I. The stranger ahead of us didn't move either. We watched, and as the credits rolled, for a while, everyone was still. Then, the stranger ahead of us slowly rose, turning just enough to exit, trying to avoid being seen by us. It was hard to be certain, but to my eyes, it was the same person who was investigating my car.

"Interesting," Atarah whispered. The stranger did not risk a glance towards us, instead heading, noticeably slowly, down the stairs to the exit. "Very interesting. Ophelia's little friend is dedicated, I see."

"Do you think it'll be a problem?" I asked her. In my own head, I believed it would be, for as long as I was planning illegal activities. I wanted Atarah's opinion, though, and she shook her head.

"We'll just be on the lookout. If we're careful, it won't matter that we're being followed."

We waited a full minute after the stranger was gone before getting up and heading towards the exit ourselves. I followed Atarah, and as she rounded the corner, she gasped. "Oh, Stephen! Hi!"

My heart felt like it stopped. I walked into Stephen's line of sight on momentum, but stopped dead on instinct. "Hey!" I stumbled into a frenzied greeting. I sounded so desperate, and I hated myself for it.

"Hi guys." Stephen's voice was noticeably forced into politeness, but it was unclear whether he was simply tired, or annoyed, or what. "Did you enjoy the movie?"

"Sure, it was good," Atarah answered; I settled for a nod, in fear of sounding desperate again. "Not much on at this time of night, though."

"No," Stephen agreed, somewhat distracted. He had a watch on one wrist and a number of bracelets on the other, which he fidgeted with. I found myself playing with the string bracelet on my own wrist, something I never did. "If you don't mind me asking, why are you two out here so late?"

Somehow, all I could think about was how cool it was

that we both wore these colourful bracelets, even while know-ing I should not care.

"We're just hanging out," Atarah answered, as I was too distracted staring at Stephen to come up with a response. "Is it that weird to be hanging out at night?"

"Oh, no." His wrist sported a few black bands with text I couldn't read, and one string bracelet that was white, blue, and pink. Mine was yellow, orange and white. "If I'm honest, I thought you two might've been on a date, or something."

His tone was strange. Nervous, somewhat, like maybe he thought it was rude to make such a statement. My reaction was visceral, and as with every reaction to him, entirely un-planned.

"No! Don't be ridiculous," I rushed to say, breathy and nervous as I laughed through the words. "No, we're not... no, Stephen, no."

His name from my lips felt like a prayer.

He smiled at me and I felt like I was falling apart. "Okay, Alex."

And my name from his felt like that prayer answered.

"Hey Stephen." Atarah stepped closer to him, pulling his attention from my eyes to hers. Some idiotic part of me resented her for that. "You're a dancer, right?"

"Yes...?" His eyebrow twitched at her question, con-fused.

"Do you have any performances coming up? Alex here used to be a gymnast, and apparently was thinking of taking up dancing soon, so I said it would be a good idea to check out what some of the schools do, and a-"

Stephen cutting her off seemed unintentional, but it was probably for the best. Her over-explaining the lie cost it a lot of credibility. "You used to be a gymnast? That's really cool. You totally should join at my school." He seemed so happy at the idea, and I was ecstatic at the expression of how much he'd enjoy me doing it with him. It was undercut by the reali-sation he was probably stretching the truth. "If you want to see a performance... yeah, I've got one coming up, in a few weeks."

"Cool, cool." I struggled to keep breathing properly. Imagining him dancing, the beauty and grace of it all, was just so inherently wonderful. "That would be amazing. And you're right, I should totally join." The thought of doing dancing was as neutral as everything else until I imagined doing it with him.

"Great!" Atarah took control of the conversation again, both a blessing and a curse. I was saved from awkwardly staring at him like I just was, but that was all I wanted to do. I found myself running over the elaborate plait Kenia had given me, hoping it looked okay still. I hated how it mattered to me. "Let us know time and place, okay? I wanna come too."

"Alright." Stephen ran a hand through his hair, pausing to look at the ground. "I guess I'll see you guys at school?"

"Yeah," both Atarah and I said at once, although Atarah's was said with a confident assurance and mine was breathy and lovestruck. I hoped he was paying attention to her, and not me, and at the same time I didn't. With the conversation officially and irrevocably ended, Atarah took my arm and led me from the theatre, as though afraid I wouldn't move if she didn't make me.

"God, you two lovebirds do nothing but stare at each other," she remarked as soon as we were out of earshot, and I found myself stuttering with some new, unpleasant emotion that made me feel slightly sick.

"We- we were not! He doesn't- he can't like me." The idea of being liked in return was terrifying. "No."

"That's new," Atarah remarked on my embarrassment with a little laugh. "I got you in to see a dance concert of his. And you can even take him up on the offer and actually join his dance school. Aren't you proud of me?"

"Not literally, but thank you." I was collecting my emotions, destroying them- or burying them as much as possible- as I spoke. "It would be, uh, helpful, to- I mean, it would be helpful. That's not a lie, it's just..."

I squinted at nothing as I tried to discern what was going on inside my brain. "I... don't know what I'm thinking. Is that common?"

"You're excited to hang out with him," she said, and I gritted my teeth. How could she know, when I didn't?

"I don't want to be." I couldn't justify why I said it. She knew it was true already, but some lingering emotion itched to be released. "I want to get rid of this sooner, rather than later."

Atarah's eye twitched. "Well, I've got the beginning of a plan, if you're interested."

"I am." The fact that this was actually going to happen caused a stutter in my heart. I had so many feelings about that, too, although they were quieter than most now.

"That door? Let's see where it goes," Atarah grinned. I followed her outside the building, and she explained as we walked. "He came in alone to the theatre when the movie was done. He was coming to clean, I think."

As we walked, Atarah checked around us, attempting to spot our little follower. I did the same, but neither of us could see anyone. She kept her voice down anyway. "So if he's alone in there after the movie, and this door leads where I think it does, this could work."

We were following a concrete driveway that lead around the rear of the building. The bins were out the back here, visible in the harsh light against the darkness of the night. There were a few doors, one of which Atarah stopped in front of. "It's this one," she said, reaching out towards it as she surveyed the area. "We can get a car in here. Yes, this is perfect."

"I think I have an idea of your plan," I told her.

She grinned. "We'll have to get lucky. It might take a few times. As long as it's just the two of us, and it's late like this, we can park the car out here and drag him out."

I began to walk back towards the car as I spoke. "I still remember how to make chloroform. We'll have to make sure that there's no cameras, or people, to see us. And we still need a plan on where we're going to take him, and how we're going to hide the evidence when I do kill him." I kept my composure, feeling nothing, right up until the last word, when my voice cracked and I almost didn't want him to die.

"Well," Atarah said, "it's definitely a start."

Chapter Eight - Alex Keen, Iterum

Stephen messaged me on social media the next day. It wasn't the first time- scrolling back, we'd had a few correspondences before. There were messages from him sending congratulations after big school events, congratulations that read as though sent to many. There were a few times he had asked me where classes had been moved to or when homework was due. Last year I had sent him a congratulations on his performance in the play, and it had led to a rather lengthy conversation about how unfairly the drama teacher treated her students and how we had hoped another teacher would take over her role. All of this was before I fell in love with him, and it wasn't unusual; as far as I could tell, he was just like that. Any message he sent me, I could always assume was casual friendliness, perhaps over-friendliness at times.

But this time, I felt blind panic like never before. I daren't even read it. My first reaction was to turn my phone off, as if I could hide from him. My second reaction was to attempt to figure out what the message said just from reading the notification. I got a vague idea, and once I'd calmed down a little, I realised it was about the dancing, the conversation that happened less than twelve hours before. I hated myself for my emotion-induced idiocy.

I paused, took a moment, and planned out a few responses before actually opening the message. As soon as he saw that I'd seen it, I needed to reply, and fast. Which was bad, because while words usually came to me easily enough, Stephen upturned everything that was usual for me.

If you're serious about coming to my performance, and Atarah wasn't just messing you around, let me know :) none of my friends ever seem interested, so I think it'd be really nice if you actually wanted to come. It'd be even nicer if you were actually going to join the school too, it'd be pretty cool to have a friend do it with me, you know?

There were many aborted attempts at replies. The one I ended up sending was not intentionally chosen; I fumbled my phone, swearing as it fell onto my bed and hoping the message I had been halfway through deleting had not just sent. It had.

I do actually want to come, haha. I think it'd be awesome to see you dance at least, from what I've seen you're actually pretty amazing at

What had been deleted read, *it, and I'd love to see it for myself :)*. Too flirty, coming on too strong. No words were right, but I'd have to live with what was sent, despite how it made me want to shrivel up and die myself.

No matter how much I told myself that embarrassment was just a stupid, lying emotion, I couldn't get rid of it.

So I just added, *it.*

He answered me almost immediately with a date and a time, and an *I hope to see you there :)*. I had to lie on my bed, face-down, for a good few minutes while I let my heart regulate itself just a little bit.

It was the worst.

The performance was a little over a week from that point, and the whole time, it hung over me. I was thinking about it in class. I was thinking about it at lunch. I was thinking about it while I followed Stephen around, and I was thinking about it while I followed Ophelia and tried to discern what the hell she was up to (and learned nothing, as she did all of her business outside of school). I was thinking about it while lying awake in bed at night, and I was thinking about it when I was hanging out with Atarah after school. She pretended not to know me that well while in class, simply because our fast friendship would've been a little suspicious, but she continuously asked to go with me while I was stalking Stephen and to do things with her afterwards. It was like an actual close friendship; at least, I imagine it was. She thought my nervousness about going to the dance was stupid, and the worst part was that I agreed, yet felt it anyway.

"He's so nice to you," Atarah remarked one of those nights. "He never sent me any of those congratulatory messages. Whenever I talk to him he's... not rude, per se, but kinda short with me. Like he wants me to go away sooner rather than later."

I couldn't be annoyed at Stephen for this slight against Atarah, even though I logically knew it was rude of him. "A lot of people don't like you. I doubt he's any different."

"Maybe not," Atarah muttered. "Or maybe he is."

And then the day came.

It was a Saturday, and I woke up in a haze. I hadn't slept well, which was strange, because sleep had always been inherently peaceful for me. I hardly remembered the dream I had, but I did remember Stephen's face in my mind. Now he was even ruining my sleep. Another reason to hurry up and get rid of these horrible feelings.

I managed to keep my composure until half an hour before I had to leave. I was examining my reflection in a fit of anxiety, picking at my skin. I was shaking ever so slightly, my throat felt dry, and there was a twisting nausea in my stomach that wouldn't relax, not even a little. I couldn't get rid of the thoughts that I didn't look good enough. I knew they were irrational, I knew it didn't matter, I knew he was going to die, but none of these thoughts helped. None of them could stop me from calling Atarah, hoping that talking to her would ease this pain.

"What's up?" Atarah answered immediately, cheery and light. I couldn't even have happiness, the light to this dark. It seemed like my emotions were wall-to-wall pain.

"I hate this, I hate this." The shaky fear in my voice was new and horrifying. "Do you think Stephen's going to notice my acne? How should I dress? What does Stephen like- should I be masculine or feminine, soft or- or what- I don't even know what he likes, Atarah. I've never seen him date anyone. But- I really need to cover up this acne, at least, just-"

"Alex." Atarah's voice cut through my rambling. It would've been embarrassing, my loss of composure, if I had room in my mind for that. "I think Stephen won't care if you have acne, or how you dress. Either he'll like you or he won't. You seemed to take badly to the idea that he did like you, so when did that change?"

It was the logic I needed. I don't know if I resented or appreciated that she neglected to mention how I shouldn't care at all, because he was going to die. "I don't know, Atarah. It didn't change. This isn't logical. I just want to get rid of this anxiety. How do I hide acne?"

"That anxiety won't fully go away no matter what you do," Atarah sighed, and the truth weighed on me. I was drowning, and she was telling me there was no way to swim. "You can lessen it, maybe, but that's it."

"I want it to go away," I answered, childishly petulant. I felt like a child; not the child I had been, an empty mirror of the people around me. No, I felt the way I imagine most children felt. Raw, experiencing things for the first time and needing guidance to handle them. Nobody but Atarah knew the reality of who I was beneath the act, and therefore nobody but Atarah could help me.

She sighed through the phone. "Put some concealer on your acne. Wear the nicest clothes you can plausibly say you'd wear casually. Remember, you're there to see him, not the other way around."

"I don't have any makeup," I answered, but as I thought through her suggestions, I felt I might be okay. It could only go so badly, right? "Can I borrow yours?"

"Not unless you're suddenly got a very drastic tan. You've got three sisters and a mother, one of them will have something close enough to your skin tone. I've got to go get ready myself, but I'll see you soon, alright?"

It was comforting, the way she spoke to me. Comforting- not an absence of discomfort, but an active soothing of it. I wondered if I was feeling, or could feel, gratitude; in amongst everything, it was hard to tell if I imagined it.

She hung up, and I went about following her advice. I spent long enough agonising over what I was wearing that by the time I'd decided- still unhappy, but knowing I had no perfect choice and no time left- I had to go. I drove to Atarah's house to pick her up, and just as I was about to text her to let her know I was outside, she was climbing into the car.

"Great timing," she said as she looked me over. "Hang on, one second."

She reached towards me and took my plait in her hands. At first, I didn't understand what she was doing, until she slipped off the tie at the end and began to free my hair.

"What are you doing that for?"

She smiled softly. "Everyone- and I mean everyone- with long hair looks better with it out." When she was done, I shook my hair free and stared at my reflection in the rear-view mirror. It was a difference for sure. My face was rounder, softer, gentler. I was less androgynous than before, more feminine, but if the way Atarah had described me as beautiful and elven was accurate to how everyone- Stephen- saw me, it worked with that.

"Thank you," I told her, and I meant it.

As we drove, Atarah talked about the video series she was working on, and it helped distract me from the anxiety of what lay ahead. She described over again how it was not just about unsolved mysteries, but more accurately, about serial killers- because of course it was. She mentioned how my story would've been perfect, if she didn't have to worry about not getting me caught. I reminded her that she was an accomplice to my next murder, and she just laughed.

My anxiety had dimmed, right up until we were at the door. It was a large building, modern in its design, intended as far as I could tell for large functions, or, I suppose, dance performances. It was well separated from its neighbouring buildings. As soon as we were at the door, it felt real, and it was scary. He was in there.

"Hello," we were greeted by a pleasant-voiced dance teacher at the door, holding a clipboard. "Welcome. Have you got tickets already?"

"Oh, shit." Atarah stopped in her tracks. "No, we haven't. Is that a problem?"

"Not at all," said the teacher, looking down at the list. "Can I have your names?"

Atarah gave hers as she frantically searched her pockets. I did the same; I hadn't thought this far ahead, not when my mind had been so occupied by irrational worry.

"Alex Keen?" questioned the teacher, and although I was confused, I nodded, trying to peer at the list myself. "Yes, there's a ticket pre-paid for you. There's only one, though, and no Atarah on this list. Whoever booked it thought you were coming alone, I suppose."

I felt, somehow, warm at the realisation that Stephen went ahead and bought a ticket for me. It was so nice, so thoughtful, so wonderful. I could almost feel guilty for what I was going to do to him.

I did feel guilty. Guilt. Minor, hidden underneath the happiness, but it was guilt. I couldn't have a single good emotion without the bad to go with it. I couldn't just enjoy this kindness done to me.

Atarah had to buy her own, which annoyed her a little, but she didn't complain about it. She was able to get one beside me, and as we made our way to the seats we were assigned, my heart was racing. "He actually went and got me a ticket," I whispered to Atarah, as if she didn't know. "That's so cute, isn't it?"

I was aware of how little I should've cared. That didn't

change how my emotions were bright and bold and cheering about what felt like the biggest win one could have. It was simply a kind gesture, but it felt like so much more than that.

"I guess it is," Atarah said, disinterested. "I didn't think he would do that kind of thing, so… I guess that's nice."

"Mmm." I barely heard her. I could've been mad that she didn't think he was that nice, but that emotion was small beside the giddiness, almost as small as the guilt. The nervous energy from before was quickly becoming excitement. I truly wanted to see him perform. It felt foreign, to want things like that.

We sat down, and there was a while before it began. Atarah pulled out her phone and began to text someone, but all I could do was stare at the curtain in front of us. I couldn't believe I was here, and I couldn't understand why I thought that going through with this would be a good idea. I was going to fall in love with him further. What if I fell in love with him so much I didn't want to kill him anymore?

I watched the room fill up with people, and when it was almost entirely full, the lights dimmed, and music began from offstage. The curtains opened, and my anticipation bubbled in my throat almost like it was physical. At first, there was no one to be seen, but as a group of younger children came on, with no Stephen, I found myself disinterested.

I mean, their dancing was good, especially for children their age- they were eleven, maybe twelve- and they didn't often make mistakes. The music was fine, something from a musical that could've been from any of the past four decades. When they were done, everyone clapped, and a teacher came out to announce that we'd just seen the under 13 elite's routine, and to introduce the next one.

"They're good for kids," Atarah muttered to me. I shrugged.

As the next group came on- under 10s, annoyingly not Stephen- Atarah whispered to me, "why do you think Stephen does dancing?"

"Because he enjoys it?" I guessed, and there was a pang of something in my chest that was mildly unpleasant. I wondered what that was like, enjoying things. Stephen was the only thing that brought me any kind of joy.

"Maybe not. You did gymnastics for years without enjoying it," Atarah mentioned, and I shrugged again. Sure, that was true, but Stephen wasn't anything like me. Stephen was normal. He could never be like me, he could never understand me.

That thought was so utterly painful to think. I wanted these feelings gone.

But before that, I wanted to feel just one little moment of happiness. I wanted to see Stephen perform. In that short time, away from the rest of the world, I was to be allowed that small pleasure. In that moment I couldn't leave, so I may as well enjoy it, right?

Just since I'd never get to enjoy anything again once he was dead.

It took a while to get there. So many dances I didn't care about went past; they went through the younger kids first, promising that the older kids and individual showcases were to come later. I was impatient- another first for me- wondering if there was anything I could do to make the proceedings move faster. I wanted to see him. He was all I came here for.

Atarah sensed my impatience, and with a hand on my knee, silently reminded me that bad emotions must be beared. Annoyed, I sat back, and sat through another dance I didn't care about in silence. The first few I could appreciate for their skill, but as I had to wait longer and longer to see Stephen, the less I could appreciate them objectively.

And then, his first group performance came on.

I located him immediately, and I cared about nothing else. I didn't know if it was his only performance that night, and thinking it might be, I drank in everything with hungry eyes. The group he was dancing with consisted of only five others, so it was easy to focus on him. They wore plain white, and as they stood, ready to perform, I saw Stephen's eyes searching the crowd. I knew he was probably looking for his parents or something, but just the suggestion that he might've been looking for me made me so indescribably happy.

When the music started, it was like he went into a trance. He reached up for the sky, and began the routine with a rolling movement of his entire body downwards, in perfect sync with those around him. The music marched on, and with every movement I grew more impressed. Objectively, this might've seemed simply mechanically impressive, or even a little silly- it achieved nothing, after all, and could be considered a waste of time. Exercise at best. That was what I might've said, a month or two ago.

But there was something beautiful about it. The fluid movements of his body, bending in ways that didn't feel mechanical or human, but instead like strokes of a paintbrush, twists in a riverbend. He seemed to meld with the music; in the slower parts of the song, he was graceful and gentle like a breeze, each movement capturing a riff of music inside of it. When the song grew faster, more urgent, so did he, and it wasn't like I was watching a human being move to sound; it was like I was watching a song take human form.

It was a song I had never heard before, but I liked it. Not because of any property of the song itself, but simply because Stephen became it.

They did two dances, that group, one more contemporary, and one that I guess was ballet. The classical music of the second dance was more recognisable to me, and I found myself getting lost in it as I watched Stephen, as I breathed him in and exhaled him out. I understood what art was in that moment. I understood why humanity devoted so much time to it, creating things simply because of the joy they sparked. I understood what it meant for something to spark joy. I understood a fundamental human drive that had always eluded me.

When they were finished, I clapped, not only because everyone else was doing so, but because Stephen needed to know how amazing I found his dancing, him. I was grinning, I realised, as the song ended. The grin fell from my face as soon as he was offstage, but that moment of pure joy was something I could hold onto.

Something good.

They went offstage for a while, I prepared to sit through the rest of whatever was going to happen, unbothered now. I had seen what I came to see, and it was wonderful. It felt like nothing could destroy this happiness, and while I knew on some level it was the deceptive lie of neurochemicals, I didn't care. I didn't want to care. I wanted to enjoy the good emotions I had while I could, before the bad returned and I was reminded of what I had to destroy.

And then the individual showcases were on, and Stephen came back on stage, alone.

My eyes were glued onto him from the second he was visible to me. He had changed, in the same white pants as before, but this time in a much tighter black shirt. I had found people attractive before- Stephen was not the first- but the fact that I loved him seemed to give those feelings meaning, context. It was not passive, this exact desire, but an active need that could only be ignored for my own sanity at this point.

"Damn," Atarah muttered beside me, an acknowledgement that his attractiveness wasn't just to me. That seemed to help, somehow.

His searching gaze connected with mine right as the music started. The look he gave me was indescribable; it was a grin of happiness, but underlying it was what might've been smugness, if I was reading it right, and I wasn't sure I was. Wishful thinking tainted everything about Stephen in my mind.

I only saw that look for a second, as he immediately dropped to the ground.

The dance was something of a mix between the two styles he'd done before, and it was mesmerising in an entirely different way. The song was very different, too- for one, the others had both been wordless, but this one had lyrics. It was energetic throughout, and he followed the music; it was dramatic, and wild, yet orchestrated, and as beautiful as always.

The song was about becoming human. A beast transforming, growing, losing control and finding themselves. Losing control and becoming human.

And as I watched him, becoming the music, I couldn't help but think that he deserved so much more than this. My attention and the gaze of a couple dozen parents wasn't enough; Stephen was a work of art, and he deserved the appreciation of the entire world.

At the same time, however, there was some part of me that wanted him all to myself. Something genuinely selfish; much like the real, emotionless me, yet different. Different because it wasn't simply what made things easiest for me.

It was what I wanted. I wanted something, and it was him, and nothing else.

It was almost comforting to know that I would kill him, and nobody else would have that privilege.

"Alex," Atarah whispered, and I ignored her, my eyes only for Stephen. He was a work of art that needed to be witnessed while I had the chance. I only regretted that I had so little time to take him in, that this dance would not go on forever.

He became the song, the song about becoming human.

When it was over, he lay against the stage, bent backwards on his knees, breathing heavily. I don't think I imagined it when I heard the crowd clap harder for him alone than they had almost anyone else. Maybe it was just my own clapping sounding so loud in my ears.

He looked at me again, then; his eyes were green in the light, his soft joy so utterly wonderful it was almost too much to bear.

Just as soon, it was gone, as he had to go offstage for the next act. Any other act was meaningless next to that.

My heart was so full, and for a while I knew what it was like for everyone else. I felt the joy that drove so many to get out of bed in the morning, to live. It was wonderful, and beautiful, and it was real. It was real. It may've just been chemicals in my brain, but I felt it as real as I felt the world around me.

It was hard to believe, in that moment, that it was an illusion. It was such a good illusion that I almost didn't care.

"Alex." As soon as Stephen went offstage, Atarah was

gently shaking my arm, trying to get my attention again. With nothing else to care about, I turned to her, and she nodded ever so slightly to the right, encouraging me to look in that direction. It took some searching up and down the rows, before I found what she was gesturing at.

"Oh, this is serious, then," I muttered to myself when I saw. Ophelia's follower was back, sitting at the very end of our row.

"What should we do?" Atarah muttered, her fingernails digging into the skin of my arm. "I haven't seen anything suspicious since last week. I thought she only hired them for like, one day or something."

"I have. Seen something." I squinted through the dark, confirming it was the same person. "A few days ago, I spotted that same person outside the school. I got a good look then, too. I think it's a man, maybe late thirties, I guess. Definitely a private investigator. If Ophelia-"

"Will you two shut up?" hissed someone in the row behind us. I closed my mouth shut on instinct, but Atarah turned around to face our accuser, her jaw set.

"Excuse me, but we're being stalked. I think that's important," she snapped, her usual disregard for her surroundings making her voice louder than she may've liked. Her words drew the judgmental gazes of several other people. Between Atarah's words and the stares, the person who shushed us decided that staying silent may've been the best choice, and left us alone.

Atarah didn't say anything after that, and neither did I, but my gaze was fully focused on the end of the row. As soon as I saw shuffling, a shadowy figure moving towards the door, I got up and followed, Atarah close behind. Shuffling past everyone slowed us down, but as I barged through the door into the hallway, I could clearly see a retreating back heading out of the building.

"Hey," I called out, hoping that being noticed would give the follower pause, enough that I could stop and question them. They instead walked faster.

So I broke into a run. "Hey! Stop," I called after them,

hoping I could at least put them off. "Wait!"

The door was slammed shut right as I reached it. "What the hell?" I heard Atarah yell behind me. She shouted, loud enough he'd be able to hear it through the door, "if you're not doing anything shifty, why are you running, huh?"

"What the hell's going on?" came a demanding voice from behind us, with footsteps fast approaching. Atarah rounded in a flurry, her dreadlocks whipping around her face, ready to meet whatever came next head-on.

There were several made-up faces of the dancers peeking around the doorframe, neutrally confused, as well as a teacher coming to sort out what the hell was happening. Atarah leaned against the door, trying to shove it open, and found it was being held shut. "We think this guy is stalking us and he's just ran off," she admitted to the teacher, anger edging into her words. "He's making sure we don't see his face."

We received a subtle eye-roll, but the dancers backstage all heard what Atarah said, and began whispering amongst themselves. "Are you sure?" asked the exasperated teacher.

"Yes," Atarah insisted, stepping away from the door. "I don't know any more than that, that's why we were following him, alright?"

As the teacher walked over to the door, I heard it, and the rest of the world was put on hold. "Alex? What's going on?"

Stephen's voice froze me. Even if I didn't want to answer him, I didn't think I would've had a choice. I looked up, and he was there, leaning against the doorframe alongside his classmates. He wore an oversized hoodie with the sleeves rolled up, and clutched a mostly-empty water bottle. I had wanted to talk to him, but not like this.

"Oh, hi. Stephen." There was a longer gap than there should've been between my words. The conversation between Atarah and the teacher was background noise, irrelevant now. "Uh, not much."

He began to walk towards me, and like a magnet, I took a step towards him, then another. He stood in front of me, and it took all of my strength not to cross the gap that remained. What that meant wasn't exactly clear; if I wanted to hug him, kiss him, somehow merge with him, I didn't know. All I knew was that this wasn't enough.

No; it just didn't feel like enough. I kept myself in check with the knowledge that everything he was to me was illusory.

I spoke before he did. "I just wanna say that you were really good." I had to tell him. That beauty I had witnessed built up inside of me and begged to be released; someone had to share in this wonderful feeling, and the best person for it to be was him. He who created it. "I'm not one for dancing, but... I enjoyed you. It."

He seemed not to notice my slipup, beaming at me, self-satisfied. His smile was already burned into my memory, a permanent scar. I couldn't help but notice every detail about that smile; the ever-so-slight, charming crookedness, the prominent cupid's bow, a little pocked scar just below his lower lip that told of a long-removed lip piercing. I didn't re-member him actually having one, but then again, I had only paid surface-level attention to him before now. Now, I want-ed to know everything about him, every single minute detail of his past.

Except I didn't, and I wanted him dead.

"I'm glad." His eyes glittered with an innocent happi-ness. "I think I'd like to see you dance, though. If you join."

I shied away from the idea. "Oh, no. I don't think I'd be any good." That was half reflexive response to a compliment, and half visceral denial that I could ever come close to every-thing he was. Would I be good? Maybe. Could I ever make art, like he had? Never, at least, not in my own mind.

"Well, it's be easy for you to pick up. How long did you do gymnastics for? Most of your life, right?" He was looking at me with a gaze that probably wasn't truly as intense as it felt. I was surprised he got it right, surprised he remembered at all. Pleasantly surprised. I thought I might've heard my name, but anything Atarah had to say to me right now felt less important than answering Stephen. Was whatever she was going on about even important? I forgot.

"Yeah, but I still don't think I'd ever be as good as you."

My words were poorly chosen, overly eager, and embarrassment flushed my cheeks as I turned away from him, looking at the floor.

Those overly revealing words motivated me to answer when Atarah called my name for the second time. "Alex, he's getting away-"

"What?" Out of the open door, Ophelia's follower could be seen running off down the road. If I moved right then, I'd have been able to catch up.

"What's going on?" Stephen asked, confused, and his voice was enough to distract me. He came to stand beside me- so close, I could feel my heart skip a beat- and when I turned my attention to the door again, the follower was too far down the road. Gone.

"Shit." Atarah stomped her feet against the carpet, annoyed. Her eyes caught Stephen's. "We were being followed. The bastard got away."

"Followed?" Stephen's eyebrows shot up, as he went to the door to look for himself. "Who? Why?"

I was about to feign uncertainty to do all I could to keep from getting Stephen involved, but Atarah answered, and I cursed her reckless honesty. "It's fucking Ophelia. Not her, but someone she hired."

"Ophelia Hough." It was a question, but the way Stephen said it was flat, in a way that could've been disbelief or anger. I didn't want it to be either. I didn't want him to be involved.

"It doesn't-" I began, but I got nowhere before Atarah was explaining further.

"She's got some weird conspiracy theories about Alex," Atarah said, and while I was struggling to figure out a way to shut her up, Stephen surprised me.

"Yeah, I know." He sounded distant, almost. "She thinks they killed her father, doesn't she?"

Atarah stared at him in disbelief, a hand on her hip. "I didn't realise you were friends with her," she said.

Stephen wasn't looking at her, instead down the street still, as though he'd be able to see anyone in the dark. "I'm not," he answered, and an invisible weight lifted off my chest. That was all he had to say about it, however, and I had questions still.

None of them got any answers, though, as the teacher from before returned. "Stephen, you need to go back inside."

With a reluctant glance towards us, and his mood considerably lowered, Stephen backed away from the door. "Well," he said, watching his teacher with careful eyes, "I guess I'll see you guys at school. I-" he paused, stuttered without knowing what to say, and gave up, following his teacher backstage again without another word.

Atarah turned to me a good few seconds after the door closed, her lips a tight line. "So we missed that one."

"That was my fault." Stephen was gone, and my emotions were waning. I was able to pull myself back into line and recognise the way my feelings had led me astray. "I could've gave chase, but Stephen distracted me. I'm sorry."

Atarah ground her teeth. "It's fine. I'm annoyed, but it's not really your fault. I just... what should we do now?"

I shrugged. "Go home, I guess. I saw all I wanted to see."

"Good." After checking that we both had everything we'd taken in with us, we did just that. Neither of us cared about the ending of the performance, and the sighting of Ophelia's follower had left Atarah on edge. She was looking every which way as we went back to my car, like someone would pop out from behind it to attack us.

"I don't think we're in danger," I told her as we climbed into our respective seats. "I don't think Ophelia wants me dead."

Atarah slammed the door shut, and checked the backseat just to be safe. "You murdered her father. Of course she'd want you dead."

"Well, she doesn't want me dead until she's sure." I couldn't bring myself to care. I felt empty and lost now that my happiness was gone, and I just didn't care about why I was being followed. Maybe that was normal for me, but it felt like a loss. I had to remind myself I was coming off of a high, that this was a lie, that in truth I had lost nothing at all.

It was hard to believe.

Atarah was silent for most of the ride home. She only spoke up once. "So I guess you don't want to talk about Stephen, do you?"

"No." She didn't speak again after that.

I dropped her off and went home. I was silent, stoic, blank right up until I fell onto my bed. With my face buried in the sheets, hidden from the outside world, I exploded.

I sobbed. My shoulders wracked, my eyes hurt, my face twisted and contorted, sobbing louder and harder than I'd ever imagined. There was a scorching friction in my throat with every movement, and it felt like I couldn't get enough oxygen. It was a painful struggle just to breathe. The sobs wracked through me like an earthquake, unstoppable. And yet, I hardly felt anything.

I knew true emptiness, and this wasn't quite it, but it was close. I didn't know what I was feeling, this faint echo of pain and sadness. I didn't know what caused this.

I didn't know it until I said it, the thought forming on my tongue before it reached my brain. I whispered it into my arm like a secret. "I don't want to fall in love."

It became like a mantra. Muttering it over and over was like a salve on this numb, yet fatal wound. "I don't want to fall in love- I don't- want- I don't want this. I don't want this."

And I just cried.

There was a small, gentle knock. I clutched the sheets in horror, terrified of anyone in my family seeing me like this. The exact identity of the knocker became clear quickly. "Alex?" It was the voice of one of the triplets- Darcy, to be exact.

I took a deep breath, steadied myself, and called back, "Yeah?"

The door inched open. Darcy had her pyjamas on, her black hair in a thin plait over her shoulder, ready for bed. She looked almost like a younger version of me, although my hair was shorter when I was her age. She should've been in bed by now, technically, although my parents were not at all strict with maintaining that. "Are you okay?" she asked, eyes widening when she actually caught sight of me.

I wish I could've told her I was fine and sent her back to bed. Nobody had ever seen me like this; the closest anyone had come was Atarah. "I don't know," I answered instead. There was no way to get her to go away. She was going to see this, and there was nothing I could do about it.

Darcy didn't say anything. She moved into the room, closing the door quietly behind her. Her bare feet were quiet on the carpet as she made her way towards me, and I sat up, prepared to tell her whatever she wanted to know. But she still said nothing.

She stood in front of me, reached out, and pulled me into a hug.

I was surprised, just a little. I moved, and she settled around my shoulders, patting my back gently. I wrapped my own arms around her, returning the hug, something I had done many times before; but this was different. It was emotionally soothing. She was close enough to absorb just enough of my pain that it became bearable.

After I stopped crying, she pulled away and looked me in the eye. "Do you wanna talk about it?" she asked, and when I shook my head, she left it there. "Well, talk to me if you need to, okay? I'm here."

She was twelve, and it felt like she shouldn't have the amount of emotional intelligence that she did. But she left, and she closed the door behind her, and I stared at the empty space where she had just been and realised she had not changed at all. It was me, growing an appreciation for the fact that she loved me.

And that made me cry anew.

I woke up without remembering when I had stopped crying. I had dried tears across my face, and I was still in my day clothes. I had never before cleaned myself up after a rough night, as I was always the responsible one, and I quickly found that I hated waking up wearing jeans, with bad breath and my hair a tangled mess. I changed, brushed my teeth twice, and untangled that mess, still not quite sure what had caused my breakdown last night.

I mean, I knew what the emotion was, and I knew the cause of it. What I did not know was why last night was any different to any night before it. And why I had felt better when Darcy offered her support.

I ignored it all, pushing every thought I had about it down. I was beginning to get the hang of that. I now could understand what everyone else went through, all the time, and it made it easier to understand others on a fundamental level that I'd never had before.

The next Monday, everything was all back to normal, as though that concert had never happened, as though everything was fine. My world felt changed, but the sun still rose, I still had to go to school, and my friends greeted me at lunch like it was the same as any other day. And I grinned and pretended it was.

I caught Atarah's eye across the cafeteria, and she gave me her usual nod of recognition. Just as I was trying to discern who it was she was sitting with, a slamming sound resounded through the room. Everyone's eyes followed the sound on instinct, and I couldn't hold back the gasp when I saw who it was. My feet moved before my brain fully caught up.

Ezra stood, red-faced and angry, over Stephen- Stephen, his arms thrown up in front of him, leaning backwards against a table, almost cowering. "You think you can say that kind of shit about my sister?" Ezra yelled, fists balled. I ran down the aisle, in that moment paying not one iota of attention to how things looked. "You wanna dance with the big boys, huh? Well I ain't afraid of you, and there's nothin' you can do to hurt me!"

"What the hell, Ezra?" Stephen yelled, just as the teachers were jumping into action. I was there first, however, skidding to a stop in front of them, discarding the reactions of my peers and my reputation in favour of protecting Stephen. In seconds, I forced myself between them, shoving Ezra away with a hard, one-handed push to the centre of his chest. My other hand searched behind me for something I didn't quite understand, until Stephen's fingers curled around my wrist, and my heart began racing so fast I thought it might give out. He took my hand, and for a moment I almost couldn't care about Ezra. A crowd began to form, a wall of schaudenfreudic students blocking the teachers from interrupting, but all I could seem to notice was Stephen's fingers against my skin.

He pulled himself up, and when every second of contact felt maddeningly long, it seemed like it took forever for him to drop my hand. Ezra's eyebrows shot up as he processed exactly who had interrupted, and he especially noticed Stephen's hand in mine.

"Step away, Ezra," I warned, in a voice with all the emptiness I normally possessed. I wasn't acting or pretending. I was angry, but it was a dry, unspoken anger that itched in my veins and begged to be let loose. If anyone touched me, I might've exploded, and Ezra would've ended up in hospital.

"Well, well, well, look at you two," Ezra smirked. "I-you- ain't this predictable."

"No it isn't. Go away." Stephen's voice sounded like I'd never heard him before. Bored, exasperated, angry. He stepped around me, as if refusing to be protected. "Leave us alone."

Ezra took one glance around him, at the forming crowd. One of his friends reached out and nudged him, and he turned back to Stephen with gritted teeth, raising a hand. "If I ever-"

As soon as I saw his hand move, I gently pushed past Stephen and stood toe-to-toe with Ezra. I knew exactly what to say to shut him down, and I didn't care about the cruelty of it. I whispered, right next to his ear, even as he tried to push me away; nobody else would get to hear this. "Touch him, and you'll go the same way as your father."

Ezra hit me without a thought, a sharp jolt to the jaw that wasn't as hard as he'd clearly intended. Disgust and anger riddled his face, and I stood completely still, unreactive. Before he had a chance to do or say anything else, the crowd was busted through by an unstoppable force. "Get away!"

yelled a voice I didn't immediately recognise as Ophelia's until I saw her face, when she grabbed her brother and pulled him away from me. "Just what is going on here?"

"You tell me," I answered, numb, but hostile somewhere beneath that. "All I saw was Ezra shoving Stephen against the table and yelling at him."

"Break it up, now, kids, break it up," a vaguely annoyed teacher called out over the heads of the crowd, as if she was changing anything. I held Stephen behind me, and Ophelia held Ezra behind her, and it was like we were animals protecting our young, circling each other and waiting for the other to attack.

"Oh, drop it, Alex." Ophelia scoffed. "I don't know what in the world's going on here, but you better leave Ezra alone."

It was then that the teacher managed to reach us. "All of you. Separate. Now."

I knew her. It was the same rather dull teacher who I'd managed to trick surrounding Amanda's death. She liked me, and she'd probably believe me if they decided to question this incident; but they wouldn't. Not when Ezra was the only troublemaker in the group, and the only one who'd done any damage.

I felt Stephen's hand on my shoulder as he began to back away, encouraging me to do so, too. I did as he implied I should, not just because it was logical, but because I would do anything he wanted.

"Thank you." Stephen whispered near my ear. "I- please- please don't do anything like that again, though. I don't want you to get hurt."

"I-" many responses came into my mind, and all of them felt wrong in some way or another. I said the first one that my mouth would let me say. "You're planning on getting into confrontations with Ezra again?"

Stephen laughed, a real laugh that resonated deep in my heart. The crowd was parting as the teacher pulled Ezra aside and Ophelia glared me down. I felt accomplished, somehow, and I couldn't even begin to stop and consider what this all looked like to anyone around me.

"Preferably not," Stephen finally answered, his voice as soft and beautiful as the rest of him. "But I definitely don't want you getting hurt."

Maybe there was a reason I fell in love with him. Maybe it wasn't random. Maybe he wasn't just anyone.

Or maybe I was blinded by my emotions so much that I couldn't see the truth anymore.

I was thankful for the bell ringing, because it meant I wouldn't have to explain to my friends why I'd run towards a fight so quickly, why I'd run towards a fight at all. I was not known for those acts, and I wasn't ready for my public persona to change.

I was not thankful for the bell ringing, because Stephen and I had to part ways. "Thank you again," he said as we deftly dodged the teacher searching the cafeteria for us. "I'll have to talk to you later."

"Goodbye," I said, and it felt bitter on the tip of my tongue.

I wanted to try and figure out what the hell had happened, but events on that Monday lunch were not yet over. I found a hand on my elbow as I collected books from my locker, even as I was still shaken up from what had just happened. It was Atarah. I had expected her to want to talk about this, of course, but I thought she would've known to wait until after school.

"What do you want?" I asked anyway, putting my questions of what Stephen had said to provoke Ezra aside for the moment. I had only just concluded that he'd asked Ezra about the follower, accused Ophelia of something, but it wasn't a lot to go off. I was still glowing from how he said he'd talk to me later, and it was distracting to imagine our next meeting.

Atarah didn't say anything. She simply handed me a piece of paper. Lined paper, folded twice.

I took it and silently opened it, expecting it to be something she had to tell me. That was not it.

Written in the middle of the paper, in thick, straight

lines, were the words:

THIS IS YOUR FIRST WARNING TO STAY AWAY FROM ALEX KEEN

Chapter Nine - Atarah Adebayo, Iterum

I didn't get long to talk to Atarah at lunch, but after school, it was all she wanted to talk about. "I can only guess it was Ophelia," she'd said first thing, with no introduction. "This is so exciting. I don't even know how to react to this. I'm certainly not going to leave you alone just because someone said to."

"You saw what happened at lunch today, didn't you?" I asked her. I was… not nervous, not apprehensive, but simply acknowledging that what I'd said to Ezra was of immediate importance. The emotions passing had shed light on my actions, and it only occurred to me now just how serious my threat had been. In my anger, my protectiveness of Stephen, I'd all but confessed. "I didn't get a chance to tell you, but-"

"Oh, Stephen's picking fights with Ezra, yeah. What about it?" She was typing away on her phone, not quite looking at me. When I looked over her shoulder, she was on social media, making a post. Presumably about the threat.

"I basically confessed to Ezra."

Atarah nearly dropped her phone, staring at me wide-eyed. "About what? Please tell me you told him you liked Stephen, not that you're planning to kill him, before-"

"I told him if he touched Stephen-" my voice broke at his name- "he'd go the same way as his father."

"Oh, oh no, he's going to kick your ass." Atarah hissed through her teeth. "Why the hell would you say that? Ophelia's been stalking us, she's sending me threats, she wants you dead as soon as she's sure you killed her dad, and you all but tell Ezra you're going to fucking kill him, *and* confess to the murder of his father?"

"He was going to hurt Stephen. I know it's not logical, but I wasn't thinking properly. You understand."

Atarah cursed under her breath. "You've got to be more fucking careful. They're going to come for revenge, Alex, and this... you're signing your own death warrant."

"You don't have to stick around," I reminded her, gazing at her screen again. The idea of getting the threat seemed to excite her more than it scared her. "I get that this is, I suppose, exciting, but you might be in danger. If Ophelia tries to-"

"Alex, you're my friend. I like you. Yes, this is fun, and it's also a little scary, but I'm going to stick around anyway because I promised I would." Atarah didn't look away from me for a word of that. "It wouldn't be fair to just leave you alone like this now that the water's getting hot. I wouldn't do that to you."

"Okay." Somehow, in some way I couldn't quite understand, hearing that made dealing with the Houghs feel doable. I don't know what I thought before, and I don't even have an idea of what I think the Houghs are going to do to me, but knowing I won't face it alone helps.

Falling in love with Stephen changed me, and I'm scared that when he dies it won't go away.

Atarah took the piece of paper out of her pocket again, looking it over. "I'm worried about what Ophelia's going to do," she muttered, running her fingers over the writing. "To you. She won't take this lightly at all."

"There's nothing to worry about until she does something," I reminded her, checking around us to make sure we were alone.

Atarah sighed. "I'm not sure I want to leave you alone tonight. I'm worried she's going to come after you."

"We've got to go home sometime," I said, eyeing her curiously.

Atarah grinned. "Not if you come over tonight. I know you don't want your parents asking any questions, but in my case, my stepfather never leaves me the fuck alone anyway. I don't care if he's asking me questions about you."

I took a moment to consider it. "As long as you're okay with that. You know, if you really think I'm in danger, they might still come after me at your house."

"My stepdad's a cop. We don't get along at all, but he'd protect us if it came to that."

"I'll have to at least take my car home," I reminded her, as we came towards the car park.

She bit the inside of her mouth, considering. "I guess we don't have a choice. And I mean, you can look after yourself, I'm not that worried, it's just..."

"Are you worried for yourself?"

Atarah stared down at the paper, reading those words yet again. "I mean... maybe? It's... you get it, you actually *do* get it, when you don't know what you're feeling? I know I can look after myself, I can, it's just... I've never been in this situation before. I've never felt like my life was in danger. You've dealt with death before, I mean, on the other end, but-"

Suddenly, she turned to me, her eyes wide. Her fingers clutched my arm, turning me towards her. She paused, uncertainty riddling her face. "I was thinking. I've seen

Ophelia's handwriting, and this isn't it. I'm worried that whoever's coming after us is bigger, more powerful, braver than either of them. Ophelia's totally nonviolent and law-abiding, and Ezra's a brash idiot. Neither of them could hurt us. Whoever Ophelia's hired won't do anything she wouldn't do. But I think this is someone else entirely. That's why I'm afraid, Alex."

"It's nothing we won't be able to deal with." I felt confident that between us, that statement was true. "I don't know of anyone else who'd want to hurt either of us, at least not yet."

"Neither do I," Atarah agreed, "but that's the issue. Anyway, just-" she gestured vaguely at my car. "-go home, and then come right over, okay? I don't want to be alone."

"Okay." Her hands were shaking ever so slightly. In light of the conversation we just had, I wanted to do what was best for her. "I will."

And I did. I told my parents I was going over to a friend's house, and they didn't ask questions. Atarah picked me up, holding her phone like she would have to call someone at any moment. She hurried me into her room before I had a chance to be met by her stepfather.

"Atarah!" called a voice that I deduced as belonging to her mother. "Before you hide in your room, come help your sister!"

"Mom, I have a friend over!" Atarah yelled back. I took the chance, while she was occupied with her mother, to read the clippings on her wall, the murder board.

The headlines were expected. *Cold Park Killer Evades Capture. Seventh Victim In Chicago Stabbings. New Lead In Zodiac Killer Case, Sixty-Five Years Later. Troy Shooting Unsolved.*

One in particular was a much smaller newspaper cutting, showing only a small paragraph. *Oliver Hough, 38, was killed on August 4th in a stabbing off Main St. The motive, police say, may have been robbery, although investigation is still underway. He is survived by his wife, Tanya, and his two children, Ophelia and Ezra.* Alongside the text was a photo of Mr Hough with his wife and his kids. Ophelia and Ezra were young then, ten and nine, holding each other's hands and smiling for the camera.

That piece of paper was old, from the original newspaper. Two newer additions to the wall, printed off from the internet, were added below it. One was the memorial page our school posted of Amanda's death, and the other was a photo from my mother's social media, such an old photo that I didn't even remember it existed. It was of the seven of us- my parents, me, my sisters, and my brother. Taken on the same trip to Lake Michigan on which he died. I had my arm around him, and we were both grinning these wide, toothy grins. My smile was fake. His was not.

I looked at the image of me and my brother, and back to the image of Ezra and Ophelia. Ophelia loved her brother. Ezra was important to her, and she'd do anything for him, much like I would for Stephen. When she was smiling, it was because being with her family made her happy.

When I was smiling, with my arm around Bailey, it was because it was expected of me.

I wished I had loved my brother.

Atarah had left the room, and I hadn't even noticed until she came back. "Sorry. We're going to have to come out for dinner later, and my mom's going to grill you, and I'm sorry about that." She shrugged off her coat, coming over to stand beside me. "I love her and all, but she's hard to deal with sometimes."

Even Atarah's casual throwaway statement was more than I could say about my own parents. It occurred to me for the first time that I wasn't just *different* from those around me; I didn't exist in some equally valid way, some neutral opposing option. I was actively missing something that everyone else around me had, and I felt it in that moment. Looking at those two images, side by side, of love I had faked and love that was real, almost made me want the real version. If I hadn't killed Bailey- if he was still alive- I could've loved him in the way Ophelia loved Ezra. It was at least a possibility.

Why did that feel like something I wanted, even when I knew it would only bring me so much more pain? Were my emotions leaking into other thoughts, tainting me, poisoning me before I had the chance to recover and return to normal?

I needed Stephen dead now, before this got out of hand.

"Atarah, have you had any ideas about the plan with Stephen? Like where we could go, perhaps?" I asked, skipping the thought process that had gotten me to that question. There was no reason in particular to do so, and it was hard to convince myself I wasn't at least a little embarrassed of my weakness. Embarrassment- another emotion. This was spreading like a sickness.

"Hmm." Atarah came over to stand beside me, gazing at her wall of clippings. "When you guys went to Lake Michigan, where did you stay? You don't have a holiday house or anything, do you?"

"No, it was a rented cabin. Besides, it's not a good idea to return to the scene of the crime. It's best if it's completely unconnected to us."

"But it's so nice and poetic," Atarah protested, leaning against my shoulder. "Full circle, you know?"

I raised an eyebrow. "There's no way in hell I'm going to get caught just because you want it to be poetic."

Atarah's eyes glittered, and she paused for a moment, looking up to the roof. "No way in hell, huh," she said, and I could tell it was a leadup to something. "Well, how about we go to Hell? That's poetic and completely unrelated."

"Hell, as in, Hell, Michigan. Very funny." I said it sarcastically, but I could definitely see the humour in it. "That's nearly a two hour drive. If I was killing him straight up, it would be perfect, but I don't know how long we're keeping him alive for."

"Oh, I doubt it'll be long. There's a bunch of lakes out there, too. The ice should last until at least March or April, so you could always bury him under the ice at the end of the night, and he won't be found for a while."

"And what if I want to keep him alive for longer than one night?" I asked her. "I'll do whatever it takes to get rid of these feelings. I don't think one night will do it."

"If you can't kill him after one night, I don't think you can kill him at all," Atarah argued, and I decided to believe her. I conceded her plan was a good one, at least for now, and we dropped it.

Atarah then left me to my own devices, explaining that she wanted to make a video. I sat with my back against the wall, working through my biology homework, as she spoke to a camera about what happened today. I was listening to her carefully chosen words. She omitted names, referring to me as her 'best friend' for what I assumed was convenience. That, or maybe she did consider me her best friend. She knew everything there was to know about me, and nothing I could find out about her would make me like her any less- short of her liking Stephen or trying to hurt me.

She was my best friend, considering she was the only one I could say I preferred to be around.

We weren't bothered by anyone in her family, excepting a black-and-white cat that seemed to know how to open the door by jumping at the handle. The sound startled Atarah, and the cat lumbering in, mewing, without seeming to care.

"Oh, you idiot cat," Atarah mumbled fondly as it launched itself onto her bed. "Come here." She took the cat into her lap and continued her story, as though nothing had happened.

I had never had pets. All I could think about when I looked at the cat in Atarah's lap was whether or not Stephen would want pets, should we live together.

It was easy to quickly dismiss the idea. He was going to die, so it wouldn't ever matter.

When Atarah was done and she was transferring the video file to her laptop, there was a knock. Atarah's mother didn't wait for an answer before opening the door. "Atarah, listen when your mother's calling you." As she spoke, her gaze turned to me. "I'm so sorry my daughter is so rude. She hasn't even introduced you to me."

"Hi," I said, realising I had no idea what to call her. "I'm Alex, and..."

"Mom, before you go any further, don't say anything embarrassing," Atarah said, fixing her mother with a stare.

She raised her eyebrows. "I was just going to say I'm

glad you've got more friends than just Maisie and-" she tried to say, before a long groan from her daughter cut her off. She rolled her eyes. "Well, anyway, dinner is ready. Come on out, you two."

Atarah's mother was nice. She introduced herself as Teash, and she had the same chatty energy about her as her daughter. Her hair was cut entirely short, and long strings of gold dangled from her ears. She led us into the dining room I'd first spoken to Atarah in, and it was there that I met Atarah's stepfather for the first time.

It was clear from half a glance that the two were not related. He was tall and wiry, pale as alabaster, and when he smiled his hazel eyes seemed to shrink back into his face. He shook my hand and introduced himself, with a genuinely happy tone, as Josh.

"It's nice to meet you," I said, subtly watching Atarah. "I'm Alex."

"Alex?" he asked, like he'd misheard me, as we were all moving to sit around the table. Atarah's little sister, Dayo, ran in from another room just before she could be called. Atarah sat down beside me, eyeing her stepfather up cautiously.

"Yeah, Alex. Just Alex," I added, wondering if that was the question he was asking. Teash was handing out plates as we spoke, and I was trying to figure out why exactly Josh was looking at me like that.

"Alexis Keen, right?" he said, and I allowed myself to appear taken aback. It was surprising, for sure, that he knew me. It was a concern, perhaps, that he was a *cop* who knew me.

I wasn't quite sure how to play it off, but I managed to sound natural when I said, "I mean- I prefer just Alex. Alexis is fine, it's just that people assume I'm-"

"No, no, that's fine, Alex, that's not what I meant to say." He seemed overly eager to make sure I wasn't offended before continuing on. "I thought I recognised your face, is all. I've heard some stories about you."

"Oh, no," Atarah whispered under her breath, before saying much louder, "Josh, please don't-"

"Well I didn't believe them, of course," Josh added, his face reddening slightly. He seemed very upset at the idea of offending anyone, even Atarah, who he must've known didn't like him very much. "I was just going to say, Alex, that there are some people who seem to have beef with you, so to speak. There was a young woman a few weeks ago that kept coming into the police station, asking if we'd open an investigation on you at her request. She said a lot of crazy things to me, and couldn't back up any of it, so don't worry, I just wonder why-"

He was interrupted by the sound of Atarah loudly stabbing a fork into her plate, acting like she'd just missed the piece of pasta she'd been aiming for and the screeching noise had been entirely accidental. It didn't surprise me that Ophelia had tried to go to the police first; she seemed to prefer doing things with the least amount of blood on her hands as possible. Atarah trying to shut her stepfather up wasn't out of the ordinary either.

"Atarah, be nice," Teash warned, and that was the end of that conversation. Josh didn't want to bring it up again, and Dayo- after saying a chipper little hello to me- began to tell him and Teash about this new game she'd been playing, and I let her take over the conversation. It was not in anyone's best interests if I were to be dodging questions about a murder I most definitely committed, even if Josh didn't believe I did.

Dinner went smoothly enough, and as Dayo talked, I began to get an impression of Atarah's family. Josh was almost sycophantic in his efforts to get along with everyone, and it was especially noticeable with Atarah. Teash, Dayo and Atarah were all similar in their gregariousness, although their interests were very different. Atarah was some intersection of goth, emo, and punk, while her mother was traditionally feminine and glamorous, and Dayo was a sporty tomboy who asked her mother if she could get a skateboard at least twice in that single dinner. She asked me how my sisters were doing and started talking about how we should all do something together. I smiled and pretended like I'd enjoy that.

It was relatively painless, yet Atarah seemed sick of it less than five minutes in. She dragged me away from the table at the earliest opportunity, and I quickly thanked her mother for the meal before I was shut back in Atarah's room.

She held her back against the door, like someone was going to push through it. "I know you don't care, but my stepdad talking to you about Ophelia trying to get you investigated was both *really* rude, and super annoying knowing what's going on right now." The scowl on her face made it clear she was speaking from a grudge. "Honestly, it just pissed me off hearing him say how nonsense he thought you killing Oliver Hough was. It's just further proof that cops are as selfish and dog-eat-dog as anyone else, they're just convinced that that's what justice is."

"I mean, if he knew the truth, he'd probably want justice," I told her, unsure of where her thought process was right then.

Atarah shook her head. "Alex, if the world was just, you wouldn't be a murderer and I wouldn't have a stepfather. All you ever did was what you had to do, which can't be said for just about anyone in the world."

I disagreed, but I kept quiet on it. My eyes kept returning to the image of my family on the wall, my arm around Bailey. I wondered if he had to die.

I didn't tell Atarah about these thoughts, exclusively because I wasn't sure if they were permanent. It was unlike me to come close to regret, and it was definitely somehow connected to Stephen, another of the tricky illusions these feelings created. I ignored it and hoped it would go away sooner rather than later.

Atarah went to have a shower not long after that, leaving me again. It was then that I began to check the notifications on my phone, and found one that instantly intrigued me. Stephen.

I clicked on it immediately, without a second thought. There was two messages, one that had been sent to many recipients and one sent after that was only for me. The first was a peppy invitation to a birthday party, his eighteenth. As

I read it, I could already feel my heart racing, and my imagination running wild. Going to his house, actually being inside of it. Being around him in some context other than school. Having a chance to maybe, maybe be alone with him.

It sounded incredibly dangerous, and irresistible.

It took me a moment to get to the second message, while I held my phone against my chest and tried to remember how to breathe. When I did read it, it absolutely did not help my beating heart.

Hi Alex :) first of all, check that ^, it'd really mean a lot to me if you could come. I also just wanted to thank you for defending me today. I didn't get a chance to talk about it, but the reason he shoved me in the first place was because I told him and his sister to leave you alone, and mentioned the person who was following you. I hope it was okay that I did that. I just think it's unfair that they're treating you like this because they're looking for someone to blame, you know?

I put the phone down and took several deep breaths. He was trying to help me. He was trying to help me, his future murderer, because he thought two people trying to get revenge for another murder of mine were wrong. And I loved him so *fucking* much for it.

Even as I brought myself back around and began to type a reply, I didn't know what to say. It was painstaking, the process of answering. Usually I was smooth and easy, erring on the side of uncaring; but nothing I could come up with seemed to do.

In the end, I had to take a moment of courage, regretting the whole time, and stab 'send' with my finger before I could change my mind again.

Of course I'll come! and it was really nice of you to stand up for me like that. you didn't have to do that. i don't know about fair w/ regards to the Houghs but if there's anything i can do for you, let me know.

It was clunky and wrong, ineloquent at best and incoherent at worst. It was the best I had, though.

I had only just got tired of rereading his previous message over and over again when he replied. *You don't owe me anything! Even if you did you'd have repaid it by defending me today. You know how violent Ezra gets, it was really brave of you. I was actually going to ask you if you wanted to hang out after school, but I saw you were with Atarah and I didn't want to interrupt you guys. It's too late now, lol.*

Shit. My hands were shaking so much it was hard to hold my phone as I typed out each word. I couldn't even fully get an idea of how I sounded, as my feelings clouded my judgement so much. I kept deleting and re-writing, and everything hurt. If Stephen was paying any attention at all to how long these responses took, he must've realised how nervous I was.

I'm still with her right now, but if you wanted to hang out another day, I could do that?

As soon as I hit send, I threw my phone down on Atarah's bed and hid my head in my hands. It was hell navigating five minutes alone with Stephen; what made me think I could 'hang out' with him? I could see that going a number of ways, most of which ended horribly. I'd have to stop myself from making a move on him, and no matter whether I did or not, I'd probably end up killing him sooner rather than later. It was simply too intense, his presence, despite how good it felt. Having emotions had taught me that too much pleasure was pain. And if it was time to care about fairness- in life and death- that was the most unfair thing of all, that pain seemed to be the endgame no matter what.

I heard my phone buzz, but I dared not look at it. Maybe if I didn't look, it would be like I never sent it at all, and things could go on like I'd ignored the message in the first place. Like I should've.

Atarah came back into the room, saw me hiding from the world, and naturally went straight to my phone. "Ah, I see," she said, squinting at the notification. "Hang on, did you ask Stephen if he wanted to hang out?"

"Read the messages," I told her. After a second's pause, I demanded, "what did he say?"

"He said Monday is the only day he has free, except that he got Saturday off for the party, but you can hang out next week maybe. I wonder if I'm invited to this party," Atarah muttered, checking her own phone. "Oh, apparently so. That's nice of him."

"He's so nice. You read what he sent to me," I said, and it sounded like a dreamy gloat; it probably was, as there was no real excuse to say it. "That's so nice."

"Yeah, it was weird. I'm certain he's not like that with anyone else," Atarah mumbled, almost to herself, taking my phone again and rereading the messages. Her skin was still somewhat wet from the shower, a pyjama shirt hanging loosely off her chest. "He must like you."

"Or, as we established, he doesn't like you," I argued back, and she shrugged. "No that it matters. I shouldn't hang out with him. I'll go to his party, because I can escape if I need to, but if I'm alone with him, I don't have a chance. I'm stupid. This was stupid."

Atarah seemed amused by how flustered I was. "It's your decision. It doesn't bother me."

Her lack of an opinion didn't make anything easier. When she gave my phone back to me, I typed out a reluctant, open-ended message to Stephen. I let him know next week wouldn't work, but sometime soon, definitely. He sent me back a reply after a little while, short and sweet. *That's fine. At least we'll see each other on Saturday :)*

I sent one last message agreeing, and then retreated into my other messages, some much less high-stakes group chat conversations that calmed my anxiety down back into a blank slate, before Atarah dragged me into watching a show she liked with her on her laptop.

I didn't know what my plan had been for sleeping, or if I'd even had one, as I never quite got around to it. As I laid beside Atarah on her bed, trying to follow along with the plot- it was a crime drama, and the main character was a detective trying to discover who was killing children in her neighbourhood- I found my mind wandering. To Stephen, as it always did. My mind never used to wander.

There were so many ideas of romance I'd heard, and when I had first fallen in love with Stephen, it was like I was overwhelmed with choice. I didn't know if a domestic fluffy marriage appealed to me more than eloping and going on an adventure, because when I imagined doing it with Stephen, it all felt the same.

But laying there next to Atarah, I knew the kind of future my feelings drove me towards. I still wanted to be a doctor, I still wanted to have many friends, but it was different to my previous ideal, with nobody close to me, and nothing to look forward to or hate. In this version, I lived with the love of my life, Stephen, and my best friend, Atarah. I'd never have to kill again, unless something somehow threatened them. I'd wake up every morning beside the man I loved, and fall asleep next to him every night. He would know me, and what I was, and love me anyway. That feeling he arose in me would still flutter in my stomach, but bearable and pleasant only, without overwhelming me and scaring me half to death. We'd go see the world on holidays, and everything would be beautiful when he was by my side. I'd give him anything he wanted, make him so happy he wouldn't know what to do with himself. Maybe he'd teach me how to dance.

Those daydreams turned to dreams, and I didn't even realise I was asleep until I woke up. A cold breeze gently shook me awake, running over the bare skin of my arms until it became uncomfortable in the haze of sleep. I shivered as my eyes opened.

It was dark, and the waning moon through the open window did almost nothing to illuminate the room. I sat up, shaking my head to clear my mind, and looked down at Atarah, who was actually under the covers, her laptop and glasses sitting on the bedside table. She had let me sleep, which was nice, although I wished I hadn't fallen asleep as I had.

With my mind a little clearer, I looked back at the open window and realised what was wrong. It was early February in Michigan; there was no way Atarah had just left the window open by accident, or on purpose. No wonder the cold had woken me up.

I stood, carefully clambering over Atarah. I padded over to the window and shut it. It wasn't broken, and the lock seemed fine- just open. That didn't reassure me, however. It was possible Atarah had just left the window unlocked, and it had blown open, but considering the threat she'd received earlier, I wasn't willing to bet that that was the case.

She was fine, fast asleep and unbothered. I locked the window, gazing through it at the dark street as though I could see anyone out there. There was movement, but it was impossible to tell if what moved was a tree in the wind, a small animal, or a person.

I cast a glance around the room, and that was when I saw it. Atarah had not left the window open at all, and this was no accident. In thick black letters across the mirror, it read:

THIS IS YOUR SECOND WARNING. THREE STRIKES YOU'RE OUT

"Atarah, wake up," I said, loud enough to make her stir in her sleep. When I turned her light on, she threw her hand over her face and groaned. "Wake up, now."

"What?" she grumbled, squinting at me as she fumbled for her glasses. "What time is it?"

"Someone broke in," I told her, and that was enough to get her moving. She jammed the glasses on her face and sat up, scrambling out of bed. "Look at the mirror."

"Oh, fuck," Atarah whispered, her hand over her mouth. "I- fuck. How'd they get in?"

"The window was open. The cold air woke me up, I got up to close it, and saw this." I wasn't afraid, not technically, but it was fair to say I wasn't sure of her safety. Afraid, in an abstract way, where I couldn't technically feel it.

"This damn fucking window- I knew it was possible to unlock it from outside. Fuck." She stood up to inspect the mirror, running her fingers over the letters. They didn't smudge. "It's nail polish, I- look, this is open." She picked up a bottle of black nail polish on her dresser, showing it to me. "They used this."

"You think it's Ophelia or Ezra?" I asked. She'd mentioned that she thought it was someone else, and with this new evidence, I thought she might be onto something. "I mean- I can't see either of them doing this."

"Are you a heavy sleeper?" she asked, returning the nail

polish to its rightful place.

"No, not at all."

"I'm not that heavy of a sleeper, either. Don't you think someone breaking in would've woken us up? See, this window can be opened from the outside- I've snuck out before, that's how I know- because of the way the lock works. Watch this." She went to the window and laid her palms against it, before moving the windowpane up and down in place. As she did, the latch began to slowly move from the 'locked' position to the 'unlocked' position, as she repeatedly shoved parts of the mechanism against one another. It made a lot of noise, however, and by the time the lock clicked open it was obvious that such an endeavour would've been incredibly hard to sleep through.

"That would've woken us up, right?" she said, and unsure of where she was going with this, I agreed.

"Unless," she said as she locked it again, "you were very, very slow, and patient." She did the same movements again, and she was able to get it to budge ever so slightly. "You could do this quietly, but it would take ages."

"So it wasn't Ezra, is what you're saying."

"Yep. And I don't think it was Ophelia, because I know her. We were friends. She wants this all done as cleanly as possible, and wouldn't break into my fucking house to threaten me. I mean, she's weird and all that, and I don't think I know her well, but… she wants revenge on you. She doesn't care about me."

"Maybe she's mad you're my friend and not hers." I went over to where I'd left my phone on the bedside table, just to check the time. "Oh. I see."

A new message, from Ophelia Hough. It was 5:42 AM- later than I thought it was- and the message was sent at 12:49. I opened it immediately, with Atarah leaning over my shoulder to read beside me.

We need to talk. Can you meet me before school, at the school bus stop? Just the two of us, no hostility.

"A surprisingly calm message, considering what it's about." Atarah tapped her face absentmindedly as she thought. "Although I suppose if it began with 'listen up ass-hole', you'd be unlikely to go. Are you going to do it?"

"I need to do some damage control, yes. Ophelia might listen to reason. Ezra's way too aggressive and irrational, so at least it's not him." I shook my head, pushing the issue aside. "Yeah, I'll go, but I think this is the more pressing issue right now," I said, pointing at her mirror. "This might be confirmation that she did this- we'll see. But what are we going to do? It seems you may not get another warning before you're harmed. I think we should stay away from each other until we figure out what's going on."

Atarah was silent for a long moment, as she pondered the words on the mirror. She walked up, ran her fingers over them, and sighed, before finally speaking. "I must say, Alex, that I don't buy the idea that you don't care about anything other than Stephen. Maybe that was true at some point in the past, but not anymore. It's great that you care about my safety, and I half-agree. After tonight, we'll keep our interaction to texting and short conversations in school, until we know who's doing this and what we can do about it. It'll make it harder to go forth with the plan, but I frankly care more about my own life than anything else."

"Okay." It was vaguely disappointing, knowing I wouldn't be able to be publicly around Atarah when she was the only person I could be honest with, but I did value her. I don't believe I valued her in the normal way anyone else would, as she seemed to imply, but I did care about her, and preferred her alive to dead. It was worth questioning whether or not those leaking emotions could've been influencing how I felt about her, too, but I didn't want to linger on it. "It's nearly six AM. Considering these new developments, and the fact I'm going to have to meet Ophelia-"

"I get it." Atarah cut me off, refusing to look at me, instead staring at the ground. "You should go. I'll take you home."

"As long as it's not too early," I said. I could guess at what she was feeling. "I'm sorry this is happening. You shouldn't be in danger because of me."

Atarah laughed then, a bittersweet laugh. "Oh, please don't just say that because you know it's what I want to hear. I-"

"I'm not just saying that. I know it's not fair. I never cared about 'fair', but now, I'm beginning to gain an appreciation for what it means. This isn't fair, and I wish there was anything other than leaving you alone that I could do to fix that."

Atarah paused, and finally looked at me, her eyes glistening behind her glasses. I could see her as she did it, so it wasn't like she did it out of nowhere, but it somehow still surprised me when she hugged me. She was warm and soft, and I wrapped my arms around her neck, pulling her against my chest. It was nice in the same way hugging Darcy was nice. It was an extremely faint kind of pleasantness, next to the feelings Stephen gave me, but at least I could appreciate it a little bit.

It was symptomatic of the problem, but it was bearable. Killing Stephen would make this small comfort disappear, but with all the pain I felt- bawling my eyes out for no reason and the terrible awkwardness of simply messaging him- it was beyond worth it, to be emotionless again.

We snuck out the front door silently after that, and Atarah drove me home. Nobody was awake when I crept up to my room, and so no questions were asked of me. I showered, changed my clothes, brushed my teeth, and took an apple to eat on the way to school; even those echoes of emotions I felt when I hugged Atarah were gone when I was alone for long enough. I felt no fear, no apprehension, no curiosity as I arrived at the bus stop Ophelia had asked to meet me at. I had sent a message confirming the meeting on the way up, and I arrived before she did. It was just a bench on the sidewalk; no shelter, just a pole with a sign on it, indicating the bus was to stop there. Nobody looked at me twice, not even when the bus arrived and I ignored it.

Ophelia took fifteen minutes. I saw someone coming out of the corner of my eye, and she sat on the bench beside me, facing the other direction. Her brown coat was lined with faux fur that partially covered her face, and her hands were stuffed deep into her pockets, trying to escape the cold.

"There's no point in lying anymore," Ophelia said, not a single emotion leaking through her words. She spoke as plainly as I. "I was trying to find proof that you killed our father, but as it turns out, if I waited long enough, you'd hand me that proof on your own. Why'd you do it, Alex?"

"I don't know what you want from me. I can't trust that you aren't recording this conversation to try and get a confession." Every word was blank, truthfully spoken. I turned to her, but she continued to look straight ahead. So, I did the same. "I have no desire to hurt you. I want to be left alone."

"I've got no desire to hurt you either," Ophelia attested, "but you should know that Ezra's never forgiven our father's murderer. I was trying to find answers for his sake. And now that he knows it's you, I'm the only thing standing in between him and your death. I'm stopping him from shooting you in the head because I don't want him going to jail for life. But what you said..."

My head was ripped back by a hand in my hair, and the tugging at my scalp burnt like hell. My neck was twisted into an incredibly painful position as Ophelia pulled me towards her, her mouth right up against my ear. "You listen to me. If you so much as *look* the wrong way at my brother, I'll kill you with my bare hands before you can even blink. I'm not gonna feel guilty for killing a murderer."

I nodded, hoping she'd let up on my poor scalp, and she let go of me with that. I leaned forward, holding my neck, and she acted like nothing had happened. "I'm not an innocent child like you were when you murdered my dad. I won't get away with it. But I don't care."

I didn't know how to address the accusations, so I just didn't. I did my best to placate her anger instead. "I don't intend to hurt Ezra. I said what I said only to scare him away..." I paused, and stopped, not wanting to admit that Stephen came into this at all. "I didn't mean it. I want to be left alone, is all."

Ophelia shook her head. "I almost forgot about Stephen. Tell me, Alex," she said, something I couldn't under-stand behind her words. "...do you love him?"

"I-" I stuttered, the question hitting me hard. I knew the answer- I'd thought it a thousand times, and it wasn't like there was any doubt. I'd just never said it aloud. "If I say yes, will you leave him alone?"

Ophelia was quiet for a moment. "As I said, Alex, all I want is Ezra's safety and happiness. I don't think I can stop him from wanting revenge, but I'm trying to get him that without harming him. Dragging Stephen into it would not help that. If it's up to me, I'll leave him alone."

"And Atarah." I wasn't encouraged by the phrasing of 'if it's up to me', but if I was going to get her promise, I was go-ing to get it for Atarah, too. I didn't want to have to avoid her just to keep her safe. "Don't hurt her, either."

Ophelia finally met my eyes then. Her face was blank, and so was mine, as we regarded each other. Both bare-facedly truthful, admitting what we cared about with no more precedent.

"If you don't hurt Ezra, I won't hurt Stephen or Atarah. But I'm still comin' after you, don't get me wrong." She stood, arranging her hands in her pockets.

"I don't care what you do to me." I knew I'd be able to find a way out for myself. I could stop them from taking any legal action against me, and I was prepared to be attacked. But I'd never had to defend someone else before. "But I won't let you get away with hurting either of them. You know what I can do, Ophelia. You know what I will do. Keep that word."

Ophelia raised her eyebrows, but her expression didn't move beyond that. She stood there, ready to walk away, be-fore she asked, "out of curiosity... I know you killed my dad. And I suspect you killed Amanda, too. How many people have you killed, Alex?"

We were alone. Nobody was at the bus stop with us, and nobody was walking past. Ophelia was calm, and looking at her, considering what she said before, I knew it wouldn't make a difference if she knew the truth.

So I raised my hand and held up three fingers.

Ophelia's expression did not change. I didn't feel any different. She walked away without another word, and I was left at the bus stop to consider how I was going to save my own life from Ezra Hough, should Ophelia fail to find justice.

And she would.

CHAPTER TEN - AMANDA MCINTOSH

Ezra gave me dirty looks pretty much all week. I still had no idea what to do in the inevitable event that he went after me, but the good news was that whatever Ophelia was doing to keep him in check, it was working, at least for now.

Atarah and I were constantly texting. It was mostly her sending me updates, although she had a lot of questions about Ophelia, and when I told her about Ophelia's behaviour, she was confused, but it made enough sense to her. *I did think it was about her own revenge, but at least we know what's going on now. I think she told you the truth.*

And I agreed, but I just couldn't focus on that. Saturday the 14th of February was all I could focus on. Stephen's birthday, and his party.

I had been to plenty of teenage parties. My casual

friends always put me on the invite list, and with everyone turning eighteen, there were a lot of parties to be invited to. Technically, nobody could drink for at least three years, but some crowds had been drinking for years already. I'd seen other drugs thrown around, too, but only once or twice. I had always avoided drinking more than one or two drinks, for the sake of keeping myself sharp; but knowing where I was going, and who I was going to be with, I thought it might almost make it more bearable to be drunk. I briefly considered not going at all, but there was an allure to the destruction of it, and I got the idea that I wouldn't be able to stay away.

Getting alcohol was easy enough for me. I was the one my friends always sent in to do it. I could only buy so many drinks for so many people, so this time around it was just Madison and Kai who came with me, although Atarah had asked me to get some as well- some I'd have sneak to her, since we were avoiding each other in public. As I sat in the driver's seat, I began to undo my plait.

"How do you do this?" Kai asked, leaning over from the back. "Mads told me you always get in and out without an ID, no problem."

I met his eyes in the rear view mirror. He and Madison were a strange match; his hair was dyed red at the ends, turning into black at the roots, and he wore a band t-shirt over a long-sleeved striped shirt, where Madison had natural, but thick make-up and carefully styled strawberry blonde hair. I made about as much sense beside them, in a pastel blue shirt and white overalls.

I took my now-loose hair and pulled it up into a high ponytail. "I'm just the right kind of androgynous that I can get away with being a fifteen year old boy or a twenty-five year old woman depending on how I look. Madison, give me your necklace, please, and if you have any makeup at all on you, that'd be great."

Kai's eyes flickered over my body as I locked Madison's choker around my neck. I continued. "Looking old enough doesn't do it on its own. You also have to act like you know exactly what you want and where you're going, and then you engage them in conversation and be really nice. That's it. Watch me have no problem."

With that, I got out of the car and made my way towards the bottle shop, everyone's money in my pocket. My confidence was, yes, put on, but I also knew I wouldn't have any problems, not realistically.

The person behind the counter didn't look twice as I went straight to the liquor cabinet and got out the requests I'd received. When it came to my own, I checked the alcohol contents of various bottles and chose the highest I could find.

I went up the counter, a confident swagger in my step. "How's it going today?" I said, trying to sound as pleasant as possible. "Busy, or no?"

The person looked up from something beneath the table. "Oh, hello. How can I help you?"

A nametag read 'George'. "Oh, just these today, George. How've you been?" I asked, smiling expectantly. He blinked, trying to throw back to where he knew me from, and drawing up blank.

"Oh, uh, fine." He seemed at a loss for how to react. He kept squinting at me, like he could see past me or something. "Do you have ID?"

Despite my recently surfacing emotions, I didn't panic. "You know I always forget my ID, George. I brought it last time, remember? Surely you remember me."

The ploy was one that had been successful in the past. Most people didn't care that much about their job, and would just let me go if it was too much trouble. George narrowed his eyes at me again. "What's your name?"

"Alex." My calm demeanour was so often enough, but I knew he wasn't believing me. I figured I'd have to put them all back and just leave, before things got out of hand.

George sighed. "And you don't have ID?" he questioned, a somewhat hostile edge to the uncertainty in his voice.

"Look, I can just go-" I began, but I felt a hand on my back and paused. There was the faintest smell of coconut and buttered popcorn, but I couldn't really believe it until he spoke.

"Is there a problem?" Stephen's hand travelled to my shoulder, so familiar, like we'd been dating for years. "Oh, hi George. How're things?"

The surprise froze me in place, as well as the fear that came with Stephen's presence. Why had I told Ophelia to leave him alone? If she'd hurt or killed him, my heart wouldn't be racing so. Although I'll admit, the idea of her touching him felt substantially worse.

It took a moment for me to fully realise that he was playing along like this had been planned the whole time.

"I-" George began, uncertain. "I can't sell you alcohol if you don't have-"

"My wife and I have been here before-" There was a twitch in Stephen's voice at 'wife', but otherwise he kept his voice even and acted well. The way my heart jumped at those words, implying we were married, was duller than it would've been if he'd used the right word, but it still multiplied the butterflies in my stomach. "...and you've never bothered asking for ID before. We always forget to bring it anyway."

His hand was still on my shoulder, and the warm weight of it sunk into the very fabric of my soul. Even as my heart raced, it was comfortable and familiar, easy. It was like sinking into a warm bath when you were cold; despite the sting on the surface, I wouldn't want to get out, not for a second.

"Can I ask what it's for?" George asked, eyeing the bottles up. "Is it for you, or-"

There was a giddiness that came from being so close to Stephen, but my lying skills returned from where my nerves had hidden them, and it was hard not to laugh as I answered his question so easily, too easily, playing off and building onto Stephen's lie. "Oh, no, it's not for me. I'm pregnant." I could feel Stephen's fingers clench as he did everything he could not to laugh at the absurdity of that statement. "It's a wedding gift for his sister," I added, nodding at Stephen behind me. I rode the feeling of invincibility that came with Stephen's touch to keep the lie going.

George passed one last judgement, and let it go. "Congratulations, to both you two and your sister," he finally said, taking the bottles and running them through the register. The fact that the man in front of me not only believed that Stephen and I were married, but that I was pregnant with his child, almost made me want to laugh; it was absurd and literally impossible, but the idea of it was, to this man, believable.

We were still selling the lie, so I shouldn't have been surprised when Stephen's hand moved from my shoulder towards my hand, but I could swear I died when I felt his fingertips graze my skin. They interlocked, and his palm was so soft, his touch so gentle. He didn't have to run his thumb over my fingers, and I swear he did it just to make my heart crumble to pieces.

Stephen added another bottle to the collection on the counter, with a very confident wink towards George. "This one's for me, though," he said, perfectly calm like nothing was at stake.

I paid with the money I'd received, Stephen adding his own into my hand, causing it to shake. George was still suspicious, but he didn't want to question us again.

I took the offered bag of alcohol, so distracted by Stephen's touch that I almost forgot where I was and what I was doing. "Thank you! See you later!" Stephen said with a grin, gently leading me out of the shop with our interlocked fingers. I could hardly breathe. It felt like we were out of the shop far too soon, as we rounded the corner and Stephen fell into bubbly laughter, finally dropping my hand to hold his stomach. It was contagious; I fell into laughter too, that ugly real laughter that was so rare in my life, only around Stephen. It felt good, in some strange way, laughing without knowing why.

"Oh my god," Stephen gasped, "that was close. I can't believe he thought you were pregnant. That's amazing."

I absolutely glowed when I realised he wasn't laughing at the idea of us being married, but I knew better than to mention it. I pretended to forget. "How did you know what I was doing? You fit in just like that was planned."

"You told me you did this kind of thing last year, at

Ben's party. You said that you'd pretend to be female when you wanted to look older, and you'd pretend to be male when you wanted to look younger. I saw you were struggling, and I thought I should probably help. Sorry for what I had to say, of course."

I had the vaguest memories of that party. At the time, it meant absolutely nothing to me, sitting in that corner of Ben's backyard with half a drink in my hands, speaking to a group that happened to have congregated. We all knew each other from queer club, and so the conversation had been on that. I remembered Stephen was there, watching me from where he sat on the grass, eyeing me with the smallest of smiles. He had meant nothing to me then; how could there be such a change, from then until now?

"Thank you." We were still close, leaning against the wall, residual traces of laughter drawing grins on our faces. Oh, it felt good to be close to him, sharing this glow of adrenalin that I wouldn't have been able to feel had he not been right there beside me.

There was a pause, where he seemed to be almost looking past me, before he said, "you look good, um, like that," he said, with the vaguest gesture towards my head. "I mean, you always do, no matter what you do, but-"

I didn't know how to react, because my feelings were bubbling up inside me and threatening to burst. He thought I looked good, Stephen liked my appearance, and that fact was something I wanted to scream. I felt like I was going into cardiac arrest, or perhaps, about to throw up. It was as amazing as it was nerve-wracking to endure, and I wanted to tell him he was wrong, or that he was only saying it, but I couldn't make my mouth move. I'm pretty sure I just blushed, and he quickly turned away. All I wanted to do was get closer, inexplicably closer.

Even though I knew that indulging in these feelings would hurt me in the long run, it was hard not to resent Madison and Kai when they interrupted us.

"What happened?" Madison asked, and I shocked myself into autopilot to answer her properly, but even as I explained, I was still riding out those feelings. I gave them their bottles and their change, and they laughed when Stephen told them what we'd said, but it was all bitter. The magic was gone now.

"I've got to go," Stephen said quickly, before Madison could drag him into some long conversation. "I'll see you guys all tomorrow, though."

"Seeya!" Madison cheerfully sent him off, but he wasn't looking at her. He caught me with a wide smile, and my heart, having barely recovered from earlier, burst again. I could only smile back; it wasn't voluntary. He just made me happy, and as unfamiliar as that was, it felt so right.

It was getting harder and harder to feel like that was a lie.

"Bye," I said, my voice breathless. "Thank you again."

When he left, everything felt empty once more. The colours faded, the noises dulled, and I was back to normal, back to plain.

I couldn't tell if I was sad that he was gone, or if the loss of happiness was just unpleasant. I wasn't sure which one I'd rather believe, either.

I texted Atarah to let her know what happened, and she responded in the same irritating way she had too many times before: *Are you sure he doesn't like you back?*

I hoped he didn't, because it would make killing him so much harder. So I told her, *he better not.*

It was harder than ever to sleep that night, and like always, my dreams were about Stephen. It was fitful and anxious, and when I finally did fall asleep, I slept for much longer than I intended to. That was fine, in all honesty; it meant there was less time to fret over the party before it started. As it was, I still had several hours, too many hours, to stress myself out over how things would go down.

You look good no matter what you do. Stephen's words kept ringing in my mind, but I couldn't believe it. Just thinking about it made my stress so much worse, and I did everything I could to ignore it. There wasn't a lot I could do, however, and I ended up on yet another phone call to Atarah, begging for her help.

"For fuck's sake, just wear what you'd normally wear to a party," Atarah groaned after I'd been complaining for five minutes. "I must remind you, this guy is going to die soon. Who cares?"

"I do." I ended up taking her advice, because of course I did; white jeans, white sneakers, and an ice-blue sweater, because, after surreptitiously stalking Stephen's social media for an hour, I discovered that was his favourite colour. Looking in the mirror, it matched my eyes, which could only help me out.

I left my hair out, like Atarah seemed to think I should, snuck my alcohol out to my car, and said goodbye to my parents. My dad told me to have fun, and I wished I could.

I sat in my car outside Stephen's house for a good long moment, contemplating if I should just turn around and leave. Tell Stephen I had to take one of my sisters to the hospital. He wouldn't check. They were triplets, impossible to tell apart unless you knew them well; if he saw her fine, he'd think it was another triplet.

There was a knock on my car window. "What the fuck are you doing?" Atarah's voice was muffled through the glass. I gestured for her to move back so I could open the door, and she did, almost stumbling over the curb.

"Don't you care about your own life?" I asked, using sarcasm to get my point across. I handed her her pack of alcohol, and she took it with a toothy grin.

"Just getting my poison." She had gold lipstick on that shimmered against her skin, although her dress and stockings were still her trademark black, aside from a gold belt. "I've avoided you all week. I think a two-second conversation is fine."

"You're the one risking it," I told her, strongly implying that I disapproved. "We should get inside. When we're in there, though, stay away from me for your own health."

"Don't worry, I will. I don't have any good friends here, but I'm good at forcing my way into conversations. A word of advice, before we part," she said, as we approached the door.

I could hear music going on inside, a song I'd heard on the radio a few weeks ago, and I felt like my heart was beating out of my chest. I'd seen this house so many times when I'd been following him home, stalking him. Now I was going inside.

"Yeah?" I asked, blinking through the haze in my mind.

Atarah had a knowing look in her eyes. "One. The Houghs weren't invited to this party, but they're still after you, so don't let your guard down. Two," she said, "...trust Stephen."

"What?" I asked, but she walked on ahead of me, pushing through the door and leaving me to follow alone. I paused and took a quick swig of my alcohol- it burned down my throat and took all my strength not to spit out- before I followed her in.

Every detail of Stephen's house felt like something I needed to memorise. The door lead into a living room with a white cloth couch and black throw rugs; the coffee table was glass with white edges, and a multicoloured rug sat underneath it, covering a wooden floor. A small white dog with hair falling in its eyes sat in front of the TV, its beady black eyes watching everyone who came in the door without moving. Two people sat on his couch, and one stood in the doorway to the kitchen, speaking to someone I couldn't see. There were stairs to my right, but I chose to head into the kitchen.

I immediately spotted him, leaning against the counter, a glass bottle in his hand as he spoke to someone in my group of friends, Chloe. His hair was, somehow, sitting perfectly; he had a red bomber jacket on, and maybe it was just because he was wearing his red uniform when I fell in love with him, but he looked so good in red.

He noticed me instantly. "Hi Alex!" he said, raising a hand and waving. Atarah was standing close to the corner, speaking to one of Stephen's friends, and I saw her smirk at me in my peripheral vision. I couldn't look at her, though; I had eyes only for Stephen.

Chloe gestured for me to come over, which only gave me a better excuse for the beeline I made towards him. "I was

just hearing about what happened with the alcohol yesterday," Chloe said, an expectant tone in her voice.

"Oh, yeah!" I grinned, falling right into my gregarious-
if-oblivious persona. I helped tell the story, and it was genuinely funny when he said it. I tried to stifle the sound of my
real laughter- it sounded so different to the fake laughter I'd
created for my whole life, and I was scared someone was going to notice.

The conversation kept changing, new people coming
and going, but I tried to stay with Stephen as much as I
could. Atarah occasionally made her way into the conversation as well, but she made sure not to be around me too
much. We still had no idea who was sending those threats,
and there was always the risk that they were here. Whatever
they wanted from me, from her, we still had no idea, but it
was better to be safe than sorry.

I never saw Stephen's parents, as much as I'd have liked
to see the kind of people he was descended from. The house
slowly filled with more and more guests; Stephen cast a large
net of friends, much like I did. Atarah had expressed surprise
that she was invited, but seeing how many people were here,
it wasn't so strange. I'm almost glad he had a big party, not a
small one; I didn't want to know how far down his list of
friends I was.

We had migrated to his living room, where the speakers
playing the music were, when one of his friends called out to
him, "hey, do something cool!"

"Like what?" Stephen asked, even as he put his drink
down and made his way over to the clearest space on the
floor. The crowd parted, giving him room, as he turned
around to face the friend who'd asked, grinning.

"You know, something cool," they said, slinking back into the crowd a little.

Stephen smirked, moved towards one end of the open
space, and warned, "you might all want to move," encouraging even more room. Then, with a grin that almost looked
like it was directed at me, he jumped. He threw his arms up
and behind him, and combined with the force from his legs,

he flipped backwards, flying through the air like a dolphin arcing above the waves, landing gracefully on his feet in the middle of the floor- and then he did it again, barely a split second between. Everyone looking on cheered, and I held my heart when he stood from the second flip, not because I was impressed- I could do that, after all, although he was so graceful- but because of the way he was smiling, fixing his hair lightly and looking around him, searching for something. His eyes landed on me, and he extended a hand towards me. It took a moment for me to understand what he was saying.

The music was upbeat, dancy, but the lyrics were about falling in love. Almost every song was about love, gaining or losing it, and only now did I know what they meant. Those who sung about lovers being fools were right, but I had to let myself be a fool, for just one moment. I couldn't turn him down, not here, not now.

"You did gymnastics, right? You've got to have something cool," he said, almost too soft for me to hear. I handed my drink to Madison, and made my way to the edge of the cleared part of the floor, cracking my knuckles.

I did the most complicated move I knew how to do; a handstand, on one hand, turning and landing in the splits. I leant over my back, reaching a hand out to Stephen behind me. I knew that people were reacting, but I cared as little about them as I always had. When he took my hand, it felt like reconnecting with a part of me I'd lost. I knew it was dangerous, treacherous, to let myself feel like this, but I couldn't seem to save myself from falling into the trap.

He pulled me up, and I didn't think about how we would end up until it happened. Holding hands, twisted again to face each other, determination in his eyes.

I let myself go. I let the smile take me, because there was no point in fighting it; not now, not tonight. As soon as the night was over, I would go ahead with the plan to kill him, but tonight, I could maybe, just maybe, see what it was like to be the fool.

He stepped forward, which pushed me back into the middle of the cleared space. He changed the hand he held me with, holding my left with his left, and then he pulled me towards him, and I let myself spin, the giddiness rising in a smile on my face. Everyone was watching, but he didn't seem to care, and I sure as hell didn't give a shit. I didn't realise quite what was going on until my arm was around his neck, and on instinct I lifted up my legs. Despite the fact that I was taller than he was, he was so strong that he made it look easy to pick me up. His arm circled under my knees, and he was carrying me, spinning still. The motion made everyone in the background seem far away, unreal; all I could see was his face, so close to mine, and his smirk, and all that seemed real was him, right there in front of me.

Oh, how I wanted to be able to love, and nothing else. How tempting it was, to put up with the pain and longing and sadness that filled me whenever he was gone, the panic that came with the anticipation, just to feel these few precious moments with him. If I could dance with him forever, and it never fell apart, and it never changed, and it was just him and me for the rest of time, I'd be happy.

But this was the bait in the trap. This was the eye of the hurricane. Because he stopped spinning, and let my legs fall to the ground, and I was just hanging in dead space, staring into his eyes, his face mere inches from mine, and the song's chorus announced, *I'm right here, baby, right here*, and I had never been more terrified in my life.

If I kissed him, what would happen?

I hit the ground. My grip on Stephen's shoulder slipped, and despite his instinctual grab to catch me, the back of my head hit the wooden floor and I groaned in pain. I could hear some people laughing and plenty more asking if I was okay; I was suddenly aware of them all again, now that the spell had been broken. It was my fault I fell- Stephen was holding me, but I forgot in that moment that anything as trivial as gravity existed.

In truth, though, it was the only way out of the situation. If I had stayed where I was, I was going to kiss him, and then my world would've changed so drastically that there would be no return. My love for Stephen was, right now, internal. A secret that, despite others knowing, felt like mine alone, since he had no idea himself. If I kissed him, it would make it real in his mind, too. It would make it material.

If he had rejected me, it would've been easier to kill him. That doesn't mean I wanted it to happen, though.

Stephen helped me back up, and it was only his words I had ears for. "Are you hurt?" he asked, his voice gentle, his touch even gentler. His skin was warm and soft, and I wanted to fall into his touch again, but I had to save myself.

I needed to lie, because I was flying too close to the sun. "Not really, but I need to sit down for a second," I said, and I watched as his face closed off slightly, and despite the smile still there, I could tell he was disappointed.

I wanted to think his disappointment was just about the dancing as I slowly walked over to the couch, faking the tiniest of limps. Madison handed me my drink back, and I fell into the empty spot beside Kai, with Madison following and sitting in his lap. I wanted to think it was just about the dancing, but how could I be certain? How could I know without kissing him?

When I looked back, someone else was doing an over-the-top dance move that had gone out of fashion just long enough ago that everyone thought it was hilarious. Stephen was leaning against the wall, a drink in his hand again. He didn't look at me, and that magical moment was gone.

Stephen and I were separated for a good while. I spoke to Madison, dulling the ache of longing with idle conversation. Every time I found myself searching around for Stephen, I took another drink, until my thoughts and feelings felt fuzzy around the edges, softer, easier to deal with. Everyone around me was getting drunker, too; time seemed to drag on so much longer when I wasn't talking to Stephen, and I could swear it had been three hours when it was only one.

The first slip of my tongue occurred when I was, again, searching the crowd for him. "Where's Stephen?" was the thought I had, and it slipped out as a quiet mutter through my teeth. It caught Madison's attention, and she furrowed her brows for only a moment, before accepting it as a question she would answer.

"I don't know. I saw him not that long ago," she said, following it up with a sip of her drink. "It's weird. He's been really chipper recently. Not like usual."

"What?" I should've held back my questions, really, but this was what alcohol did to people. I could blame it on that, at least. "He's usually happy when I talk to him."

Madison chuckled. "I think he likes you. I've thought that for a while. I don't think he's your type, though." The irony, the bitter irony of her words. I bit my lip and said nothing. "You know, you never seem to like anyone, Alex. It's always people liking you. Ava really liked you, you know."

"I know," I said, having never wanted a conversation about it less in my life.

"You two would've made a good match. Hey, you and Kai dated, didn't you?" she grinned at her now boyfriend. He raised a hand to hide his face, shaking his head, not because she was wrong, but because he didn't want to talk about it.

"Freshman year doesn't count for anything," Kai groaned, but the surface of mild annoyance was a lie.

"What, you're embarrassed you dated Alex? There's nothing wrong with-"

"It's not that. The circumstances sucked," he said, and I could feel myself sinking into the couch to hide. The last thing I wanted was to talk about Amanda, even less than I wanted to talk about Ava. "You remember."

"Oh. Yeah. With... fucking Amanda. I forgot you were dating her, oops." Madison played it off with a bit of a laugh.

"I was literally telling you about therapy yesterday." It seemed to come out of nowhere, but I now understood that emotions did that. Kai's hands were shaking, and there was a hint of redness at the edges of his dark eyes, a wet glisten. He was doing his best to keep his voice down, but he couldn't stop the words from tumbling out. "I ignored it for three years, and I'm only just getting over it now. You have no idea how shit it feels to know you're responsible for someone's death, Mads. It's my fault she's dead. It's not funny."

In that moment I felt almost, almost the same about him

crying in front of me as I would have felt before I fell in love; there was just the smallest, tiniest twinge in my heart that would never have been there before. "What do you mean? You had nothing to do with it." I killed her. "She killed herself."

"Yeah, because of me." The venom Kai spat was self-hatred. "She said so in her note."

I remember writing that the breakup had contributed to her suicide. At the time, I had used Kai to sell her suicide, and that was all he'd meant to me, and even now, I didn't care for him. He'd been upset, but so had everyone, right? When I killed Amanda, I thought everyone would be upset and then move on, and the pain they went through couldn't have mattered.

But now I understood even a tiny fraction of it, and it was unimaginable how any human being could get through that. I would not care about anyone in a way that would make me grieve, but if I did, it would be such torture that I couldn't bear it. I couldn't bear being sad for fifteen minutes when Stephen and I parted ways; Kai was still not over it, years later. Years.

"Look, it's not that bad, I'm getting over it, just-" he covered his face with his hand again. "I just- wish it didn't happen like it did."

I almost wanted to tell him that he had nothing to do with it. That I killed Amanda McIntosh because she made my life difficult, and that was all there was to it.

If anyone else at all thought like I did, I'd be dead. With grief, I had made Kai's life a thousand times more difficult than Amanda had ever made mine when I killed her. How could Atarah think that was fair? I never cared about fair, I never cared about just- but I knew what it was, and what it wasn't. For Kai, everything was worse because Amanda was dead.

I didn't care, not really. I didn't feel anything when I looked at Kai. I didn't feel guilt, or even sympathy; not that I knew how that felt. But something was still wrong.

"I need a minute," I said, and even though I felt numb

still, there were emotions lurking beneath the numbness. The first thing I said was the truth; the second was a lie. "I'll be right back."

I couldn't immediately see a bathroom to convincingly escape to, but when I stumbled up the stairs I found one, unoccupied. I shut myself inside of it before anyone could notice.

When I used to look in the mirror, I saw Alex Keen, someone who had never lived for anything in their life, and didn't mind it that way. Before this party, all I'd seen is an ugly, undesirable person who could never attract someone as perfect as Stephen Minett.

Now, I wondered what everyone else saw. If Kai knew the truth, if he knew what I'd done, he'd never blame himself again. He'd see me as Amanda's murderer, and never anything else. All Ezra and Ophelia saw me as was their father's killer. If my parents, and my sisters, knew the truth, would they disown me? Would it have been unforgiveable, the fact that I murdered my brother? Of course it would have been.

What did Stephen see when he looked at me?

And what would he see if he knew the truth?

I stared into my own eyes like my reflection would give me the answer. I had never cared about the fact that my life was built on lies; and I still didn't, at least, not where my family and friends were concerned. But Stephen- our friendship was a lie. I was in love with him and plotting his kidnap and murder. He didn't know any of that, and I was betraying him, I was absolutely betraying him, and I felt like a monster for it.

There was no way we could be together. It wasn't just because I couldn't handle the feelings he'd give me, although that was the biggest reason why. Even if I got over it, and I managed to keep a lid on my heart, and it became bearable- I was a murderer. I killed Amanda. I killed Mr Hough. I killed my own brother. Who could forgive someone like that? Stephen wasn't like Atarah, with twisted morals and strange obsessions. I couldn't lie to him in the long run- my heart wouldn't be able to take it. I couldn't tell the truth, or he'd leave me, and he'd have to die anyway.

Killing him was my only option.

A buzz from my pocket distracted me. It was, of course, Atarah. *Where are you?*

If I'd fallen in love with Atarah, or someone like her, everything might've been fine. But I didn't fall in love with someone like that. I fell in love with Stephen Minett, who, despite how extraordinary he was, had all the morals of a normal person and could never love a killer.

I'm in the upstairs bathroom, I texted Atarah back. Madison also texted me, but I ignored her; it was too much effort right now. It only took about fifteen seconds before Atarah knocked gently on the door, and I let her in.

"Why are you hiding up here?" she asked without introduction, closing the door behind her and sitting on the edge of the bath. "I was talking to Maybelle, that girl who sits in the art room all day, and she claimed you two dated sophomore year and she took your virginity. I don't believe it, is it true?"

The way I looked at Atarah, eyes hooded and tired, made her reconsider her tone a little, but as always, I answered her anyway. "Yes, we dated, no, we never had sex. I didn't have sex until last year. As for your first question, I'm hiding here because Kai and Madison started talking about Amanda's death, and all I could think about was how I'm a murderer and Stephen could never accept that."

"Do you feel guilty?" Atarah asked, taking a long drink of something clear that I did not buy for her. "Has it gone that far, yet?"

"Don't say yet, and no." I followed her example, downing a ton of my own drink. It hurt like hell; why did people do this? "I just felt like shit, 'cause I was lying to Stephen."

"You feel like shit for lying to him, but not for planning to kidnap and murder him," Atarah deadpanned.

I stared at the tile beneath my feet, and despite the fact that I didn't like it, I took another sip of my drink and just shrugged. "I know it makes no sense."

There was a moment of silence, where all I could do was stare at my feet and wonder what I would ever do next. What day should I kidnap him on? I was starting to care less and less if the plan was perfect. "Can we talk about the plan?"

"Sorry, I didn't realise you wanted to talk about it." Atarah polished off her drink; she smelled of alcohol, but so far wasn't too affected. "What's your plan to get rid of the cameras and make sure nobody sees us? Also, are we using your car, or-"

"Just break the cameras with a rock or something. I don't care. I want Stephen dead sooner rather than later and I don't have time for elaborate plans." I held my hand to my face, feeling the heat of my own skin. "I want to do it soon. Next week. Maybe if I kill him before Ezra snaps and goes after me Ezra will be scared off."

"We're both tipsy, this is never gonna be a good time to plan," Atarah suggested, rubbing her eyes. "If you want to do it next week, let's just... it's not a great plan, but we can just break the cameras and hope nobody notices. Done."

I nodded, hoping I'd remember this tomorrow. "I know what days he works, so we'll just go as soon as we can."

"Yes, great, good, done. Can we go snoop around Stephen's room now?" Atarah said, completely nonchalant towards our plan to kidnap and murder a classmate.

She stood, extending her hand to me. She ended up grabbing my wrist when I hesitated, and dragged me out of the bathroom, almost bumping into a line of people heading downstairs. I spotted Stephen at the bottom of the stairs, and he immediately caught my gaze for a long second before Atarah pulled me away. There was an upstairs living area with a few people in it, but we avoided that, as Atarah chose the first closed door and hid us behind it.

"This isn't Stephen's room," I said before even looking. It didn't smell like him. When I did check, I quickly identified it as his parent's bedroom, with a big double bed and a wooden dresser. I didn't see much more than that, as I was dragged back out and across the hall.

The next room we entered was his room, and I knew immediately. It was dark, the curtains pulled shut, but I could still make out the outlines of the bed, a desk, a bookshelf. It all became clear when Atarah flipped on the light and closed the door.

Stephen's bed was a plain white frame with black and red bedsheets; it was a double, the two pillows skewed against the headboard. A skateboard peeked out from under the bed, along with a cardboard box that Atarah made a beeline for. An easel sat against one corner, an empty canvas on it, with several canvases turned backwards behind. Stephen's wardrobe was closed, and mirrors on the sliding doors reflected my own morbid curiosity back at me. There was a desk, mostly clean, with only a few pens laying out. Classical books and art supplies filled the bookshelf. I had thought Stephen was an artist, from vague memories of years prior, but now I was sure, and I wanted nothing more than to see the art he'd created.

And so I went over to the easel, moved it aside, and picked up the closest painting, turning it around to admire it. It used only three shades, a dark, light and medium grey. It depicted someone from behind, a light back, dark grey hair cascading down it. Some clumsily copied Chinese characters in the same dark grey cut off the body, spelling out 'ideal', or perhaps 'perfect'. I knew nothing about art to comment on the technical skill, but what I did know is that it was beautiful.

I put that one back where I found it and picked up the next one. This one was done in shades of blue and white, a sky and a frozen lake, with grey rocks and a city skyline I couldn't pin down on the horizon. It looked like it might've been one of the Great Lakes, although whether the city was Chicago, Detroit or something else, I couldn't be sure. There was only one tiny splotch of colour, two people in the distance with red coats, although it was too small to make out any details at all.

I put that one back, too. They were amazing, and I wanted to take them with me; they made me feel happy, warm inside in a way little else did. It wasn't quite as amazing as watching him dance- these paintings were abstracted from him, after all- but it was still nice. I put them back only because I was afraid of being caught.

"Hey, this box doesn't fucking open," Atarah said, whacking it with her fist. I came over beside her to see what she meant. It was evident she'd been pulling at the lid for ages, and there were a few nail marks in the cardboard that she'd surely created. "What could he have in here that's so secret? I want to know."

"Why does it matter?" I asked her, wondering how my drink got half empty. "What could it be that would make a difference?"

Atarah blew a raspberry at me and shoved the box back under the bed. "I wanna find something secret and interesting. I don't care what it is."

"Not everyone has a wild secret." I sat down on Stephen's bed, feeling the sheets through my fingers. They smelled so strongly of him; coconut shampoo, buttered popcorn, a twist of the unique smell that only he could have, like a fingerprint. I took a drink of the bitter, burning alcohol; how many drinks was I on? "No. Stephen doesn't. Just because I did."

Atarah plopped herself on the ground, her hand against her forehead. I leaned slowly sideways, so slowly I didn't even realise I was doing it, until I was laying on Stephen's bed, curling my fingers in the sheets that felt so nice against my cheek. It was just... nice. I let my eyes drift closed.

"We're really gonna do it in a week, huh." Atarah smacked her lips together, considering. "I've never committed to this kind of shit before. Fuck, what if the cops find us?"

"I'll take full responsibility, it's fine." I was barely paying attention to a word she said. "It's my murder."

Those words were whispered against the sheets, and it was the last thing I remembered saying. All the stress, the anxiety was getting to me in the form of falling asleep; and although I did remember Atarah talking for a while, saying she felt we would get away with it but unsure if I would be safe following it- something about Ezra, I wasn't listening- when I woke up, she was gone. I felt a weight on the bed beside me, wondering if perhaps she'd moved. "At..." I began to ask her what was happening, but I felt a hand on mine, and as I looked down at it, I realised it wasn't her. Atarah's skin was the colour of obsidian and her fingers decorated with golden rings; this hand was a honeyed tan, slender but strong, inviting. Stephen.

My heart stopped in my chest. I turned over and saw him, gazing at me with a radiating warmth that was both emotional and physical, and it didn't feel quite real. The smile on his face shone through his watery blue eyes, and it was contagious. I couldn't stop myself from smiling if I wanted to. "Tired, huh?" he said, and it was the most obvious joke to make, but it was still so funny to me. I bit my lip to hold back the ugly laugh, but it still shook in my chest.

It occurred to me a little late that I probably shouldn't be in his room. "Oh, I'm sorry, I didn't- I mean- I-" I stuttered through even the simplest of apologies, when he was looking at me with that stupid smile and I couldn't think straight. "Yeah, I'm sorry."

"Sorry for what?" Stephen asked in a voice so pretty and soft that it struck me silent. His fingers glided over my skin, and I shivered, immediately hoping he wouldn't notice. How could he not notice? I shifted, laying on my back, thinking maybe it would be a little less compromising to do so, but now he was leaning over me, our hands touching, and I was in his bed, and also unable to speak.

I shook my head, having already forgotten the question. Stephen smelled of alcohol, which was usually something un-pleasant, but when I was still halfway intoxicated myself and *it was Stephen*, I couldn't be put off by it if I wanted to be.

He leant closer, ever so slightly; it almost seemed acci-dental. "You can stay. I don't mind." His voice was quiet, almost a whisper. My heart was racing out of my chest. Those words woke me up completely. I was on fire inside, and every action took so much of my energy; all I could think about was how much I hoped he wouldn't notice my nerves, and how certain I was that he had. I managed to muster up the strength to turn my hand over, just to see what would happen when our palms touched. Slowly, like he didn't want me to notice, his fingers interlocked with mine.

"You don't?" I breathed. It was the immediate, instinctual response, and it showed the deep fear within me that he didn't love me back. It was a deep fear that ran counter to what I really wanted. I wanted him to hate me, so I could kill him easier, without the strain on my heart.

"Never." He was so close that I could make out every detail on his face with extreme clarity; each individual eyelash, every freckle, the pink hue over his cheeks. I felt like I was flying. This was the most dangerous drug I could've possibly taken. The fear was disappearing, replaced with euphoria, and it was as poisonous as it was perfect.

It was a snapshot of how life could be- if I wasn't a murderer.

I knew I was selfish. It was a neutral descriptor to me. I made every decision based on what was best for me, with everyone else coming second. That was, at least, how I'd always made decisions. I killed people when it made my life easier.

I had never thought that all of that would catch up to me, and my own selfish decisions would be all the worse for me. Not just in the form of Ophelia knowing the truth and Ezra one small step away from hunting me down, but also in the form of never, ever being able to be with Stephen.

I wasn't imagining it; he was getting closer. Any second our noses would touch, and I'd be powerless to resist. "Stephen," I gasped, and I meant to tell him to stop, but it would only sound like a plea for him to continue. That was all my heart wanted, and we both knew it. He was staring at my lips, and the tiniest of smiles began to tug on his; until he looked in my eyes again, and his brow furrowed.

"Alex?" he asked, his fingers brushing against my face. I felt the wet tears between our skin then. I reached up with my free hand, still shaking from head to toe. I took his face in the palm of my hand, burning hot from alcohol and proximity, hot enough to burn me. Concern spread through all his features. "Did I do something... wrong?"

I choked on the tears as more came out. He couldn't love a murderer, not until hell froze over. He wouldn't do this if he knew what I'd done.

I didn't want to say it, but these emotions were overwhelming, and I wanted to know, more than anything, whether I would ever have a chance. Whether the real, honest me could ever be loved by someone like Stephen. I needed to know, and if I ruined everything, it felt like the end of the world, but not knowing was somehow so much worse.

So I chose the most present, and the most justifiable, of the three, and I sputtered it through the tears. "I killed Amanda McIntosh."

Chapter Eleven - Bailey Stern

I had no expectations at all, so I would be surprised no matter what he did. His first reaction was blinking denial. "Sorry?" he said with the same furrowed brow of concern. And I thought- for one delicious moment- that he'd say *I know and I don't care*- but I knew that would never happen. "What- why- I don't- now?"

"I couldn't..." I tried to speak, but I could barely get two words out. The sounds wouldn't come. My throat wouldn't make them. I had just confessed one of my murders to the only human being I had ever loved; what was there to say?

Stephen backed up, and I felt so cold and broken. "I'm sorry, I- did I misunderstand?" he said, almost to himself, whispered into his hand. He looked at me, looked at us in the in mirrors on his wardrobe, and then covered his eyes with his hand. "You- weren't supposed to, you... oh. Oh. No, I..." He wouldn't look at me. He wouldn't look at me.

I knew he couldn't love a murderer. Somehow, that was all I could think, and it was a numb kind of affirmation. It felt numb. Numb and normal.

He took a sharp breath, and slowly lowered his hand. His other hand was still holding mine, but I was sure it was by accident. "I'm so sorry," he said, and I could almost laugh at how he was apologising to me over this. "Clearly, I misunderstood. You... are not in a good way right now. This was not a good time. I'll... let you go, and we'll talk later, or... something." He stared at his fingers, and even though I was numb, I wanted to cry, harder, for reasons I couldn't figure out.

It was clear send off. "I'm sorry," I choked, and I ran. It felt like ripping a band aid off, but I ran. It was more of a scramble, reaching his door and slamming it behind me; the party wasn't over, and there were still groups of tired, drunk teenagers hanging around, but it was over for me. I caught a few eyes as I ran down the stairs and outside, but I ignored them all. There would be some rumours about what happened, and a lot of questions- I'd make up some lie about my family, it didn't matter. I needed to be out of Stephen's house before my heart exploded.

He was as nice about it as he possibly could've been, pretending not to understand, pretending he misheard me. Would he say something to anyone else? Maybe, maybe not. I had no way of knowing. Maybe I'd kill him before he did.

I stood outside his house, panting and leaning on my knees. It was official now; he had to die. There was no hope for me to keep these horrible feelings without the pain tearing me apart. A shame, really, I thought to myself; what a waste of human life. An absolutely necessary waste.

The pain was there, quiet and hidden, but there. Trying to act nonchalant about killing him didn't do as much as I had hoped to combat it.

Nobody followed me out of the house. Wherever Atarah was, she hadn't seen me, and nobody else cared enough. I could see Stephen's window from here, but the curtains were drawn. They didn't move, no matter how long I stared at them.

I looked up and down the street, searching for anyone who might see my breakdown. The tears were coming again, slowly but surely, and I was determined to keep them private. There was only one person, a silhouette across the street, sitting and staring at a blue phone screen. In the dark, I could make out nothing more than that. I watched the stranger hold the phone up to their ear, and with the light the phone cast over their face, I recognised who it was.

"Oh, no you don't," I hissed, focusing all of that horrible energy into this. Ophelia told me to leave Ezra alone; she said nothing about the person she hired to follow me.

I ran across the street at full tilt. It might've been terrifying, to see me running with a frustrated scream in my throat, if I wasn't stick-thin and crying. I tackled Ophelia's follower, pinning their shoulders to the sidewalk.

"Give me your name," I demanded, the numb, empty, default voice of mine tinged with anger. Anger I wanted to direct at Stephen, but couldn't.

"Mr. Bailey Stern, P.I.," he said, more self-satisfied than anything despite the fact I had him pinned to the ground. Of course Ophelia hired a private investigator; well, what did I expect? "Do you mind getting off of me, Alex?"

He wasn't even slightly intimidated by me. He was about my height, with scruffy brown hair and a patchy beard that didn't quite meet with his moustache. I felt the strangest turn of nausea to learn that he had the same name as my brother. Did he know about that? Had Ophelia told him?

"I do mind. What the fuck are you doing here? I know Ophelia sent you, but I don't know what you think you're going to learn. Why don't you tell me?" I was angry, so angry, and I imagined punching the man beneath me, as though it was his fault Stephen had turned me away. As though it had nothing to do with me.

He laughed, and it was the most annoying laugh I'd ever heard. He wasn't the least bit intimidating, and maybe his laugh might've been normal to any other person at any other time, but when Stephen and I could not be together, everything was annoying. "Let me reach my phone, and I'll show you."

I let up just enough for him to grab the phone that I'd

knocked clean out of his hands before. The emotional part of me absolutely didn't want to give this dickhead anything he was after, but the logical, real part of me knew I needed this information.

He pressed a few things I didn't see, before holding the phone up to my ear. It was garbled and difficult to understand, but I heard my own voice, saying, *"I killed Amanda McIntosh,"* and my reaction was almost, almost, emotional. I was angry, and I knew I was in trouble, and the two things separately added together to place my hands around his throat, ready to choke him at any moment.

"That's going to be deleted," I informed him, staring him down. He still had that horribly smug grin on his face. I considered killing him there and then; it would satisfy the anger, but oh, what a shame it was that I wouldn't get away with it.

"Oh, it's interesting, but it's not the most interesting thing I've found," he said, raising an eyebrow. Reaching around my arms, he pressed a few more buttons and relayed another bit of audio back to me. My voice, messed up through the recording, saying what I knew to be, *"...and all I could think about was how I'm a murderer and Stephen could never accept that,"* and then, Atarah: *"Do you feel guilty? Has it gone that far, yet?"*

I stared down at Stern, and the shit-eating grin on his face. My own voice, all casual; *"Don't say yet, and no. Just felt like shit, 'cause I was lying to Stephen."*

And then, just clear enough to feel like a punch in the gut, *"You feel like shit for lying to him, but not for planning to kidnap and murder him."*

He pressed pause on the audio. "Not only do I have you on tape confessing to the murder of Amanda McIntosh, but I'm sure Stephen Minett would find the fact that you're plotting to kill him very interesting-"

The reaction was guttural. I ripped his phone out of his hands and bashed him in the nose with it, and although it wasn't anywhere near as hard as I'd have liked to hit him, I saw blood. I just did it again without even thinking. Stephen would not know. This slug of a man would never speak to him. There was blood on my hands, blood making the phone slippery, but the phone itself was still intact; and that wouldn't do. I threw it at the sidewalk and scrambled to grab it as Stern cried out in muffled pain, gripping his broken nose. I hit it against the concrete again and again until the glass was shattered, and then I stood and kicked it with the heel of my foot until it had splintered into pieces. Just as Stern was rising to his feet, I picked up what remained of the wreckage and threw it in the sewer.

"Fuck you," was all I had to say to him, wiping his blood on my already soiled sweater. Holding his bruised face, he looked out onto the street to frantically find where I'd thrown it, but it was no use.

"Nice try," he said, and although he tried to make it sound confident and suave, his voice was nasally and choked with the blood. He winced as he moved. "Ophelia and Ezra already heard what I found."

"But you lost the recording." The sound of anger in my voice was still new, and surprising, and ugly, but I couldn't stop myself. Now, Stern was angering me all on his own- he'd invaded Stephen's house just to stalk me, and Stephen was being affected. That was much, much too far for my new-found emotional side to deal with.

"Maybe, but now they know-" Stern began, but he didn't get far. I channelled the anger into a swift kick to his ribs, feeling the slightest relief and satisfaction when he doubled over in pain. I wanted to do it again, but I knew the logic in restraining myself, and kept it back.

"Yeah, they do know, dumbass." Not about Stephen, but I bluffed on it. "I spoke to Ophelia. I'm going to need you to stay the hell away from Stephen. I don't care what Ophelia told you to do, *stay away*. I'm not afraid to hurt you much, much worse."

"So I guessed," he said as he rose to his feet. He was a little less smug now, far more serious as he glared. "You're a murderer, and you're going to do it again. Why? What made you do it?"

"I'm not stupid. I'm not answering your questions. Just leave! Get away! Leave Stephen alone!" That anger was bristling under my skin again, burning in my blood, and I followed it forward, shoving him in the chest. The cries scratched my throat, bordering on hysterical. "Go away! Leave!"

"You're going to kill him and you're telling *me* to leave him alone?" Stern's incredulous tone was still remarkably calm for the situation. He didn't view me as much of a threat, despite the fact I'd broken his nose and he knew I was a murderer. At this point, I couldn't chalk it up to my appearance of frail epicene softness, but instead his own headstrong overconfidence.

I knew that my wily, uncontrollable emotions were affecting my actions, to matter how little I wanted them to. I knew that anything to do with Stephen had the potential to make me angry, and I knew that all of my anger was born from Stephen. Even so, I couldn't figure out what drove me to punch him. It was a moment of blinding, agonising anger that demanded to be released all in his fucking face until he was unrecognisable.

I had never physically fought anyone before, and it shouldn't have surprised me when he was able to grab my wrist. His blood was slick on his skin, making his grip unstable, and yet, I couldn't find a way to wrench out of it. He was strong, that was for sure.

"Why do you want to kill Stephen?" he asked, quiet and threatening. I sized him up, feeling like a pack animal forced to submit. Yet, I refused, raising my chin in defiance. With all this rage coursing through my veins, I didn't care if he hurt me. Somewhere beneath that anger was a despair at Stephen's rejection that almost invited Stern to kill me, or at the very least, make me hurt.

"I'll ask you one more time," he said, all smugness gone, no longer pathetic or patient, edging on pissed. "Why are you going to kill Stephen?"

I tilted my head ever so slightly, and I could see the anger tick up in a twitch of his lip at my nonchalant response. I watched the scowl grow, the movement of his fist towards my stomach, until I doubled over in pain. The pain was forgotten in favour of surprise when I heard the clunk of something hard hitting his skull, and saw the rock hit the ground.

"Who threw-" he began, but he didn't get far before there was an arm around his neck and he was stumbling off-balance, letting me go. I saw a face like an angel, albeit twisted in anger, and his eyes red and raw. After what just happened, it was hard to believe that Stephen had just come to save me.

He wasn't alone. A fist quickly met Stern's already bloodied face, and although Atarah couldn't jump on his back in the same way as Stephen had, she did her part. She had that wild energy about her that drew her to these situations in the first place, to react with excitement where others did fear and repulsion. "Get away from Alex! My stepdad is a cop, and I'll get him to arrest you!"

Stephen said nothing, but when he looked at me I could see the tormented choice he'd just made. I feel like there was something in that gaze I didn't quite have the capacity to understand- some emotion that was out of my reach just yet- but whatever it was, it overrode the emotions that had kept him away from me.

He brought Stern to the ground with his weight, and Atarah gleefully leapt on him, yelling, "This is what you get for being a creep! Leave my friends alone!" as she hit at him with her hands. She wasn't truly aiming to cause him any grievous injury, but even with his hands up to protect him, it might've still hurt.

Stephen rolled away from the confrontation, rising gracefully to his feet and brushing himself off. It was surely not far above zero degrees outside, and Stephen had lost his bomber jacket somewhere along the way, but he didn't seem to notice. He didn't waste time looking at Atarah and Stern; his attention was on me. There was hesitance in his voice, but not in his actions, as he stepped up close to me and asked, "are you alright, Alex?"

I couldn't help but wonder what was going on inside his

head. February 14th, Valentine's Day, Stephen's birthday. He had almost kissed me for a second time that night when I confessed that I was a murderer. And now, he had rushed to my defence?

His hair was ruffled and bits of it were sticking up in all directions. The whites of his eyes were red, evidence he had been crying, and there was a worrisome twitch in the corner of his lips. Ice from the sidewalk he'd landed on wet the collar of his white t-shirt, causing it to stick to the nylon underneath, and below that, his skin. I wished, in that moment, to kiss him right now; but he had already rejected me, and saving me from Stern hadn't changed that. Kissing him could only make things worse.

"I- I'm fine," I answered, possessed with the ghost of politeness, not feeling fine nor like that was what was important right now. "I'm sorry, it's my fault he's here, I should go-"

Stephen's brow furrowed ever so slightly. "You," he called, and at first I thought he was talking to me, until he turned his head towards Stern. "What's your name and why are you here?"

Stern sputtered through blood, his voice still choked up a little, "get her off me and I'll tell you!"

Atarah was, at this point, more laughing than attacking, and when Stephen fixed her with a gaze, she clambered up without having to be asked, stumbling over to me and using me as a support. Her fingernails dug into my arm, and Stephen watched us out of the corner of his eye, but most of his attention was on Stern.

Stern clambered to his feet. "My name is Mr Bailey Stern, P.I.," he said, and at hearing his first name, Atarah paused and let forth the laugh that I could've had myself. "Stephen Minett, am I right? I have some information-"

My heart stopped at those words, but it beat again as Stephen waved dismissively and cut him off. "Nope. I don't care. I want to know why you were attacking my friend."

Friend. A murderer was not someone Stephen would consider romantically, but a murderer was still someone he could be friends with. That made him exceptional; but was that the act of a good person, or a bad one? Forgiveness, or apologism?

Friend. What did he mean when he said that?

Was I worth defending? Were his morals even half as messed up as Atarah's? Did he even believe me when I told him what I'd done?

Stern spat blood onto the frozen sidewalk. "If you'll hear me out, I think you'll find what I have to say about your friend here useful information. Your life could depend on it-"

"Shut up," Stephen snapped, and in each sound there was a kind of contempt I had never, ever, since the day that I'd met him, heard from Stephen. Contempt that he didn't show me, knowing I was a murderer. "I'm not interested."

"Someone's coming," Atarah whispered near my ear, nodding to the darkness behind Stern. I squinted over his shoulder, trying to make out the figure in the dark, recognising the curly hair in the streetlights before anything else.

"Ezra," I whispered back, as Stern made another futile, rebutted attempt to get Stephen to listen. "Stern did say he was in contact. He must've somehow got his attention before I got here."

Stephen noticed, too, before Ezra got too close. "This is about Mr Hough, isn't it? Why is Ezra here?" he asked the man in front of him. Stern turned, caught Ezra's eye, and something that was, perhaps, relief came over him. He didn't fear *me*, but he feared *us*.

I felt a visceral kind of terror when Ezra's face came into view, and his hand came out of his pocket, but I wasn't scared for myself. I was scared for Stephen. As soon as I saw the silhouette of a silenced pistol, even before he had it pointed at Stephen's chest, I was terrified beyond belief.

Stephen began to slowly raise his hands, but Ezra kept walking at him, encouraging him to walk backwards until he was standing beside Atarah and I. The gun was pointed at all three of us then, with Stern slowly moving away. Ezra's face was the kind of blank that came with dry rage, a second away from snapping at any given moment; honestly, not far from Stephen's own expression. Atarah began to giggle low in her throat, almost unaware of the lethal weapon that could, at any moment, tear a hole through her.

"Alex," Ezra said finally, making it clear who he was addressing, although his eyes were fixed on Stephen. Watching him for threats. "Does Stephen know you're gonna kill him?"

"Oh, fuck off," Stephen scoffed, dismissing it out of hand. "Do you really think Alex could, or would, kill anyone? Seriously, Ezra?"

And with those words, the truth became clear. He couldn't possibly have been lying to Ezra to protect me; he simply didn't believe I was a murderer. He couldn't see it, even in my confession.

What a lovable fool.

"You fuck off. Didn't they literally say it to you? *I killed Amanda McIntosh?*" Ezra said, mocking my voice with his words. "You-"

"First of all, I heard Kai say pretty much the exact same thing earlier tonight. Survivor's guilt does that to people." When I thought about it, he was right- Kai said it was his fault she was dead. The leap of logic to think I was in his situation wasn't far. How kind of him to give me the benefit of the doubt. "I wouldn't be surprised if you managed to convince them your dad's death was somehow their fault, too, or that some accident that happened when they were a child was murder. Now I'm supposed to die? Don't try to feed me your lies."

I tried not to let my surprise show. In one fell swoop, Stephen made excuses to disbelieve every murder I had and would commit, discounting all of my wrongdoings as forever unbelievable. It was either stupidity or a good-natured belief in the kindness of humanity that would come back to bite him in the end.

"Second of all," Stephen said, his teeth gritting in annoyance, "did you bug my fucking house?"

Ezra didn't seem to properly process Stephen's words. "If you'll stop and listen, Stephen, we got proof. We caught those two-" he gestured between me and Atarah with the pointed gun- "...planning it."

"I don't give a shit. You bugged my house?" Stephen wasn't backing down, and my heart was bursting with so many feelings that all bore his name. He couldn't believe I was a murderer, so much so that he wouldn't listen to a messenger of the truth. Somewhere in all that love and amazement was pity. He would die for trusting me over Ezra.

Ezra blinked back his confusion, the gun lowering slightly. "It was his idea, not mine. If you'll listen, you'll understand why we-"

"For fuck's sake, shut up!" I had never seen Stephen as angry as he was in that moment. He stepped forward, and in a moment of bravery, grabbed Ezra's gun. Stern was slipping away, but nobody seemed to care.

The following second was another that seemed to last forever. Stephen pushed the gun upwards, pulling it towards him, trying to overwhelm Ezra and rip the gun away; and in the same second, Ezra pulled it back, wrenching it away from Stephen. The barrel had been pointed at me, but when Stephen grabbed it, he'd skewed Ezra's aim towards Atarah.

On instinct, I shoved Atarah sideways onto the sidewalk and dived towards Ezra, ducking under the line of the gun and aiming for his chest. Stephen was taller and probably stronger than Ezra was, and probably could've won the contest; but it was the perfect moment to help.

I heard the shot go off as soon as I connected with Ezra's chest, both of us falling to the ground. The gun clattered out onto the asphalt of the street, but before I grabbed it, I turned around to check. Stephen was standing above me, breathing heavily, and sitting where I'd pushed her was Atarah. She was staring at the air above her, at the very place she'd been standing mere moments before. She wasn't hit, but I could tell from her expression alone that it had been close.

Looking at them had cost me a few seconds that Ezra took advantage of. He was quick, and I felt the cold metal press into the side of my head before I saw anything.

"Get off your high horse, Alex." I don't know what he thought that meant, and it could've been funny, if I could feel anything at all about my impending death. I met Stephen's eyes; there was nothing but fear in them. Oh, I almost wanted to be able to feel fear; it would protect me from the reckless mockery sitting on the edge of my tongue that could very well get me killed. "Give me one reason why I shouldn't kill you right now."

If I were afraid right now, I would've lost the perfect words I needed to save my own life. "Because your sister loves you. She doesn't want to see you go to jail. Killing me right now, right here, will put you in jail for life." As I spoke, I watched Stephen. He backed up, silently watching Ezra for a reaction, before going over to Atarah and pulling her to her feet. He whispered something in her ear, and she immediately pulled out her phone and began to text.

"Don't get me wrong. I'm gonna be your murderer." Ezra whispered it harsh against my hair. I was frozen in place, propped up over him with a gun against my head, unable to move lest he accidentally shoot me. "I've got a plan to bring you to justice. Not just for my dad, but for Amanda too, and your other victim. What was their name, huh? The third person you killed?"

"You don't want to kill me, not really." I couldn't see his face, but I felt the barrel press harder into the side of my head. A non-verbal warning.

"I promised her I'd wait one more week. That's it. You've got until next Saturday to live the rest of your life. So make it work." I gritted my teeth; I found nothing funny, but somehow it was still difficult to keep from mentioning his misphrasing. "That's when I'll hunt you down. You're right; I don't wanna kill you. But I want revenge more than I wanna keep my hands clean. Don't underestimate me."

He shoved me off onto the pavement, and as I rolled away and began to take my surroundings in again, the reasons became clear. A few people had left Stephen's house to gather on the sidewalk, taking photos, with one person making a call. Nobody had yet decided to actually cross the road, but the confrontation hadn't gone unnoticed.

"Don't forget it," Ezra growled at me as he rose to his

feet, one last warning before he took off into the night, in the same direction he came. I lay there on the sidewalk, collecting my thoughts, as both Atarah and Stephen ran to my side. I tried my best to look at the stars above me instead of staring at Stephen like I wanted to. I was scared to see his reaction to all of this.

"I had just texted Josh to get here as fast as he could. Now it's for nothing," Atarah bemoaned, falling to the sidewalk beside me. She was exhilarated, not a hint of fear on her face. "What did he say?"

Stephen gave Atarah a weird glance, an obvious judgement of her reaction, thinking neither of us would see. I didn't blame him for judging her. "I want to know what he said, too," he admitted.

Even in a moment like that, my heart fluttered at the sound of his voice. Atarah needed to know the truth, but I had no idea if it was better to lie to Stephen. I supposed it hardly mattered; I didn't care if he liked Ezra. So I told the truth. "He said I have one more week before he kills me."

"He's crazy," Stephen said immediately, sinking down to sit beside me. I had been tempted to get up, as the cold was beginning to seep through my sweater and into my skin, but having Stephen beside me felt nicer. "Don't worry. He won't get a chance to hurt you."

It was such an empty platitude. Stephen had no way of stopping him, and neither did I. I suppose I could try and press charges for assault, and maybe drag the police into it, but not only would that take far too long, it wouldn't stop him from killing me.

I could run away, start again somewhere else. Of course, it wasn't that simple- I'd have to figure out where my family would fit in with this, how to get a job, and where to go where he wouldn't find me. I'd have to kill Stephen first or take him with me, lest I miss him constantly or put myself in danger trying to see him again. I suppose I could live with him as my eternal prisoner, but then again, there'd be a whole investigation. And what of Atarah? I wouldn't miss her, but I'd never meet another like her, who'd accept me for what I was.

"I don't know what to do," I confessed into the silence when neither of them spoke. "He's going to kill me."

"You know what I think we should do," Atarah said, and it sounded like an introduction to a plan, but she didn't finish the sentence. When the silence was left up to interpretation, I heard her implication. Kill him first.

"We can't come up with a plan in seven days that would keep both of the Houghs away from me." Around Stephen, I coded my language, but Atarah understood me completely. Kill Ezra, and Ophelia would kill me, no questions asked. They had to both die, and soon, and it just didn't feel plausible to me.

"Hey." Stephen grabbed my attention, and when I met his eyes, they were so naively warm and gentle. "Two things. First- give me your sweater now, before the cops show up. You don't want them to see you covered in blood."

The surprising clarity with which he spoke, the calmness about him, was enough to get me to follow his instructions. I sat up and lifted it over my head, shivering as the cold air met my bare arms and my stomach where my t-shirt lifted up. I handed the sweater to him, looking for guidance on what to do next.

"I'll get it back to you on Monday," he said, all casual, like we had just had English class and not a near-deadly confrontation, followed by news of my imminent demise. "Second of all. Believe me when I say we'll find a way to save you- he's seventeen, and no matter how angry he is, he doesn't want to be a murderer." It might've been more believable if I didn't know just how easy it really was. "I- I get that you might not feel safe right now. Would it make you feel safer to stay here tonight?"

I was so dumbstruck by the idea that I almost didn't hear him continue. "You won't be alone, and I won't... make you uncomfortable. I just want to make sure you're going to be safe."

I was frozen in uncertainty. I was being given a second chance, offered to me almost like an apology; *this time, don't blurt that you're a murderer.* It felt so much more important than dealing with Ezra. What if I had one week to indulge in my feelings, and then I just... died? Before I could feel any of the pain that came with this love?

"We've got a week." Atarah's interjection was entirely unwelcome. "You're both still tipsy. My stepdad's coming, and the cops are almost certainly going to be here separately. We're all going to the station whether we like it or not."

"I don't want to." Most times, I would restrain my natural, emotionless reactions when someone else was around, but Stephen distracted me, and I forgot. "It's a waste of time."

"I hate cops. You know this. But I can see his car. Maybe if we all go to the station with him, we can avoid being interrogated."

"We all?" Stephen raised his eyebrows at her, scrambling to his feet. I followed on instinct, and Atarah rose wearily, just to keep up. "I'm not going anywhere."

"Well, you can try that," Atarah argued. I was distracted, watching a white car I was fairly certain belonged to Josh drive towards us.

"One minute," Stephen grumbled, clearly unhappy, before running across the road and into his own yard. He called out to the people standing around, explaining in a hurry that the police were coming, and that they should all head home.

"Jesus," Atarah muttered in my ear as soon as he was out of earshot. "I think if you politely told him to jump off a cliff, he'd do it. He thinks the world of you. He wouldn't think for a second that you could ever do anything wrong. Did you actually tell him you killed Amanda?"

"Yes." I couldn't believe it either. "He was about to kiss me, Atarah. For the second time tonight."

"Fuck," Atarah whispered under her breath. "He loves you back."

"I know." The words tasted so, so bitter on my tongue. "It makes it so much worse." I knew we couldn't be together; I'd established that tonight. It hurt like hell.

Stephen ran inside, and quickly came back; when he returned, it was without my sweater. As Josh finally found somewhere to park and got out to speak to us, Stephen met us back on the opposite side of the road, ready for whatever our fate might be.

Josh's concern was immediate and obvious. "What happened? Atarah, are you alright? I saw people heading off that way- is that...?"

"Oh, just a kid with a gun who was going to fucking kill Alex." How thrilled Atarah was shone through every feature of her face. Josh cringed slightly at her odd but predictable reaction, checking Stephen and I to see if we were put off. He was met with my blankness, and was put off himself. "It's okay, he's gone now. But I think someone else called the cops."

"Let me deal with them. Alex, do you feel like you're in danger?" he asked. I could feel Stephen's gaze, and Atarah's as well. Everyone was waiting, and I didn't know how to answer.

I was in danger. "Yes." The words were true, but the affect had to be forced on. I copied the fear I'd seen in others' faces a thousand times before, and with my hands held close to my stomach, I pinched the skin on the underside of my wrist. The pain made me scrunch my eyes up and I looked down to the ground, pinching harder until the tears began to come out of my eyes. I may as well commit. "I think he's going to kill me and I don't know what to do." I choked on the words, gazing up at Josh like I was begging for help.

I had a good idea of his character. Despite how much Atarah disliked him, he answered her call immediately. I saw the same care for her when I ate dinner with them. Despite what he did for a living, and how much Atarah hated it, he was generally kind, and he cared about her. He'd likely become a cop out of a desire to emulate the naive, childish idea to protect and serve, nothing like Atarah's experience. He was a compassionate person, and stupid.

So he'd play right into my lies.

"You can stay with us again tonight, if it makes you feel safer," he said softly, stepping forward to place a gentle hand on my shoulder. "You know who that kid is, right?"

I nodded slowly, as Atarah blurted his name. "Ezra

Hough."

"You don't have to do it tonight, but we can take a statement, and I'll see what I can do about a restraining order." His hand on my shoulder was supposed to be comforting, but unlike the one comforting touch I'd received in my entire life, there was nothing to comfort.

I pinched myself harder and the salty tears tracked down my skin. "Thank you," I gasped, looking up at him through the haze in my eyes.

To my surprise, I heard my favourite voice right beside me, in an emotion I'd never heard before. "Can... I come, too?"

Stephen wasn't far off from crying himself. He held his hand over his face, and it shook. "I... someone just pointed a gun at me? He shot at my friends? He bugged my house. I don't want to be here right now. I want to be anywhere but here."

"I mean, that makes sense," Josh said, looking between the two of us as the gears turned inside his brain. I wanted nothing more than to hug Stephen at that point, but I couldn't quite convince my limbs to move; all I could do was stare through quickly-drying tears of pain. My wrist hurt. "We have a spare mattress somewhere, it'll be fine. Atarah, can you take them to the car?"

Why he said that became clear when I looked across the road. A police car, sirens off, was pulling up to Stephen's address. Josh sighed, gave me a gentle pat on the shoulder, and added, "...while I deal with them."

Atarah was already at the car. "Come on, you two."

The idea was sinking in that I was going to sleeping over with Stephen- at Atarah's house, sure, but with Stephen- and the nervous sickness lacing through my intestines made it hard to speak, hard to move. Stephen walked towards her, turning back to me with an unreadable expression, and that was what drove me forward. That, and I was cold.

"What about the bugs at your house? You could do something about that," I said weakly, as a fleeting thought that came into my mind. "I mean, like, press charges, or..."

"I'm mad about that, yeah, but I'm way madder about what he's doing to you," Stephen answered. Good, kind, thoughtful Stephen, thinking way, way, way too much of me.

"You shouldn't be." It's justified. It's even honourable. Movies are made about kids like Ezra and Ophelia, and they're always the heroes. Me, I'm the villain in every single one. And I'm the villain of this movie, too; I knew that, but when I didn't care about right or wrong, it didn't matter to me.

A small part of me wanted to be the hero. The hero always gets the girl. But Stephen wasn't the girl, I could never be a hero, and I was going to kill him. This was all wrong. And unless I had a time machine to stop myself from killing Bailey and starting on this path, it could never be right. I had ruined my happy ending forever.

When we got into the car, we were sitting barely a foot apart from each other, and we were both freezing, and I was so in love with him. It took everything I had not to inch closer and wrap my arms around him, to breath him in like smoke. Smoke from this new, horrible drug that would be so, so amazing, but contribute to my slow, painful death. The symptoms were difficult to bear. My heart racing in my chest, the sickness in my stomach, the awkward headache that I got from trying so hard not to look at him. My shaking hands, my locked-up throat, the tugging behind my sternum that was so heavy and hurt so much to carry.

If I didn't kill Stephen, and Ezra didn't kill me, I'd probably kill myself just to escape this feeling.

"I think I've said this already, but I'll say it again, because I mean it," Stephen said quietly, possibly hoping Atarah wouldn't pay attention, but I knew she was listening. She was tapping away on her phone, but I felt the buzzing in my pocket. "I won't let him hurt you, Alex."

"I don't mean to be rude when I say this." The last thing I wanted was to hurt Stephen's feelings, murder plots aside. "...but why do you care so much? Ezra in the cafeteria, and just now- you didn't have to help me. Nobody else has. And maybe you're just a better person than everyone else, but..."

"Maybe nobody else cares about you like I do."

My heart fluttered, and every bad feeling inside of me shattered into pieces. I was floating. It was better than the tastiest food I'd ever eaten, better than the most pleasant smells. It was better than beautiful artworks in wonderous colours, and the most magnificent scenery I'd ever laid eyes on. It was better than the most outstanding, evocative music I'd ever listened to. It was better than the best sex I'd ever had. Nothing in my mandatively mediocre existence had ever felt as wonderful and beautiful as Stephen Minett saying that short sentence.

It was blissful, imagining a world where he could say something like that to me every day. I would never get sick of it. If only such a world was possible.

He was looking out the window, unable meet my eyes. I couldn't blame him, after saying something like that.

I realised my night of letting go wasn't quite over yet. After tonight, when he went home, I'd go back to planning his murder- and hopefully I'd do it soon, so I could escape Ezra's justice with my heart removed once again. But just for this brief moment, I could have this feeling, before I surgically cut him out. Before the consequences reached me.

So I offered my hand across the car seat.

And Stephen took it.

Chapter Twelve - Bailey Keen

"God, get a fucking room, you two." I would say Atarah's interjection ruined the mood, but I was still holding Stephen's hand, so I had absolutely no complaints about the situation. Soft, warm, smooth, strong. I felt guilty, deep down, for playing his emotions like this, for letting him naively believe in my goodness, just so he could love me. That guilt was the sharp end of the stick.

"Oh, fuck off," Stephen muttered, but he was smiling. His thumb was gently moving across my skin, and I was in heaven.

With my free hand- there was no way I would ever sacrifice touching Stephen- I took my phone out of my pocket to read Atarah's messages.

Stop flirting with each other, you're going to kill him.

Is he dumb, lovestruck, or both? I think both.

He's definitely got to be dumb. Or Ezra is just that much of an un-likable twat that he couldn't possibly believe him.

All of the above.

Are you two fucking holding hands?

I ignored absolutely all of those text messages. It was for the best, because her insulting of Stephen, however objectively accurate, pissed me off, and the one time I'd shown her my anger had been unpleasant. "I'm just going to tell my parents what's going on," I said, mostly for Stephen's benefit. When I texted my mother, I made it relatively vague, telling her I was staying at a friend's house and leaving it at that. I didn't want my parents involved in the Ezra situation until absolutely necessary. By the time Atarah texted me again, asking *Serious-ly, are you?*, my anger had faded, and I answered her with a simple, smug reply.

yes

And I was so smug about it. I was giddy, and excited, and amazed that Stephen Minett- the single remarkable human being on this planet- wanted me, of all people. Of anyone he could have, he wanted me. He'd never dated any-one before- if we were to date, I'd be the first. The only person thus far he'd deemed good enough to date him.

And that feeling was absolutely everything. It overshad-owed all the bad that I knew would come later, the bad that kept my murder plans in place. In the moment, it was won-derful.

When Josh got back into the car and drove us home, he was talking, but I wasn't listening. I was staring out of the window, because if I looked at Stephen, I wasn't sure I'd be able to cope. It was too much happiness all at once. Holding his hand was hardly bearable. There was no free space in my mind for anything other than the fact that he was touching me.

And it was stupid, and I was a fool for letting it happen, but for just this one night, I let myself be happy.

When I had to let go of him to get out of the car, I felt loss weighing on my shoulders and I remembered why I hated feelings again. The happiness was fleeting, always fleeting.

Atarah lead the way into her house, followed by Stephen, myself, and Josh. A cat wound its way around Atarah's legs, stopping her in the hallway as she leaned down to pet it, but Stephen sidled past her, opening the door to her bedroom and heading through it, allowing me in after him. Atarah picked up the cat and followed us in, after thanking Josh for picking us up. He said it was nothing and smiled at her in a way that said, *I'm trying my best.*

I sat down on the bed, pulling a blanket around my shoulders to try and warm up. Atarah looked at Stephen curiously, and at first, I couldn't figure out why, until she said, "how did you know which one is my room?"

Stephen stared at her in return for a long second before answering. "There's an A on your door."

"Oh. Right." Atarah threw her coat off on her chair, the side-eye she was giving Stephen quickly dropping. He was casually observing all the decorations in Atarah's room, hands in his pockets. He was a gazelle in the lion's den, and watching the confidence he had about him was almost sad. It was unearned, built on a fragile and misguided trust in me. A trust that was, in some part, due to the fact that he liked me. I tried not to get too happy about that.

"What's all this?" Stephen asked, drawing Atarah's attention. He was standing in front of the collection of newspaper clippings, skim-reading each of them. There was a flash of fear that hit me when I realised all of my murders were there, too, but I did my best to ignore it. He didn't believe a direct confession, and besides; him finding out just meant it would be easier to crush him when the time came.

Would I stab him? Shoot him? Drown him? Leave him to freeze to death underneath the ice? What was the right way to kill Stephen Minett?

"Oh, I'm interested in true crime. I do a video series on it." I'd never watched her videos; it occurred to me then that I probably should, considering she was my best friend. Even if I had no interest, for the sake of others. Our friendship was getting hard to hide, after all- Stephen at the very least knew.

"I keep a lot of this stuff."

Stephen's questions were innocent and kind. "What interests you about it?" he asked, running his fingers over the various clippings. His eyes were naturally drawn to the corner with my murders on it, because of course. The fear spiked, and I remained fixed in place, staring at the side of his head, afraid to say or do anything.

"It's just the psychology of why people do those kinds of things." Atarah stared at me out of corner of her eye, her brow furrowing at my expression, until she turned back to Stephen and saw his fingers lingering over the photo that absolutely didn't belong. My family on summer vacation when I was seven. Bailey.

"If it's not rude to ask," Stephen said, like he shouldn't already be demanding answers, "why's this here?"

I swallowed back terror, hard and thick, and looked to Atarah to explain herself. I wanted to be mad at her for putting me in this position, but this wasn't enough to trigger my rare anger. It was only fear, clogging my judgement and making it hard to speak.

She did her best to explain it. "Well, not many people know this, so consider yourself lucky," she said, clearly buying herself time to perfect the lie. She tapped Bailey's face, picking him out from the crowd. "But Alex had a brother. And he, uh, went missing when he was little. Nobody really knows what happened to him. I thought it was interesting enough to belong here, even if it's not a murder."

It sounded true, and that was all she needed to achieve. Stephen turned to me, and I forced my face blank with the effort it took to move mountains. "I thought there was an accident, and he drowned."

It was impossible to keep my shock hidden. How did Stephen know that? Had I been better friends with him than I thought, or was it common knowledge? How could he possibly know what happened to Bailey? Most people didn't even know he had existed. I never mentioned him to my friends, my sisters never knew him, and it was painful for my parents to talk about. It wasn't a secret- I'd told Atarah, after all- but it pretty much never came up. "How... did you... hear that?"

"I don't remember where I heard it," Stephen said, innocent as ever. "I think I heard it a long time ago, I don't know."

"Well, that's what they tell everyone, because really, nobody knows what happened." Atarah easily followed through on the lie, trying to draw attention away from the wall and towards her. "That's what they think happened, but his body was never found."

"Oh." Prior to this, I would've thought Stephen smart, or at least, smart enough. But there were three suspicious deaths surrounding me now, one of which several people were sure I'd committed, one of which we were gaslighting him about, and one of which I legitimately confessed to having done, to his face. And yet, the look he gave me was soft, and caring, and kind. "I'm sorry. If you want to talk about... anything..."

"Thank you." I lowered my head, refusing to push this matter any further than it had to go. I sure hoped Atarah had something planned to break all this tension, because I didn't. Stephen opened his mouth to say something, but decided against it.

So Atarah spoke. "It's pretty late, so we should probably all just sleep. I'll go ask Josh where the spare mattress is, and we'll figure something out." Nobody commented on the math: two mattresses, three people. Nobody wanted to. "In the meantime, would either of you like a shower? Alex, you've still got..." she trailed off, gesturing at my hands. There was dried blood smeared across the back of my hands, between my fingers, under my fingernails. Stephen had held my hand like this. It didn't paint me in a great light.

Thankfully, Stephen's skull was pretty thick.

"Yeah, that's probably for the best." Atarah and I were nowhere close to being able to share clothes, so I'd have to put the same ones back on; but she gave me a towel and showed me where the bathroom was, leaving me with a short joke about how she'd take care of Stephen. Despite the fact that I trusted and knew her, and it was a joke, the knife of jealousy twisted in my stomach. I let the door shut on her just to keep my reaction silent.

With Stephen gone, I was empty again. It was both disappointing and relieving. It was easy without him. For that precious stretch of time, there was nothing, and there wouldn't be anything until I walked back through Atarah's bedroom door.

There was no use in lying to myself. I did, strictly speaking, enjoy myself more, and feel better, when I was sitting in the back of Josh's car, holding Stephen's hand. But everything else- that fear of him finding out, the guilt of lying to him, the pain of rejection, that jealousy when Atarah so much as mentioned the fact that she would be with him when I was not? Emptiness was preferable to that.

When I did walk back through Atarah's door, ready to face my emotions again, I wasn't prepared. Stephen was sitting on Atarah's bed, leaning up against her wall, a hand on his stomach and a fading laugh on his face at some joke Atarah was finishing up telling. "...I mean, what is he going to do, throw a tantrum until Alex just drops dead? He won't do shit! Hey, Alex," she said, seamlessly transitioning into greeting me. "We were just making fun of Ezra."

"He did have a gun," I reminded her, stern for a moment, "...but he may be a few bullets short of a full chamber himself. Or, maybe, a few pencils short of a toolbox." The wry grin on my face was for Stephen. It wasn't the best joke I'd ever made, but all I wanted was to make him laugh.

And he did, a beautiful, angelic sound that echoed in my mind. The sound of his laugh was so, so wonderful, and unforgettable. I was already a wreck, and it felt good. It was hard to regret leaving the emptiness behind.

On the floor was a single mattress, and the calculations quickly began in my head, returning error codes. Atarah winked, telling me she had a plan, but I realised that no matter what she did, it would be bad. I'd be jealous if he slept beside her, upset if he was on the floor alone, and kept awake by constant churning anxiety if she gave us her bed. There was no good solution, and I was anxious just thinking about it.

"Jeez. Don't worry about Ezra, Alex." Stephen rose, walking over to me and patting my shoulder. The contact froze me, electrocuted me. It didn't matter that we'd almost kissed twice tonight, or that we'd held hands maybe ten minutes ago. His touch was as new and exciting as it had ever been. "He's full of it."

I couldn't help but smile, regardless of how empty his words were. It wasn't as infuriating as it had once been, these emotions, but I still felt completely out of control. Stephen turned to Atarah, an expectant look on his face. "May I have a shower as well? It'd probably make me feel better."

"Of course," Atarah grinned, rising to her feet. As she took Stephen to the bathroom, I sat on her bed and pulled out my phone, first finding Atarah's video blogging channel and saving it for later perusal, before opening my social media.

I searched my profile for the word 'Bailey', and it didn't turn up. I checked both of my parents as well; it was only mentioned once, in the description of the very picture Atarah had printed out and stuck on her wall. Someone would've had to thoroughly look into me to find out that he even existed, let alone how he died. Who was spreading rumours about him through the school? Ezra mentioned Amanda and Mr Hough by name; he would've mentioned Bailey if he knew. There was no way I could think of for Stephen to find out how Bailey died. That was something I'd never fully told anyone but Atarah, and that I was sure of.

As far as I was aware, Atarah was the only person who knew the truth. When she came back, I asked her. "You never told Stephen about Bailey, did you?"

"No. I don't talk to him, usually. If I'm honest, I have no idea why I was even invited to his party." Atarah shrugged, plopping herself down on the single mattress. She removed her shoes and began to roll her stockings off under her dress as she spoke. "I'm stumped as to how he knew, too, unless you told anyone else."

"I didn't, and that's the thing. The only people who

know specifically that he drowned are you, my family, and a few family friends from the time. It was in a brief newspaper obituary, I think, but who our age would've found that? You'd have to be looking for it. Even if Stephen was stalking me and learning every possible morsel of information he could, he shouldn't be able to find that out, right? Not even the Houghs know that, and they've been stalking me almost that close."

"I would normally say you're overthinking this, but it *is* weird," Atarah agreed. "Your sisters could have told someone, but it's unlikely. My best guess is that you did tell someone and just forgot."

"Maybe," I conceded, but it felt like there was more to explore. "I just fear that someone other than the Houghs might be after me, and they found it out somehow."

"I mean, those threatening letters were un-Ophelia-like, and Ezra's too dumb. I still don't believe it was them." Atarah bit her lip. "For now, we should focus on the Houghs. We have a deadline of one week until Ezra's officially hunting you down, and we know nothing else about this hypothetical other person. They can wait."

I sighed, looking at the photo on my screen. Bailey's smile was so wide and genuine beside my utterly fake one. "Okay, I agree. Priorities are: murder Stephen, figure out a plan to deal with Ezra and Ophelia, and then deal with... that."

"Speaking of." Atarah laid down on the single bed on the floor, making herself comfortable. "What the fuck happened with you and Stephen? I mean, it sounded a whole hell of a lot like you confessed to him, and he's still on your side. Please explain."

"Well, you remember our conversation in the bathroom." I gestured vaguely at her, and she nodded. "And I realised Stephen could never love a murderer, right? Well, after I fell asleep, and you left to wherever you went-"

"Oh, before you continue, you should know. Stephen came in not long after you fell asleep. He asked me to go downstairs, but he let you stay since you were asleep. Or at least, that's the excuse he gave. I went downstairs and chatted up one of his friends for a while, and then saw him running outside after you."

"Alright." My voice was empty and it sounded sarcastic, but she understood. "He woke me up. And then, well... we almost kissed." It made me blush to mention it, despite how it was simple, factual truth. The butterflies in my stomach stirred at the memory, even though he wasn't here, now.

"Almost?" Atarah was smiling, leaning forward expectantly for the rest of the story.

"Yeah. I... I didn't, and don't, want to get in a relationship with him if I'm going to kill him. It will only make it harder. And I don't want to *not* kill him, because most of these feelings are horrible, and I want them gone. But... those feelings? When he's about to kiss me, or he's holding my hand—they're better than nothingness. And in that moment it made sense to me to think that if I did get in a relationship with him, and I just made sure he never left or fought with me... somehow... that that would be preferable to killing him."

"So why didn't you just kiss him? He's clearly both into you and dumb enough to easily manipulate into staying. Then we don't have to kill him, and instead, he can help us kill Ophelia and Ezra." Atarah shrugged like it was obvious. "Tell him it has to be done, whatever."

"Because even if he's dumb, he's certainly a good person, and my feelings won't let me lie to him. Guilt is the worst emotion of them all, Atarah, and even if I'm embracing these emotions I still have to eliminate that one. I wouldn't be able to keep the truth from him, about who I am and what I've done. And once he knows that, nothing short of kidnapping him could make him stay." I watched the realisation on her face sink in. "So I figured that if he took it badly, he still wouldn't tell anyone, and I just told him the truth. Amanda was on my mind, because of Kai, so that's what I said. And he didn't believe me."

"Oh." Atarah pauses as the gears turn in her head. "I mean, what exactly did you say?"

"I said it plainly. *I killed Amanda McIntosh.* And he said

something like, *I'm sorry, I misunderstood*, and I ran away. I ran outside, found Stern- the P.I.- and was only talking to him for about five or ten minutes before you two showed up."

Atarah hummed for a moment. "Okay. Timelines are a little weird there, unless Stephen left and came back or you were talking to him for ages... but it doesn't matter. So the P.I. had bugged the house, heard you say that, and... there isn't a recording, is there?"

"Ezra and presumably Ophelia heard everything, but it sounded like he lost the record of it when I destroyed his phone." That information was so easily forgotten in amongst everything.

Atarah hissed through her teeth. "I think you should talk to Ophelia. Technically, she broke her deal. Almost twice."

I raised an eyebrow at her, encouraging an explanation. She stared, like it should be obvious. "I would say that bugging Stephen's house was hurting him, or at least not leaving him alone. And if you hadn't shoved me out of the way, Ezra would've shot me. Thanks for that, by the way." She had a self-satisfied grin that didn't immediately make sense to me, until she said something about it. "I guess you do care, on some level."

"Maybe. I don't feel anything about you, but you dying would've been a bad thing as far as I'm concerned." I let her have her satisfaction. I didn't want to consider whether or not loving Stephen had changed me, so I didn't consider it. "As for Ophelia... I don't think either of those things was necessarily her breaking her word. She only promised not to hurt you two, and she's been trying to uphold that. But I could always pretend it was, and tell her that if she goes to the police with what she found, I'll break my side of the deal."

"I like the way you're thinking." Atarah nodded decisively. "I could also fake an injury and claim Ezra did it. Or the P.I., she'd probably believe that first. But for now, send her that threat."

I took my phone up again, and went to Ophelia's social media. Her profile picture was a year or two old, her and her brother outside a theme park, wide white-toothed smiles and summer clothes. Her bio was simple: name, age, school, sexuality. No hobbies or interests listed, no personalised flair.

I drafted a message, showed it to Atarah for approval, and sent it. *You broke your promise to me. There were listening devices in Stephen's house, and Ezra would've shot Atarah if I didn't step in. I mean this is the nicest, most diplomatic way: go to the police, and I'll break my promise.*

I closed the page without waiting for a response. "Let's hope that's that dealt with," Atarah said. She muttered something about forgetting to take off her makeup before standing up and heading over to the dresser. I opened up my phone, closed Ophelia's page, and headed to Stephen's.

His profile picture was a selfie taken in his bedroom at sundown, the red and pink colours cascading across his face and lighting up the greens and blues in his eyes. I had the picture saved, along with pretty much every picture of him I could find. I had resisted the urge to make it my screen background, preferring to forget him where possible. His bio wasn't dissimilar to Ophelia's, but it felt a lot more creative than hers did. *Stephen - he/him - 18 - artist & dancer - persist.*

I already knew pretty much everything about him. He was an only child, but he had a lot of cousins. His mother loved to take pictures of him. He didn't have a lot of friends until a few years ago. He'd deleted all photos from primary school, but his mother kept them up, and I'd downloaded them from there. Objectively speaking, Stephen didn't stand out, and he wasn't noteworthy. My emotions lied, as always.

There were a lot of posts from friends wishing him a happy birthday. More than anyone usually got- he was popular, although he had no close friends. A lot like me. Most of them fell into a similar pattern, talking about how they can't believe he's an adult, wishing him a good birthday, inside jokes, some awkward photos they'd collected over the past year. I downloaded all of those.

There was one that hinted at him being attractive, and the anger it filled me with was irrational. Since it came from someone I'd never spoken to before, I blocked her, just so I wouldn't have to read her words again.

The 'post' button was itching to be pressed, but I had no words. I opened it up and stared at the white emptiness where words should be, wondering why the hell I was doing this. He was in the next room; if I had something to say to him, I could just say it. I didn't have to do this.

But I wanted to.

Happy birthday, Stephen. I hope it's been a good one; you deserve it.

I felt numb as I posted it. It was uncharacteristic of my persona, the way I spoke, but I truly did want him to have enjoyed his birthday. And to enjoy the next few days. Right up until his death.

Maybe if he enjoyed the next few days, his death wouldn't be so bad.

Posting it eased the hidden well of guilt in the tiniest way. A hidden well of guilt I did not want coming to the forefront of my mind right now, but it was happening. I didn't want to kill him, and it felt wrong to do it. It was doing him a disservice. I shouldn't kill him.

I remember looking at that picture of Bailey, and wondering if he really needed to die. Not because I felt guilty, but because I knew what love felt like. I saw what it looked like for Ezra and Ophelia, and I knew I could've had that. Right now, I had love- romantic, not familial, but it made no difference- and I was about to kill to destroy it.

So why did I long to love? Why did I want to test if Stephen could love me when I supposedly didn't want him to? Why did I think Bailey being alive, being loved, would be a good thing?

I wanted Stephen dead- the logical part of me knew it was the right thing to do, the rational decision. But I felt guilty about killing him, and I longed for him to love me, and this pain, this contradiction, was unbearable.

I wished he was already dead so I wouldn't feel this terrible guilt. I wished Ezra had shot him, or I'd gone with my initial plan to somehow get him in an accident, before Atarah had gotten involved.

I wanted him dead so I'd stop feeling guilty about killing

him.

"So." Atarah's voice caught me out of my thoughts; I wanted to thank her for that, almost. "I want your guess on who's leaving these notes. Someone who could've found out about Bailey somehow, and would want to keep me away from you."

"Nobody that I know of meets that description, and nobody could. If they know about Bailey, and they're threatening you to stay away from me... I can't figure out a motivation that connects those two things."

Atarah sighed. "It can't be two separate people. Are you sure you didn't just casually mention it once, by accident?"

"Even if I did, who would've spread it enough that Stephen heard? I wasn't ever close to Stephen. I know I never brought up Bailey to him, because I never stop thinking about him."

Atarah saw my insistence and let it go. "You know why this is on my mind, right?"

I took a moment to consider. Atarah had been warned to leave me alone, hadn't she? "...well, you aren't exactly leaving me alone."

"Three strikes, you're out, it said." Atarah went over to her window and locked it. She seemed perfectly calm in her actions, but her voice was low and serious. "You may have a week, but I have no idea how long I have. I still think we should prioritise the Houghs, but... that doesn't stop me from being scared, you know?"

"I'm sorry for being self-centred." It was said in the same calm tone as everything else I say, but after a second of thought, it caught Atarah's attention. "If we're working as a team, we should devote equal time to solving each other's issues. You can't help me kidnap Stephen if you're dead. I propose that-"

The door opening snapped my mouth shut. Stephen's wet hair clung to his forehead in tight curls, tighter than normal. He'd put his white shirt back on, and it clung to the form of his body, every curve of his chest, like a sculpture, his bare skin hardly hidden. I hoped he didn't listen through the door for even half a second, and also that he wasn't paying attention to the fact that I was staring at him.

"What's up?" he said casually. He took the towel from around his neck and dropped it in Atarah's wash basket, wandering over towards the bed. "Thanks, Atarah."

"It's fine." She blinked herself back into the swing of things. I still needed to talk to her, without Stephen. He sat right beside me, making it impossible for me to sneakily text her. "I should probably shower too, but I can't be bothered." Atarah sat back down on the single mattress, perhaps sealing my fate.

"Ah, well." Stephen said, leaning back in Atarah's bed. "I don't blame you. I'm tired, too." He yawned, stretching out. I hated how much I liked the fact that he seemed so comfortable with the idea of sleeping in the same bed as me.

And then Atarah made it official. "You and Alex can have my bed. I'm going to go to sleep now, so if you don't mind, keep it down." She took her glasses off and put them on top of her phone on her bedside table. "Can I turn the lights off, or are you two going to stay up?"

"I, uh." As I was about to tell her, I didn't plan to sleep at all tonight. Along with the fact that I'd sobered up and I'd already slept some, Stephen's presence would make that impossible. Maybe if we were sleeping in separate beds I'd be able to drift off, but like this? There was no way. "I'm good either way."

"Turn it off if you want." Stephen was looking at me, but I couldn't meet his eyes. I didn't know, or want to know, what that stare meant.

"You turn it off," Atarah said, throwing a blanket over her head.

Stephen's presence was like a fire. Warming, enticing, drawing me in towards him; but at the same time, it burned, and I knew if I touched him, it could only be painful. So I got up and went to the door, feeling the distance like cool air between us. Cold, alone, but relieving.

I found my way slowly back to the bed with the light off. Atarah may've not known I was going to stay up all night, on the lookout for her stalker, but I would do it regardless.

Stephen wouldn't let me sleep anyway.

I sat back down on the bed, gingerly finding where I could safely be. My hand found Stephen's leg- on the other side of the covers, thankfully, to save my fragile heart- and as my eyes adjusted to the moonlight through the window, I could see the outline of him, laying on the pillow closest to the wall. Silently, I laid down beside him, gingerly sliding under the covers.

The whole room smelled like Atarah, and her bed even more so, but I could smell coconut and buttered popcorn and it kept my eyes wide open. I wondered if he could see my eyes in the dark. I was laying on my back, determined not to look at him; I didn't want to invite any feelings in if I could avoid them. I knew it was unavoidable, but even a futile attempt was something.

"Alex?" The sound I most dreaded couldn't even feel unpleasant to my ears. It was a quiet whisper, so soft that Atarah wouldn't have been able to hear it.

Soft, so gentle into the darkness, I answered him. "Yeah?"

"I..." Stephen's words were carefully chosen. Every second of silence was as excruciating as every syllable he spoke. "A lot's happened tonight. Things have changed."

"Yeah." My heart was racing, but my mind wasn't quite up to speed. My mind was blank.

"And..." Sincerely honest, the man I loved, my future victim, opened his heart to me. "...I just want to make it clear where we stand."

"Yeah?" I didn't know what to say. My mouth was dry. I realised that no, my mind was not blank: it was full of so much that it all faded into background noise, any one thought incapable of being distinguished from another.

"So." He sounded fearful, so fearful. He should be afraid of me murdering him, not of me rejecting him. "...where do we stand?"

"Oh. You're asking me." I was genuinely surprised; something I've been, in theory, but I was interested to notice that there was an actual emotion associated with the vague uncertainty that hit me when suddenly approached with new information. "Oh. I need a moment to think."

And that was true. I was going to kill him in a few days; I couldn't exactly say the full truth and confess my love to him, or killing him would quickly become impossible. But it was also clear that he liked me, and rejecting him would make the next few days far more painful than I was willing to sit through. I couldn't break Stephen's beautiful, fragile heart. Not right before his murder, not ever.

I constructed the closest thing I could to the truth. A few words that would buy me the time I needed to kill him. "Frankly, I'm surprised you're standing by me as a friend after tonight, let alone... you know. I'll be honest with you." The butterflies churned in my stomach, and all those thoughts were forcing their way to the surface, pushing up against the inside of my eyes as welling-up tears. "I..."

It burst out of me in the barest whisper, but I felt so exposed. I felt like a specimen pinned to a board, and the words were the blood spilling from the open wound, the first cut of my dissection. "I like you, Stephen." And there were the tears, quiet and overwhelming. "I like you."

And then came the lies, and they were so, so easy to tell compared to that. It took so much strength, but still, lies were easier than the truth. "But I- you saw what happened tonight. I need some time to sort all of this out. I can't give you any of the attention you deserve while I'm trying to avoid being killed. Once this is all over, I'll..."

I knew this was the best case scenario. I knew it was better than rejecting him, or putting myself through the heartbreak of getting involved right before he was to die. But lying to him still hurt like hell. And inevitably, the truth came out, even if it was all just to sell the lie. The truth came out in a devastating flood, each word dripping with emotion. I hated it.

"I want you to feel like the most gorgeous and important thing in the world. Like a prince. I want you to look out at the world around you from some great height and realise that you're so much better, so much more perfect than anyone or anything else in all of creation. I want you to feel like a god on Earth. You are so beautiful, so good, so resplendent that it's hard for me to believe you could ever be anything as lowly as a god. You're something else, Stephen. You're the only thing in the universe that matters. I don't deserve you. Nobody does. Nobody could ever come close to deserving you. I want you to feel like you're beautiful and perfect because that is all you could ever possibly be, and if it's even possible for someone to disagree, only utter delusion could lead them to that conclusion. I want you to feel like that every day, Stephen. Every waking moment. And I want to be the one to give that to you, if only I deserved to do something anywhere near as magnificent as that."

I felt the back of his hand gently wiping away my tears, and it only made me cry all that much harder. There was a long, long silence before he spoke, and I heard his own crying in his voice. "Alex," he whispered, "...you mean that?"

"Oh, god, I do." I choked on the words. He shifted, sitting up on one elbow, and I turned my head away from him. He wanted to kiss me, and that was my fault. If I let him, I'd lose control completely. I was barely holding on as it was. Telling just that tiny piece of the truth helped me breathe, but it was risky. "I mean it. Believe me when I say I want to be with you, and I'm not making excuses. I just... need you to give me some time."

He took a deep, sharp, breath. "Okay." I risked a glance at him, and I thought I glimpsed a wide smile in the moonlight, right underneath those tears. "You're sure we can't cheat, and start a little early?"

"Give me two weeks. If Ezra's true to his word, it'll be dealt with one way or another by then." He nodded, and the grim implication of my own potential death was ignored. He thought I was the only one in danger, and it was best kept that way.

And with that, we laid down beside each other, still crying. In his mind, we were whole new people with a new, shared future. Nothing had changed for me, except that he had had a glimpse into how I felt, and my heart was that much lighter.

"Just one thing," I whispered into the dark before committing to silence.

"Mm?" Stephen answered, his weariness showing through. It appeared evident that he would sleep, leaving me alone in the dark by myself. Alone in darkness summarised my whole life, and that was fine by me. In fact, it was what I was desperate to return to.

"Why do you like me?" It was the simple, honest question that I needed answered. It was self-interested, but what, honestly, wasn't?

He thought on it for a moment. "Well... I'll probably be able to answer that someday soon." It was a cryptic way of saying what I best guessed to be, 'I can't figure out the words right now'. "...but, I guess I could ask you the same question."

And oh, how I wished I knew the answer. I felt like there was something special about Stephen, but in truth, he was just as much a person as anyone else. There was no rhyme or reason behind this reckless, horrific, all-encompassing love, and that made it all the more frustrating.

Passing time used to be simple, but every second that Stephen was beside me seemed to go excruciatingly slowly. One can't just make oneself sleep. Sitting there like that, staring at the roof and trying not to get any closer to Stephen, was exhausting, but I still couldn't rest.

I made the best of it. I planned every aspect of his kidnapping in my head. The timing, how we'd get him in the car, where exactly we'd go, how I'd kill him, how I'd keep my family ignorant of what I was doing.

The Houghs were the biggest problem. Ezra would kill me in a week, if Ophelia didn't prove my guilt by then. They'd immediately blame Stephen going missing on me. If I managed to kill not one, but both of the Houghs, at the same time, before the week was up, and get away with it, I could go free. But only then. In every other situation, it was a choice between life without parole, and death.

I knew which one I'd rather have. Killing the Houghs

might be possible, but getting away with it was a whole other story. I supposed I could kill them and just go to jail if that was what I needed to do; but I'd have liked a better plan. I didn't want just a small chance of freedom, and I knew I could do better.

This was all happening because I killed their father. Mr Hough was important to them, so important that it was worth revenge eight years later, when they finally knew for sure who had done it. They were important to each other, as well. Logically, it followed that their mother was important to them, too.

Killing her would be of absolutely no help to me, but it wasn't the only thing I could do. The idea that came to me wasn't a long-term solution, but it would buy me time to kidnap Stephen and come up with a full, better plan.

I'd talk to Atarah about it in the morning, but that night, I planned Stephen's kidnapping, Mrs Hough's 'accident', and my subsequent escape and/or murder of Ophelia and Ezra. I kept my eye on the window, watching as I had silently promised for any break-ins, but nothing happened throughout the whole night. Stephen got up and climbed over me at one point, thinking I was asleep- I closed my eyes and laid still just long enough for him to be convinced of it- and went to the toilet, but that was it. He tripped over Atarah's bag on the way back in, and it took all of my energy to refrain from asking if he was okay, to keep up my facade of being asleep. After a moment of shuffling on the floor, while my eyes stayed closed, he climbed back over me, his proximity burning in my awareness.

But the sun came up, and Atarah's window stayed locked, and nobody entered. Atarah was safe for at least one more day. Her persecutor had, as far as I could be aware, decided to be merciful.

By the time Atarah was awake, I was tired through and through, but it was still impossible to sleep. I got out of bed, leaving the sleeping Stephen where he was- as painful as it was to put any distance between us- and sat beside Atarah, quietly telling her the plan. With a yawn, she agreed it was a good idea. When I told her about the fact that there was no disturbance last night, she seemed surprised that I'd actually stayed up the whole time.

"You didn't have to do that just for me," she said softly around big sips of water. "That's adorable. You're sure you don't care about me?"

I sighed. "I wouldn't have been able to sleep anyway."

It took a while for Stephen to wake up, and I couldn't help but smile when I saw him gently raise his head, his hair falling in his eyes. I loved him, and it was the worst.

"So," he muttered, staring through half-open lids, "my head fucking hurts."

"You want some water?" Atarah said, offering him her water bottle. He shuffled over to take it and quickly finished it off. Atarah made a face that he didn't see; it was obvious that she was hungover, too, and regretting the loss. I also felt like shit physically, but lack of sleep was the main cause.

"Fucking hell. I'd have thought I dreamt last night if I wasn't here," Stephen muttered. "Ezra's crazy."

"Yeah." I appreciated how strongly he was on my side, but the sentiment wasn't exactly helpful. "It was... an experience."

"I promise you, it'll be fine." Stephen sounded sure, repeating that for what must be the fifth time. I didn't have any use for empty platitudes, although I couldn't possibly think any less of him for it. I just nodded and let him believe he'd helped.

Going home was a chore. We went back to Stephen's house to drop him off and pick up our cars, and I dealt with the pain of saying goodbye to him- and the exciting promise in the smile he gave me, even though I knew I would kill him before that promise was fulfilled. And then I had to drive home without falling asleep at the wheel and crashing.

When I did get home safely, I went straight to bed. I'd texted my parents last night to explain, so I was saved that questioning; and maybe they'd want to know more later, but for now, they let me sleep.

I woke up at dinnertime with a worse headache than I'd

gone to sleep with.

Sunday was pretty much wasted. I had until Saturday to make this work.

I needed to get started.

Chapter Thirteen - Stephen Minett, Iterum

Originally, I had planned to poison Mrs Hough. I was going to find a fungus or a mould that was bad to ingest and put it in her food, to send her to the hospital for a few days. That, however, proved to be nearly impossible, once I considered how I'd access her food. After following Ophelia home from work on Monday night at a distance, I got their address. They had two cars, one of which Ophelia had been driving, so it was easy to figure out which was her mother's. As far as I knew, Mrs Hough didn't have a job; she made her money off of property and rent. When Mr Hough was alive, he'd worked in a corporate position to add to their riches and finance all that property in the first place, and she hadn't had to work. It was possible that Mrs Hough would've gotten a job since then, but I didn't believe it.

Ideally, she would've been hurt right as Stephen was being kidnapped, but I couldn't possibly have timed it. Stephen worked Thursday, Friday and Saturday, and the kidnapping was to happen one of those three days, so I gave myself a buffer of one day. On Tuesday night, I drove to the Hough's house and cut the brake line on Mrs Hough's car. It wasn't the perfect solution, but if nothing had happened by Wednesday night, I could always try to break into their house and poison her.

When I got home, I sat in my bathroom mixing a batch of chloroform. It was easier than it should have ever been to make, pouring one bottle from my mother's cupboard into one from the laundry room and waiting. There were less than forty-eight hours to go until Stephen was dead, and interestingly, I felt nothing about it. It wasn't an empty nothing; my suspicion was that too many emotions were cancelling each other out.

My phone ringing was unexpected. Atarah was frantic and buzzing when I answered, spouting that there had been a new development.

"So you remember how nobody came after me after the party?" she said. We had risked speaking exactly once since the party. I'd told her what had happened that night we slept over, what I'd talked to him about, and she'd laughed about it. Apparently, she'd heard most of what I'd said to him, and I was glad I couldn't have been embarrassed about that fact.

"Of course, yes," I said, to prompt her to continue.

"Well, that doesn't mean someone's not paying attention. Guess what I found in the bottom of my schoolbag."

"...not a threat, surely? Three strikes, you're out? That's what it said?"

"I'll read it to you." Atarah clears her throat. "*I am still watching. Consider yourself lucky. Don't forget - Alex is mine.*"

"*Alex is mine?*"

"I don't know, but this isn't Ophelia. It could be Ezra warning me to stay away so I don't get hurt, but then this implies that he thinks I'm going to kill you, to take his murder away from him. I doubt it was him, but the point is, I think

I'm safe. Regardless of who sent this, they did away with their 'three strikes' thing."

"Well, that's good news." I looked down at the mixture in front of me; the fumes were obnoxious, so I backed away. "I cut Mrs Hough's brake line tonight, so if you can think of any way to make sure she gets in her car Thursday morning, that'll be great."

"You should've cut the brake line on Ophelia's car too. Hopefully they'll all go on a family trip down the highway or something." Atarah sounded far too cheery for the sentence she was saying. "I mean, I don't honestly feel bad if Mrs Hough dies. Eat the rich."

"She won't die. Nobody drives fast in the winter. She'll crash, and go to the hospital, and then Ezra and Ophelia will be too distracted to notice when we kidnap Stephen. And then I can escape, and they won't kill me, and I won't go to jail."

"Do you have a plan?" Atarah asked, and I wanted to tell her I did.

"I was hoping you'd come with me, but beyond that, I have no plan."

Atarah paused for a moment. "I... want to say things will be fine, but we'll have to see. In a lot of ways, the ball's not in our court. We're going forward with the Stephen plan, though, right?"

I took a deep breath. "Yeah. No matter what, I can't live with these emotions. At least if I go to jail, I won't be in agony missing him all the time."

"Okay. I've got to go, but we'll talk tomorrow," she said, and hung up.

When the chemicals finished reacting, I hid the chloroform in my wardrobe. It was an unclean reaction, and the mix would've been contaminated with side-products, but it would do. It would take longer to knock him out, but chloroform takes several minutes to work anyway. With Atarah's help, being caught wasn't the issue I would face. It would be holding Stephen, struggling, for at least five minutes and not being able to fend off the guilt telling me to let him go.

This was a pattern I'd been in before. Bailey was quick, but Mr Hough and Amanda took time to kill. I had spent days sitting at the dinner table with my parents when I knew I was about to kill someone and I acted normal. When they asked how school was, I had told them lies that sounded the same as my truths. But those times, when I was emotionless, it made complete sense that it was easy. When I was apprehensive, guilt-ridden and scared, it shouldn't have been as easy. But it was. My parents didn't even twig that anything was different.

On Wednesday, Ophelia wasn't at lunch. I spotted Ezra, and watching him carefully, I noticed when he first checked his phone and his laugh dropped. I knew my plan had worked. Ezra promptly left, and neither of them were at school the next day.

My encounters with Stephen in the leadup to kidnapping him were strange, to say the least. He spoke to me a few times, and each time, he was kind and gentle, making me laugh, and making me feel safe and protected. I knew enough about people to know that he was doing it deliberately. He'd talk about a hypothetical, long-distance future where we went to college together, and he'd casually put his arm around me. It made my heart flutter, and I took some comfort in the fact that my heart would stop fluttering tomorrow.

His death was so, so, tantalisingly close.

Atarah sent me a bunch of frenzied texts on Thursday morning, demanding to know if I was ready. I told her it felt the same as it always did, and she called me a liar.

Stephen came by my locker in the morning. He was standing in front of me, eyes glittering, dressed in a tight grey shirt and a gold-coloured jacket. He was real, but it didn't feel like it. It felt like a dream. It felt like a day that should never have come.

Ezra and Ophelia weren't there; I could only hope I'd bought myself enough time. I knew their mother wasn't all that bad off- she'd posted on social media thanking people for their support in her recovery, showing off her sling and forehead gauze. I was scared it wasn't enough.

I met up with Atarah after school, and she was buzzing. I didn't know what I was feeling, but it wasn't anything positive. "Do you think something is wrong with you?" I asked her as we walked towards the gates. "Considering what you're excited about doing?"

"Who gives a shit?" Atarah answered, her grin stretching across her whole face. "Let's fucking go."

"It's the last movie of the night. We still have a few hours," I reminded her. "Don't jump the gun."

Time felt like it shouldn't be passing. I realised as I sat at home, trying to focus on homework and being unable to do so, that I wasn't ready. Unreadiness. Not a feeling I had expected, and not one I liked.

I didn't have another day to wait, though. I needed as much time as possible to deal with the Houghs, and I needed these emotions gone. I felt nothing about the fact that I'd be emotionless soon; and even though that didn't feel like the normal state of affairs anymore, it was safe. Being empty was safe, and it meant being without pain. I needed that again.

I wore black to the theatre. So did Atarah, but that was usual for her. Stephen was working, but we knew that. He looked at me a little strangely as we came in, but the furrow in his brow quickly straightened out. We walked up to him, and it was obvious that I was nervous; but when hadn't I been, when he was around?

"Is this a new tradition of yours?" he asked as I handed him the money, not even needing to specify what we wanted. Only one movie was playing this late. "Last movie of the night?"

I surprised myself with what I said- was able to say. "Maybe I'm just coming to see you."

It was something strong and strange, having the gall to flirt with him hours before his kidnapping and subsequent murder, but I couldn't put my finger on what to call it. Stephen smiled, and I enjoyed the last happy moment I was going to get before my emotions were gone.

"You're cute," he said mischievously, and I tried to ignore the fluttering in my heart. He slid us the tickets, and although I wanted to hang around longer, Atarah's fingers on my forearm reminded me that that was a bad idea.

"See you later," I said quietly as we walked away. Stephen's eyes went to Atarah's grip on my arm, and then my clothes again. If he couldn't work out that I was a murderer, given all the evidence- including a literal confession- then he couldn't work out that something was going on.

We slid into the correct theatre, and found that we were alone. I was prepared for that to not be the case, but it made things easier.

"Hang on," Atarah said as I tried to head to a seat. "You go sit down. I'm going to go repark the car in the right place, and break the cameras."

In carefully crafted conversations with Stephen, I'd learned that only two employees were in the theatre each night, and they cleaned at the same time. They only ever checked the tapes in the morning. Breaking the cameras would be a safe way of hiding our actions from anyone.

"Alright. Be quick," I told her. Atarah left through the door we'd identified, and I sat with my nervous apprehension, and wondered if I'd really be able to go through with this. I had a water bottle full of chloroform and a cloth. I had a hoodie and a bandana to cover my face just in case the cameras couldn't be broken. I had the experience and the need to get this done.

But I fundamentally didn't want to do it, in my heart. As much as I wanted him dead, my deepest baseline instinct was to keep him alive. Instinct. A useless phenomenon I'd never had before, that was urging me to keep him alive.

I didn't let it interfere with the cold rationality of the truth. Stephen Minett needed to die if I were to function on any real level ever again.

The previews started, and then Atarah came back through the door, giving me a big thumbs up. As she got to where I was sitting, she explained. "Easy. I climbed up on some bins and bashed the glass in with a rock. Jammed the rock in there just to be sure. There was only two of them, and I covered my hair with my hoodie just in case they could catch anything, but they should be pretty much destroyed right now."

"Good. Great." My nerves were showing, but Atarah was kind enough not to comment on them.

The movie started, and I kept losing track of what was going on on the screen in front of me. It was a romantic comedy, which was terrible. It was about a cynical man going through a divorce and falling in love with a ballerina girl. Stephen was not a ballerina girl and I was not a man going through a divorce, but when he stared at her with wonder in his eyes before turning away, certain he could never have her, I understood. I felt that. I felt like that when I watched Stephen dance for the first time. When I watched him confess that he loved her, despite feeling like she could never love him back- for very different reasons than mine- I began to cry. Atarah looked at me strangely, but realisation soon dawned on her, and she let me be.

In this movie, all ended well, and she loved him anyway. Stephen couldn't love me, not in the way he thought he could. I was sure of it.

As soon as the credits rolled, reality hit me like a speeding truck. It wasn't just days, or hours, until we were going to kidnap Stephen. It was minutes.

"Fuck yes," Atarah whispered under her breath. She stood and walked towards the front of the theatre, and I steeled my heart. It was time.

There was still the possibility that Stephen would not be the one cleaning this theatre tonight, and although we had a failsafe for that, it would've been a great excuse to walk away. To say this plan wasn't going to work, and we had to leave.

But despite how common they were now, I recognised that this was simply an emotion holding me back. Fear was as fake as anything else. My plan with Amanda, although it occurred five years ago, was no less bold than this one. I had done it before.

Stephen walked into the theatre, right in front of Atarah.

"Hey, Stephen, can I talk to you for a minute?" Atarah said, gesturing for him to come closer to her. The door swung shut, and I opened my bottle of chloroform, pouring it out onto the cloth. There was no going back, as soon as I did this.

Atarah had drawn Stephen's attention, and his back was to me. I slowly, silently began to walk down the aisle towards him. "About what?" he asked, casual, unbothered.

"Alex." I told Atarah to say whatever works, and although I hadn't expected her to talk about me, it did seem to grab Stephen's attention. "You and Alex, to be exact."

"Is there a problem?" Stephen asked, more confused than anything, although I could hear a tinge of annoyance. He had never, ever spoken to me with that tinge of annoyance, but I'd overheard it enough times in his conversations with others. I was close now, only a few more steps until I'd be upon him.

"Oh, no. I just want to ask you how you feel, what's going on between you two, you know, I'm curious. Alex won't tell me anything." Although Atarah wouldn't directly look at me, she could see that I was close, and talked just long enough for me to reach.

When I clamped the cloth over Stephen's mouth, the deed was done, and we'd have no choice but to go through with it.

His hands came up to grip at mine, and I watched Atarah's eyes go wide and her grin stretch with excitement. Stephen should've been so much stronger than me- this should've been so difficult- but his attempts at self-defence were surprisingly weak. He gripped my hand with both of his and tried to kick back at me, but it almost felt half-hearted. He leaned back, eyes up, trying to get a glimpse of me. Was he really as stupid as that, to not realise it was me?

I didn't want to look him in the eyes, because I knew what I'd see was betrayal. I closed my eyes and tried not to cry again.

"How long does this take?" Atarah asked impatiently, poking her head out of the door. Stephen made a noise- why was he not screaming for help already?- and kicked at her. She stepped easily out of his reach.

"A few minutes. I'm not sure how long it'll last until he

wakes up." My voice was soft and regretful, but if Stephen had any doubt it was me, he knew now. "This isn't the most effective way of doing this, but it's the easiest to get away with. You have to hold a struggling person still for several minutes. It's difficult."

"How'd you do it with Amanda?" Atarah asked, completely cool with having a casual conversation as I held Stephen close to my chest and smothered him with chloroform. Stephen made another noise, some attempt to speak, but I squeezed with the arm around his neck that held him in place, and the words disappeared.

"She was a lot weaker than this, but even then, she... fought." It was almost suspicious, how easy this was, and Atarah noticed, too.

Stephen kept trying to speak, but seemed to be struggling to breathe properly. He was choking on every breath, and he seemed to be drifting off. "I told you, you probably could've just told him to get in the car and he would've done it. Kidnapping him didn't have to be this difficult."

"Well, we're doing it now. It's probably so easy because chloroform is a euphoriant. I don't know." There was an odd numbness that covered every horrible emotion I had about what was going on. I could smell coconut, buttered popcorn, and chloroform. It was so, so terrible, but it was also fine.

Atarah shrugged. It was just like every murder I'd committed before, except she was here and I felt something. That something was horrific guilt and sadness.

Every movement he made was a reminder of my betrayal. And yet, when he went still, it was even worse.

As soon as I lowered the cloth, Atarah came to my side, and we held him up like we were helping a drunk friend as we carried him to the door. She kicked the door open, and together, we dragged Stephen's unconscious body to the car. Lights illuminated the asphalt, striking weird shadows across everything, and the feeling of unreality returned again. This was just like every other murder, except it wasn't at all.

With some difficulty, we managed to get him into the shotgun seat, and Atarah ran back inside to make sure all of our stuff was removed from the theatre. I got into the driver's side and stared at the boy beside me, like his unconscious form would tell me everything was fine.

I reached across and gently brushed his hair out of his eyes. Chloroform is not the most effective sedative, not really, but he was completely out of it, unmoving. He was still gorgeous, still amazing, still the best person I'd ever known.

What if I killed him and it wasn't enough? What if I missed him for the rest of time? What if someone else came along who reminded me of him, and I fell in love with them?

It was too late to change my mind, though. Stephen would not forgive me for this, even if he wasn't smart enough to see it coming. I would rather him dead than hating me.

Atarah soon returned, climbing into the backseat with the rest of my chloroform and her bag. "Right, let's go to Hell," she said. "What are you going to do when you get there?"

"I guess my original plan was to beat him up or something, but I don't know." I swallowed back the disgust I felt. That, too, would disappear soon enough. "He'll wake up on the way, and we'll probably have to knock him out again. Let's just go."

Leaving the city was physically easy, but emotionally, every mile we travelled felt like another weight on my chest. I knew I was doing what had to be done, but the emotional side of me wanted nothing more than to turn around and go home. It was like forcing a dog into a bath. The bath was necessary and good, but the dog couldn't understand that, and did everything possible to escape the water. I was both the dog and the person bathing it. Every mile to Hell was an inch closer to the water, and the dog was screaming to be spared this experience.

Stephen did wake up at one point, and Atarah gleefully knocked him back out again with the rest of the chloroform. I was grateful that I didn't have to do it.

"However you're going to kill him," Atarah remarked at one point, "don't get any blood in the car. That's always what gets people caught. Also, make sure he didn't leave some hair behind or something. Are you going to kill him violently? I think you should."

"I think that's just what you want to see," I told her, and she shrugged.

"We became friends because that's what I wanted to see. At least choke him out or something."

"I'll consider it." The road was dark and empty between towns. Each place seemed to go by far too quickly; I could swear it was further to Battle Creek. I realised I was speeding and dialled it back down, but even then, Jackson came up quickly on us.

"We don't have to go all the way to Hell. There's plenty of lakes around here that we can stop at," Atarah said with a yawn. I quickly shook my head.

"We can't stop anywhere with people. Especially if you want a violent death. There's a lake north-west of Hell with no residential areas around it. That's where we're going," I told her, and she accepted it with a shrug.

Every so often, I looked over at Stephen, at his peaceful face in sleep. Would he be so pretty and peaceful when he was dead? Would I even be able to look down at his gorgeous face and squeeze the life out of it?

I almost missed the turnoffs I had to be taking. "I didn't think it would take this long to get out here," Atarah complained, as we exited the highway. "Can I go through his phone?"

"Can you wait until we stop? Twenty minutes."

"You don't want to waste any time, do you?" Atarah asked, leaning on the back of my seat. "Are you excited to kill him?"

"No. I want it over." I gritted my teeth around the words. "This pain has gone on long enough. I can't love him anymore."

"I hope this works, for your sake," Atarah said, patting me gently on the shoulder. Her touch sparked annoyance in me, and that mingled with every emotion in existence swirling in my chest. I didn't want to think about it. I didn't want to think at all until these emotions were gone and I was back to being myself again.

'*Myself*' was empty, but that was fine. That was safe.

In the darkness, it was hard to find the road. If it wasn't for a little sign under the trees signalling access to the lake, I'd have missed it. I swerved the car onto the road at the last second, and Stephen groaned numbly. The dirt road jostled the car, waking him up further. I'd never been to this lake before, but I'd been through the area and presumed it to be empty enough. Thankfully, it was.

I drove to the very end of the road and stopped the car. The sound of it braking on the dirt and the stillness in the frozen air sounded like finality. There was no more waiting. There was only time for action.

Atarah was having far more fun than I was. "Great." She climbed out of the back seat and opened Stephen's side door, as I sat there trying to catch my breath. I could feel myself close to tears, but I couldn't explain why. "Give me his phone. I'm going to snoop while you figure out what you want to do."

"Thank you," I said. I was unsure how she'd anticipated I'd need time, but grateful she had. As grateful as I could be, anyway. "Just a few minutes."

Stephen moaned lightly and tried to sit up. Atarah shoved him back against the seat as she fished in his pockets for his phone. She opened it up, the bright blue light illuminating her face. When she identified it took a fingerprint to open, she took his hand- although he tried to tug it away, she simply gripped tighter- and pressed the button against his finger. I found myself getting annoyed with how callously she handled him, before I remembered that I was about to murder him.

"Okay, I'll be out here. Don't kill him without me," she said, before slamming the door shut and walking out towards the lake.

Stephen muttered something, turning to face me. I had no idea what to do, but I didn't like that he was moving and speaking again. I had imagined, back when I'd first planned to kill him, that I'd want to see him suffer. That if I took out my anger with violence, I'd enjoy getting rid of these feelings he didn't deserve, and that would be the end of it.

I still thought he didn't deserve my feelings, but now, it was because I was nowhere near as good as he was. He deserved much, much better. Such a death was unfair. Now, I wanted him to die as quickly, quietly, and painlessly as possible; it would end in less guilt, and I could move on faster.

That, and I knew him as far too kind of a person to die.

"Alex." That time, I understood what he said. No, this wouldn't do. I had to knock him out again.

We were out of chloroform, so I'd have to do it myself.

Every movement was emotionally devastating, but I did what I had to do. I climbed over into the passenger's seat, but to do so, I had to straddle him, and the warmth of his skin, even through two layers of clothes, was burning hot and terrifying. I wanted to run away. This proximity, even in this context, scared the hell out of me.

Stephen looked up at me with his watery, blue-grey eyes, and his expression was entirely unreadable, mostly disoriented. His voice sounded hoarse, but the words were clear. "Listen to me," he said. We were so close, as close as we were in his bed, closer even. My hands found their way to his throat, and he gripped my wrist with one hand. I think I began to cry around then.

I pushed, hard. I watched his eyes pop in surprise, the pressure waking him up even more. That was the opposite of what I wanted. "Stop," he choked out, and it hurt, it hurt so bad. "-for just a moment-!"

"Stephen," I whispered, nigh involuntarily. I saw one of my tears land on his face. His face, slowly turning red and purple. One of his hands clenched my wrist harder, and the other came to grip at the back of my head. How he thought to fight me like that, I couldn't process.

I couldn't process anything properly, it seemed, because I was looking at his lips, and there were the upturned edges of what almost could've been a smile. I must've been delirious at that stage of emotion, imagining him smiling up at me as I choked him out.

I wasn't sure if I would be able to stop when he passed out. I might've just killed him like this.

I felt his hand pulling me, and the idea of what he could've been doing came to me, but it felt like another delirium. It felt completely, categorically impossible. At best, an escape ploy. No, he couldn't have meant to pull me closer, he couldn't have been smiling. He couldn't have whispered my name the same way he spoke to me in his bedroom, when we almost kissed.

I didn't believe it until he actually kissed me.

His lips burned like fire against mine, cold like ice, and I melted so easily into him. It wasn't by choice; my heart was captured in an inescapable net and tethered so closely to his it was impossible to separate where he ended and I began. I wasn't aware of anything except the fact that Stephen Minett was kissing me. Desperately. His hands scrabbled at me to pull me closer, and as my hands naturally fell from his throat, he moved away from me for barely a second to cough and regain his lungs before pulling me back in. I didn't have a chance to think. That kiss sucked the air from my lungs and the life from my body. In that moment, he killed me. He kissed me like his life depended on it- and it did.

When he broke away, his hands were gently holding either side of my face, and he had the softest smile that reached all the way to his eyes, the way I'd have expected him to look at me after the kiss we almost had in his bedroom. In that second, I re-evaluated the situation and realised I was in far, far, far over my head. I was drowning. If he was playing the game, finding a way to escape- he had won. I'd let him take the victory.

I needed a moment to think.

Me scrambling out of the car was not the reaction Stephen had expected. "Alex, don't-" he cried, but I hit the icy dirt road and pulled myself to my feet. I was still crying, I realised when my vision was blurry. I didn't need to see where I was going. I found my way onto the ice of the lake, and there I ran into the only other person on Earth who would be able to help me.

"Stephen's- oh, he's probably about to escape," I told her, rubbing the water out of my eyes. Something in my throat caused me to choke and hiccup. It was a sob. I could still feel Stephen's lips burning against mine, even now. "I can't kill him, Atarah."

"He's... not about to escape," she said, cautious and confused. I felt so cold, everywhere but my lips. It took a moment for me to understand what Atarah had even said, with how many thoughts were swirling in my head. "He's not going anywhere."

"...why do you say that?" I finally found words through the haze of emotions. Beneath them, somewhere in my logical brain that Stephen had just murdered, an answer was forming, but it didn't make sense. It couldn't make sense.

"I knew something was up." Atarah had the same triumphant tone in her voice that she did when she confronted me about being a murderer. "He acts different around you. To you, he's kind, thoughtful, gentle, all that shit, but he was never that nice to me, and the thing is, I didn't think I was the odd one out. I thought you were. But I was never sure. He definitely liked you- I was trying to push you towards him because I was sure he liked you- but I should've realised I was picking up on more than just that. You remember how he knew which room was mine?"

"You have an A on your door. That's how he could tell."

"It sounded like an excuse. And it was an excuse. It's because he's been in my room before. He's not so blindingly stupid that he'd think you're innocent when you confessed to his face, Alex."

"Then why did he pretend he misunderstood? It doesn't make sense." My lips burned and my fingers were so cold. I could feel hope brewing and I wanted to squash it. Why was my immediate reaction to squash it?

"I don't know. I don't think he knew we were going to kidnap him until recently, but he's always known you were a murderer, Alex. I don't know if he's exactly like you, like he's emotionless, but he's in love with you. Maniacal, obsessive love, the same way you love him. *He* was leaving the threats, because he thought I was a rival. Look."

And she showed me the screen she had open on Stephen's phone. It was an album full of just pictures of me. Photos downloaded from the internet, selfies we'd taken together at various parties throughout the years, candid photos I hadn't even realised he'd been taking. There was even several drawings of me that he'd done in that folder, including one of the paintings I'd seen in his room. A person with long black hair, above the Chinese character meaning 'perfect'. I started to cry again.

"And look at this copycat," she grinned, showing me something else that it took a moment to understand. It was clearly a draft of a suicide note, but as I read through, I realised just whose suicide note it was supposed to be, with mentions of loving his sister and missing his father. Stephen was writing Ezra's suicide note.

When I turned around to look, the love of my life was walking towards us, weak on his feet for understandable reasons. He held out his arms to me, and I couldn't stop myself from running towards him. Touching him was too much, though. I could only stop to stand and stare with tears in my eyes, waiting for something I didn't know. An acknowledgement that this was a joke, or that I'd misunderstood, or perhaps some sign that this was all a dream.

But all I got was Stephen Minett, trying to fight back a hopeful smile. With an upbeat tone, he asked, "can we talk?"

Chapter Fourteen - Alex and Stephen, Iterum

I fell to my knees on the ice. It wasn't a dream. He wasn't about to tell me this was all fake. This was real.

Stephen Minett knew I was a murderer, and he loved me anyway. He loved me far beyond that.

All I could feel was joy, and it came out of me in a burst of bubbly, ugly laughter. Stephen knelt in front of me; his gentle touch on my fingers still burnt, but it was real. It was honest.

Loving Stephen, and building a world alongside him, was possible.

But I needed answers. When the laughter stopped shaking my chest, and I'd wiped the tears from my eyes, I demanded them. "I don't understand this at all," I confessed. "Please explain. From the beginning. The whole truth."

Stephen took a deep breath. "Should I start from the day I fell in love with you, or before that?"

"No, before." My heart sung when I heard him say he

loved me. "What are you like, Stephen? Are you like me?"

"No. You're completely emotionless, or, you were. I'm not." His emotions didn't drop from his voice when he was being honest like mine did. "I don't care for anyone in the world except you, I can't feel empathy, and I never get sad, just angry. I can't remember if I'm a psychopath or a sociopath, but it's one of the two. I don't know if there's a difference."

"Depends who you ask," Atarah interjected, before realising what she was interrupting. "Sorry, continue."

Stephen pretty much ignored her. "For as long as I can remember, I was kind of disgusted by humanity. Everyone else was weak and boring and useless, and nobody except me was worth my time. I made friends only to use them, and sometimes I played them off against each other because it was fun." He stopped for a second, gauging my reaction. "That doesn't bother you, right? Even with your new emotions? I want to be sure-"

"Nothing you could ever do could ever bother me. I assure you. It does not matter what you say or what you confess to. I am in love with you and there is nothing I can do about it."

"Good." Stephen took a deep breath. "I have a lot of things to tell you. I've been in love with you a very, very long time, Alex. I thought this day would never come."

"How long?" The question was breathed into the freezing air, barely audible, barely heard. Stephen was still smiling, and it was beautiful.

"Always." My heart could hardly take hearing it. "You probably don't remember the day we met. Freshman year, orientation day, I saw you for the first time. You had the beauty and grace of an ancient deity, and for the first time in my life, I felt like there was something truly beautiful for me to appreciate. Not just exciting, or fun, or interesting, but beautiful." He spoke with reverence, and it was almost too much. I wasn't sure if I had stopped crying- I could hardly pay attention to my own body- but I definitely started crying again, or harder. One of the two.

"And I kept an eye on you. We spoke the next day, and you were just... there was nothing I could put my finger on, but everything you said, everything you did, everything you are... it was all just so perfect, and so much better than anyone else. Everyone else sucks, except you. You're the only person I truly feel is worth anything in this world, besides me. I was searching for something better than me, and I found it in you."

He paused to let me process his words, and I needed it, because I was beyond sobbing. He knew better than to try and touch me any more than he already was. He was easily overwhelming.

"I think I was in love with you at first sight, but it just kept getting stronger." His voice choked a little. "It snowballed. You quickly became the only thing I was living for, and you still are. I kept up the appearance of normalcy, but everything I did, I tried to angle it to make you fall in love with me. I didn't get too close that you'd consider me a friend first and a lover second. I didn't date anyone else- although I wouldn't have anyway, because everyone else is gross, and nobody but you deserves to be so close to me, let alone have sex with me. The whole idea of sex is pretty disgusting to me, actually, unless it's with you." He said it completely deadpan, honest. "I did everything based around you. I joined queer club because of you, changed into every elective you were in, befriended your sisters- ask them about me if you want. Ellis was the one who told me about Bailey, that's how I knew. I found out what you did pretty early on, and between that and a lot of paying close attention, I figured out what you were like. And honestly, it was as good as it was bad for me, because I knew you'd have the genuine, honest me, if you'd have anyone- but you wouldn't love me unless a miracle came around."

"How'd you find out?" It was Atarah who asked, not me. Stephen gave her a cursory glance before turning his gaze back to me, but he answered her.

"I remember when Amanda died." Stephen was so nonchalant about the whole thing. "I saw her bullying you. I know you were good at stopping her friends from really joining in, but I did everything I could to help. I tried to be discreet about helping you, because at that point, I wasn't sure about your personality. But when you dated Kai, I knew something was going on. It's hard to explain the feeling I got, aside from the frustrating, heartbreaking jealousy. But I knew you had a plan. Amanda went off the rails, and I heard about what happened in the bathroom. I almost turned them in, but when I was following you I overheard your conversation with the teacher and I knew exactly what you were about to do. And I honestly wanted to help. I told a different teacher the exact same thing. And when she 'killed herself', that was only impressive. Because you got away with it."

I was silent, listening to his explanation. I simply nodded for him to continue. The tears were drying up, and it was impossible to deny how this was the best thing that could've possibly happened to me. I didn't think there would be a murder tonight. Fuck returning to how things were. I knew I was being emotional right now, but all I could think about was how great this was.

"I found out about Ezra and Ophelia's dad not much later, and Bailey too. It didn't change how I felt. It never could. These feelings only got stronger, and worse. They began to change me. I used to be impulsive, but I couldn't take any risks when it came to you- I had to be sure you were comfortable, and you loved me back, before I could do anything. If you rejected me, I would've killed myself without a second thought. That is how little I care about everything that isn't you. I was, and am, extremely wary of anyone who comes close to you. Every time you dated someone, I did a little social engineering. I got people to make Kai like someone else, Maybelle was told you were planning to break up with her so she'd do it first, and I got a friend to make Beth cheat on you. Knox had to be threatened and bribed, but that was it. And Atarah, well." He acknowledged her properly for the first time. "I saw how close you two got so quickly, and it terrified me. I thought you fell in love with me when I helped you outside the theatre, and that made it hurt even worse that you might've found someone else. So I skipped straight to the threats. I was wrong about that. So, Atarah. Sorry." He didn't sound like he meant it, but he didn't have to say it for my benefit, so it was probably genuine. Even knowing he was a psychopath, he still came across as so sweet.

"I have so many fucking questions," Atarah whispered, her eyes wide open in awe. We were still crouched on an icy lake just outside of Hell, but not a single one of us cared about that at that moment.

"Yeah." Stephen shrugged. "I was planning on killing you, to be honest. Never done it before, but I think I'd have managed. Now I'm going to kill Ezra tomorrow. I mean, I won't let him hurt you, Alex. No way."

"You can't kill Ezra." Oh, I had subjects I needed to return to, but this was important too. "Ophelia will come after me if he dies. They have to both die if we're going to kill them. And- I'm struggling to find a way to make their deaths inconspicuous. I put their mother in hospital to buy myself some time."

"That was smart," Stephen said, eyes glowing. "How about you go get an alibi and I'll just blow up their house? I think I know how to make-"

"Can we discuss plans on the way home?" Atarah interrupted, standing and yawning. "I'm cold."

Stephen looked to me for an answer. It surprised me that he wanted to check if I was okay with something as obvious as going home, and I had to wonder if this was really what he'd been like all along, throughout the whole time I'd known him.

One thing was clear: He was never stupid. He was just pretending.

I got up and began to follow Atarah to the car, wordlessly signalling to Stephen that he should follow too. "Why did you pretend to be normal?" I asked him as he fell into step beside me.

"I needed to make you fall in love with me. I thought I could just make it clear I'd be useful to you, but that wouldn't make you love me, and that would be immeasurable pain." I could imagine that pain. It was a magnitude millions of times stronger than any pain I'd felt, but I'd imagined it, when I thought of Stephen rejecting me. "When you did love me, I had to be certain. I had no idea how you'd react to loving someone, so I had to be careful. I gently pursued you, and made it clear that I liked you back. When you told me you killed Amanda, I- I thought what was happening was that you had begun to feel everything, and the guilt was tearing at you, so I figured it would be bad to just... pretend it was fine. I thought I'd let you deal with your emotions, and when you'd come to terms with them, I could explain that I knew. Was I wrong?"

"Yes." I climbed into the car and prepared to drive home; the adrenalin kept me wide, wide awake. I'd have trouble staying awake tomorrow, though. "I hated feeling things. Most of them were bad. Missing you, longing for you, being sad when you weren't around, being angry when other people got near you. It was terrible."

"I promise you," he said, reaching a hand across the console and gently touching my leg. I froze up with the electricity it sent across every nerve. "I will do everything in my capacity to make you happy, and get rid of those bad emotions. From here on out, it only has to be good."

"I want that," I whispered, blind to the world around me except for him. His hand gently rubbed my thigh, and I shivered. I moved away from it, just for some relief. "But- I'm easily overwhelmed. Everything is new and my emotions are raw. I love you so much that it hurts when you get too close. I'm getting better, but I need you to be careful with me."

His understanding smile melted me. He took his hand away. "Take it slow. I get it."

Atarah was staring at me in the rear-view mirror, grinning like a maniac. Honestly, I think she preferred this outcome to a murder; two fucked up people, turning out to fit perfectly together.

"I was going to murder you," I told Stephen, and he laughed. He just laughed. "I'm serious. I thought the only way to get rid of these horrible feelings was to murder you. And then, I thought, maybe if you could love me despite the fact that I was a murderer, I could... live with that. So I confessed to see how you'd react."

"Oh." Stephen's eyes were wide. I started up the car and turned around on the dirt road; it was the same scene we saw coming in, but every single thing about this situation was incredibly different. "My mistake."

"I only have feelings in regard to you. Or at least I think so. I used to feel like these feelings were lies, and clouding my judgement, and I mean, they are, but I couldn't kill you anymore even if I wanted to." I felt my voice breaking ever so slightly, torn with emotion. "Maybe I'll just be normal from now on. I don't even know where to begin with doing that."

"You won't be normal." I hear Stephen say it first, but Atarah echoed it at pretty much the same time. She finished her sentence first. "-because you're still a murderer who's in love with a psychopath and you're being hunted down by vengeful twins. Sorry, siblings."

"Because you're the only human being I'm capable of loving," Stephen finished. We pulled out onto the road, and I tried to keep my racing heart from distracting me.

There was silence for a moment as I tried to collect my thoughts. "I think I can live with this," I said, soft and uncertain. I was cautious in saying happiness would be better than nothing, because I couldn't be sure I'd be happy- but I had to give it my best shot. "I think I want to."

On the drive home, we filled Stephen in on the truth, the whole truth. He told us he'd figured out he was about to be kidnapped the night we all slept over- he hadn't trusted Ezra, but he'd been listening in on our conversation. We told him about Ophelia, and the threat she'd made to my life if Ezra came to harm. He was visibly pissed off.

"So they have to both die then. So be it. My plan was originally to make him shoot himself, but I was thinking we could lure him out to an empty parking lot and hit him with a car."

"In something high-impact, like a car accident, material is exchanged. Pieces of your car would be on his body and vice-versa. You can get away with it if the cops are lazy, but when he's rich, I doubt it. I only got away with killing his dad because I was ten." With the script so suddenly flipped, and Stephen working beside me, it was strange, but it all felt doable.

"What they said," Atarah adds from the back. "We need something clean."

I sighed. "I don't want to kill the Houghs if I don't have to."

"And what's the alternative? You die, or confess and go to prison for life? No. Not now, not ever." Stephen scowled at the very idea. "What's different now, compared to when you killed their dad?"

"I didn't care about anything then. It's not that I care about them, but I can't ever lose you. I want a solution with less risk."

"Is that it though?" Atarah questioned, and I ignored her. The Houghs didn't deserve to be the targets of any new sympathy I'd gained; I refused to give it to them. I didn't want to kill them because it was messy. Except that's not what I said.

"It's messy," I added, even if it was only to justify it to myself.

"So then, what? Running away isn't going to work. They'll find us." Stephen wasn't helping my logical thought process. We were already back on the highway; I didn't even know where everyone would go when we got home. I didn't want to be apart from Stephen, not for a second.

"There's three of us and two of them," Atarah said, and actually, that was helpful. "Oh, shit, there's the P.I., too. But that just makes it evenly matched. Assuming he's still helping them."

"We could split up," I suggested, following the idea Atarah gave me. "Watch them and see what they do."

"No way am I leaving your fucking side," Stephen protested, bristling with anger, fear and love. "I don't care what Atarah does, but I'm staying with you."

"And if we watch them and discover that they're coming

to murder you as planned, we've learned nothing," Atarah added, and again, she was right. "We need a preventative strategy. We need to stop them before they get to you."

"In that case, we have to run." It was the only conclusion I could come to. "We can't do anything to hurt them without getting caught, until we have a better plan. We'll come up with something to tell our parents, like we're... going camping together, or something, I don't know. We'll take a few days and come up with a plan."

"We can only buy so much time," Atarah reminded me, and the truth stung. Finally, I felt fear about the encroaching threat of the Houghs, and it was because Stephen might be separated from me.

There were a few more ideas thrown around, but in the end we agreed upon waiting. Stephen wanted to throw himself into the line of fire for me, but I couldn't accept that, and he refused to accept me putting myself in danger. Atarah had less gusto in suggesting she be the one to act, but I told her no just as much. I didn't want her to go to jail, even if it wouldn't devastate me in the same way.

Stephen insisted we stay together, and I absolutely did not complain about that. He told me he'd make up a story to his parents, and that was all I needed to hear. I'd deal with explanations in the morning. I just needed Stephen to stay by my side forever.

"Tomorrow night, we'll meet up and go somewhere out of town," I said, confirming the plan, when we were past Battle Creek and only ten or fifteen minutes from home. "I distracted them, so we'll probably have more time than that, but I'd rather be safe than sorry."

"Alright," Atarah agreed with a yawn. "I still vote we kidnap them for fake ransom and then kill them. But fine. Just drop me off at home, and I'll meet up with you guys after school."

"Okay." The idea of being alone with Stephen still terrified me to my core, but I knew, logically, that if I told him the truth he'd be sensitive to it. One thing I was sure of, from the short hour or so I'd spent with an honest Stephen, was that he'd do anything to make me happy.

Before him, I'd have said I didn't believe in the concept of things being 'deserved'. But now, when I looked at him and caught him already staring at me with this loving, almost reverent look in his eyes, all I could think of was how I didn't deserve him.

When we dropped Atarah off, she left us with a "have fun!" and a wink. I was already lightheaded from how fast my heart was racing, and that didn't help. I was frozen trying to remember how to drive.

"It's fine," Stephen whispered, a calming voice allowing me to breathe again. "Anything is fine."

"*I'm* fine," I said, but it was at least somewhat a lie. "I- I just... it's a lot of emotions."

"I know," he offered quietly, helping me to finally snap out of it and pull out from the curb. "I waited years for you to love me. I can wait however long it takes for you to be ready for *anything*. Even if it takes years for you to hold my hand again."

I wanted to cry with how much his kindness meant to me. I didn't deserve him. That was an honest fact, and just because it took emotion to understand what 'deserve' meant didn't mean that what I deserved was an emotional lie.

Emotions could be lies. My fear at being alone with him was completely lying, misinterpreting the situation and twisting it in my mind. Without emotions, though, there are so many things I'd have never understood. Emotions were a whole sense I'd had missing, and now that sense had opened up, and I was seeing the world in a way I'd never been able to understand before. It was like seeing colour or hearing sound for the first time, and the brightest, loudest emotions were overwhelming, but they still showed a perspective on the world I'd never had before.

"I love you," I reminded him, just to make sure he knew. His wide smile was everything.

"I love you too."

Even if I wanted to kill him, I wouldn't be able to. Not anymore.

I drove back to my house and snuck him in through the back door. Predictably, everyone was asleep.

He was awestruck at the sight of my room. Not that there was much personal flair- I didn't have much of a real personality yet, since I didn't care about anything until recently- but he seemed to love it anyway. He went to sit on my bed as he admired my stuff, looking over every book on the bookshelf and every piece of clothing in my wardrobe. It felt extremely personal inviting him in here, for reasons it was almost impossible to explain. I'd had countless friends over here before, including partners. It's just that those people were inconsequential, and Stephen was the world.

"I never thought I'd be in here," Stephen finally said, so softly I almost didn't hear him.

"We should sleep." My nerves made it difficult to talk normally, to think normally. "I mean, we don't have to, I just-"

"Alex." His reassuring voice was welcome, but it hardly helped my anxiety. "It's fine."

I could feel the emotions pressing at the edges of my eyes. "It's just that I'm scared and I don't know why. I'm not scared of you, but you make me so nervous and I don't- want to mess up somehow, or embarrass myself, or..."

He stood, approaching me. When I looked at him, it took everything I had to keep the tears from escaping. He was so gentle with me, light fingers on my arms that strangely did help calm me down. "I get it," he said, so softly. "Emotions are dumb like that. We'll just go to sleep, okay? Nothing else. You don't even have to talk to me or acknowledge me. Baby steps."

And then I did cry. "You're so nice," I choked out. "How are you a psychopath when you're so nice?"

"Loving you made me better," Stephen said, reaching to wipe a tear from my face and changing his mind. He really was doing all he could to be careful with me. "I mean... I only care about being nice because of you. I can't not be nice to you. But I know *how* to be nice because of you, even if I don't always act like it to anyone else."

"You apologised to Atarah. I think that's nice," I said, smiling through the tears.

"I guess it was." Stephen shrugged. He seemed unbothered by the subject. "Anyway, if we're going to sleep, can I get changed?"

"Oh, shit, of course." I'd forgotten about the obvious details, with how Stephen had distracted me. "Do you want... to borrow some clothes? I don't know if you'll like my style, but some of my bigger clothes would probably fit you."

"Honestly, now's a good time to mention it. I was never actually planning on returning your sweater. I wanted something that smelled like you." I realised only as he said it that he'd had that for nearly a week. I'd just forgotten about it. "Basically, uh, without being weird- I want to borrow something. Preferably not with blood on it this time."

I think we passed 'weird' when he broke into Atarah's room to write a threat on her mirror. He and I were the exact same level of fucked up and weird.

I gave him a shirt from my closet and some pyjama pants, throwing them in his direction. He caught them easily, and his face showed a wild mix of emotions, all of which he tried to hide. He wasn't quite there yet, either.

I began to take my shoes off, refusing to look at him directly and instead watching him out of the corner of my eye. Looking at him directly would be like staring into the sun. I saw the red button-up shirt slide off of his shoulders and hit the ground. I deliberately fumbled with my laces so it would be longer until I had to look upwards. When I saw a black binder lifted over his head and bare skin underneath, I still refused to look. I would go blind.

With my shoes off and my jacket shed, I risked a look back at him. He was sitting on my bed, wearing my clothes, and he looked amazing. He was always amazing, and I wanted to melt into his arms.

It took me a moment to realise I could.

I sat on the bed beside him. He was quiet, saying nothing, but I could see the slightly nervous twisting of the sheets in his right hand. Slowly, cautiously, like his touch might burn me, I laid my head on his shoulder. I let out a deep, shuddering breath, and felt my heart warm.

Gently, he put his arm around me, and I settled into him. My head fit perfectly in the crook of his shoulder, and it was wonderful. Everything was wonderful.

It would take a long time to get used to living with emotions. But if it felt as nice as this all the time, I could do it.

Knowing that I was in control helped ease my emotions a lot. Sleeping still took a long time, but I was able to just lay beside him, my fingers lightly intertwined with his. After some amount of time staring at the darkness above his face, my weariness got the better of me. I closed my eyes with my face buried in his shoulder, and when I opened them, I was lying face down with my hair obscuring my face, and I could hear Stephen's voice.

"...yeah, I'm really sorry. I had an emergency at home and I didn't even think before just taking off. My mother's really sick, you know." When I looked at the clock, I realised I only had about half an hour to get ready for school, and that kicked me into gear, getting me to scramble out of bed. I must've slept through my regular alarm. If Stephen had woken up, he'd decided to let me sleep- which was cute, but unhelpful.

When I looked at him, he immediately burst into a smile. "I know," he said to a person who I assumed was his co-worker, "I have no idea how that happened. Again, I'm really sorry. I'll make it up to you, just let me know how."

I realised he was technically apologising for being kidnapped, and there was something funny about that, even to me.

While he was on the phone, I grabbed the clothes I needed and had a lightning-quick shower. It helped to make me feel less like I'd just been trekking in the snow in the middle of the night, and also, I didn't have to get changed in front of Stephen. That was not something I was anywhere close to being prepared for.

When I got back, he was dressed in the jeans he wore yesterday and the shirt I'd given him. "So my co-worker's not too mad that I ditched her, my boss is giving me tonight and the weekend off- on the same lie, so they probably won't question it- and my parents aren't freaking out about me not coming home last night. I pretended that I forgot to tell them I was staying at yours tonight."

I nodded slowly as I took in the information. "Okay, well, good." It seemed every loose end was covered up. Nobody would learn what I'd almost done. "Do you, uh, want a shower? You probably feel like shit. My fault, obviously."

He shook his head. "We'll be late to school. That's important to you, right? You want to be a doctor?"

It was a little strange for him to not be asking me these questions, but checking that the answers he had were correct. Luckily for him, I doubted weirding me out was possible. "Yes."

"Can I ask how you decided what you wanted to do when you didn't care at all?" His words were not so much careful, as respectful, somehow treating me like a superior. Like I was better than him. I had absolutely no idea how to feel about that. I was feeling something, but it was as vague and hard to understand as it could possibly be.

"Of course, yeah." I wondered if that would change. "I wanted to make a lot of money and to be respected in my work. Being an engineer or a physicist doesn't play to my strengths very well, and doctors can often be something of heroes. And also... Why not save lives? If it doesn't affect me, I always choose to help others, just because they appreciate it."

Stephen's admiring gaze was never something I could get used to. "Believe it or not, that's noble. I mean, I dance because I enjoy the attention. Even if you made that decision without emotions, it's still noble."

I've always known I was capable of noble acts, in the same way I'm capable of evil acts. I can't claim to be a noble person when I'm a murderer, though.

"I'm glad you think so," was all I could figure to say.

To avoid my parents- because I had no excuse for Stephen's presence, and would've preferred not to have to come up with one- we snuck out through the back door. He suggested stopping somewhere for breakfast, offering to buy me something when I told him I had no money on me. When I reminded him he'd skipped showering so we could get to school on time, he quickly gave up on the idea. I could tell he just wanted to sit and eat with me, and that made my heart melt in the same way as his loving smile did. I was, slowly, beginning to get used to feeling like this. He would never stop making me feel so much love all the time, but feeling love was becoming bearable. Excruciatingly slowly, but it was.

He apparently didn't need to go home to pick anything up. I wasn't entirely sure if he was telling the truth or not, but the nonchalant way he said it tracked with it being honest. I parked and got out with my bag; it was warmer than previous days today, the long freeze of winter not yet snapping, but bending somewhat. I didn't believe in anything beyond the physical, no deity and no fate, but the outer world happened to reflect how I felt inside. I was not so cold and alone anymore, and although it was tentative, the warmth was creeping in.

And I was letting it.

Chapter Fifteen - Oliver Hough

"**S**omething's wrong," Stephen said, eyes narrowing as he gazed around the carpark.

"What?" Looking around, everything seemed fine. We were one of the last people into school, and nobody was nearby.

"Because Atarah always parks there," he said, gesturing towards an empty parking space. When I considered it, it was true; I just hadn't paid attention to that exact detail. "Where is she?"

"It's more likely she's fine than not," I reminded him, trying to puzzle through it myself. It had only been maybe six or seven hours at most since I last saw her; she wasn't suddenly sick or injured, and she wouldn't have walked or taken the bus to school. "...but I have no explanation."

"I don't care if she's fine, I care that the Houghs are going after you and they're the only people who might've hurt her. What if they did something to her to try and get to you?" Stephen was rapidly looking around the carpark as he spoke. "No, her car isn't here. Something is wrong."

When I looked to the school gate, I saw an unwelcome sight. Ophelia Hough leant against the mesh of the fence, impatiently tapping her foot on the sidewalk. She was also looking back and forth for something, and with the truth open in the air between us, I wasted no time and made a beeline for her.

She saw me right as I was upon her. "Where's Ezra, and what has he done with Atarah?" I didn't feel the same fear or anger that I did when Stephen was involved, but I was quick and direct and urgent. If Atarah was in danger, it only made sense to hurry in getting her out of it. There was always the concern that I was not like this before my emotions began, but that was quiet among my other current concerns.

"I should ask you what Atarah's done with Ezra," Ophelia hissed, distraught. "We figured out your little stunt with the brake line. It made him furious. Last night he ran off, and I haven't seen him since."

"*We* figured it out?" Stephen's mocking tone was unfamiliar to me. I'd always thought it uncharacteristic of him, but Atarah had disagreed. It turned out she was right. "We all know your brother's a terminal idiot, don't act like he figured anything out."

"I would stay silent if I were you." Ophelia's words were a dangerous whisper. She turned to me then. "That was bold of you, you know. We're closing in on you from both sides and you decide the best thing to do is attack our mother? Explain that one."

I ignored her. "We don't know where Ezra is, but Atarah isn't here either. I haven't spoken to her since last night. If she's done anything with Ezra, I don't know about it. Which is why I think he's done something with her."

"Call him," Stephen told Ophelia dismissively.

"Don't you think I've been trying?" Ophelia snapped at him. "He's not picking up. Call Atarah."

She was talking to Stephen, but I was the one to act. I saw Stephen's eye twitch at her tone, but he said nothing. I quickly located Atarah's contact and pressed it, and the phone began to ring.

Both Ophelia and Stephen were watching me as I held the phone up to my ear. Each consecutive ring made Ophelia's stare more intense. When it went to voicemail and I lowered the phone in defeat, Ophelia let out a short noise of rage, her face twisted in anger. "Fine! I'll find him myself!" she professed, turning on her heel and heading off down the sidewalk.

Not yet discouraged, I touched the contact again. Again, the phone rang out.

"Maybe she just stayed home and forgot to tell us. She didn't say she'd be at school. I think she might be fine," Stephen said, even though he'd been the one to suggest something was wrong.

"Don't lie to me for even a second, Stephen. You have to be honest with me. All the time." I caught what he was trying to do easily. He thought I was worried. "I'm not worried. I just want to know if Ezra's done anything to her."

"Okay. He very obviously has and I don't know what we should do about it." He parroted my monotone voice back to me. "What would you suggest?"

Before I could suggest anything, my phone rung in my hand. *Atarah Adebayo Calling.*

Stephen eyed it warily, but I answered pretty much immediately. "Hello?"

"Alex." The voice that met me was not Atarah's. It wasn't particularly hard to figure out what was going on, but I was unprepared. We were supposed to have at least one more day before this happened. "Lookin' for Atarah?"

"What do you want with her? It's me you're after." I turned away from the school gates, heading back towards my car. Stephen followed.

"You told Ophelia not to harm her, right?" Ezra spoke with a strange calmness I had never heard from him before. It wasn't a natural calmness, though. It was forced and emotional underneath. "We're at the empty dance academy. Stephen'll know where it is. You've got three hours to get here before I kill her."

He hung up with that. I didn't have the time, and hardly the capacity, to be shocked or surprised. I shoved my phone into my pocket and unlocked my car, staring at Stephen.

"What's going on?" he asked, brows furrowed. "I'm guessing that's not her."

"Ezra has her at the dance academy. He's going to kill her in three hours if we- or I, I guess- don't show up."

Stephen paused. I started to open the car, wondering why he wasn't automatically following. Gently, the corners of his lips started to turn up, and I could only be confused. I asked, "do you know something I don't?"

"I mean, I don't think so." Stephen spread his arms wide, gesturing at the carpark around us. "This is our chance. We've got warning to get out."

I processed it, and it struck like a sickness in my gut. The feeling was, technically, still connected to Stephen- the betrayal of Atarah was his- but in that moment I could no longer deny that I had changed far beyond just him. "We can't let her die. We're going to save her."

He was hit with a dumbstruck expression. "But- Ezra's given us three hours to get out of here. He's dumb, he's caught the person we can leave behind. I know it's not great, but if you show up, he'll kill you, Alex. He probably won't even kill her. He's a coward."

I tried to think of any good reason at all that I wanted to save Atarah. I mean, she was my best friend, but that wasn't worth putting my own life in danger, was it? Was it because she'd do the same for me? I mean, she *would* do the same for me, but she'd probably do it because she loved being in danger. Was it because nobody else in the world could understand me like she did? Stephen would, someday, but he was different. It couldn't be because a life without her would be worse than death, because that wasn't true. I couldn't even imagine feeling sad after her death. I didn't think I cared about Atarah in any emotional way, even when I was the most honest with myself I could possibly be.

I would save her because I wanted to. I wanted to in the same way I had always wanted to wear pastel colours and grow my hair long and eat strawberry ice cream instead of chocolate. There was no emotion behind it; I just wanted to be good in a way I never had before. And I didn't know if it was emotions, or love, or finally experiencing consequences for my terrible actions that made me feel that way. All that was important was that I wanted to be good and I didn't want to leave Atarah to die.

"I'm sorry." I opened my car door and got into the front seat. Looking like a scared and bewildered dog, Stephen followed. "Loving you has changed me, and I can't explain why, but I can't just run away."

"While I would prefer we do that," Stephen said, biting the inside of his cheek, "I'll follow you to the ends of the earth. If you say we save Atarah, we save Atarah."

"Great." I put the car into drive and prepared to enter the lion's den. "Let's go."

Stephen was noticeably nervous the whole drive. "We should have a gun or something," he said. "Or at least a bulletproof vest. Let me go in and deal with the situation. Don't go near him."

"Stephen, I need you to focus." My voice seemed to snap him out of it, at least somewhat. "You're clever, and I need you to use that cleverness to figure out how we're going to deal with Ezra instead of freaking out."

"You're right." He sat back forcefully against the seat. "It's my worst fear that you're going to die. That's all. I'll be fine. It's fine."

"Stephen." I spoke as calmly as possible, and he took a few deep breaths, centring himself. When he opened his eyes again, he looked determined. That made me confident, which was a wonderful and entirely new feeling that I had to guess from context. I reached my hand towards him and he gratefully took it; the rush of endorphins only made the confidence stronger. It was the opposite of fear, and I almost *wanted* to fight Ezra.

He thought for a moment and rattled off a plan. "So, chances are he's on stage, because he's not going to hide. He's got these delusions of a western, and this is his big showdown. That also means he's not going to shoot you the second you step through the front door, but I will not take any chances. There's a side door that will get us behind the backdrop, and if we're quiet and move slowly, he won't even see. We can get on either side of him, he goes for you, I attack him from behind."

He certainly sounded different than he had before, when he was deferring to anything I said. Now I saw the extreme self-confidence he'd described himself with, and I was far from hating it. "No idea which way I like you more," I muttered, more to myself. When he gave me a curious look, I waved him away. Not a great time to distract him. "Nothing. Let's do it."

We pulled up to the building, and I was struck by the memory of coming to watch Stephen dance. It looked different in the morning sunlight, but I distinctly remembered sitting in almost this exact car spot when Atarah took my hair out and told me Stephen would like it. I turned to him as I parked the car. "Do you think my hair looks nicer when it's out?" I asked.

He was visibly confused, but answered anyway. "I mean, you always look good, but... I guess so. Why'd you ask?"

I was smart. I got away with three murders, and I was on track to becoming a doctor- maybe with some cheating, but I wasn't dumb. Stephen was smart too; he'd figured out what I'd done and what I was like. So had Ophelia, for what it was worth. He'd done that through close inspection, however, as had she.

Atarah only took a few weeks of mild interest to figure it out. She had been onto Stephen in a way that I, at least, had not, and that I doubted anyone else was. I could tell she knew something I didn't about him ever since she spoke to me before his party. She may not have been doing as well in school, and she may not have known where she was going with her future, but she was the smartest one of all of us.

"Before we go in," I told Stephen, "do me a favour. Trust Atarah."

He nodded solemnly. He was afraid, that much was obvious. It wasn't for himself, or her.

When I got out of the car, I took notice of the only other car in the carpark- Atarah's. He must've stopped her and forced her to drive here, and that meant he had a gun to threaten her with.

"He has a gun," I told Stephen as soon as the thought occurred to me. Stephen followed my gaze to Atarah's car, and put together the same clues.

"I think she told him to go here. I don't think he chose it," he added. "He wouldn't have known that it was going to be empty and unlocked at this time of day. But I remember telling you guys about it. She'd have known."

"So she predicted we'd save her." She'd been making comments about my emotions changing for a while. Of course she knew I'd save her. "Like I said. Trust her."

Stephen sighed. "I know. Let's go."

He led me around to the side door, and as he said, it was unlocked. He opened it outwards, very slowly, and inside of it I could see only a thick black curtain. I creeped through and saw that the curtain stretched from wall to wall, with gaps on either side that still lead to darkness. It was the backdrop of a stage, for performers to sneak behind, and the perfect way to ambush him.

I could hear Atarah's voice. "Oh, come on, E-Z. They're not coming. You know Alex is emotionless and doesn't care about anyone." She didn't sound sad or upset, but then again, she wouldn't even if she thought she were about to die. I trusted that she knew I was coming.

"I still don't believe you." Ezra sounded oddly conversational, and very audibly confused. "I'm trying to figure out why the hell you're acting like this. It ain't working."

Stephen gently, silently, shut the door behind him. He gestured with his head in one direction behind the backdrop, and I nodded. He began to head down that way with silent footsteps, and, slow so as not to make a sound, I went in the other direction.

"I'm not trying to pull something on you. I'm serious. Why do you think I hang around Alex? Hey, why are you lowering the gun?"

I wished I could see what was going on. Whatever Atarah was doing, it was already sounding successful.

"Please stop." Ezra's voice was high-pitched and embarrassed. "You're a hostage."

"I know." Atarah's voice was almost too soft to hear, but it was decidedly sultry. "This is like, my number two fantasy."

I looked back at Stephen, and he was silently laughing, clutching the wall and trying to keep from making a sound. Atarah's strategy was, I had to admit, creative, and honestly believable. I almost found it funny, too, but my sense of humour was critically underdeveloped.

"I... what's number one?" Ezra was probably not intending to flirt back- he sounded more scared than anything. I finally reached the edge of the wall and felt along it; light from the stage showed me where I'd be visible, and I was careful not to enter that spot. From where I was, I could only see the very bottom of Atarah's legs, laying on the wooden floor. She was turned towards me, but I still couldn't see where Ezra was.

"That depends on how I feel. Either you've got a knife and you're cutting me up, or we're cutting someone else up together." She was speaking about it so casually, managing to keep her voice honest and without a hint of irony. So much so that I was beginning to question her previous denials that her interest in serial killers was sexual. To my best guess, she wasn't a great actor.

"Oh, fuck off," Ezra muttered, almost under his breath. Looking around me, I could see a ladder used to reach the lighting rig, and briefly wondered if another plan could be achieved. "You're fucked up."

"You kidnapped me, Inigo Montoya. Shoddy kidnapping, by the way. I kidnapped someone last night and it was way better than this."

"I *knew* y'all were gonna kidnap Stephen." Ezra sounded

vindicated, like he hadn't literally heard me confess to doing it. "What'd you do with him? Is he dead?"

The plan had been that I'd step out and distract Ezra, so that Stephen could come up behind him. "I'm right here," said Stephen, and along with the sudden fear for Stephen's safety, I was hit with the need for a new plan. Luckily, I already had an idea.

"What the fuck?" Trusting that Ezra had turned to him, I crept past the opening in the curtains. I got a glimpse of the scene as I went past; Atarah was lying on the floor, her hands taped together behind her back, facing me. In the brief second I got to look at her, I met her eyes, and she smiled. Ezra's back was to me; he held the same gun he'd threatened us with outside Stephen's party, and the way he held it told me that he was confident. He knew how to use it. Stephen stood in front of him, face blank. "What're you doing here? You're not kidnapped?"

I went to the ladder, careful to make every step silent. Stephen absolutely ignored the questions. "Ezra, put the gun down. This isn't a game. You don't want to kill Atarah, and you know she doesn't deserve to die."

Atarah sounded like she was enjoying this an awful lot. "Aww, thanks, Steve."

"Call me Steve again and I'll kill you myself," he snapped. I used the chance to begin climbing the ladder, conscious of the noise every step made. It was excruciatingly difficult to try and be wholly silent, and on the metal ladder I couldn't guarantee anything.

"That ain't gonna work out how you intend, I'll tell you that," Ezra said, somewhat uncomfortable still, and Atarah laughed. Unfortunately, Ezra couldn't be distracted for long. "So where's Alex?"

"I wouldn't know." Stephen shrugged. He, unlike Atarah, was a very, *very* good liar. "Why do you assume I would?"

"Because you're... here?" Ezra was perfectly correct in his reasoning, but Stephen's confidence shook his certainty. "Besides, ain't you on Alex's side? They asked Ophelia to leave you alone, just like Atarah. You keep defending them.

I'm not as stupid as you think I am."

"I don't think you're stupid." Even in his act, Stephen could hardly keep from sounding sarcastic. I finally reached the top of my silent ascent of the ladder; from there, I could reach the rigging for the stage lights. With some acrobatics, I'd be able to pull myself on top of it. "You were right. I was wrong not to trust you. Alex is evil."

Ezra's stunned silence prickled in the air. I reached my hands up for the bar; I could grip it, but I didn't have anywhere near the strength to deadlift my entire weight up. I was, however, a gymnast. With some swinging I could easily get on top. The only problem was, that would be loud, and the silence in this place was currently deafening.

"You're saying you're here to help me?" Ezra said after a long moment. I gripped the metal tight in my hands and slowly stepped off the ladder, testing the sound; even just the little bit of momentum had my hands squeaking against the metal. I held my breath, waiting, and I didn't like the silence that followed.

"Yes," Stephen said, almost too confident. "I should've-"

Ezra cut him off. "Or are you just saying that to distract me? Alex is here, ain't they?"

"You're right. He's lying." Atarah cut through it easily. "Do you know the truth, Ezra? The truth is that Alex and Stephen are both fucked up psychopaths and they're working together."

"What the fuck?" Stephen's anger was almost a screech. "Atarah, you're supposed to help me! I'm trying to save you!"

As he yelled, the sound was loud enough to drown out the shaking of the bars and the friction of skin on metal. I swung back and forth, bringing myself higher each time.

"You're so fucking stupid, Stephen!" Atarah yelled back at him, and there was the sound of her moving on the floor, scrambling as though to her feet. "I know exactly what's happened! You want to know, Ezra? Guess what? We were going to kidnap and kill Stephen because Alex couldn't stand being in love with him! And now Alex has sent him here, alone- don't try to say they're here, Stephen, we'll both know you're lying- so that they can run off alone! Alex doesn't care about either of us, you were tricked!"

There was the tiniest gap in response that told me Stephen was thinking. Ezra wouldn't have picked up on it, but I did. "Fuck off and fuck you, Atarah!" Stephen yelled, and I wasn't sure if he'd caught on or not until the next sentence. "Alex would never leave me, and we're going to meet up in Canada as soon as I get you out of here!"

I swung up and launched myself onto the rigging, landing with grace. Their shouting match was so effective that I heard it louder than the noises right by my head. Stephen trusted Atarah, and it worked perfectly.

"Both of you, shut up, before I shoot you!" Ezra screamed over the top of both. I took advantage of the noise to quickly scamper along the rigging, stopping to be a little quieter when Ezra was finished. I could see them now; for the tiniest moment, Stephen looked up at me, but he was able to play it off by adding a groan and throwing his head back in annoyance. Ezra was pointing the gun at him, but not as confidently as before. Atarah was lying down again, and she was able to look up at me directly without it being suspicious. She raised an eyebrow at me, and I nodded a thanks back to her.

"Oh, no, don't shoot me," Atarah deadpanned.

"Shut up." Ezra pointed the gun at her for a moment, and then thought better of it and pointed it at Stephen. "You two better explain what's going on right now. You're telling me Alex *did* just leave Atarah to die?"

"Well, no, I'm here." Stephen treated Ezra with the contempt he clearly wanted to, even when he was acting. "Do I need to walk you through it step-by-step? Draw a flowchart? Or is that too advanced for you?"

Stephen was buying time, and I used it to crawl along. I couldn't get directly above Ezra; he was maybe a foot or two to my left. The drop wasn't far, and at best it would hurt in my ankles and shins if I were just to fall to the floor. Considering I weighed a hundred and forty pounds at most, I doubted Ezra would be very injured. It would, however, knock the gun out of his hand- and right now, all I needed was for that gun to not be pointed at Stephen.

"Are you trying to get shot?" Ezra was beyond pissed now. I rarely saw him anything but angry or confused, and I could only wonder what he was like otherwise. I'd seen pictures of him with Ophelia where he seemed happy, and he enjoyed himself around his friends. It was an alien idea to me.

I caught Atarah's eye and made the symbol for a gun with my fingers. She gave the briefest of nods.

"You should totally shoot him." Atarah was all casual about it, and Stephen was disgusted, surprised and annoyed all at once. Trusting her didn't come naturally to him. "That'd be pretty hot, I think. You're cute, pointing a gun like you think you can use it, but you're not a killer."

"I don't wanna be a fucking killer," Ezra snapped, falling for her trick easily. "I'm not killing anyone for no fucking reason. I'm only gonna kill Alex. So one of you had better call Alex and make them come here right now."

"I mean, sure. I'm on your side now, baby." Atarah shifted, trying to sit up. Ezra stepped back and away from her, holding the gun pointed at the ground.

I took the chance the moment it was handed to me. My feet hit Ezra sharp in each shoulder, and he went down, the gun clattering away and towards Stephen. Ezra cried out, but it was more surprise than pain. He struck the wood and I fell back off him. He opened his eyes, laid them on me, and nearly bit his tongue off in rage.

"How the fuck?" he cried, immediately scrambling for the gun. Stephen kicked it away and stomped on Ezra's hand. I backed up, ready to leap on him again if necessary. "Fuck you guys! Fuck!"

"It's over," Stephen declared incredibly pre-emptively, but his confidence was enough to give Ezra pause. "We're taking Atarah, and we're leaving."

Ezra reached for the gun again, and Stephen tried to kick him out of the way with a swift blow to his shoulder. I leapt after him, and with Stephen keeping Ezra down, I managed to stumble to the gun and gather it clumsily in one hand. I'd never held a gun before. It was cold and heavier than I had imagined a gun would be, and the fact it was made for killing didn't seem to really sink in, just looking at it.

I pointed it at Ezra and he immediately froze in place. He still looked angry, but there was fear in there too.

Atarah gestured to Stephen. "Untie me?"

Stephen rolled his eyes, but went to help. Ezra glared at her, but he didn't take his eyes off of me for long. He slowly raised himself up from where he lay on the wooden stage. Rage and fear turned to determination in his eyes.

"Ezra, I don't want to kill you." I said carefully, keeping my voice level.

"Why not?" He shrugged. He looked kind of pathetic sitting there, in a black hoodie that was a little too big. His hair looked like he hadn't had a shower in a few days. "You killed my father, and you nearly killed my mother. Why wouldn't you kill me?"

There were logical reasons, there were. I could swear they existed. "Because there's been enough senseless death," I said.

He snorted a humourless laugh. "I know how you are, Alex. Be honest."

"I would get away with it. This is your gun. All I'd have to do it shoot you, wait until Ophelia gets here, shoot her as well, clean the gun and put her fingerprints on it, and leave it as a mystery for the detectives. Honestly, Ezra, you've given me a perfect scenario to get away with killing both of you. We'd be able to finish school and move away before anyone even connected us to this crime scene."

"So why not?" Ezra cried out. His eyes were glossy, and he knew as well as I did that I was only stalling for time. "Why won't you just shoot me?"

"Because I don't want to!"

CHAPTER SIX-
TEEN - ALEX
KEEN, TERTIUM

Ezra blinked in surprise, furrowing his brow like he'd misheard me. Stephen was ripping the duct tape off Atarah's wrists, and both of them paused to look at me for a moment. Stephen's face fell into an almost sympathetic understanding, and Atarah just rolled her eyes. I ignored her completely inappropriate reaction, as I always did.

I slowly lowered the gun. "I'm going to tell you the truth, the whole truth, and hope that you make the decision to spare me."

"What the fuck are you doing?" Stephen said incredulously, coming to stand by my side. Atarah followed. "He's going to kill you no matter what you do."

"Well, we can always shoot him after," Atarah said, and Stephen, grumbling, agreed and waved for me to continue.

"Fuck you too, Atarah. I knew you were only saying that

shit to try and get away," Ezra scowled at her.

"So you admit it worked." Atarah grinned, pointing at him like she'd just caught him out. "Because I was only half lying. You're not quite as cute as your sister, but I like a fiery personality."

"Don't talk about Ophelia like that," Ezra snarled. He then turned to me, impatient. "And you said you were gonna tell me. So tell me."

"Fine." I looked at Atarah to check that she was done, and she nodded for me to go on. "I don't know how much you've figured out, or you think you have, so I'll start from the beginning. For as long as I can remember, Ezra, I haven't been able to feel emotions."

"So you're a psycho. I knew that," he said, unimpressed.

"No, I'm not. I couldn't feel anything at all. I couldn't be happy, or sad, or angry, and I couldn't feel love or hate. I didn't know what anger even was, I just knew how to mimic it." Now I was getting his attention. "I felt the same every single day, no matter what happened. Killing people was just a thing I could do if my life would be easier without them. That was all I felt about it."

At this revelation, Ezra didn't look so mad anymore. Sure, the lingering traces of anger remained, but the beginnings of tears that sat in his eyes were beginning to well up stronger, and all I could see was the same sad little boy I'd glimpsed so briefly around the time I killed his father.

"The first person I killed was my own brother. You wouldn't even know he existed. His name was Bailey, he was two years younger than me, and he was a nuisance. And... I can tell you honestly, that now, today? I wish I had loved him." I still felt the same about it now. That was the truth. "I pushed him into Lake Michigan, and he drowned. And I felt as much nothing as I did before."

Ezra opened his mouth to speak, but no noise came out. Instead, a single tear crept down his skin.

"And then, when I was ten- your dad was our landlord. He was increasing our rent, and on the money my parents made back then, we couldn't afford it. We'd be priced out. I saw an opportunity to save us from losing our house, and I took it. I didn't think or care about anything else. That was why I killed him."

"Why're you telling me this?" Ezra asked softly. He was broken back down into something sad and pathetic, and I felt something stir in my chest, almost, almost like pity. That was certainly impossible, but I let it go. I knew I would never feel any emotion like he was right now, not unless Stephen died, and that stirred something up from the depths.

I imagined Stephen dying and realised it was sympathy.

"Because you deserve to know the truth." There it was: *deserve*. I saw Atarah raise her eyebrow out of the corner of my eye. She knew as well as I did that this was new, uncharted territory for me.

I knelt down to meet Ezra's eye level; he was kneeling on the wood, shoulders hunched, eyes puffy like this was the fifth time he'd cried in the past day. That may well have been true. "I killed Amanda, too, because she was bullying me, and it was the only way I could think of to make it stop. And, skipping ahead a bit, I did put your mother in hospital, only because I needed to buy myself some more time before you hunted me down. Obviously, that backfired."

I paused, feeling like he was supposed to say something, but he just finally began to sob, his body wracking with the effort. His eyes were scrunched up shut, red and puffy, and his mouth pulled into a terrible grimace of pain as tears streaked down into it. Five minutes ago, he was fuming, and now, the simple truth was tearing him apart.

I went on, knowing he was still listening. His heart was busted wide open now. "But the thing is, recently, that has all changed. I'm not emotionless anymore. I fell in love with Stephen, and now I'm feeling for the first time everything I missed out on. I resisted it- that's why I was going to kill him- but when I found out he loved me back, I stopped resisting. I've accepted that I have emotions now. And for some reason- some reason I can't understand, but maybe you might- having emotions makes me want to be a good person. I don't want to kill you. I don't want to kill anyone ever again, for any reason. I never will. All I want is to be able to live the rest of my life with Stephen. And, well, Atarah, because she's my best friend. And I don't know how that's working with my emotions, but it is. All I'm asking is you let us all go, and I can promise you on my life that nobody else will get hurt."

The silence in the hall was deafening. Stephen and Atarah had watchful eyes on Ezra, and even though the gun was lowered, Ezra was still staring at it. His sobs were dying out, and after a long, long second, his gaze flickered up to me.

"How do I know-" his words were interrupted by the lingering hiccups from crying- "how do I know you're telling the truth?"

I looked to Stephen and Atarah. Both looked nervous, Stephen exponentially more so than Atarah. "Do you trust me?" I questioned them, feeling confident in my decision.

"Of course," Stephen whispered, clutching at his chest, and Atarah just nodded.

"Then step away," I told them, as I took the barrel of the gun in my fingers and held the handle out to Ezra.

Stephen cried out in primal terror, and Atarah hissed through her teeth. Ezra's brows furrowed, and he sat up straighter to reach for the gun. Stephen went to grab him, but Atarah threw up a hand to stop him. It looked like it was incredibly difficult for him to sit back and do nothing, but he managed to stop himself with a look of great pain.

"I did swear on my life," I said, a little brush of humour. I had always been able to make jokes, I'd just never appreciated them. I thought about how Stephen might've found that funny, had he not been so terrified, and it brought a little smile to my face.

I was afraid to die, because I didn't want to leave Stephen behind; but that concept of *deserve* just seemed to echo in my mind. If anyone deserved to kill me, it was Ezra Hough. Well, him as much as Ophelia, Mrs Hough, Kai, Amanda's brother, her parents, her friends, and my own parents and sisters. The ghosts of all I'd killed would drag me to hell with them, and maybe I'd finally have a relationship with my brother. Knowing him, I imagined he'd take a long time to properly forgive me, lording his moral high ground over me for probably centuries. He'd eventually get over it, though.

I didn't really believe there was an afterlife; I had no opinion on the subject. It would be kind of nice, though, to see Bailey again and get a second chance.

"I should kill you." Ezra's voice was shaking. He raised the gun, aiming it square between my shoulders. "I should. You deserve it."

If hell was real, Amanda was in it. She was rotten and cruel. I imagined if I saw her again, she'd probably continue to treat me like trash. I could only wonder what had made her so angry and bitter. Ezra was made angry and bitter by the death of his father, and his resentment was fed by the entitlement he got from being rich and spoiled by his sister, and probably his mother too. I never learned what had made Amanda so mean. Perhaps she had good reason.

"You're a murderer," Ezra said, more to himself than anything. Remnants of his sobs still wracked his shoulders every so often. "You killed my dad."

If hell was real, Mr Hough was in it too, and it was where I was going. I could only imagine we'd end up torturing each other. It would be a constant business meeting, with just him and the child version of me. I would have absolutely nothing to do except miss Stephen, which would be the closest experience I could have to torture, and he'd be forced to explain complicated topics to a child for eternity. He hated children, all children except his own.

"Tell me one more thing," Ezra demanded. He was shaking, but the gun was held steady. He would not miss if he shot me. "What were my father's last words?"

I remembered it well, Mr Hough's shaking voice in the dark. He sounded a lot like Ezra.

"*I love my family.*"

"Bullshit," Ezra whispered under his breath, a sentence I was not supposed to hear. He slowly shook his head, and I saw him mouth something; as I was trying to process what, I was suddenly burning alive.

There is something about the word *excruciating* that almost, but not quite, gets across the way a bullet wound feels. It felt like Atarah stabbing Stephen, or perhaps Stephen punching me, or maybe even Stephen dying in a fire right in front of me and me being unable to help, except all that pain was localised underneath my right collarbone. I heard several things in some sequence, but it was difficult to tell the exact order through the red haze in my mind. One was my own voice screaming. One was the sound of footsteps running. One was Stephen's scream, and Atarah's, and Ezra's; Stephen's and Atarah's blended. One was a separate, closer sound of footsteps. One was the sound of a door being kicked open. One was the sound of flesh crushed under a blunt object. One was a warning shot fired into the roof. I also felt like I could hear my own blood, but that was neither here nor there.

I processed Ezra's mouthed words very late. *I can't kill you.*

It took me some time to realise I still had vision. When I opened my eyes, I was staring at the slightly-blurry roof and suffering a whole hell of a lot. The pain was constant and taking up every sphere of focus. I tried to figure out where Stephen was, but the pain distracted me. I tried to figure out who had just entered, but the pain distracted me. I tried to think, but the pain distracted me.

I attempted to sit up, and the pain smacked into me, like rubbing salt in the wound. I grimaced and fought it just enough to lean on my elbow. When I had felt the pain of moving my shoulder, the pain I had when sitting still was a little more bearable. With the haze clearing, I was at least a little able to think, and look around me.

Ezra's face was bloody, his nose unrecognisable and one eye jammed shut with how swollen it was. Stephen was pointing the gun at him, and keeping a close watch on someone behind me. Atarah had kneeled to come to my side, but backed away. Everyone was looking behind me.

"If you shoot, I'll shoot," Stephen snarled. I think some things were said while I was listening to my own bleeding.

"The same goes for you." I figured out, a moment later

than I should've, that a gun was pointing at me. It also took me longer than it should have to recognise that voice as Ophelia's. "I see we're at a stalemate."

"Oh, for fuck's sake, Ezra's already tried to kill Alex. Just put the gun down and we'll call it a day." Atarah didn't sound impressed. She stood, moving towards where Ophelia must be. I didn't want to move to check. "I mean, I did go into this wanting a murder, but this is getting old pretty quick."

"Hang on-" I tried to say, but I was reminded of the pain again, and my elbow fell out from under me. I forgot what I was trying to say when the pain shocked me like that. I resorted to just lying on the ground and accepting that this was a horrible situation. Strangely enough, I didn't regret going to save Atarah, even though it got me shot.

"What?" Ophelia asked, impatient. She was usually quiet and meek, or so I was told. When it came to her family, she was the exact opposite, and with me, it was always about her family.

I struggled to think what I was saying. Then, I remembered what Ezra had mouthed as he shot me. "He wasn't-" I groaned through another stab of pain, but gritted my teeth and forced myself to speak again. "He wasn't trying to kill me."

Ezra made a noise, but he seemed to be in a worse position than me, at least from a consciousness perspective. From what I'd seen, Stephen had only punched him a few times, compared to how I'd been shot, but at least I didn't have a probable concussion. I wasn't even bleeding that badly- the bullet was still in there, blocking up my blood vessels.

"Killing you is all he's wanted ever since we found out it was you who killed our dad. We waited eight years until I could get control of our inheritance, hired a private investigator to make sure it was you, tried and failed to get you arrested, and all throughout that time he's said, whenever anyone asked, that he'd kill our father's murderer without a doubt. And you're telling me *he wasn't trying to kill you*?"

Atarah was out of my line of sight, but when I looked down I could see Stephen looking at me in disbelief. I believed Ezra had wanted me dead, right up until the moment he had to pull the trigger. Holding a gun and threatening to kill someone is very different to actually doing it- at least, when you had morals it was.

The pain of the gunshot wound was going from excruciating and sharp to excruciating and dull, and I was at least able to form full sentences uninterrupted now. "Your brother, for all his talk, is a good person." It was something I'd known from the beginning, and something I honestly should have trusted. I was never in any real danger from Ezra. "He didn't miss when he shot me. He's not a murderer, Ophelia."

"I am."

I heard the gunshot go off and my eyes instinctively shut. For a moment, I genuinely thought I was dead. I saw darkness and heard ringing in my ears. But then, I felt the pain in my right shoulder, and realised it was the only pain I felt.

I thought perhaps it was Stephen who had shot, but I heard him yell, "you are so, so lucky your brother is still alive right now!"

"Hah!" Atarah let out a triumphant cry, and I pieced together what happened. I sat up on my elbow again, grimacing and lightly swearing through the agony, and followed the sound of her voice to see her, having clumsily landed on one knee, holding the gun that had been Ophelia's. Atarah was the reason her shot had missed. "Nice try!"

"Great," Stephen said, reassuming the confident leadership that came easily to him. "Let's kill them both and get out of here."

"Kill him and you won't get a chance to get out of here," Ophelia growled, her voice truly angry, far surpassing her brother in how extreme her rage was. Atarah had the gun pointed at her, and it felt like that was the only reason she wasn't attacking me right now. Ophelia was so mad, it paralleled only my anger when Stephen was threatened.

"Okay, but you saw what I just did, right?" Atarah said with a laugh. "I mean, you were pretty badass, all *I am* and shit. I rescind what I said about-"

"*Shut up.*" Ophelia made a lunge for the gun in Atarah's

hand, and Atarah had to dance away, backing up onto the stage. I saw Ophelia's face and recognised that emotion.

I took the distraction to slowly rise to my feet, as much as it hurt; I could see the way out of this, now. If only I had known it was all going to be this simple. Sure, I had gotten shot, but considering I could've died or gone to prison for life, I was feeling rather positive.

It was strange, watching Ophelia be so enraged. She was normally quiet, meek and a little odd. It was only when it came to her brother that she got anywhere near this mad or defensive. She didn't care about killing me.

"Stephen." I called his name as soon as I was sitting up, although it came out slightly infused with the agony it took to move. He immediately paid attention. "Drop the gun and let's go."

He cast a nervous glance to Ophelia, who had paused upon hearing me speak. I saw Atarah put the pieces together in her mind, but then, her brow furrowed again.

"If we don't hurt Ezra, Ophelia won't hurt us." I looked over my shoulder at Ophelia. She straightened up, listening. "Isn't that right?"

"He wants you dead. I'm going to kill you for him," she insisted, taking a step closer. Atarah also stepped up and held the gun a little straighter, giving Ophelia pause.

"So he doesn't go to jail. I get it." I had a suspicion. A suspicion that I was surprised Atarah hadn't gotten to first, except maybe she had. "If Stephen wanted someone dead I'd probably try and kill them first, too. But if you just let us all go to the hospital-" I groaned through the pain, clutching at my shoulder like that would do anything- "when he wakes up, he'll have realised he can't do it. And I'm sure you don't care if I'm dead or not. If he wants to kill me, he can kill me afterwards."

I think Atarah came to the same conclusion as soon as I put the pieces together like that. Ophelia's face had that familiarly blank expression as she thought it over, stepping away. I saw it when we spoke at the bus stop, and I could only wonder how I didn't see it sooner.

"Fine." I almost hadn't expected Ophelia to relent, and I had to admit, I felt relief. "We're going to the hospital. I expect both of our guns back at some point." She headed up to the stage, ignoring Atarah's gun still pointed at her. With all guns put away, tucked into waistbands, Stephen rushed to my side. His arm slid under my left shoulder, and while it still jostled the wound and caused physical pain, having him touch me made so much difference it was unbelievable. He helped lift me to my feet, and behind us, Atarah helped Ophelia to carry Ezra. Ophelia tried to wake him, and he responded to her with a few barely understandable words.

Walking was a little difficult, which may have seemed odd for a shoulder injury, but my whole body has filled with a dull ache. I was able to stumble, and I would've been able to walk on my own, but I certainly appreciated having Stephen's help.

"Such a gentleman," I said as he helped me into the passenger seat of my car, and he laughed.

When he got in to drive, he turned to me with that tender smile I loved so much. My shoulder hurt like the fires of hell were burning in it, but that smile was a pretty good anaesthetic.

"You had me so worried," he finally said, and he was laughing, but it was in relief. "How did you *know* he was going to shoot you non-fatally?"

"I..." I realised that Stephen thought I had planned to survive that. I obviously wanted to survive, but when I handed Ezra the gun, I wasn't sure at all that he wasn't going to kill me. In fact, I believed I was going to die. "I didn't know what he would do."

For my whole life, all I'd ever cared about was how to make my life easier. My life was the only thing I had that I cared about losing. I couldn't come up with a logical reason that I had almost thrown it away. I couldn't come up with any reason at all.

"So you lied to Ophelia? Ezra might still kill you?" Stephen's face fell. I remembered- there was a heart-twisting sweetness to the idea- that all he cared about was me.

"No. Ezra didn't miss." I reached across and gently took his hand. His eyes sparkled with hope, and it was wonderful. "We're in the clear, Stephen."

He was smiling as he drove me to the hospital.

I'd been in hospital before, but only once, when Amanda's friends made me swallow razorblades. Upon entry, I was rushed to the ER, and so was Ezra. As soon as there was a needle in my arm giving me painkillers, I took the chance to pass out. I wanted none of this agony, even dulled, for any longer than I had to suffer it. They were probably going to knock me out later, to take the bullet out of my shoulder, so I may as well.

I woke up feeling like no time had passed, and perhaps like time itself was a viscous fluid I was suspended in. Every muscle felt overencumbered. When I pulled my heavy eyelids open and adjusted to the yellow light reflecting off the wall, I saw that around me were my parents, Atarah, and of course, Stephen.

"Alex, you're awake, thank God," my dad exclaimed, reaching over to hug me. I winced and hissed in pain as he jostled the wound, and he quickly backed away. I gave him a smile of thanks anyway, and he sat back down.

"We were so worried," my mother said, taking my hand in hers. She then switched to her native Mandarin for the next few sentences, deliberately excluding Stephen and Atarah and making it hard for my dad to follow. "I can't believe that you got shot! Who are those kids and why did they shoot you? Explain to me what's going on right now. And if you don't mind explaining who your friends here are, I'd like to hear that too."

I didn't really have a good lie to tell my parents as to why Ezra Hough had shot me. In my story, I had to come as close to the truth as possible, without telling them I murdered Mr Hough. When I reminded them that they were the children of our old landlord- telling the story in English so my dad could keep up easily- recognition flickered across their eyes. They fully bought the idea that the Houghs were searching for someone to blame, and blamed me. I explained that

that was why Ezra Hough had shot me, but we'd spoken after the fact and everything was fine now. Stephen had badly concussed him, so we called it even.

"You don't even want to file a police report?" my dad confirmed, and I shook my head weakly.

He patted me on the shoulder. "You're so noble, Alex."

I found it hard to believe that I could be noble. I never saw myself as evil, purely neutral, but these feelings had changed my programming in such a way that all I could see in my past were evil acts. I wanted to change that. For reasons I couldn't explain, I wanted to be the noble person my dad thought I was.

Maybe I was becoming good.

CHAPTER SEVEN- TEEN - EZRA AND OPHELIA

"**W**ho are these people?" my mother asked me in Mandarin, pointing at Stephen and Atarah with her eyes. "How come I've never met them before, but you save her and he beats up the guy who shot you?"

"Atarah is my friend. I've been to her house before, I've just never brought her over," I told her in English, for the other's sake. She avoided looking at them. "And Stephen," I said in English, before switching to Mandarin for the actual words, "is my boyfriend."

She gasped and stared at him, which made my attempt to keep him from understanding pointless. "As of yesterday!" I added quickly, in English, which confused the others for just a second before they put the pieces together. I didn't exactly make it hard for them. "I didn't get a chance to tell you!"

My father knew enough Mandarin to have understood completely. "Well, it's nice to meet you, young man," he said, offering Stephen a hand to shake. Stephen put on his charming, lying smile and took it. "I'm sorry that the first thing I heard about you was that you gave someone a concussion, but considering it was in defence of my Alex, I think I can conclude you're a good kid."

He offered Atarah a nod as well. "And you're always welcome in our home. Just so you know."

Atarah nodded with a soft smile. She was relatively quiet, which may've been unusual, but I'd give it to the fact that she'd never met my family before. It occurred to me that she'd first offered not friendship, but help in kidnapping and killing Stephen. When that fell through, and it was clear I had some, however basic, sense of morality now, I couldn't guess what she might've been thinking. It was possible she wouldn't want to hang around anymore. I sincerely hoped that wasn't true.

Stephen looked very tired, and I could tell the stress had been wearing on him. His hand laid at the very edge of my bed, like he wanted to support me without openly making a gesture of affection. It was cute. Everything he did was cute to me. Objectivity had left the building a very, very long time ago.

My parents asked me questions for some time, throughout which Atarah and Stephen stayed. My sisters, my parents said, were still in school, which told me it hadn't been more than a few hours since I'd been shot. After a lot of questions- I answered with the truth where possible, which meant at least half of my answers were lies- my dad announced that he was going to go get lunch. Stephen perked up for just a moment, thinking perhaps we'd get a chance to talk alone, before my mother said she'd stay with us.

It was barely half a minute after my father left before someone was leaning in to look at us. I had been moved to the ICU while I was asleep, so I was in my own little side-room off the main area, but there were no doors, which meant Ophelia couldn't hide. She stood completely still, not fidgeting, no expression on her face. Not lying or putting on an act. Being honest, like I'd been with her.

It unsettled my mother. "Do I know you?" she demanded, furrowing her brow. "Are you Ophelia?"

"I'm only here to talk to Alex," Ophelia said, switching on her persona when she realised it would benefit her. Suddenly, she was meek, uncertain, a little shy. I understood exactly what was going on in her head now. She was never angry when it wasn't about Ezra; loud, hot anger went counter to the persona she'd built.

"I think not," my mother snapped, standing and using her height to intimidate Ophelia. She had a graceful elegance even in her anger that made the fiercest adversary feel small.

"*Māma*," I said, drawing her attention to me. I then said in Mandarin, "yes, that's her, but I want to hear what she has to say. She couldn't hurt me even if she wanted to. Can you go, just so I can talk to her? She won't be entirely honest with me if she knows you're here. I promise I'll tell you exactly what she says."

With all of that said to her in confidence, my mother accepted the premise. She nodded, and with a stern glare towards Ophelia, almost like a warning, she left.

Ophelia waited until her footsteps were most of the way down the hall before she turned to me. The persona was dropped again; now that I was looking for it, it was obvious.

"So." We hadn't had a chance to talk about it, so I was unsure of how much Stephen and Atarah had caught on. "To what extent are you and I the same, Ophelia?"

"I see you've noticed." Ophelia walked over and sat in the seat my mother had just vacated. Her face carried the same entirely neutral expression that one so rarely saw on any given person's face. I was only used to seeing it in the mirror. "Ezra told me everything you said. You were born without emotions, and developed them when you fell in love with Stephen, correct?"

"Correct." Atarah was staring at the two of us like she couldn't quite believe what she was seeing. "One day, Stephen ran into me and caught me as I was falling. And suddenly, for no reason I could understand, I loved him. Ever since then I've had emotions, but only in relation to him."

Ophelia nodded her understanding. "I am the exact opposite."

Atarah gasped, but it wasn't so much surprise as excitement. It was the same excitement I'd heard when she and I had our first honest conversation. Stephen stared at Ophelia with mild disapproval and even milder disbelief.

She began to clarify. "I was born normal. I liked reading, science, and horses. My favourite colour was green and country music was my guilty pleasure. I was normal, until my dad died and I didn't care."

She paused, confusion like searching for a lost memory crossing her face. "I know I loved him. In fact, we were very close. He spent all his spare time with me and Ezra. He took me horse-riding and read all the terrible poems I wrote. He carried them in his wallet. I loved him and he loved me, but when he died, I didn't care. I couldn't care. There was just nothing. I only felt sad when I looked at my brother crying."

"I see." The other two stayed silent; they understood that this was between Ophelia and I. "Ezra is your Stephen, isn't he?"

"Yes. Obviously, I love him as my brother, and not as you love Stephen," she said, gesturing between Stephen and I, "but he's the only person who can make me feel anything. I grew incredibly overprotective of him, and I probably give him too much. Anything he wants, I get for him. I work because I'm going to give him our whole inheritance. He wanted to find out who killed our father, so I investigated it as soon as I had the means. And then he wanted you dead, so I helped. I wanted you to go to jail because it meant neither Ezra nor I would have to risk getting ourselves arrested, and therefore being separated. If it wasn't for Atarah, I would've gotten away with that plan."

That didn't make immediate sense, so I turned to my best friend, looking for an explanation. She shrugged, playing with her sleeves, almost embarrassed. "When Ophelia went to the cops, I told Josh it was only because she was harassing you for being friends with me. He got her case thrown aside in the police department itself."

"I thought you hated your stepfather," I said, simply not understanding.

She shrugged again, shrinking in on herself. I could tell it wasn't me; she was having an internal conflict. "I hate the fact that he's a cop. Cops don't represent justice. I hate the fact that he's a cop even more because a cop killed my actual dad, and my mom apparently doesn't give a shit about that, but-" Atarah stopped herself from going on a rant with a sharp intake of breath. "...but Josh is alright as a person. He's totally misguided in his sense of justice, but he's…well, trying."

I nodded, making a note in my mind to talk to her about it later. For now, though, Ophelia was here, and despite knowing she was empty inside I didn't want to talk about private matters in front of her. I gave her my attention again. "So you talked to Ezra?"

"He told me he couldn't shoot you. I've come to conclude that he'd feel guilty if you died, so yes, we'll be leaving you all alone from now on." She gave me that information neutrally, but glared at Stephen. "He's been vomiting constantly, because he has *a very serious concussion*, but he told me all about it."

"Let's be fair, Ophelia. I gave him that concussion after he'd just shot Alex," Stephen retorted with serious disdain.

"I understand. I'm not happy about it, but I understand." Ophelia sighed. "Alex, I have a question for you."

"Go on." Despite being hazy from painkillers, I felt relatively alright. It was strange just how clear my head was.

She bit her lip. "How did you deal with being emotionless? And, a follow-up question: why were you so desperate to return to that state? I hate this. I'm so protective of Ezra because if anything were to happen to him, my heart would stop existing entirely. I don't wanna lose my heart. Why did you?"

I closed my eyes and tried to imagine what my life had been like before that fateful day, when I'd fallen for Stephen. I used to analyse everything and find the easiest path through life because I had nothing else to do. I wanted it back because it was easy, and because pain was horrible.

"Because I felt grief, and longing, and sadness, and emptiness was better than that." It felt weak when I said it. I felt weak. "I thought happiness was an illusion and clouding my judgement. I thought feeling emotions was unnatural for me, and wrong. And..."

I remembered how Atarah had cried when she talked about her dad's death, and how Ophelia had raged knowing her brother was being hurt, and how Stephen had longed for me for years. "...it's just hard. Feeling things all the time. Emotions are so intense, and I didn't want to deal with them." After a second, I remembered who I was talking to. "Not that you'd have that problem."

Ophelia took a deep, shuddering breath. "I mean, I'm not missing very much. I can still have the simple joys of eating an ice cream or watching the sunset when I'm doing it with my brother. I just... don't understand why you'd give that away, is all. All the pain in the world is worth it to see him smile, to me."

I gazed at Stephen and offered him my hand. When he took it, the touch sparked my heart to life again, and I understood exactly what she meant. At least, I was starting to.

"I have a question for you, Ophelia," Atarah said, leaning across the bed to look her in the eye. "When Alex said, 'Ezra's not a murderer,' you said, 'I am,' and tried to shoot them in cold blood. I get you were acting in that emotionless, careless way, and you would've been totally fine with murder as long as Ezra was, but... did you mean you *could* be, or did you mean you *were*?"

"Good pickup," Ophelia said, still in that flat tone I was only used to hearing from myself. "I say this with caution, because I'm very aware of what you're like, but I am not innocent, no. I trust that I can tell you three. There was a girl from town who took a great deal of interest in Ezra- which would be fine by me, so long as she didn't hurt him- except he turned her down, and she wouldn't take no for an answer. She was banging on our front door demanding to talk to him, and he was terrified. I chased her away that night, and she followed him around town the next day. I found out where she lived, beat her to death and burned her body. She was a junkie, so nobody ever properly investigated her disappearance. I simply told him I'd chased her away. I felt bad lying to him, but never, ever would I risk losing him by telling him the truth. He still doesn't know."

"Holy shit," Atarah whispered under her breath; she had a quickly spreading grin. All I could think about was the irony of the situation. "Hey, so, out of interest-"

"No. It's not you, I am simply never going to date anyone when they can't bring me happiness." Ophelia rose then, heading towards the door, as Atarah was sputtering with indignation.

"That is not what I was about to say! Why does everyone assume I want to fuck any killer at all? I have standards, for fuck's sake!" Atarah almost yelled, as both Stephen and I gestured for her to keep her voice down. She quickly quieted herself mid-sentence, but Stephen was still left with his face in his palm from second-hand embarrassment.

"You're not helping your situation at all," Ophelia said dryly, before turning back to me. "Alex, if you want to speak more, you know where to find me. Thank you for talking to me. I may come to you for advice in the future, if that's okay."

"That's more than fine," I nodded, and she took her leave. That just left an embarrassed, indignant Atarah, and an embarrassed, annoyed Stephen. Stephen's annoyance quickly melted away as he looked at me.

"I've been waiting all fucking day," he said almost under his breath, leaning closer to me. "Can I kiss you?"

I felt like shit, and Stephen was medicine. "Please."

His fingers brushed my cheek as he leant in to press his lips to mine; it was careful and soft, doing everything he could to make sure I felt okay. It brought a smile to my face, and my head felt clear. He pulled away and leant his forehead against mine, and everything was good.

It wasn't just fine, okay, normal. It was good.

"Are we going to talk about what the fuck just happened?" Atarah interrupted. I tried not to react emotionally, moving just enough that Stephen could lean on my shoulder instead.

"What about it?" I asked like I didn't know exactly what she meant. I wanted to know what she was thinking, what she thought was important. There was a lingering possibility I wanted to avoid, and that was the possibility that she didn't want to be my friend anymore.

"I mean, Ophelia's like you. I didn't see that coming!" She gestured hugely with her hands, like this was some big deal. Was it? I'd never searched for someone like me, and I'd never been bothered by being alone. I guess it was interesting. "She's a better liar than even you. I bet it was because she'd had emotions before. Do you reckon Ezra knows? Should I tell him?"

"Of course he doesn't know. Honestly, it would be cruel to tell him." I shrugged. "Let him be happy in his ignorance, and let her be happy in keeping him close. They probably deserve to be happy."

Bringing up that word- deserve- caused a ripple to spread between the three of us. I hadn't shared my thoughts with them yet, but they both knew things had changed in no uncertain way. All I could hope was that I wouldn't lose either of them for it.

"We should talk about this," Stephen said, glancing towards Atarah. She curtly nodded, and it occurred to me that they'd had an uncertain amount of time to speak since I'd fallen unconscious. I couldn't know what they'd said. What conclusions they'd come to.

"Alex." And as soon as Atarah said that, I knew something was up for sure. "You were about to give your life up to Ezra. You... don't do that."

"Yeah." She wasn't wrong. I didn't do that. I didn't know how to respond except to tell her she was right; she probably wanted an explanation, but I didn't have one.

"And you came to save me." Atarah leaned forward; the look on her face was one of uncertain, soft awe. "You would never. Or at least, an emotionless Alex- even an emotionless

Alex who only cared about Stephen- would never."

"I told her the truth," Stephen added. "That it was you who wanted to save her, and not me."

"I don't know what to tell you." I stared at my hands, the idea of confronting the truth incredibly unpalatable, but also unavoidable. "I felt... I felt like I couldn't leave you behind. And I don't know if that's guilt, morality, or... friendship, but whatever it is, I followed it, and I liked following it."

Atarah had the tiniest of smiles, almost undetectable to anyone. "I get it. I like it. But you let yourself get shot? You gave him the gun."

I had a feeling she wasn't asking me questions because she didn't know the answer. She was asking me questions because she wanted to hear the truth from my mouth. She wanted it to be me who told Stephen. She knew it was true before I did.

"The reason I gave him the gun wasn't because I knew he wouldn't kill me. I know that now, but when I'm honest..." it was hard to say, which was stupid, because it was just words, and these shouldn't have had emotions behind them. I didn't feel anything about them; they were just hard to say. "...when I'm honest, I gave him the gun because I thought I deserved to die. I thought it was... fair." I looked at Atarah when I said that, because it was her who knew about what was fair, her who knew about what was deserved. "Was it fair? Did I deserve it?"

"I didn't think so, because you never acted to hurt anyone, but..." Atarah trailed off, before taking a deep breath and starting again. Her eyes welling up happened so suddenly it took me by surprise. "You nearly died. I was numb and fuelled by adrenaline at the time, but I kept thinking of that moment when Ophelia raised the gun and for a split second I just imagined you dying. I thought you were dead before I got there. I heard the gun go off and I thought you were gone. I had to double-take, and I just... it scared me to death."

"You and me both," Stephen breathed as she spoke, squeezing my hand. It physically hurt, but I did nothing to stop him.

"Alex, you're the only person in my life who doesn't get sick of me, who knows everything about me and isn't repulsed, who trusts me so completely that you were ready to commit a crime with me. I saw your death in my mind and it was as horrible as my father's death. And you came to save me when you really should've run away. I don't want you to ever be in that kind of danger again, and I don't want to lose you. I'm hoping that the fact you saved me means you still want to be my friend despite all of this."

I wanted to say that what I felt was relief, but it was so weak and distant that I wasn't yet sure of whether it was a real emotion or not.

I rested my hand on top of Atarah's; physical intimacy with friends was her thing, not mine, but it felt appropriate. "I was thinking I was about to lose you. For as long as you want to stay, Atarah, I'm lucky to have you."

Stephen nodded. "I don't know you very well, and we started off quite badly, but any friend of Alex's is a friend of mine. Just so you know."

Atarah smiled through the silent stream of tears that drew a line down her cheeks. She had had some bright blue eyeliner on, stark against the backdrop of her skin, but the water made it run, causing an effect not unlike a painting.

There was a moment of silence before Atarah looked to Stephen, and I realised there was more to ask me. "What is it?" I said pre-emptively. There was a concern in my mind that something was still wrong, that something threatened the future I wanted to build alongside Stephen and Atarah.

Stephen turned to me, seeming a little less certain of himself than Atarah did, but asking it anyway. "So… where do we go from here?"

It wasn't the question I expected. The three of us seemed solid as a team, even though we were all people who had never been part of a team before each other. This was new. Before, Atarah and I had functioned with the goal of kidnapping Stephen, and after, for that brief time, we'd had ourselves set on finding a way to escape the Houghs. Now that we'd done that, it made sense to feel directionless.

"All I know is what I want." I spoke it to them at the same time as I figured it out myself. "I know I want both of you around. I know I have a moral compass now, and following it feels good. I want to follow it. I think I'm still going to study to be a doctor, but beyond that... building a life is all I want."

"I'm guessing no more murder," Atarah said, fixing her glasses. "Not saying that's a bad thing. I really need to find a healthier way to get my kicks."

"You do," Stephen agreed dryly.

I shrugged in response to her. "Maybe my moral compass will lead me there, but I doubt it. If I couldn't kill to save my own life, I can't think of when murder might be right. I've been bad in the past when it suited me, but from now on I want to choose to be good, even though I don't know how and I haven't done it before."

Stephen's touch calmed me, and I could barely feel pain whenever he spoke. It was just so nice, to have a presence of comfort like his. "I don't know how to be good, either. I don't feel empathy, and I don't know how to act good. That, and nobody seemed like they deserved it. They still don't, for the most part." His fingers ran up and down over my skin, so casual like he didn't realise he was doing it. "You make me want to be good, too. Even though I don't care about the people I'm being good to."

"I mean, if we're doing confessional hour, I haven't exactly been the best either. It's like Stephen said, people don't deserve it." Atarah was wiping at the eyeliner that streaked down her face like she'd only just realised she'd cried it off. "It's just that... I thought Ezra deserved to die, and I was totally for killing him, and Ophelia too. But when we all escaped alive, it's just so much nicer. I mean, I wish everyone got that mercy- especially the innocent- but I guess we can't change the past. Nobody deserves kindness when we're in such a cruel world, but it felt strangely nice to give it to them."

"We all got here because I was going to kidnap Stephen

and murder him to avoid loving him," I said, "and here we are, declaring how we're all going to be good."

"Because of you," Stephen responded with fervour. "If it weren't for you I'd be a bored psychopath and Atarah would be a freaky loner. I mean, I don't think either of us is going to change overnight. I'm still going to be disgusted by everyone, I'll just be nice to them as well, and I won't hurt anyone. That's basic decency, not goodness."

"And I'm still going to do whatever I want, except maybe not kidnap or murder people. Not hurting people seems like such a basic thing, but you'd be surprised how many people don't follow even that. You're doing well to just try and do the right thing." Atarah offered Stephen a friendly pat on the shoulder, which he quickly shrugged off. She apologised quickly. "For example, I won't do that in the future."

He gave a brief nod and settled back into my shoulder. I let go of his hand only so that I could reach up and run my fingers through his hair; the jolt to my heart was almost too much, but when I was careful and took it slow, I could touch his soft golden curls, and feel good without feeling overwhelmed. Slowly, someday, we'd get there. I'd managed to kiss him without running away; that was a start.

"All I know," I thought aloud, "is that following my moral compass feels better than fighting it. That's all I think I need to know right now."

I had the man I loved and I had my best friend. Nobody was going to kill me, and things were nice. Things were capable of being nice at all. I changed my mind: pain was worth it to sit here like this. Pain was worth it for Stephen's head on my shoulder.

Maybe I didn't deserve to live. It was impossible to know for sure. What I did know for sure was that I was grateful to live, because now I had a life ahead of me where anything at all mattered.

Chapter Eighteen - Alex, Stephen and Atarah

Whenever I woke up alone, I always had an irrational fear that Stephen had disappeared somewhere. I knew it was never the case, but his disappearance was all I had nightmares about. The fear, when it came, only ever lasted half a second, and it was always rare; usually he had just shuffled to the other side of the bed, or I'd fallen asleep on the couch instead of in bed. This time, when I sat up straight and clutched the cotton sheets to my chest in a moment of panic, I was in bed alone.

I stood up cautiously, like I'd be burned by the floor. I knew it was irrational, but seeing him would ease the ache in my chest and I'd start feeling fine again.

"Stephen?" I called out. I knew he wasn't anywhere in our bedroom, and I didn't hear the shower running, but somehow, I felt like calling him might reveal him. When I was quiet for a moment, I could hear sound outside of the bedroom door. Movement in the kitchen.

As soon as I opened the door and caught sight of him down the hallway, my heart immediately eased. He was in the kitchen, mixing something up in a bowl. I admired him in the morning light; a ray of sun fell across his face, somewhat blocked by a dividing wall between the kitchen and the living room. He didn't seem to notice me looking at him, and he hadn't heard me call his name until I repeated it. "Stephen."

He was broken from his trance with a slightly annoyed look, until he registered that it was me. He instantly melted into softness, as surely and steadily as he had for months now.

I padded up to him, disregarding whatever he was doing. I wanted attention, after all. "I didn't know where you were," I said in the cutesy tone that always made him do what I wanted, with a little pout of mock sadness. "I thought you'd disappeared."

He tucked a lock of hair behind my ear, following the path of it down to rest his palm on my shoulder and run his fingers over my scar. It was an impressive thing, a star-shaped dint in my shoulder with a longways slash through it, where they'd sliced me to get the pieces out. I told everyone at school I got caught in the crossfires of a shooting I had nothing to do with, and along with making a more believable story, it was my little favour to Ophelia. And Ezra too, but he wasn't exactly grateful for it.

"I was making you breakfast," he said, playful. He looked at me through his lashes, in a way that easily made my knees weak and my heart tremble. I still felt every look, every touch the same; it was just that now, I could withstand it, and the happiness that he gave me was just that.

"Why were you-" I began to ask, before I realised what day it was. I took the nearest object with which I could check, which happened to be Stephen's phone, and turned it on.

The screen read the eleventh of September, as I'd thought.

Stephen's hands cupped my face, bringing my eyes back to his. He constantly swore he was getting taller, but he was always about an inch shorter than me. "Happy birthday," he said softly, kissing me with all the sweetness of pure love. Sometimes it was still hard to believe I had a love like that. It was even harder to believe I hadn't wanted it.

If I had killed Stephen, I'd still be mourning months later. I'd still be mourning in years. The pain would have driven me mad.

"Thank you," I said, almost breathless. "What were you making?"

"Pancakes. And you've got to stop distracting me from them," he said, fake sternness in his voice. "Or you'll never get to eat them."

"Fine." I gave him a quick kiss to satisfy me before stepping away and walking around to the other side of the bench. I leaned across far enough to physically obstruct him, and he raised an eyebrow at me, which I met with a little laugh and a refusal to move. He just held the bowl above my head and kept mixing. I sat back then, just so I could stare at him while he worked.

He was always happy whenever I was around. Atarah attested that there were times when he was grumpy or irritable, but only ever when he'd come home from work while I was out. I always tried to be home whenever he was, because neither of us could bear to be without each other very long. I was starting college in two weeks, and the worst part of it was always going to be missing him every moment we weren't together. That sadness couldn't be turned off like most of my emotions could be, although it could be dampened.

Right now, though, I was just happy to be with him.

I watched him as he went about cooking the pancakes. He hadn't known a thing about how to cook back when our relationship began, but he was a quick learner. He was teaching me how to paint and learning partner dances with me, saying one day he wanted to enter a competition. I privately knew it would take a while for me to be that good, and he knew the same, although he never said it. In return, I taught him to cook, and I was slowly teaching him Mandarin. Of the three languages I spoke that he didn't, he was the most interested in Mandarin, because it would allow him to understand my mother. He swore to learn them all eventually.

When I finally managed to drag my eyes away from him, I walked over to the other bedroom in the apartment. I knocked, loud enough to wake her up. "Atarah?"

When she didn't answer, I called again. "Atarah. Do you want breakfast or not?"

"Maybe she didn't come home last night," Stephen said offhandedly.

I opened the door to check, and while her room was a mess- clothes that weren't put away, her bag just dropped on the floor and half spilling open, several books stacked up on the floor while we procrastinated buying her another shelf- she wasn't in it. "She said she'd gotten an interview for her video series," I commented to Stephen. Considering she wasn't big enough to get her channel verified just yet, that was a big deal for her. "I'm not sure why that would mean she wouldn't come home."

Stephen laughed. "Maybe it was more than that."

I turned around to face him, unable to resist the urge to come interrupt his cooking again. I slipped an arm around his waist, instantly drawing his attention to me. "While she's gone, why don't you tell me about our plans for tonight?"

"Our plans?" He raised an eyebrow, only turning away for long enough to flip the pancake, lest it burn. "You're asking me for plans on your birthday?"

"Well," I dragged it out as long as I could, hoping the message would get across without me having to say it. "...you implied you had a surprise for me."

He chuckled. "I said that two weeks ago." Despite how he spoke, he knew we were both that obsessed with each other. It would've probably been incredibly unhealthy, had our outrageous attachment not been in equal measure. I was already figuring out our wedding- postponed only for appearances and financial reasons- and flip-flopping back and forth on whether we should have kids. Everything even remotely related to Stephen was wonderful, and I knew I'd love any children of ours simply because they belonged to Stephen; but at the same time, it meant his attention taken away from me, and mine from him. That wouldn't do, not for one moment.

"Well," he said, leaning forward and pressing me against the counter. My heart still raced as fast as it did the moment I literally fell for him, but that underlying fear was gone. "I got tonight off work, for one. I was thinking."

When he didn't finish the sentence, I leaned in, close enough that it was almost like I was about to kiss him. "Oh, you were," I said, grinning mischievously. It took me weeks to get used to kissing him, just about as long to be able to comfortably sleep beside him, and weeks longer to even talk about going any further than that. I was almost there, though. Almost.

"Maybe." He sounded like he had something to say, but he paused to kiss me, although it was a little difficult with how much I was smiling.

This was the world I had thought I'd never get to.

The sound of an opening door didn't quite convince me to break it off, but Atarah's loud, deliberate coughing did. There was relief I didn't realise would be waiting for me to know she was okay, although I'm told some fears are unnoticeable until they're gone.

"Where were you?" I asked immediately, as Stephen took the chance to return to the pancakes before any burnt. I knew Atarah well; she dressed in pretty much entirely black, with accents of red or purple or gold or white. When I looked at her, she wore a grey sweatshirt with a New York design on it; it wasn't something she owned, and I knew it instantly.

Atarah dropped her keys by the door. "I told you guys. I was interviewing for my channel. I don't yet know what exactly I'm going to call this one, but something like 'my experience with a killer?' or something else clickbait-y."

"Hang on, you're not making one about Alex, are you?" Stephen said, incredulous. *"You can't."*

"Ah, you see, it's clickbait-y because it's not exactly true. I'm not making one about Alex, or at least any of their murders." She walked up to us as she spoke, peering into Stephen's bowl. "I'm talking about the almost-murder where Alex was the victim. I'm making one about Ezra."

"Well, he never killed anyone, so that's clearly misleading," I said. There was a feeling somewhere in my chest that, at best guess, might've been dread. I turned it off like turning off a light. I was getting good at doing that, choosing what I wanted to feel- when it wasn't Stephen, of course.

"So which one of them did you interview? And sleep with?" Stephen asked, completely straight-faced. He was messing with her, and she knew that, but she gave him the reaction he wanted anyway.

"I did not sleep with him!" she protested, smacking the counter.

"That answers my question," Stephen smirked.

Atarah threw her hands up, exasperated. "Whatever. Take my word for it or don't. I got the interview, we talked for a bit, ended up smoking, and I was too high to drive home. That's the answer."

"At least you're not driving dangerously," I said, shrugging. I felt the stirrings of another emotion, and indulged it just long enough to figure out what it was. Something like sadness or disappointment, with Atarah. At first, I thought it was because she was hanging out with Ezra, someone who would never speak to me again; but I didn't care about that, not really. After I'd gained the ability to feel, I started being able to have subjective, meaningless opinions about people, and I found that I didn't like Ezra that much anyway.

"Are you forgetting something?" Stephen said defensively, and I realised why I felt a little sad. I was able to turn the emotion off, so it didn't really matter, but it certainly annoyed an over-protective Stephen.

"Oh, I didn't forget," Atarah said, perfectly calm. When I flipped that internal switch again, all I felt was relief and love for Atarah. I knew there was a reason she was my best friend- well, *still* my best friend, now that first degree murder was no longer a shared interest of ours. "It's just that you bombarded me as soon as I walked through the door. Hang on."

Atarah slipped into her room and came back out with an envelope in her hand. She pulled me into a hug; she needed a shower, but the hug felt nice, so I didn't mind. "Happy birthday," she said softly, handing me the envelope.

It was plain white, and my name was handwritten on it in Atarah's sharp lettering. I was used to doing one of two things; playing the persona I'd created, which would mean opening it cautiously but eagerly, or doing the most efficient thing and just tearing it open. But, when I allowed myself to feel, I was excited to know what she'd got me, and it led to a slower, messier, somewhat ruder way of tearing it open. Fake Alex and Emotionless Alex were both incredibly different to Real Alex, and it was still disconcerting, enough to give those around me whiplash on occasion. It turns out, when I didn't mute all my emotions, I cried at dog movies and found poetry strangely insightful. I loved attention and I liked wearing sweaters that were a little too big. Baby blue was my favourite colour and I was a cat person. Some of those facts had lingered in my emotionless self, and I wondered now which side of me came first. Did I enjoy dressing in pastel fashions now because I had always done that in the persona I had built? Or was there an inherent enjoyment of the colours and aesthetic that existed my whole life and affected my decision making, that I'd just never been aware of until I unearthed it?

I was staring at the envelope that I'd just opened without taking anything out of it. I was a stranger to myself, and often it hit me at times like this, when I did something out of character for any version of me that I knew. I didn't open envelopes frantically, and it was enough to throw me.

There was a card inside, and as I took it out and read it over, a feeling of joy rose inside me. I got the vague gist, seeing the name of a spa I'd driven past before, but I felt Atarah would need to explain it. "I... what is it?"

"Just a few hours with nothing but each other. It's two hours for two people. I didn't think there was a material thing you'd want, and I know all you really want to do is be stuck to Stephen's side, so I thought it would be a good idea." She seemed happy with herself, and I pulled her into another hug on instinct. It wasn't the kind of hug I used to give back when I was pretending to be normal. It was much clumsier, yet more intimate than that.

"Thank you," I said softly against her ear. She squeezed me a little before letting me go.

"We'll have to go soon, before you start school," Stephen suggested, coming over to me. Atarah stepped aside to give him space. "Not tonight, though, because I-" he grabbed me by the waist again, pulling me close enough that our noses touched- "am taking you on a date."

"Anyone ever tell you two you're gross?" Atarah mocked us, but we both ignored her. She gave me a gentle pat on the shoulder as she walked past and sat at the table. I paid her no mind.

I chose to focus on Stephen, his blue eyes with veins of grey around the pupils and hints of green edging around the outside of his iris. His long and elegantly beautiful eyelashes, the golden blonde of his curly hair, his grip strong enough to hold my entire weight if he wanted to. "Where are we going?" I asked, sweetness permeating every word.

"What if I want it to be a surprise?" he replied, eyebrow raised.

I was perfectly ready to take on that challenge, tilting my head and putting on my best smile. "What if I don't?"

"You're burning the pancakes," Atarah called from the dining room table.

Embarrassment burned in my cheeks and I quickly turned it off, shuffling away so that Stephen could return to cooking. I forced myself to sit at the dining table instead of bothering him further. It was difficult.

"So." Atarah's familiar, mischievous grin slowly grew on her face. "I have a question."

"You don't always have to say it like that, you can just ask," I told her.

She poked the dint in my shoulder. It didn't really hurt

anymore, but it felt strange to be reminded I was missing flesh. "How is it, really, becoming a normal person? How do you feel about it?"

"It's odd, developing a personality this late." I shrugged. "It's a great escape that I can turn off my emotions at will, when it doesn't have to do with Stephen. Parts of it do suck, though, like I thought they would. I'm never going to watch any movies with any dogs in them whatsoever, *ever again*, for any reason." I was so emphatic about it that it made her laugh loudly. "...but, honestly, Ophelia was right. The good parts are worth the bad. I've just got to find the good parts, and make them."

"...and the good parts are mostly being in love?" she asked, in a way that was hard to interpret. I'd have to judge her reaction once I answered.

"While that is amazing," I said, catching Stephen's eye for just a moment, "there are other things, too. Like making a joke that all my friends laugh at, or buying new clothes that fit perfectly and make you look amazing, and seeing a cat on your way home that comes up and gets you to pet it. And," I said, making sure she knew I was speaking about her, "when your best friend gets you the perfect birthday gift. There's so many things I would've never experienced if I'd really gone through with our plan. And the first thing I ever did just because I wanted to was saving Ezra's life, so you should thank *me* for last night," I teased with a grin, laughing as she lightly whacked my good shoulder.

"Piss off," she said, but she was laughing too.

"You forgot the best thing that you never would've had if you killed me," Stephen called, and I stared at him as he approached with a plate in his hand, waiting for the joke to hit.

"And what is that?" I asked.

He leaned down and looked me in the eye, holding the plate high just so he could dramatically place it in front of me with that beautiful little smile he had, the same one he gave me the very first time we kissed, and he revealed the truth, and I finally came to conclude that I couldn't ever kill him. The plate hit the table with a soft noise. "Pancakes."

Other titles by the authors that you may enjoy:

Soul of a Vampire
By Silencio Marquez

Kris Kellman is a vampire living in Calgary, Canada who works as a detective at the Magical Laws Division. It's his job to solve crimes committed by magical people like himself. When his former lover, Zeke Yonah, shows up on his doorstep covered in blood and asking for help, Kris is conflicted. Is he a vampire first, or is he a cop?

As he begins to investigate the murder that Zeke doesn't remember committing, things get really complicated when Kris realizes that Zeke is being set up for murder.

Charles Anderson is in charge of the vampire community, and he has a plan to enslave all mankind. The only thing standing in his way are people like Zeke and Kris, a vampire whose loyalty can't be bought. Kris's ridiculous dragon-shifter boyfriend isn't making things easier either.

Kris realizes that if he can't stop Charles, it will mean war between humans and vampires. He knows that it's not just humans that will suffer, but vampires like him who won't just sit by and let Charles get away with genocide. Will Kris do what's right and bring Charles to justice before it's too late?

Arc City Stories
By various authors

Welcome to Arc City.

A city that exists in a world beyond governments, where war and climate change have destroyed the old order. Corporations are now the authorities of the surviving city states. The elite live in luxury above the clouds in their towers, everyone else lives further down, based on their corporate and economic worth.

Arc City Stories is an exciting, action-packed collection of nine cyberpunk tales, written by eight authors, of various citizens each trying to survive, in their own way, this brave new world.

Prester John
By Richard Denham

He sits on his jewelled throne on the Horn of Africa in the maps of the sixteenth century. He can see his whole empire reflected in a mirror outside his palace. He carries three crosses into battle and each cross is guarded by one hundred thousand men. He was with St Thomas in the third century when he set up a Christian church in India. He came like a thunderbolt out of the far East eight centuries later, to rescue the crusaders clinging on to Jerusalem. And he was still there when Portuguese explorers went looking for him in the fifteenth century.

He went by different names. The priest who was also a king was Ong Khan; he was Genghis Khan; he was Lebna Dengel. Above all, he was a Christian king who ruled a vast empire full of magical wonders: men with faces in their chests; men with huge, backward-facing feet; rivers and seas made of sand. His lands lay next to the earthly Paradise which had once been the Garden of Eden. He wrote letters to popes and princes. He promised salvation and hope to generations.

But it was noticeable that as men looked outward, exploring more of the natural world; as science replaced superstition and the age of miracles faded, Prester John was always elsewhere. He was beyond the Mountains of the Moon, at the edge of the earth, near the mouth of Hell.

Was he real? Did he ever exist? This book will take you on a journey of a lifetime, to worlds that might have been, but never were. It will take you, if you are brave enough, into the world of Prester John.

A Storm of Magic
By Ashley Laino

Being brought back from the dead is an impressive trick, even for magician Darien Burron. Now he must try and use his sleight of hand to swindle modern-day witch, Mirah, to sign her power away, or end up a tormented demon in the afterlife.

Meanwhile, sixteen-year-old Mirah is starting to lose control of her powers. After an incident at her aunt's Witchery store, Mirah is sent to a secret coven to learn to control her abilities.

While away, Mirah meets up with a soft-spoken clairvoyant, a brazen storm witch, and the creator of dark magic itself. The young woman must learn to trust in herself before she loses herself entirely to the darkness that hunts her.

Consumed
By Justin Alcala

Sergeant Nathaniel Brannick is trapped in Victorian London during a period of disease, crime, and insatiable vices. One night, Brannick returns from work to find an eerie messenger in his flat who warns him of dark things to come.

When his next case involves a victim who suffered from consumption, he uncovers clues that lead him to believe the messenger's warning. Despite his incredulity, he can't help but wonder if the practical man he once was has been altered by an investigation encompassed in the paranormal. That is, until he meets the witch hunters, and everything takes a turn for the worse.

www.ingramcontent.com/pod-product-compliance
Lightning Source LLC
Chambersburg PA
CBHW012012050726
47590CB00009B/3159